Anthology of Fairy Tales (Illustrated)

Hans Christian Andersen
Andrew Lang
Jacob Grimm & Wilhelm Grimm

Edited by Yona Rodrigue Cohen

Anthology of Fairy Tales (Illustrated)

Published by
ELL Reading, LLC
P.O. Box 1137
Mason, OH 45040, USA

Library of Congress Control Number: 2014955898

ISBN: 9780984409891

Printed in United States of America

Table of Contents

FAIRY TALES OF HANS CHRISTIAN ANDERSEN

Hans Christian Andersen

The Tinder-Box

A SOLDIER came marching along the high road: "Left, right—left, right." He had his knapsack on his back, and a sword at his side; he had been to the wars, and was now returning home.

As he walked on, he met a very frightful-looking old witch in the road. Her under-lip hung quite down on her breast, and she stopped and said, "Good evening, soldier; you have a very fine sword, and a large knapsack, and you are a real soldier; so you shall have as much money as ever you like."

"Thank you, old witch," said the soldier.

"Do you see that large tree," said the witch, pointing to a tree which stood beside them. "Well, it is quite ***hollow*** inside, and you must climb to the top, when you will see a hole, through which you can let yourself down into the tree to a great depth. I will tie a rope round your body, so that I can pull you up again when you call out to me."

"But what am I to do, down there in the tree?" asked the soldier.

"Get money," she replied; "for you must know that when you reach the ground under the tree, you will find yourself in a large hall, lighted up by three hundred lamps; you will then see three doors, which can be easily opened, for the keys are in all the locks. On entering the first of the ***chambers***, to which these doors lead, you will see a large ***chest***, standing in the middle of the floor, and upon it a dog seated, with a pair of eyes as large as teacups. But you need not be at all afraid of him; I will give you my blue checked apron, which you must spread upon the floor, and then ***boldly seize*** hold of the dog, and place him upon it. You can then open the chest, and take from it as many pence as you please, they are only copper pence; but if you would rather have silver money, you must go into the second chamber. Here you will find another dog, with eyes as big as mill-wheels; but do not let that trouble you. Place him upon my apron, and then take what money you please. If, however, you like gold best, enter the third chamber, where there is another chest full of it. The dog who sits on this chest is very dreadful; his eyes are as big as a tower, but do not mind him. If he also is placed upon my apron, he cannot hurt you, and you may take from the chest what gold you will."

"This is not a bad story," said the soldier; "but what am I to give you, you old witch? for, of course, you do not mean to tell me all this for nothing."

"No," said the witch; "but I do not ask for a single penny. Only promise to

---

hollow: empty
chambers: rooms
chest: box
boldly: bravely; without fear
seize: grab

bring me an old ***tinder-box***, which my grandmother left behind the last time she went down there."

"Very well; I promise. Now tie the rope round my body."

"Here it is," replied the witch; "and here is my blue checked apron."

As soon as the rope was tied, the soldier climbed up the tree, and let himself down through the hollow to the ground beneath; and here he found, as the witch had told him, a large hall, in which many hundred lamps were all burning. Then he opened the first door. "Ah!" there sat the dog, with the eyes as large as teacups, staring at him.

"You're a pretty fellow," said the soldier, seizing him, and placing him on the witch's apron, while he filled his pockets from the chest with as many pieces as they would hold. Then he closed the lid, seated the dog upon it again, and walked into another chamber, and, sure enough, there sat the dog with eyes as big as mill-wheels.

"You had better not look at me in that way," said the soldier; "you will make your eyes water;" and then he seated him also upon the apron, and opened the chest. But when he saw what a ***quantity*** of silver money it contained, he very quickly threw away all the coppers he had taken, and filled his pockets and his knapsack with nothing but silver.

Then he went into the third room, and there the dog was really ***hideous***; his eyes were, truly, as big as towers, and they turned round and round in his head like wheels.

"Good morning," said the soldier, touching his cap, for he had never seen such a dog in his life. But after looking at him more closely, he thought he had been ***civil*** enough, so he placed him on the floor, and opened the chest. Good gracious, what a quantity of gold there was! enough to buy all the sugar-sticks of the sweet-stuff women; all the tin soldiers, whips, and rocking-horses in the world, or even the whole town itself. There was, indeed, an ***immense*** quantity. So the soldier now threw away all the silver money he had taken, and filled his pockets and his knapsack with gold instead; and not only his pockets and his knapsack, but even his cap and boots, so that he could ***scarcely*** walk.

He was really rich now; so he replaced the dog on the chest, closed the door, and called up through the tree, "Now pull me out, you old witch."

"Have you got the tinder-box?" asked the witch.

"No; I declare I quite forgot it." So he went back and fetched the tinder-box, and then the witch drew him up out of the tree, and he stood again in the high road, with his pockets, his knapsack, his cap, and his boots full of gold.

"What are you going to do with the tinder-box?" asked the soldier.

"That is nothing to you," replied the witch; "you have the money, now give

---

tinder-box: a box used for lighting a fire
quantity: amount
hideous: very ugly
civil: polite
immense: huge
scarcely: hardly

me the tinder-box."

"I tell you what," said the soldier, "if you don't tell me what you are going to do with it, I will draw my sword and cut off your head."

"No," said the witch.

The soldier immediately cut off her head, and there she lay on the ground. Then he tied up all his money in her apron and slung it on his back like a bundle, put the tinder-box in his pocket, and walked off to the nearest town. It was a very nice town, and he put up at the best inn, and ordered a dinner of all his favorite dishes, for now he was rich and had plenty of money.

The servant, who cleaned his boots, thought they certainly were a ***shabby*** pair to be worn by such a rich gentleman, for he had not yet bought any new ones. The next day, however, he ***procured*** some good clothes and proper boots, so that our soldier soon became known as a fine gentleman, and the people visited him, and told him all the wonders that were to be seen in the town, and of the king's beautiful daughter, the princess.

"Where can I see her?" asked the soldier.

"She is not to be seen at all," they said; "she lives in a large copper castle, surrounded by walls and towers. No one but the king himself can pass in or out, for there has been a ***prophecy*** that she will marry a common soldier, and the king cannot bear to think of such a marriage."

"I should like very much to see her," thought the soldier; but he could not obtain permission to do so. However, he passed a very pleasant time; went to the theatre, drove in the king's garden, and gave a great deal of money to the poor, which was very good of him; he remembered what it had been in olden times to be without a shilling. Now he was rich, had fine clothes, and many friends, who all declared he was a fine fellow and a real gentleman, and all this ***gratified*** him ***exceedingly***. But his money would not last forever; and as he spent and gave away a great deal daily, and received none, he found himself at last with only two shillings left. So he was obliged to leave his elegant rooms, and live in a little garret under the roof, where he had to clean his own boots, and even mend them with a large needle. None of his friends came to see him; there were too many stairs to mount up. One dark evening, he had not even a penny to buy a candle; then all at once he remembered that there was a piece of candle stuck in the tinder-box, which he had brought from the old tree, into which the witch had helped him.

He found the tinder-box, but no sooner had he struck a few sparks from the flint and steel, than the door flew open and the dog with eyes as big as teacups, whom he had seen while down in the tree, stood before him, and said, "What orders, master?"

"Hallo," said the soldier; "well this is a pleasant tinder-box, if it brings me

---

shabby: worn out
procured: obtained
prophecy: prediction; foretelling a future event
gratified: pleased
exceedingly: extremely

all I wish for."

"Bring me some money," said he to the dog.

He was gone in a moment, and presently returned, carrying a large bag of coppers in his month. The soldier very soon discovered after this the value of the tinder-box. If he struck the flint once, the dog who sat on the chest of copper money made his appearance; if twice, the dog came from the chest of silver; and if three times, the dog with eyes like towers, who watched over the gold. The soldier had now plenty of money; he returned to his elegant rooms, and reappeared in his fine clothes, so that his friends knew him again directly, and made as much of him as before.

After a while he began to think it was very strange that no one could get a look at the princess. "Everyone says she is very beautiful," thought he to himself; "but what is the use of that if she is to be shut up in a copper castle surrounded by so many towers. Can I by any means get to see her. Stop! Where is my tinder-box?" Then he struck a light, and in a moment the dog, with eyes as big as teacups, stood before him.

"It is midnight," said the soldier, "yet I should very much like to see the princess, if only for a moment."

The dog disappeared ***instantly***, and before the soldier could even look round, he returned with the princess. She was lying on the dog's back asleep, and looked so lovely, that everyone who saw her would know she was a real princess. The soldier could not help kissing her, true soldier as he was. Then the dog ran back with the princess; but in the morning, while at breakfast with the king and queen, she told them what a singular dream she had had during the night, of a dog and a soldier, that she had ridden on the dog's back, and been kissed by the soldier.

"That is a very pretty story, indeed," said the queen. So the next night one of the old ladies of the court was set to watch by the princess's bed, to discover whether it really was a dream, or what else it might be.

The soldier longed very much to see the princess once more, so he sent for the dog again in the night to fetch her, and to run with her as fast as ever he could. But the old lady put on water boots, and ran after him as quickly as he did, and found that he carried the princess into a large house. She thought it would help her to remember the place if she made a large cross on the door with a piece of chalk. Then she went home to bed, and the dog presently returned with the princess. But when he saw that a cross had been made on the door of the house, where the soldier lived, he took another piece of chalk and made crosses on all the doors in the town, so that the lady-in-waiting might not be able to find out the right door.

Early the next morning the king and queen accompanied the lady and all the officers of the household, to see where the princess had been.

"Here it is," said the king, when they came to the first door with a cross on it.

"No, my dear husband, it must be that one," said the queen, pointing to a second door having a cross also.

---

instantly: immediately

"And here is one, and there is another!" they all exclaimed; for there were crosses on all the doors in every direction.

So they felt it would be useless to search any farther. But the queen was a very clever woman; she could do a great deal more than merely ride in a carriage. She took her large gold scissors, cut a piece of silk into squares, and made a neat little bag. This bag she filled with buckwheat flour, and tied it round the princess's neck; and then she cut a small hole in the bag, so that the flour might be scattered on the ground as the princess went along. During the night, the dog came again and carried the princess on his back, and ran with her to the soldier, who loved her very much, and wished that he had been a prince, so that he might have her for a wife. The dog did not observe how the flour ran out of the bag all the way from the castle wall to the soldier's house, and even up to the window, where he had climbed with the princess. Therefore in the morning the king and queen found out where their daughter had been, and the soldier was taken up and put in prison. Oh, how dark and disagreeable it was as he sat there, and the people said to him, "To-morrow you will be hanged." It was not very pleasant news, and besides, he had left the tinder-box at the inn. In the morning he could see through the iron grating of the little window how the people were hastening out of the town to see him hanged; he heard the drums beating, and saw the soldiers marching. Everyone ran out to look at them, and a shoemaker's boy, with a leather apron and slippers on, galloped by so fast that one of his slippers flew off and struck against the wall where the soldier sat looking through the iron grating. "Hallo, you shoemaker's boy, you need not be in such a hurry," cried the soldier to him. "There will be nothing to see till I come; but if you will run to the house where I have been living, and bring me my tinder-box, you shall have four shillings, but you must put your best foot foremost."

The shoemaker's boy liked the idea of getting the four shillings, so he ran very fast and fetched the tinder-box, and gave it to the soldier. And now we shall see what happened. Outside the town a large gibbet had been erected, round which stood the soldiers and several thousands of people. The king and the queen sat on splendid thrones opposite to the judges and the whole council. The soldier already stood on the ladder; but as they were about to place the rope around his neck, he said that an innocent request was often granted to a poor criminal before he suffered death. He wished very much to smoke a pipe, as it would be the last pipe he should ever smoke in the world. The king could not refuse this request, so the soldier took his tinder-box, and struck fire, once, twice, thrice,— and there in a moment stood all the dogs;—the one with eyes as big as teacups, the one with eyes as large as mill-wheels, and the third, whose eyes were like towers. "Help me now, that I may not be hanged," cried the soldier.

And the dogs fell upon the judges and all the councillors; seized one by the legs, and another by the nose, and tossed them many feet high in the air, so that they fell down and were dashed to pieces.

"I will not be touched," said the king. But the largest dog seized him, as well as the queen, and threw them after the others. Then the soldiers and all the people were afraid, and cried, "Good soldier, you shall be our king, and you shall marry the beautiful princess."

So they placed the soldier in the king's carriage, and the three dogs ran on in front and cried "Hurrah!" and the little boys whistled through their fingers, and the soldiers presented arms. The princess came out of the copper castle, and became queen, which was very pleasing to her. The wedding festivities lasted a whole week, and the dogs sat at the table, and stared with all their eyes.

The Princess and the Pea

ONCE upon a time there was a prince who wanted to marry a princess; but she would have to be a real princess. He travelled all over the world to find one, but nowhere could he get what he wanted. There were princesses enough, but it was difficult to find out whether they were real ones. There was always something about them that was not as it should be. So he came home again and was sad, for he would have liked very much to have a real princess.

One evening a terrible storm came on; there was thunder and lightning, and the rain poured down in torrents. Suddenly a knocking was heard at the city gate, and the old king went to open it.

It was a princess standing out there in front of the gate. But, good gracious! What a sight the rain and the wind had made her look. The water ran down from her hair and clothes; it ran down into the toes of her shoes and out again at the heels. And yet she said that she was a real princess.

"Well, we'll soon find that out," thought the old queen. But she said nothing, went into the bed-room, took all the bedding off the bedstead, and laid a pea on the bottom; then she took twenty mattresses and laid them on the pea, and then twenty eider-down beds on top of the mattresses.

On this the princess had to lie all night. In the morning she was asked how she had slept.

"Oh, very badly!" said she. "I have scarcely closed my eyes all night. Heaven only knows what was in the bed, but I was lying on something hard, so that I am black and blue all over my body. It's horrible!"

Now they knew that she was a real princess because she had felt the pea right through the twenty mattresses and the twenty eider-down beds.

Nobody but a real princess could be as sensitive as that.

So the prince took her for his wife, for now he knew that he had a real princess; and the pea was put in the museum, where it may still be seen, if no one has stolen it.

There, that is a true story.

Little Tiny or Thumbelina

THERE was once a woman who wished very much to have a little child, but she could not ***obtain*** her wish. At last she went to a fairy, and said, "I should so very much like to have a little child; can you tell me where I can find one?"

"Oh, that can be easily managed," said the fairy. "Here is a barleycorn of a different kind to those which grow in the farmer's fields, and which the chickens eat; put it into a flower-pot, and see what will happen."

"Thank you," said the woman, and she gave the fairy twelve shillings, which was the price of the barleycorn. Then she went home and planted it, and immediately there grew up a large handsome flower, something like a tulip in appearance, but with its leaves tightly closed as if it were still a bud. "It is a beautiful flower," said the woman, and she kissed the red and golden-colored leaves, and while she did so the flower opened, and she could see that it was a real tulip. Within the flower, upon the green velvet stamens, sat a very delicate and ***graceful*** little maiden. She was scarcely half as long as a thumb, and they gave her the name of "Thumbelina," or Tiny, because she was so small. A walnut-shell, elegantly polished, served her for a cradle; her bed was formed of blue violet-leaves, with a rose-leaf for a counterpane. Here she slept at night, but during the day she amused herself on a table, where the woman had placed a plateful of water. Round this plate were wreaths of flowers with their stems in the water, and upon it floated a large tulip-leaf, which served Tiny for a boat. Here the little maiden sat and rowed herself from side to side, with two oars made of white horse-hair. It really was a very pretty sight. Tiny could, also, sing so softly and sweetly that nothing like her singing had ever before been heard. One night, while she lay in her pretty bed, a large, ugly, wet toad crept through a broken pane of glass in the window, and leaped right upon the table where Tiny lay sleeping under her rose-leaf quilt. "What a pretty little wife this would make for my son," said the toad, and she took up the walnut-shell in which little Tiny lay asleep, and jumped through the window with it into the garden.

In the swampy margin of a broad stream in the garden lived the toad, with her son. He was uglier even than his mother, and when he saw the pretty little maiden in her elegant bed, he could only cry, "Croak, croak, croak."

"Don't speak so loud, or she will wake," said the toad, "and then she might run away, for she is as light as swan's down. We will place her on one of the water-lily leaves out in the stream; it will be like an island to her, she is so light and small, and then she cannot escape; and, while she is away, we will ***make haste*** and prepare the state-room under the marsh, in which you are to live when you are married."

Far out in the stream grew a number of water-lilies, with broad green leaves, which seemed to float on the top of the water. The largest of these leaves

---

obtain: get; attain

graceful: charming; attractive; elegant

make haste: rush; be quick

appeared farther off than the rest, and the old toad swam out to it with the walnut-shell, in which little Tiny lay still asleep. The tiny little creature woke very early in the morning, and began to cry bitterly when she found where she was, for she could see nothing but water on every side of the large green leaf, and no way of reaching the land. Meanwhile the old toad was very busy under the marsh, decking her room with rushes and wild yellow flowers, to make it look pretty for her new daughter-in-law. Then she swam out with her ugly son to the leaf on which she had placed poor little Tiny. She wanted to fetch the pretty bed, that she might put it in the bridal chamber to be ready for her. The old toad bowed low to her in the water, and said, "Here is my son, he will be your husband, and you will live happily in the marsh by the stream."

"Croak, croak, croak," was all her son could say for himself; so the toad took up the elegant little bed, and swam away with it, leaving Tiny all alone on the green leaf, where she sat and wept. She could not bear to think of living with the old toad, and having her ugly son for a husband. The little fishes, who swam about in the water beneath, had seen the toad, and heard what she said, so they lifted their heads above the water to look at the little maiden. As soon as they caught sight of her, they saw she was very pretty, and it made them very sorry to think that she must go and live with the ugly toads. "No, it must never be!" so they ***assembled*** together in the water, round the green stalk which held the leaf on which the little maiden stood, and ***gnawed*** it away at the root with their teeth. Then the leaf floated down the stream, carrying Tiny far away out of reach of land.

Tiny sailed past many towns, and the little birds in the bushes saw her, and sang, "What a lovely little creature;" so the leaf swam away with her farther and farther, till it brought her to other lands. A graceful little white butterfly ***constantly*** fluttered round her, and at last ***alighted*** on the leaf. Tiny pleased him, and she was glad of it, for now the toad could not possibly reach her, and the country through which she sailed was beautiful, and the sun shone upon the water, till it glittered like liquid gold. She took off her girdle and tied one end of it round the butterfly, and the other end of the ribbon she fastened to the leaf, which now glided on much faster than ever, taking little Tiny with it as she stood. Presently a large cockchafer flew by; the moment he caught sight of her, he seized her round her delicate waist with his claws, and flew with her into a tree. The green leaf floated away on the brook, and the butterfly flew with it, for he was fastened to it, and could not get away.

Oh, how frightened little Tiny felt when the cockchafer flew with her to the tree! But especially was she sorry for the beautiful white butterfly which she had fastened to the leaf, for if he could not free himself he would die of hunger. But the cockchafer did not trouble himself at all about the matter. He seated himself

---

assembled: gather
gnawed: chewed
constantly: all the time
alighted: landed

by her side on a large green leaf, gave her some honey from the flowers to eat, and told her she was very pretty, though not in the least like a cockchafer. After a time, all the cockchafers turned up their feelers, and said, "She has only two legs! how ugly that looks." "She has no feelers," said another. "Her waist is quite slim. Pooh! she is like a human being."

"Oh! she is ugly," said all the lady cockchafers, although Tiny was very pretty. Then the cockchafer who had run away with her, believed all the others when they said she was ugly, and would have nothing more to say to her, and told her she might go where she liked. Then he flew down with her from the tree, and placed her on a daisy, and she wept at the thought that she was so ugly that even the cockchafers would have nothing to say to her. And all the while she was really the loveliest creature that one could imagine, and as tender and delicate as a beautiful rose-leaf. During the whole summer poor little Tiny lived quite alone in the wide forest. She wove herself a bed with blades of grass, and hung it up under a broad leaf, to protect herself from the rain. She sucked the honey from the flowers for food, and drank the dew from their leaves every morning. So passed away the summer and the autumn, and then came the winter,— the long, cold winter. All the birds who had sung to her so sweetly were flown away, and the trees and the flowers had ***withered***. The large clover leaf under the shelter of which she had lived, was now rolled together and shrivelled up, nothing remained but a yellow withered stalk. She felt dreadfully cold, for her clothes were torn, and she was herself so ***frail*** and delicate, that poor little Tiny was nearly frozen to death. It began to snow too; and the snow-flakes, as they fell upon her, were like a whole shovelful falling upon one of us, for we are tall, but she was only an inch high. Then she wrapped herself up in a dry leaf, but it cracked in the middle and could not keep her warm, and she shivered with cold. Near the wood in which she had been living lay a corn-field, but the corn had been cut a long time; nothing remained but the bare dry stubble standing up out of the frozen ground. It was to her like struggling through a large wood. Oh! How she shivered with the cold. She came at last to the door of a field-mouse, who had a little den under the corn-stubble. There dwelt the field-mouse in warmth and comfort, with a whole roomful of corn, a kitchen, and a beautiful dining room. Poor little Tiny stood before the door just like a little beggar-girl, and begged for a small piece of barley-corn, for she had been without a morsel to eat for two days.

"You poor little creature," said the field-mouse, who was really a good old field-mouse, "come into my warm room and dine with me." She was very pleased with Tiny, so she said, "You are quite welcome to stay with me all the winter, if you like; but you must keep my rooms clean and neat, and tell me stories, for I shall like to hear them very much." And Tiny did all the field-mouse asked her, and found herself very comfortable.

"We shall have a visitor soon," said the field-mouse one day; "my neighbor pays me a visit once a week. He is better off than I am; he has large rooms, and

---

withered: dried up

frail: weak

wears a beautiful black velvet coat. If you could only have him for a husband, you would be well provided for indeed. But he is blind, so you must tell him some of your prettiest stories."

But Tiny did not feel at all interested about this neighbor, for he was a mole. However, he came and paid his visit dressed in his black velvet coat.

"He is very rich and learned, and his house is twenty times larger than mine," said the field-mouse.

He was rich and learned, no doubt, but he always spoke slightingly of the sun and the pretty flowers, because he had never seen them. Tiny was obliged to sing to him, "Lady-bird, lady-bird, fly away home," and many other pretty songs. And the mole fell in love with her because she had such a sweet voice; but he said nothing yet, for he was very cautious. A short time before, the mole had dug a long passage under the earth, which led from the dwelling of the field-mouse to his own, and here she had permission to walk with Tiny whenever she liked. But he warned them not to be alarmed at the sight of a dead bird which lay in the passage. It was a perfect bird, with a beak and feathers, and could not have been dead long, and was lying just where the mole had made his passage. The mole took a piece of phosphorescent wood in his mouth, and it glittered like fire in the dark; then he went before them to light them through the long, dark passage. When they came to the spot where lay the dead bird, the mole pushed his broad nose through the ceiling, the earth gave way, so that there was a large hole, and the daylight shone into the passage. In the middle of the floor lay a dead swallow, his beautiful wings pulled close to his sides, his feet and his head drawn up under his feathers; the poor bird had ***evidently*** died of the cold. It made little Tiny very sad to see it, she did so love the little birds; all the summer they had sung and twittered for her so beautifully. But the mole pushed it aside with his crooked legs, and said, "He will sing no more now. How miserable it must be to be born a little bird! I am thankful that none of my children will ever be birds, for they can do nothing but cry, 'Tweet, tweet,' and always die of hunger in the winter."

"Yes, you may well say that, as a clever man!" exclaimed the field-mouse, "What is the use of his twittering, for when winter comes he must either starve or be frozen to death. Still birds are very high bred."

Tiny said nothing; but when the two others had turned their backs on the bird, she stooped down and stroked aside the soft feathers which covered the head, and kissed the closed eyelids. "Perhaps this was the one who sang to me so sweetly in the summer," she said; "and how much pleasure it gave me, you dear, pretty bird."

The mole now stopped up the hole through which the daylight shone, and then accompanied the lady home. But during the night Tiny could not sleep; so she got out of bed and wove a large, beautiful carpet of hay; then she carried it to the dead bird, and spread it over him; with some down from the flowers which she had found in the field-mouse's room. It was as soft as wool, and she spread some of it on each side of the bird, so that he might lie warmly in the

---

evidently: obviously

cold earth. "Farewell, you pretty little bird," said she, "farewell; thank you for your delightful singing during the summer, when all the trees were green, and the warm sun shone upon us." Then she laid her head on the bird's breast, but she was alarmed immediately, for it seemed as if something inside the bird went "thump, thump." It was the bird's heart; he was not really dead, only benumbed with the cold, and the warmth had ***restored*** him to life. In autumn, all the swallows fly away into warm countries, but if one happens to linger, the cold seizes it, it becomes frozen, and falls down as if dead; it remains where it fell, and the cold snow covers it. Tiny trembled very much; she was quite frightened, for the bird was large, a great deal larger than herself,—she was only an inch high. But she took courage, laid the wool more thickly over the poor swallow, and then took a leaf which she had used for her own counterpane, and laid it over the head of the poor bird. The next morning she again stole out to see him. He was alive but very weak; he could only open his eyes for a moment to look at Tiny, who stood by holding a piece of decayed wood in her hand, for she had no other lantern. "Thank you, pretty little maiden," said the sick swallow; "I have been so nicely warmed, that I shall soon regain my strength, and be able to fly about again in the warm sunshine."

"Oh," said she, "it is cold out of doors now; it snows and freezes. Stay in your warm bed; I will take care of you."

Then she brought the swallow some water in a flower-leaf, and after he had drank, he told her that he had wounded one of his wings in a thorn-bush, and could not fly as fast as the others, who were soon far away on their journey to warm countries. Then at last he had fallen to the earth, and could remember no more, nor how he came to be where she had found him. The whole winter the swallow remained underground, and Tiny nursed him with care and love. Neither the mole nor the field-mouse knew anything about it, for they did not like swallows. Very soon the spring time came, and the sun warmed the earth. Then the swallow bade farewell to Tiny, and she opened the hole in the ceiling which the mole had made. The sun shone in upon them so beautifully, that the swallow asked her if she would go with him; she could sit on his back, he said, and he would fly away with her into the green woods. But Tiny knew it would make the field-mouse very grieved if she left her in that manner, so she said, "No, I cannot."

"Farewell, then, farewell, you good, pretty little maiden," said the swallow; and he flew out into the sunshine.

Tiny looked after him, and the tears rose in her eyes. She was very fond of the poor swallow.

"Tweet, tweet," sang the bird, as he flew out into the green woods, and Tiny felt very sad. She was not allowed to go out into the warm sunshine. The corn which had been sown in the field over the house of the field-mouse had grown up high into the air, and formed a thick wood to Tiny, who was only an inch in height.

"You are going to be married, Tiny," said the field-mouse. "My neighbor has

---

restored: brought back

asked for you. What good fortune for a poor child like you. Now we will prepare your wedding clothes. They must be both woolen and linen. Nothing must be wanting when you are the mole's wife."

Tiny had to turn the spindle, and the field-mouse hired four spiders, who were to weave day and night. Every evening the mole visited her, and was continually speaking of the time when the summer would be over. Then he would keep his wedding-day with Tiny; but now the heat of the sun was so great that it burned the earth, and made it quite hard, like a stone. As soon, as the summer was over, the wedding should take place. But Tiny was not at all pleased; for she did not like the tiresome mole. Every morning when the sun rose, and every evening when it went down, she would creep out at the door, and as the wind blew aside the ears of corn, so that she could see the blue sky, she thought how beautiful and bright it seemed out there, and wished so much to see her dear swallow again. But he never returned; for by this time he had flown far away into the lovely green forest.

When autumn arrived, Tiny had her outfit quite ready; and the field-mouse said to her, "In four weeks the wedding must take place."

Then Tiny wept, and said she would not marry the disagreeable mole.

"Nonsense," replied the field-mouse. "Now don't be obstinate, or I shall bite you with my white teeth. He is a very handsome mole; the queen herself does not wear more beautiful velvets and furs. His kitchen and cellars are quite full. You ought to be very thankful for such good fortune."

So the wedding-day was fixed, on which the mole was to fetch Tiny away to live with him, deep under the earth, and never again to see the warm sun, because he did not like it. The poor child was very unhappy at the thought of saying farewell to the beautiful sun, and as the field-mouse had given her permission to stand at the door, she went to look at it once more.

"Farewell bright sun," she cried, stretching out her arm towards it; and then she walked a short distance from the house; for the corn had been cut, and only the dry stubble remained in the fields. "Farewell, farewell," she repeated, twining her arm round a little red flower that grew just by her side. "Greet the little swallow from me, if you should see him again."

"Tweet, tweet," sounded over her head suddenly. She looked up, and there was the swallow himself flying close by. As soon as he spied Tiny, he was delighted; and then she told him how unwilling she felt to marry the ugly mole, and to live always beneath the earth, and never to see the bright sun any more. And as she told him she wept.

"Cold winter is coming," said the swallow, "and I am going to fly away into warmer countries. Will you go with me? You can sit on my back, and fasten yourself on with your sash. Then we can fly away from the ugly mole and his gloomy rooms,—far away, over the mountains, into warmer countries, where the sun shines more brightly—than here; where it is always summer, and the flowers bloom in greater beauty. Fly now with me, dear little Tiny; you saved my life when I lay frozen in that dark passage."

"Yes, I will go with you," said Tiny; and she seated herself on the bird's back, with her feet on his outstretched wings, and tied her girdle to one of his strongest feathers.

Then the swallow rose in the air, and flew over forest and over sea, high above the highest mountains, covered with eternal snow. Tiny would have been frozen in the cold air, but she crept under the bird's warm feathers, keeping her little head uncovered, so that she might admire the beautiful lands over which they passed. At length they reached the warm countries, where the sun shines brightly, and the sky seems so much higher above the earth. Here, on the hedges, and by the wayside, grew purple, green, and white grapes; lemons and oranges hung from trees in the woods; and the air was fragrant with myrtles and orange blossoms. Beautiful children ran along the country lanes, playing with large gay butterflies; and as the swallow flew farther and farther, every place appeared still more lovely.

At last they came to a blue lake, and by the side of it, shaded by trees of the deepest green, stood a palace of dazzling white marble, built in the olden times. Vines clustered round its lofty pillars, and at the top were many swallows' nests, and one of these was the home of the swallow who carried Tiny.

"This is my house," said the swallow; "but it would not do for you to live there—you would not be comfortable. You must choose for yourself one of those lovely flowers, and I will put you down upon it, and then you shall have everything that you can wish to make you happy."

"That will be ***delightful***," she said, and clapped her little hands for joy.

A large marble pillar lay on the ground, which, in falling, had been broken into three pieces. Between these pieces grew the most beautiful large white flowers; so the swallow flew down with Tiny, and placed her on one of the broad leaves. But how surprised she was to see in the middle of the flower, a tiny little man, as white and ***transparent*** as if he had been made of crystal! He had a gold crown on his head, and delicate wings at his shoulders, and was not much larger than Tiny herself. He was the angel of the flower; for a tiny man and a tiny woman dwell in every flower; and this was the king of them all.

"Oh, how beautiful he is!" whispered Tiny to the swallow.

The little prince was at first quite frightened at the bird, who was like a giant, compared to such a delicate little creature as himself; but when he saw Tiny, he was delighted, and thought her the prettiest little maiden he had ever seen. He took the gold crown from his head, and placed it on hers, and asked her name, and if she would be his wife, and queen over all the flowers.

This certainly was a very different sort of husband to the son of a toad, or the mole, with my black velvet and fur; so she said, "Yes," to the handsome prince. Then all the flowers opened, and out of each came a little lady or a tiny lord, all so pretty it was quite a pleasure to look at them. Each of them brought Tiny a present; but the best gift was a pair of beautiful wings, which had belonged to a

---

delightful: wonderful
transparent: see-through

large white fly and they fastened them to Tiny's shoulders, so that she might fly from flower to flower. Then there was much rejoicing, and the little swallow who sat above them, in his nest, was asked to sing a wedding song, which he did as well as he could; but in his heart he felt sad for he was very fond of Tiny, and would have liked never to part from her again.

"You must not be called Tiny any more," said the spirit of the flowers to her. "It is an ugly name, and you are so very pretty. We will call you Maia."

"Farewell, farewell," said the swallow, with a heavy heart as he left the warm countries to fly back into Denmark. There he had a nest over the window of a house in which dwelt the writer of fairy tales. The swallow sang, "Tweet, tweet," and from his song came the whole story.

The Little Mermaid

FAR out in the ocean, where the water is as blue as the prettiest cornflower, and as clear as crystal, it is very, very deep; so deep, indeed, that no cable could fathom it: many church steeples, piled one upon another, would not reach from the ground beneath to the surface of the water above. There dwell the Sea King and his subjects. We must not imagine that there is nothing at the bottom of the sea but bare yellow sand. No, indeed; the most singular flowers and plants grow there; the leaves and stems of which are so pliant, that the slightest ***agitation*** of the water causes them to stir as if they had life. Fishes, both large and small, glide between the branches, as birds fly among the trees here upon land. In the deepest spot of all, stands the castle of the Sea King. Its walls are built of coral, and the long, gothic windows are of the clearest amber. The roof is formed of shells that open and close as the water flows over them. Their appearance is very beautiful, for in each lies a ***glittering*** pearl, which would be fit for the diadem of a queen.

The Sea King had been a widower for many years, and his aged mother kept house for him. She was a very wise woman, and exceedingly proud of her high birth; on that account she wore twelve oysters on her tail; while others, also of high rank, were only allowed to wear six. She was, however, deserving of very great praise, especially for her care of the little sea-princesses, her grand-daughters. They were six beautiful children; but the youngest was the prettiest of them all; her skin was as clear and delicate as a rose-leaf, and her eyes as blue as the deepest sea; but, like all the others, she had no feet, and her body ended in a fish's tail. All day long they played in the great halls of the castle, or among the living flowers that grew out of the walls. The large amber windows were open, and the fish swam in, just as the swallows fly into our houses when we open the windows, excepting that the fishes swam up to the princesses, ate out of their hands, and allowed themselves to be stroked. Outside the castle there was a

---

agitation: shaking
glittering: shining brightly

© Pushkin/Dreamstime.com

beautiful garden, in which grew bright red and dark blue flowers, and blossoms like flames of fire; the fruit glittered like gold, and the leaves and stems waved to and fro continually. The earth itself was the finest sand, but blue as the flame of burning sulphur. Over everything lay a peculiar blue radiance, as if it were surrounded by the air from above, through which the blue sky shone, instead of the dark depths of the sea. In calm weather the sun could be seen, looking like a purple flower, with the light streaming from the calyx. Each of the young princesses had a little plot of ground in the garden, where she might dig and plant as she pleased. One arranged her flower-bed into the form of a whale; another thought it better to make hers like the figure of a little mermaid; but that of the youngest was round like the sun, and contained flowers as red as his rays at sunset. She was a strange child, quiet and thoughtful; and while her sisters would be delighted with the wonderful things which they obtained from the wrecks of vessels, she cared for nothing but her pretty red flowers, like the sun, excepting a beautiful marble statue. It was the representation of a handsome boy, carved out of pure white stone, which had fallen to the bottom of the sea from a wreck. She planted by the statue a rose-colored weeping willow. It grew splendidly and very soon hung its fresh branches over the statue, almost down to the blue sands. The shadow had a violet tint, and waved to and fro like the branches; it seemed as if the crown of the tree and the root were at play, and trying to kiss each other. Nothing gave her so much pleasure as to hear about the world above the sea. She made her old grandmother tell her all she knew of the ships and of the towns, the people and the animals. To her it seemed most wonderful and beautiful to hear that the flowers of the land should have ***fragrance***, and not those below the sea; that the trees of the forest should be green; and that the fishes among the trees could sing so sweetly, that it was quite a pleasure to hear them. Her grandmother called the little birds fishes, or she would not have understood her; for she had never seen birds.

"When you have reached your fifteenth year," said the grand-mother, "you will have permission to rise up out of the sea, to sit on the rocks in the moonlight, while the great ships are sailing by; and then you will see both forests and towns."

In the following year, one of the sisters would be fifteen: but as each was a year younger than the other, the youngest would have to wait five years before her turn came to rise up from the bottom of the ocean, and see the earth as we do. However, each promised to tell the others what she saw on her first visit, and what she thought the most beautiful; for their grandmother could not tell them enough; there were so many things on which they wanted information. None of them longed so much for her turn to come as the youngest, she who had the longest time to wait, and who was so quiet and thoughtful. Many nights she stood by the open window, looking up through the dark blue water, and watching the fish as they splashed about with their fins and tails. She could see the moon and stars shining faintly; but through the water they looked larger than

---

fragrance: pleasant smell

they do to our eyes. When something like a black cloud passed between her and them, she knew that it was either a whale swimming over her head, or a ship full of human beings, who never imagined that a pretty little mermaid was standing beneath them, holding out her white hands towards the keel of their ship.

As soon as the eldest was fifteen, she was allowed to rise to the surface of the ocean. When she came back, she had hundreds of things to talk about; but the most beautiful, she said, was to lie in the moonlight, on a sandbank, in the quiet sea, near the coast, and to gaze on a large town nearby, where the lights were twinkling like hundreds of stars; to listen to the sounds of the music, the noise of carriages, and the voices of human beings, and then to hear the merry bells peal out from the church steeples; and because she could not go near to all those wonderful things, she ***longed for*** them more than ever. Oh, did not the youngest sister listen ***eagerly*** to all these descriptions? And afterwards, when she stood at the open window looking up through the dark blue water, she thought of the great city, with all its bustle and noise, and even fancied she could hear the sound of the church bells, down in the depths of the sea.

In another year the second sister received permission to rise to the surface of the water, and to swim about where she pleased. She rose just as the sun was setting, and this, she said, was the most beautiful sight of all. The whole sky looked like gold, while violet and rose-colored clouds, which she could not describe, floated over her; and, still more rapidly than the clouds, flew a large flock of wild swans towards the setting sun, looking like a long white veil across the sea. She also swam towards the sun; but it sunk into the waves, and the rosy tints faded from the clouds and from the sea.

The third sister's turn followed; she was the boldest of them all, and she swam up a broad river that emptied itself into the sea. On the banks she saw green hills covered with beautiful vines; palaces and castles peeped out from amid the proud trees of the forest; she heard the birds singing, and the rays of the sun were so powerful that she was obliged often to dive down under the water to cool her burning face. In a narrow creek she found a whole troop of little human children, quite naked, and sporting about in the water; she wanted to play with them, but they fled in a great fright; and then a little black animal came to the water; it was a dog, but she did not know that, for she had never before seen one. This animal barked at her so terribly that she became frightened, and rushed back to the open sea. But she said she should never forget the beautiful forest, the green hills, and the pretty little children who could swim in the water, although they had not fish's tails.

The fourth sister was more ***timid***; she remained in the midst of the sea, but she said it was quite as beautiful there as nearer the land. She could see for so many miles around her, and the sky above looked like a bell of glass. She had seen the ships, but at such a great distance that they looked like sea-gulls. The dolphins sported in the waves, and the great whales spouted water from their

---

longed for: wanted very much
eagerly: keenly; enthusiastically
timid: shy and nervous

nostrils till it seemed as if a hundred fountains were playing in every direction.

The fifth sister's birthday occurred in the winter; so when her turn came, she saw what the others had not seen the first time they went up. The sea looked quite green, and large icebergs were floating about, each like a pearl, she said, but larger and loftier than the churches built by men. They were of the most singular shapes, and glittered like diamonds. She had seated herself upon one of the largest, and let the wind play with her long hair, and she remarked that all the ships sailed by rapidly, and steered as far away as they could from the iceberg, as if they were afraid of it. Towards evening, as the sun went down, dark clouds covered the sky, the thunder rolled and the lightning flashed, and the red light glowed on the icebergs as they rocked and tossed on the heaving sea. On all the ships the sails were reefed with fear and trembling, while she sat calmly on the floating iceberg, watching the blue lightning, as it darted its forked flashes into the sea.

When first the sisters had permission to rise to the surface, they were each delighted with the new and beautiful sights they saw; but now, as grown-up girls, they could go when they pleased, and they had become ***indifferent*** about it. They wished themselves back again in the water, and after a month had passed they said it was much more beautiful down below, and pleasanter to be at home. Yet often, in the evening hours, the five sisters would twine their arms round each other, and rise to the surface, in a row. They had more beautiful voices than any human being could have; and before the approach of a storm, and when they expected a ship would be lost, they swam before the vessel, and sang sweetly of the delights to be found in the depths of the sea, and begging the sailors not to fear if they sank to the bottom. But the sailors could not understand the song; they took it for the howling of the storm. And these things were never to be beautiful for them; for if the ship sank, the men were drowned, and their dead bodies alone reached the palace of the Sea King.

When the sisters rose, arm-in-arm, through the water in this way, their youngest sister would stand quite alone, looking after them, ready to cry; only that the mermaids have no tears, and therefore they suffer more. "Oh, were I but fifteen years old," said she: "I know that I shall love the world up there, and all the people who live in it."

At last she reached her fifteenth year. "Well, now, you are grown up," said the old dowager, her grandmother; "so you must let me adorn you like your other sisters;" and she placed a wreath of white lilies in her hair, and every flower leaf was half a pearl. Then the old lady ordered eight great oysters to attach themselves to the tail of the princess to show her high rank.

"But they hurt me so," said the little mermaid.

"Pride must suffer pain," replied the old lady. Oh, how gladly she would have shaken off all this grandeur, and laid aside the heavy wreath! The red flowers in her own garden would have suited her much better, but she could not help herself: so she said, "Farewell," and rose as lightly as a bubble to the surface of the water. The sun had just set as she raised her head above the

---

indifferent: uninterested

waves; but the clouds were tinted with crimson and gold, and through the glimmering twilight beamed the evening star in all its beauty. The sea was calm, and the air mild and fresh. A large ship, with three masts, lay becalmed on the water, with only one sail set; for not a breeze stiffed, and the sailors sat idle on deck or amongst the rigging. There was music and song on board; and, as darkness came on, a hundred colored lanterns were lighted, as if the flags of all nations waved in the air. The little mermaid swam close to the cabin windows; and now and then, as the waves lifted her up, she could look in through clear glass window-panes, and see a number of well-dressed people within. Among them was a young prince, the most beautiful of all, with large black eyes; he was sixteen years of age, and his birthday was being kept with much rejoicing. The sailors were dancing on deck, but when the prince came out of the cabin, more than a hundred rockets rose in the air, making it as bright as day. The little mermaid was so ***startled*** that she dived under water; and when she again stretched out her head, it appeared as if all the stars of heaven were falling around her, she had never seen such fireworks before. Great suns spurted fire about, splendid fireflies flew into the blue air, and everything was reflected in the clear, calm sea beneath. The ship itself was so brightly ***illuminated*** that all the people, and even the smallest rope, could be ***distinctly*** and plainly seen. And how handsome the young prince looked, as he pressed the hands of all present and smiled at them, while the music resounded through the clear night air.

It was very late; yet the little mermaid could not take her eyes from the ship, or from the beautiful prince. The colored lanterns had been extinguished, no more rockets rose in the air, and the cannon had ***ceased*** firing; but the sea became restless, and a moaning, grumbling sound could be heard beneath the waves: still the little mermaid remained by the cabin window, rocking up and down on the water, which ***enabled*** her to look in. After a while, the sails were quickly unfurled, and the noble ship continued her passage; but soon the waves rose higher, heavy clouds darkened the sky, and lightning appeared in the distance. A dreadful storm was approaching; once more the sails were reefed, and the great ship ***pursued*** her flying course over the raging sea. The waves rose mountains high, as if they would have overtopped the mast; but the ship dived like a swan between them, and then rose again on their lofty, foaming crests. To the little mermaid this appeared pleasant sport; not so to the sailors. At length the ship groaned and creaked; the thick planks gave way under the lashing of the sea as it broke over the deck; the mainmast snapped asunder like a reed; the ship lay over on her side; and the water rushed in. The little mermaid now perceived that the crew were in danger; even she herself was obliged to be careful to avoid the beams and planks of the wreck which lay scattered on the water. At one

---

startled: scared
illuminated: lit with bright lights
distinctly: clearly
ceased: stopped
enabled: made possible
pursued: followed

moment it was so pitch dark that she could not see a single object, but a flash of lightning ***revealed*** the whole scene; she could see every one who had been on board excepting the prince; when the ship parted, she had seen him sink into the deep waves, and she was glad, for she thought he would now be with her; and then she remembered that human beings could not live in the water, so that when he got down to her father's palace he would be quite dead. But he must not die. So she swam about among the beams and planks which strewed the surface of the sea, forgetting that they could crush her to pieces. Then she dived deeply under the dark waters, rising and falling with the waves, till at length she managed to reach the young prince, who was fast losing the power of swimming in that stormy sea. His limbs were failing him, his beautiful eyes were closed, and he would have died had not the little mermaid come to his ***assistance***. She held his head above the water, and let the waves drift them where they would.

In the morning the storm had ceased; but of the ship not a single fragment could be seen. The sun rose up red and glowing from the water, and its beams brought back the hue of health to the prince's cheeks; but his eyes remained closed. The mermaid kissed his high, smooth forehead, and stroked back his wet hair; he seemed to her like the marble statue in her little garden, and she kissed him again, and wished that he might live. Presently they came in sight of land; she saw lofty blue mountains on which the white snow rested as if a flock of swans were lying upon them. Near the coast were beautiful green forests, and close by stood a large building, whether a church or a convent she could not tell. Orange and citron trees grew in the garden, and before the door stood lofty palms. The sea here formed a little bay, in which the water was quite still, but very deep; so she swam with the handsome prince to the beach, which was covered with fine, white sand, and there she laid him in the warm sunshine, taking care to raise his head higher than his body. Then bells sounded in the large white building, and a number of young girls came into the garden. The little mermaid swam out farther from the shore and placed herself between some high rocks that rose out of the water; then she covered her head and neck with the foam of the sea so that her little face might not be seen, and watched to see what would become of the poor prince. She did not wait long before she saw a young girl approach the spot where he lay. She seemed frightened at first, but only for a moment; then she fetched a number of people, and the mermaid saw that the prince came to life again, and smiled upon those who stood round him. But to her he sent no smile; he knew not that she had saved him. This made her very unhappy, and when he was led away into the great building, she dived down sorrowfully into the water, and returned to her father's castle. She had always been silent and thoughtful, and now she was more so than ever. Her sisters asked her what she had seen during her first visit to the surface of the water; but she would tell them nothing. Many an evening and morning did she rise to the place where she had left the prince. She saw the fruits in the garden ripen till they were gathered, the snow on the tops of the mountains melt away;

---

revealed: showed
assistance: help

but she never saw the prince, and therefore she returned home, always more sorrowful than before. It was her only comfort to sit in her own little garden, and fling her arm round the beautiful marble statue which was like the prince; but she gave up tending her flowers, and they grew in wild confusion over the paths, twining their long leaves and stems round the branches of the trees, so that the whole place became dark and gloomy. At length she could bear it no longer, and told one of her sisters all about it. Then the others heard the secret, and very soon it became known to two mermaids whose intimate friend happened to know who the prince was. She had also seen the festival on board ship, and she told them where the prince came from, and where his palace stood.

"Come, little sister," said the other princesses; then they entwined their arms and rose up in a long row to the surface of the water, close by the spot where they knew the prince's palace stood. It was built of bright yellow shining stone, with long flights of marble steps, one of which reached quite down to the sea. Splendid gilded cupolas rose over the roof, and between the pillars that surrounded the whole building stood life-like statues of marble. Through the clear crystal of the lofty windows could be seen noble rooms, with costly silk curtains and hangings of tapestry; while the walls were covered with beautiful paintings which were a pleasure to look at. In the centre of the largest saloon a fountain threw its sparkling jets high up into the glass cupola of the ceiling, through which the sun shone down upon the water and upon the beautiful plants growing round the basin of the fountain. Now that she knew where he lived, she spent many an evening and many a night on the water near the palace. She would swim much nearer the shore than any of the others ventured to do; indeed once she went quite up the narrow channel under the marble balcony, which threw a broad shadow on the water. Here she would sit and watch the young prince, who thought himself quite alone in the bright moonlight. She saw him many times of an evening sailing in a pleasant boat, with music playing and flags waving. She peeped out from among the green rushes, and if the wind caught her long silvery-white veil, those who saw it believed it to be a swan, spreading out its wings. On many a night, too, when the fishermen, with their torches, were out at sea, she heard them relate so many good things about the doings of the young prince, that she was glad she had saved his life when he had been tossed about half-dead on the waves. And she remembered that his head had rested on her bosom, and how heartily she had kissed him; but he knew nothing of all this, and could not even dream of her. She grew more and more fond of human beings, and wished more and more to be able to wander about with those whose world seemed to be so much larger than her own. They could fly over the sea in ships, and mount the high hills which were far above the clouds; and the lands they possessed, their woods and their fields, stretched far away beyond the reach of her sight. There was so much that she wished to know, and her sisters were unable to answer all her questions. Then she applied to her old grandmother, who knew all about the upper world, which she very rightly called the lands above the sea.

"If human beings are not drowned," asked the little mermaid, "can they live forever? do they never die as we do here in the sea?"

"Yes," replied the old lady, "they must also die, and their term of life is even shorter than ours. We sometimes live to three hundred years, but when we cease to exist here we only become the foam on the surface of the water, and we have not even a grave down here of those we love. We have not ***immortal*** souls, we shall never live again; but, like the green sea-weed, when once it has been cut off, we can never flourish more. Human beings, on the contrary, have a soul which lives forever, lives after the body has been turned to dust. It rises up through the clear, pure air beyond the glittering stars. As we rise out of the water, and behold all the land of the earth, so do they rise to unknown and ***glorious*** regions which we shall never see."

"Why have not we an immortal soul?" asked the little mermaid ***mournfully***; "I would give gladly all the hundreds of years that I have to live, to be a human being only for one day, and to have the hope of knowing the happiness of that glorious world above the stars."

"You must not think of that," said the old woman; "we feel ourselves to be much happier and much better off than human beings."

"So I shall die," said the little mermaid, "and as the foam of the sea I shall be driven about never again to hear the music of the waves, or to see the pretty flowers nor the red sun. Is there anything I can do to win an immortal soul?"

"No," said the old woman, "unless a man were to love you so much that you were more to him than his father or mother; and if all his thoughts and all his love were fixed upon you, and the priest placed his right hand in yours, and he promised to be true to you here and hereafter, then his soul would glide into your body and you would obtain a share in the future happiness of mankind. He would give a soul to you and ***retain*** his own as well; but this can never happen. Your fish's tail, which amongst us is considered so beautiful, is thought on earth to be quite ugly; they do not know any better, and they think it necessary to have two stout props, which they call legs, in order to be handsome."

Then the little mermaid sighed, and looked sorrowfully at her fish's tail. "Let us be happy," said the old lady, "and dart and spring about during the three hundred years that we have to live, which is really quite long enough; after that we can rest ourselves all the better. This evening we are going to have a court ball."

It is one of those splendid sights which we can never see on earth. The walls and the ceiling of the large ball-room were of thick, but transparent crystal. May hundreds of colossal shells, some of a deep red, others of a grass green, stood on each side in rows, with blue fire in them, which lighted up the whole saloon, and shone through the walls, so that the sea was also illuminated. Innumerable fishes, great and small, swam past the crystal walls; on some of them the scales glowed with a purple brilliancy, and on others they shone like silver and gold. Through the halls flowed a broad stream, and in it danced the mermen and the

---

immortal: live forever
glorious: wonderful
mournfully: sadly
retain: keep

© Ateliersommerland/Dreamstime.com

mermaids to the music of their own sweet singing. No one on earth has such a lovely voice as theirs. The little mermaid sang more sweetly than them all. The whole court applauded her with hands and tails; and for a moment her heart felt quite gay, for she knew she had the loveliest voice of any on earth or in the sea. But she soon thought again of the world above her, for she could not forget the charming prince, nor her sorrow that she had not an immortal soul like his; therefore she crept away silently out of her father's palace, and while everything within was gladness and song, she sat in her own little garden sorrowful and alone. Then she heard the bugle sounding through the water, and thought—"He is certainly sailing above, he on whom my wishes depend, and in whose hands I should like to place the happiness of my life. I will ***venture*** all for him, and to win an immortal soul, while my sisters are dancing in my father's palace, I will go to the sea witch, of whom I have always been so much afraid, but she can give me counsel and help."

And then the little mermaid went out from her garden, and took the road to the foaming whirlpools, behind which the sorceress lived. She had never been that way before: neither flowers nor grass grew there; nothing but bare, gray, sandy ground stretched out to the whirlpool, where the water, like foaming mill-wheels, whirled round everything that it seized, and cast it into the fathomless deep. Through the midst of these crushing whirlpools the little mermaid was obliged to pass, to reach the dominions of the sea witch; and also for a long distance the only road lay right across a quantity of warm, bubbling mire, called by the witch her turfmoor. Beyond this stood her house, in the centre of a strange forest, in which all the trees and flowers were polypi, half animals and half plants; they looked like serpents with a hundred heads growing out of the ground. The branches were long slimy arms, with fingers like flexible worms, moving limb after limb from the root to the top. All that could be reached in the sea they seized upon, and held fast, so that it never escaped from their clutches. The little mermaid was so alarmed at what she saw, that she stood still, and her heart beat with fear, and she was very nearly turning back; but she thought of the prince, and of the human soul for which she longed, and her courage returned. She fastened her long flowing hair round her head, so that the polypi might not seize hold of it. She laid her hands together across her bosom, and then she darted forward as a fish shoots through the water, between the supple arms and fingers of the ugly polypi, which were stretched out on each side of her. She saw that each held in its grasp something it had seized with its numerous little arms, as if they were iron bands. The white skeletons of human beings who had ***perished*** at sea, and had sunk down into the deep waters, skeletons of land animals, oars, rudders, and chests of ships were lying tightly grasped by their clinging arms; even a little mermaid, whom they had caught and strangled; and this seemed the most shocking of all to the little princess.

She now came to a space of marshy ground in the wood, where large, fat water-snakes were rolling in the mire, and showing their ugly, drab-colored

---

venture: risk
perished: died

bodies. In the midst of this spot stood a house, built with the bones of shipwrecked human beings. There sat the sea witch, allowing a toad to eat from her mouth, just as people sometimes feed a canary with a piece of sugar. She called the ugly water-snakes her little chickens, and allowed them to crawl all over her bosom.

"I know what you want," said the sea witch; "it is very stupid of you, but you shall have your way, and it will bring you to sorrow, my pretty princess. You want to get rid of your fish's tail, and to have two supports instead of it, like human beings on earth, so that the young prince may fall in love with you, and that you may have an immortal soul." And then the witch laughed so loud and disgustingly, that the toad and the snakes fell to the ground, and lay there wriggling about. "You are but just in time," said the witch; "for after sunrise to-morrow I should not be able to help you till the end of another year. I will prepare a draught for you, with which you must swim to land tomorrow before sunrise, and sit down on the shore and drink it. Your tail will then disappear, and shrink up into what mankind calls legs, and you will feel great pain, as if a sword were passing through you. But all who see you will say that you are the prettiest little human being they ever saw. You will still have the same floating gracefulness of movement, and no dancer will ever tread so lightly; but at every step you take it will feel as if you were treading upon sharp knives, and that the blood must flow. If you will bear all this, I will help you."

"Yes, I will," said the little princess in a trembling voice, as she thought of the prince and the immortal soul.

"But think again," said the witch; "for when once your shape has become like a human being, you can no more be a mermaid. You will never return through the water to your sisters, or to your father's palace again; and if you do not win the love of the prince, so that he is willing to forget his father and mother for your sake, and to love you with his whole soul, and allow the priest to join your hands that you may be man and wife, then you will never have an immortal soul. The first morning after he marries another your heart will break, and you will become foam on the crest of the waves."

"I will do it," said the little mermaid, and she became pale as death.

"But I must be paid also," said the witch, "and it is not a trifle that I ask. You have the sweetest voice of any who dwell here in the depths of the sea, and you believe that you will be able to charm the prince with it also, but this voice you must give to me; the best thing you possess will I have for the price of my draught. My own blood must be mixed with it, that it may be as sharp as a two-edged sword."

"But if you take away my voice," said the little mermaid, "what is left for me?"

"Your beautiful form, your graceful walk, and your expressive eyes; surely with these you can enchain a man's heart. Well, have you lost your courage? Put out your little tongue that I may cut it off as my payment; then you shall have the powerful draught."

"It shall be," said the little mermaid.

Then the witch placed her cauldron on the fire, to prepare the magic draught.

"Cleanliness is a good thing," said she, scouring the vessel with snakes, which she had tied together in a large knot; then she pricked herself in the breast, and let the black blood drop into it. The steam that rose formed itself into such horrible shapes that no one could look at them without fear. Every moment the witch threw something else into the vessel, and when it began to boil, the sound was like the weeping of a crocodile. When at last the magic draught was ready, it looked like the clearest water. "There it is for you," said the witch. Then she cut off the mermaid's tongue, so that she became dumb, and would never again speak or sing. "If the polypi should seize hold of you as you return through the wood," said the witch, "throw over them a few drops of the potion, and their fingers will be torn into a thousand pieces." But the little mermaid had no occasion to do this, for the polypi sprang back in terror when they caught sight of the glittering draught, which shone in her hand like a twinkling star.

So she passed quickly through the wood and the marsh, and between the rushing whirlpools. She saw that in her father's palace the torches in the ballroom were extinguished, and all within asleep; but she did not venture to go in to them, for now she was dumb and going to leave them forever, she felt as if her heart would break. She stole into the garden, took a flower from the flower-beds of each of her sisters, kissed her hand a thousand times towards the palace, and then rose up through the dark blue waters. The sun had not risen when she came in sight of the prince's palace, and approached the beautiful marble steps, but the moon shone clear and bright. Then the little mermaid drank the magic draught, and it seemed as if a two-edged sword went through her delicate body: she fell into a swoon, and lay like one dead. When the sun arose and shone over the sea, she recovered, and felt a sharp pain; but just before her stood the handsome young prince. He fixed his coal-black eyes upon her so earnestly that she cast down her own, and then became aware that her fish's tail was gone, and that she had as pretty a pair of white legs and tiny feet as any little maiden could have; but she had no clothes, so she wrapped herself in her long, thick hair. The prince asked her who she was, and where she came from, and she looked at him mildly and sorrowfully with her deep blue eyes; but she could not speak. Every step she took was as the witch had said it would be, she felt as if treading upon the points of needles or sharp knives; but she bore it willingly, and stepped as lightly by the prince's side as a soap-bubble, so that he and all who saw her wondered at her graceful-swaying movements. She was very soon arrayed in costly robes of silk and muslin, and was the most beautiful creature in the palace; but she was dumb, and could neither speak nor sing.

Beautiful female slaves, dressed in silk and gold, stepped forward and sang before the prince and his royal parents: one sang better than all the others, and the prince clapped his hands and smiled at her. This was great sorrow to the little mermaid; she knew how much more sweetly she herself could sing once, and she thought, "Oh if he could only know that! I have given away my voice forever, to be with him."

The slaves next performed some pretty fairy-like dances, to the sound of beautiful music. Then the little mermaid raised her lovely white arms, stood on the tips of her toes, and glided over the floor, and danced as no one yet had been able to dance. At each moment her beauty became more revealed, and her expressive eyes appealed more directly to the heart than the songs of the slaves. Everyone was enchanted, especially the prince, who called her his little foundling; and she danced again quite readily, to please him, though each time her foot touched the floor it seemed as if she trod on sharp knives.

The prince said she should remain with him always, and she received permission to sleep at his door, on a velvet cushion. He had a page's dress made for her, that she might accompany him on horseback. They rode together through the sweet-scented woods, where the green boughs touched their shoulders, and the little birds sang among the fresh leaves. She climbed with the prince to the tops of high mountains; and although her tender feet bled so that even her steps were marked, she only laughed, and followed him till they could see the clouds beneath them looking like a flock of birds travelling to distant lands. While at the prince's palace, and when all the household were asleep, she would go and sit on the broad marble steps; for it eased her burning feet to bathe them in the cold sea-water; and then she thought of all those below in the deep.

Once during the night her sisters came up arm-in-arm, singing sorrowfully, as they floated on the water. She beckoned to them, and then they recognized her, and told her how she had grieved them. After that, they came to the same place every night; and once she saw in the distance her old grandmother, who had not been to the surface of the sea for many years, and the old Sea King, her father, with his crown on his head. They stretched out their hands towards her, but they did not venture so near the land as her sisters did.

As the days passed, she loved the prince more fondly, and he loved her as he would love a little child, but it never came into his head to make her his wife; yet, unless he married her, she could not receive an immortal soul; and, on the morning after his marriage with another, she would dissolve into the foam of the sea.

"Do you not love me the best of them all?" the eyes of the little mermaid seemed to say, when he took her in his arms, and kissed her fair forehead.

"Yes, you are dear to me," said the prince; "for you have the best heart, and you are the most devoted to me; you are like a young maiden whom I once saw, but whom I shall never meet again. I was in a ship that was wrecked, and the waves cast me ashore near a holy temple, where several young maidens performed the service. The youngest of them found me on the shore, and saved my life. I saw her but twice, and she is the only one in the world whom I could love; but you are like her, and you have almost driven her image out of my mind. She belongs to the holy temple, and my good fortune has sent you to me instead of her; and we will never part."

"Ah, he knows not that it was I who saved his life," thought the little mermaid. "I carried him over the sea to the wood where the temple stands: I sat beneath the foam, and watched till the human beings came to help him. I saw the pretty maiden that he loves better than he loves me;" and the mermaid sighed deeply, but she could not shed tears. "He says the maiden belongs to the holy temple, therefore she will never return to the world. They will meet no more:

while I am by his side, and see him every day. I will take care of him, and love him, and give up my life for his sake."

Very soon it was said that the prince must marry, and that the beautiful daughter of a neighboring king would be his wife, for a fine ship was being fitted out. Although the prince gave out that he merely intended to pay a visit to the king, it was generally supposed that he really went to see his daughter. A great company were to go with him. The little mermaid smiled, and shook her head. She knew the prince's thoughts better than any of the others.

"I must travel," he had said to her; "I must see this beautiful princess; my parents desire it; but they will not oblige me to bring her home as my bride. I cannot love her; she is not like the beautiful maiden in the temple, whom you ***resemble***. If I were forced to choose a bride, I would rather choose you, my dumb foundling, with those expressive eyes." And then he kissed her rosy mouth, played with her long waving hair, and laid his head on her heart, while she dreamed of human happiness and an immortal soul. "You are not afraid of the sea, my dumb child," said he, as they stood on the deck of the noble ship which was to carry them to the country of the neighboring king. And then he told her of storm and of calm, of strange fishes in the deep beneath them, and of what the divers had seen there; and she smiled at his descriptions, for she knew better than anyone what wonders were at the bottom of the sea.

In the moonlight, when all on board were asleep, excepting the man at the helm, who was steering, she sat on the deck, gazing down through the clear water. She thought she could distinguish her father's castle, and upon it her aged grandmother, with the silver crown on her head, looking through the rushing tide at the keel of the vessel. Then her sisters came up on the waves, and gazed at her mournfully, wringing their white hands. She beckoned to them, and smiled, and wanted to tell them how happy and well off she was; but the cabin-boy approached, and when her sisters dived down he thought it was only the foam of the sea which he saw.

The next morning the ship sailed into the harbor of a beautiful town belonging to the king whom the prince was going to visit. The church bells were ringing, and from the high towers sounded a flourish of trumpets; and soldiers, with flying colors and glittering bayonets, lined the rocks through which they passed. Every day was a festival; balls and entertainments followed one another.

But the princess had not yet appeared. People said that she was being brought up and educated in a religious house, where she was learning every royal virtue. At last she came. Then the little mermaid, who was very anxious to see whether she was really beautiful, was obliged to acknowledge that she had never seen a more perfect vision of beauty. Her skin was delicately fair, and beneath her long dark eye-lashes her laughing blue eyes shone with truth and purity.

"It was you," said the prince, "who saved my life when I lay dead on the beach," and he folded his blushing bride in his arms. "Oh, I am too happy," said he to the little mermaid; "my fondest hopes are all fulfilled. You will rejoice

---

resemble: look like

at my happiness; for your devotion to me is great and sincere."

The little mermaid kissed his hand, and felt as if her heart were already broken. His wedding morning would bring death to her, and she would change into the foam of the sea. All the church bells rang, and the heralds rode about the town proclaiming the betrothal. Perfumed oil was burning in costly silver lamps on every altar. The priests waved the censers, while the bride and bridegroom joined their hands and received the blessing of the bishop. The little mermaid, dressed in silk and gold, held up the bride's train; but her ears heard nothing of the festive music, and her eyes saw not the holy ceremony; she thought of the night of death which was coming to her, and of all she had lost in the world. On the same evening the bride and bridegroom went on board ship; cannons were roaring, flags waving, and in the centre of the ship a costly tent of purple and gold had been erected. It contained elegant couches, for the reception of the bridal pair during the night. The ship, with swelling sails and a favorable wind, glided away smoothly and lightly over the calm sea. When it grew dark a number of colored lamps were lit, and the sailors danced merrily on the deck. The little mermaid could not help thinking of her first rising out of the sea, when she had seen similar festivities and joys; and she joined in the dance, poised herself in the air as a swallow when he pursues his prey, and all present cheered her with wonder. She had never danced so elegantly before. Her tender feet felt as if cut with sharp knives, but she cared not for it; a sharper pang had pierced through her heart. She knew this was the last evening she should ever see the prince, for whom she had forsaken her kindred and her home; she had given up her beautiful voice, and suffered unheard-of pain daily for him, while he knew nothing of it. This was the last evening that she would breathe the same air with him, or gaze on the starry sky and the deep sea; an eternal night, without a thought or a dream, awaited her: she had no soul and now she could never win one. All was joy and gayety on board ship till long after midnight; she laughed and danced with the rest, while the thoughts of death were in her heart. The prince kissed his beautiful bride, while she played with his raven hair, till they went arm-in-arm to rest in the splendid tent. Then all became still on board the ship; the helmsman, alone awake, stood at the helm. The little mermaid leaned her white arms on the edge of the vessel, and looked towards the east for the first blush of morning, for that first ray of dawn that would bring her death. She saw her sisters rising out of the flood: they were as pale as herself; but their long beautiful hair waved no more in the wind, and had been cut off.

"We have given our hair to the witch," said they, "to obtain help for you, that you may not die to-night. She has given us a knife: here it is, see it is very sharp. Before the sun rises you must plunge it into the heart of the prince; when the warm blood falls upon your feet they will grow together again, and form into a fish's tail, and you will be once more a mermaid, and return to us to live out your three hundred years before you die and change into the salt sea foam. Haste, then; he or you must die before sunrise. Our old grandmother moans so for you, that her white hair is falling off from sorrow, as ours fell under the witch's scissors. Kill the prince and come back; hasten: do you not see the first red streaks in the sky? In a few minutes the sun will rise, and you must die." And then they sighed deeply and mournfully, and sank down beneath the waves.

The little mermaid drew back the crimson curtain of the tent, and beheld the fair bride with her head resting on the prince's breast. She bent down and kissed his fair brow, then looked at the sky on which the rosy dawn grew brighter and brighter; then she glanced at the sharp knife, and again fixed her eyes on the prince, who whispered the name of his bride in his dreams. She was in his thoughts, and the knife trembled in the hand of the little mermaid: then she flung it far away from her into the waves; the water turned red where it fell, and the drops that spurted up looked like blood. She cast one more lingering, half-fainting glance at the prince, and then threw herself from the ship into the sea, and thought her body was dissolving into foam. The sun rose above the waves, and his warm rays fell on the cold foam of the little mermaid, who did not feel as if she were dying. She saw the bright sun, and all around her floated hundreds of transparent beautiful beings; she could see through them the white sails of the ship, and the red clouds in the sky; their speech was melodious, but too ethereal to be heard by mortal ears, as they were also unseen by mortal eyes. The little mermaid perceived that she had a body like theirs, and that she continued to rise higher and higher out of the foam. "Where am I?" asked she, and her voice sounded ethereal, as the voice of those who were with her; no earthly music could imitate it.

"Among the daughters of the air," answered one of them. "A mermaid has not an immortal soul, nor can she obtain one unless she wins the love of a human being. On the power of another hangs her eternal destiny. But the daughters of the air, although they do not possess an immortal soul, can, by their good deeds, procure one for themselves. We fly to warm countries, and cool the sultry air that destroys mankind with the pestilence. We carry the perfume of the flowers to spread health and restoration. After we have striven for three hundred years to all the good in our power, we receive an immortal soul and take part in the happiness of mankind. You, poor little mermaid, have tried with your whole heart to do as we are doing; you have suffered and endured and raised yourself to the spirit-world by your good deeds; and now, by striving for three hundred years in the same way, you may obtain an immortal soul."

The little mermaid lifted her glorified eyes towards the sun, and felt them, for the first time, filling with tears. On the ship, in which she had left the prince, there were life and noise; she saw him and his beautiful bride searching for her; sorrowfully they gazed at the pearly foam, as if they knew she had thrown herself into the waves. Unseen she kissed the forehead of the bride, and fanned the prince, and then mounted with the other children of the air to a rosy cloud that floated through the aether.

"After three hundred years, thus shall we float into the kingdom of heaven," said she. "And we may even get there sooner," whispered one of her companions. "Unseen we can enter the houses of men, where there are children, and for every day on which we find a good child, who is the joy of his parents and deserves their love, our time of probation is shortened. The child does not know when we fly through the room that we smile with joy at his good conduct, for we can count one year less of our three hundred years. But when we see a naughty or a wicked child, we shed tears of sorrow, and for every tear a day is added to our time of trial!"

The Emperor's New Suit

MANY, many years ago lived an emperor, who thought so much of new clothes that he spent all his money in order to obtain them; his only ambition was to be always well dressed. He did not care for his soldiers, and the theatre did not amuse him; the only thing, in fact, he thought anything of was to drive out and show a new suit of clothes. He had a coat for every hour of the day; and as one would say of a king "He is in his cabinet," so one could say of him, "The emperor is in his dressing-room."

The great city where he ***resided*** was very gay; every day many strangers from all parts of the globe arrived. One day two ***swindlers*** came to this city; they made people believe that they were weavers, and declared they could ***manufacture*** the finest cloth to be imagined. Their colours and patterns, they said, were not only exceptionally beautiful, but the clothes made of their material ***possessed*** the wonderful quality of being ***invisible*** to any man who was unfit for his office or unpardonably stupid.

"That must be wonderful cloth," thought the emperor. "If I were to be dressed in a suit made of this cloth I should be able to find out which men in my empire were unfit for their places, and I could ***distinguish*** the clever from the stupid. I must have this cloth woven for me without delay." And he gave a large sum of money to the swindlers, in advance, that they should set to work without any loss of time. They set up two looms, and pretended to be very hard at work, but they did nothing whatever on the looms. They asked for the finest silk and the most precious gold-cloth; all they got they did away with, and worked at the empty looms till late at night.

"I should very much like to know how they are getting on with the cloth," thought the emperor. But he felt rather uneasy when he remembered that he who was not fit for his office could not see it. Personally, he was of opinion that he had nothing to fear, yet he thought it advisable to send somebody else first to see how matters stood. Everybody in the town knew what a remarkable quality the stuff possessed, and all were anxious to see how bad or stupid their neighbours were.

"I shall send my honest old minister to the weavers," thought the emperor.

---

resided: lived
swindlers: con-artists; crooks
manufacture: produce; make
possessed: had
invisible: unseen
distinguish: tell apart

"He can judge best how the stuff looks, for he is intelligent, and nobody understands his office better than he."

The good old minister went into the room where the swindlers sat before the empty looms. "Heaven preserve us!" he thought, and opened his eyes wide, "I cannot see anything at all," but he did not say so. Both swindlers requested him to come near, and asked him if he did not admire the ***exquisite*** pattern and the beautiful colours, pointing to the empty looms. The poor old minister tried his very best, but he could see nothing, for there was nothing to be seen. "Oh dear," he thought, "can I be so stupid? I should never have thought so, and nobody must know it! Is it possible that I am not fit for my office? No, no, I cannot say that I was unable to see the cloth."

"Now, have you got nothing to say?" said one of the swindlers, while he pretended to be busily weaving.

"Oh, it is very pretty, exceedingly beautiful," replied the old minister looking through his glasses. "What a beautiful pattern, what brilliant colours! I shall tell the emperor that I like the cloth very much."

"We are pleased to hear that," said the two weavers, and described to him the colours and explained the curious pattern. The old minister listened ***attentively***, that he might relate to the emperor what they said; and so he did.

Now the swindlers asked for more money, silk and gold-cloth, which they required for weaving. They kept everything for themselves, and not a thread came near the loom, but they continued, as hitherto, to work at the empty looms.

Soon afterwards the emperor sent another honest courtier to the weavers to see how they were getting on, and if the cloth was nearly finished. Like the old minister, he looked and looked but could see nothing, as there was nothing to be seen.

"Is it not a beautiful piece of cloth?" asked the two swindlers, showing and explaining the magnificent pattern, which, however, did not exist.

"I am not stupid," said the man. "It is therefore my good appointment for which I am not fit. It is very strange, but I must not let anyone know it;" and he praised the cloth, which he did not see, and expressed his joy at the beautiful colours and the fine pattern. "It is very excellent," he said to the emperor.

Everybody in the whole town talked about the precious cloth. At last the emperor wished to see it himself, while it was still on the loom. With a number of courtiers, including the two who had already been there, he went to the two clever swindlers, who now worked as hard as they could, but without using any thread.

"Is it not magnificent?" said the two old statesmen who had been there before. "Your Majesty must admire the colours and the pattern." And then they pointed to the empty looms, for they imagined the others could see the cloth.

"What is this?" thought the emperor, "I do not see anything at all. That is terrible! Am I stupid? Am I unfit to be emperor? That would indeed be the most dreadful thing that could happen to me."

---

exquisite: superb; wonderful
attentively: carefully; with interest

"Really," he said, turning to the weavers, "your cloth has our most gracious approval;" and nodding ***contentedly*** he looked at the empty loom, for he did not like to say that he saw nothing. All his attendants, who were with him, looked and looked, and although they could not see anything more than the others, they said, like the emperor, "It is very beautiful." And all advised him to wear the new magnificent clothes at a great procession which was soon to take place. "It is magnificent, beautiful, excellent," one heard them say; everybody seemed to be delighted, and the emperor appointed the two swindlers "Imperial Court weavers."

The whole night previous to the day on which the procession was to take place, the swindlers pretended to work, and burned more than sixteen candles. People should see that they were busy to finish the emperor's new suit. They pretended to take the cloth from the loom, and worked about in the air with big scissors, and sewed with needles without thread, and said at last: "The emperor's new suit is ready now."

The emperor and all his barons then came to the hall; the swindlers held their arms up as if they held something in their hands and said: "These are the trousers!" "This is the coat!" and "Here is the cloak!" and so on. "They are all as light as a cobweb, and one must feel as if one had nothing at all upon the body; but that is just the beauty of them."

"Indeed!" said all the courtiers; but they could not see anything, for there was nothing to be seen.

"Does it please your Majesty now to graciously undress," said the swindlers, "that we may assist your Majesty in putting on the new suit before the large looking-glass?"

The emperor undressed, and the swindlers pretended to put the new suit upon him, one piece after another; and the emperor looked at himself in the glass from every side.

"How well they look! How well they fit!" said all. "What a beautiful pattern! What fine colours! That is a magnificent suit of clothes!"

The master of the ceremonies announced that the bearers of the canopy, which was to be carried in the procession, were ready.

"I am ready," said the emperor. "Does not my suit fit me marvellously?" Then he turned once more to the looking-glass, that people should think he admired his garments.

The chamberlains, who were to carry the train, stretched their hands to the ground as if they lifted up a train, and pretended to hold something in their hands; they did not like people to know that they could not see anything.

The emperor marched in the procession under the beautiful canopy, and all who saw him in the street and out of the windows exclaimed: "Indeed, the emperor's new suit is ***incomparable***! What a long train he has! How well it fits him!" Nobody wished to let others know he saw nothing, for then he would have been unfit for his office or too stupid. Never emperor's clothes were more

---

contentedly: with satisfaction
incomparable: unique; having no equal

admired.

"But he has nothing on at all," said a little child at last. "Good heavens! Listen to the voice of an innocent child," said the father, and one whispered to the other what the child had said. "But he has nothing on at all," cried at last the whole people. That made a deep impression upon the emperor, for it seemed to him that they were right; but he thought to himself, "Now I must bear up to the end." And the chamberlains walked with still greater dignity, as if they carried the train which did not exist.

The Brave Tin Soldier

THERE were once five-and-twenty tin soldiers, who were all brothers, for they had been made out of the same old tin spoon. They shouldered arms and looked straight before them, and wore a splendid uniform, red and blue. The first thing in the world they ever heard were the words, "Tin soldiers!" uttered by a little boy, who clapped his hands with delight when the lid of the box, in which they lay, was taken off. They were given him for a birthday present, and he stood at the table to set them up. The soldiers were all exactly alike, excepting one, who had only one leg; he had been left to the last, and then there was not enough of the melted tin to finish him, so they made him to stand firmly on one leg, and this caused him to be very remarkable.

The table on which the tin soldiers stood, was covered with other playthings, but the most attractive to the eye was a pretty little paper castle. Through the small windows the rooms could be seen. In front of the castle a number of little trees surrounded a piece of looking-glass, which was ***intended*** to ***represent*** a transparent lake. Swans, made of wax, swam on the lake, and were reflected in it. All this was very pretty, but the prettiest of all was a tiny little lady, who stood at the open door of the castle; she, also, was made of paper, and she wore a dress of clear muslin, with a narrow blue ribbon over her shoulders just like a scarf. In front of these was fixed a glittering tinsel rose, as large as her whole face. The little lady was a dancer, and she stretched out both her arms, and raised one of her legs so high, that the tin soldier could not see it at all, and he thought that she, like himself, had only one leg. "That is the wife for me," he thought; "but she is too grand, and lives in a castle, while I have only a box to live in, five-and-twenty of us altogether, that is no place for her. Still I must try and ***make her acquaintance***." Then he laid himself at full length on the table behind a snuff-box that stood upon it, so that he could peep at the little delicate lady, who continued to stand on one leg without losing her balance. When evening came, the other tin soldiers were all placed in the box, and the people of the house went to bed. Then the playthings began to have their own games

---

intended: planned
represent: stand for; symbolize
make her acquaintance: meet her for the first time

together, to pay visits, to have sham fights, and to give balls. The tin soldiers rattled in their box; they wanted to get out and join the amusements, but they could not open the lid. The nut-crackers played at leap-frog, and the pencil jumped about the table. There was such a noise that the canary woke up and began to talk, and in poetry too. Only the tin soldier and the dancer remained in their places. She stood on tiptoe, with her legs stretched out, as firmly as he did on his one leg. He never took his eyes from her for even a moment. The clock struck twelve, and, with a bounce, up sprang the lid of the snuff-box; but, instead of snuff, there jumped up a little black goblin; for the snuff-box was a toy puzzle.

"Tin soldier," said the goblin, "don't wish for what does not belong to you."

But the tin soldier pretended not to hear.

"Very well; wait till to-morrow, then," said the goblin.

When the children came in the next morning, they placed the tin soldier in the window. Now, whether it was the goblin who did it, or the draught, is not known, but the window flew open, and out fell the tin soldier, heels over head, from the third story, into the street beneath. It was a terrible fall; for he came head downwards, his helmet and his bayonet stuck in between the flagstones, and his one leg up in the air. The servant maid and the little boy went down stairs directly to look for him; but he was nowhere to be seen, although once they nearly trod upon him. If he had called out, "Here I am," it would have been all right, but he was too proud to cry out for help while he wore a uniform.

Presently it began to rain, and the drops fell faster and faster, till there was a heavy shower. When it was over, two boys happened to pass by, and one of them said, "Look, there is a tin soldier. He ought to have a boat to sail in."

So they made a boat out of a newspaper, and placed the tin soldier in it, and sent him sailing down the gutter, while the two boys ran by the side of it, and clapped their hands. Good gracious, what large waves arose in that gutter, and how fast the stream rolled on for the rain had been very heavy. The paper boat rocked up and down, and turned itself round sometimes so quickly that the tin soldier trembled; yet he remained firm; his ***countenance*** did not change; he looked straight before him, and shouldered his musket. Suddenly the boat shot under a bridge which formed a part of a drain, and then it was as dark as the tin soldier's box.

"Where am I going now?" thought he. "This is the black goblin's fault, I am sure. Ah, well, if the little lady were only here with me in the boat, I should not care for any darkness."

Suddenly there appeared a great water-rat, who lived in the drain.

"Have you a passport?" asked the rat, "give it to me at once." But the tin soldier remained silent and held his musket tighter than ever. The boat sailed on and the rat followed it. How he did gnash his teeth and cry out to the bits of wood and straw, "Stop him, stop him; he has not paid toll, and has not shown his pass." But the stream rushed on stronger and stronger. The tin soldier could already see daylight shining where the arch ended. Then he heard a roaring

---

countenance: face; expression

sound quite terrible enough to frighten the bravest man. At the end of the tunnel the drain fell into a large canal over a steep place, which made it as dangerous for him as a waterfall would be to us. He was too close to it to stop, so the boat rushed on, and the poor tin soldier could only hold himself as stiffly as possible, without moving an eyelid, to show that he was not afraid. The boat whirled round three or four times, and then filled with water to the very edge; nothing could save it from sinking. He now stood up to his neck in water, while deeper and deeper sank the boat, and the paper became soft and loose with the wet, till at last the water closed over the soldier's head. He thought of the elegant little dancer whom he should never see again, and the words of the song sounded in his ears—

"Farewell, warrior! ever brave,
Drifting onward to thy grave."

Then the paper boat fell to pieces, and the soldier sank into the water and immediately afterwards was swallowed up by a great fish. Oh how dark it was inside the fish! A great deal darker than in the tunnel, and narrower too, but the tin soldier continued firm, and lay at full length shouldering his musket. The fish swam to and fro, making the most wonderful movements, but at last he became quite still. After a while, a flash of lightning seemed to pass through him, and then the daylight approached, and a voice cried out, "I declare here is the tin soldier." The fish had been caught, taken to the market and sold to the cook, who took him into the kitchen and cut him open with a large knife. She picked up the soldier and held him by the waist between her finger and thumb, and carried him into the room. They were all anxious to see this wonderful soldier who had travelled about inside a fish; but he was not at all proud. They placed him on the table, and—how many curious things do happen in the world!—there he was in the very same room from the window of which he had fallen, there were the same children, the same playthings, standing on the table, and the pretty castle with the elegant little dancer at the door; she still balanced herself on one leg, and held up the other, so she was as firm as himself. It touched the tin soldier so much to see her that he almost wept tin tears, but he kept them back. He only looked at her and they both remained silent. Presently one of the little boys took up the tin soldier, and threw him into the stove. He had no reason for doing so, therefore it must have been the fault of the black goblin who lived in the snuff-box. The flames lighted up the tin soldier, as he stood, the heat was very terrible, but whether it ***proceeded from*** the real fire or from the fire of love he could not tell. Then he could see that the bright colors were faded from his uniform, but whether they had been washed off during his journey or from the effects of his sorrow, no one could say. He looked at the little lady, and she looked at him. He felt himself melting away, but he still remained firm with his gun on his shoulder. Suddenly the door of the room flew open and the draught of air caught up the little dancer, she fluttered like a sylph right into the stove by the side of the tin soldier, and was instantly in flames and was gone. The tin soldier melted down into a lump, and the next morning, when the maid

---

proceeded from: caused by

servant took the ashes out of the stove, she found him in the shape of a little tin heart. But of the little dancer nothing remained but the tinsel rose, which was burnt black as a ***cinder***.

The Swineherd

ONCE upon a time lived a poor prince; his kingdom was very small, but it was large enough to enable him to marry, and marry he would. It was rather bold of him that he went and asked the emperor's daughter: "Will you marry me?" but he ventured to do so, for his name was known far and wide, and there were hundreds of princesses who would have gladly accepted him, but would she do so? Now we shall see.

On the grave of the prince's father grew a rose-tree, the most beautiful of its kind. It bloomed only once in five years, and then it had only one single rose upon it, but what a rose! It had such a sweet scent that one instantly forgot all sorrow and grief when one smelt it. He had also a nightingale, which could sing as if every sweet melody was in its throat. This rose and the nightingale he wished to give to the princess; and therefore both were put into big silver cases and sent to her.

The emperor ordered them to be carried into the great hall where the princess was just playing "Visitors are coming" with her ladies-in-waiting; when she saw the large cases with the presents therein, she clapped her hands for joy.

"I wish it were a little pussy cat," she said. But then the rose-tree with the beautiful rose was unpacked.

"Oh, how nicely it is made," exclaimed the ladies.

"It is more than nice," said the emperor, "it is charming."

The princess touched it and nearly began to cry.

"For shame, pa," she said, "it is not ***artificial***, it is natural!"

"For shame, it is natural" repeated all her ladies.

"Let us first see what the other case contains before we are angry," said the emperor; then the nightingale was taken out, and it sang so beautifully that no one could possibly say anything unkind about it.

"Superbe, charmant," said the ladies of the court, for they all prattled French, one worse than the other.

"How much the bird reminds me of the musical box of the late ***lamented*** empress," said an old courtier, "it has exactly the same tone, the same execution."

"You are right," said the emperor, and began to cry like a little child.

"I hope it is not natural," said the princess.

---

cinder: ashes
artificial: non-natural
lamented: mourned

"Yes, certainly it is natural," replied those who had brought the presents.

"Then let it fly," said the princess, and refused to see the prince.

But the prince was not discouraged. He painted his face, put on common clothes, pulled his cap over his forehead, and came back.

"Good day, emperor," he said, "could you not give me some employment at the court?"

"There are so many," replied the emperor, "who apply for places, that for the present I have no ***vacancy***, but I will remember you. But wait a moment; it just comes into my mind, I require somebody to look after my pigs, for I have a great many."

Thus the prince was appointed imperial swineherd, and as such he lived in a wretchedly small room near the pigsty; there he worked all day long, and when it was night he had made a pretty little pot. There were little bells round the rim, and when the water began to boil in it, the bells began to play the old tune:

"A jolly old sow once lived in a sty,
Three little piggies had she," &c.

But what was more wonderful was that, when one put a finger into the steam rising from the pot, one could at once smell what meals they were preparing on every fire in the whole town. That was indeed much more remarkable than the rose. When the princess with her ladies passed by and heard the tune, she stopped and looked quite pleased, for she also could play it—in fact, it was the only tune she could play, and she played it with one finger.

"That is the tune I know," she exclaimed. "He must be a well-educated swineherd. Go and ask him how much the instrument is."

One of the ladies had to go and ask; but she put on pattens.

"What will you take for your pot?" asked the lady.

"I will have ten kisses from the princess," said the swineherd.

"God forbid," said the lady.

"Well, I cannot sell it for less," replied the swineherd.

"What did he say?" said the princess.

"I really cannot tell you," replied the lady.

"You can whisper it into my ear."

"It is very naughty," said the princess, and walked off.

But when she had gone a little distance, the bells rang again so sweetly:

"A jolly old sow once lived in a sty,
Three little piggies had she," &c.

"Ask him," said the princess, "if he will be satisfied with ten kisses from one of my ladies."

"No, thank you," said the swineherd: "ten kisses from the princess, or I keep my pot."

"That is tiresome," said the princess. "But you must stand before me, so that nobody can see it."

The ladies placed themselves in front of her and spread out their dresses, and she gave the swineherd ten kisses and received the pot.

---

vacancy: available job

That was a pleasure! Day and night the water in the pot was boiling; there was not a single fire in the whole town of which they did not know what was preparing on it, the chamberlain's as well as the shoemaker's. The ladies danced and clapped their hands for joy.

"We know who will eat soup and pancakes; we know who will eat porridge and cutlets; oh, how interesting!"

"Very interesting, indeed," said the mistress of the household. "But you must not ***betray*** me, for I am the emperor's daughter."

"Of course not," they all said.

The swineherd—that is to say, the prince—but they did not know otherwise than that he was a real swineherd—did not waste a single day without doing something; he made a rattle, which, when turned quickly round, played all the waltzes, galops, and polkas known since the creation of the world.

"But that is *superbe,"* said the princess passing by. "I have never heard a more beautiful composition. Go down and ask him what the instrument costs; but I shall not kiss him again."

"He will have a hundred kisses from the princess," said the lady, who had gone down to ask him.

"I believe he is mad," said the princess, and walked off, but soon she stopped. "One must encourage art," she said. "I am the emperor's daughter! Tell him I will give him ten kisses, as I did the other day; the remainder one of my ladies can give him."

"But we do not like to kiss him" said the ladies.

"That is nonsense," said the princess; "if I can kiss him, you can also do it. Remember that I give you food and employment." And the lady had to go down once more.

"A hundred kisses from the princess," said the swineherd, "or everybody keeps his own."

"Place yourselves before me," said the princess then. They did as they were bidden, and the princess kissed him.

"I wonder what that crowd near the pigsty means!" said the emperor, who had just come out on his balcony. He rubbed his eyes and put his spectacles on.

"The ladies of the court are up to some mischief, I think. I shall have to go down and see." He pulled up his shoes, for they were down at the heels, and he was very quick about it. When he had come down into the courtyard he walked quite softly, and the ladies were so busily engaged in counting the kisses, that all should be fair, that they did not notice the emperor. He raised himself on tiptoe.

"What does this mean?" he said, when he saw that his daughter was kissing the swineherd, and then hit their heads with his shoe just as the swineherd received the sixty-eighth kiss.

"Go out of my sight," said the emperor, for he was very angry; and both the princess and the swineherd were ***banished*** from the empire. There she stood and cried, the swineherd scolded her, and the rain came down in torrents.

---

betray: deceive
banished: sent away

"Alas, unfortunate creature that I am!" said the princess, "I wish I had accepted the prince. Oh, how ***wretched*** I am!"

The swineherd went behind a tree, wiped his face, threw off his poor attire and stepped forth in his princely garments; he looked so beautiful that the princess could not help bowing to him.

"I have now learnt to ***despise*** you," he said. "You refused an honest prince; you did not appreciate the rose and the nightingale; but you did not mind kissing a swineherd for his toys; you have no one but yourself to blame!"

And then he returned into his kingdom and left her behind. She could now sing at her leisure:

"A jolly old sow once lived in a sty,
Three little piggies has she," &c.

The Angel

WHENEVER a good child dies, an angel of God comes down from heaven, takes the dead child in his arms, spreads out his great white wings, and flies with him over all the places which the child had loved during his life. Then he gathers a large handful of flowers, which he carries up to the Almighty that they may bloom more brightly in heaven than they do on earth. And the Almighty presses the flowers to His heart, but He kisses the flower that pleases Him best, and it receives a voice, and is able to join the song of the chorus of bliss."

These words were spoken by an angel of God, as he carried a dead child up to heaven, and the child listened as if in a dream. Then they passed over well-known spots, where the little one had often played, and through beautiful gardens full of lovely flowers.

"Which of these shall we take with us to heaven to be ***transplanted*** there?" asked the angel.

Close by grew a slender, beautiful, rose-bush, but some wicked hand had broken the stem, and the half-opened rosebuds hung faded and ***withered*** on the trailing branches.

"Poor rose-bush!" said the child, "let us take it with us to heaven, that it may bloom above in God's garden."

The angel took up the rose-bush; then he kissed the child, and the little one half opened his eyes. The angel gathered also some beautiful flowers, as well as a few humble buttercups and heart's-ease.

"Now we have flowers enough," said the child; but the angel only nodded, he did not fly upward to heaven.

---

wretched: miserable
despise: hate
transplanted: moved
withered: dried up

It was night, and quite still in the great town. Here they remained, and the angel hovered over a small, narrow street, in which lay a large heap of straw, ashes, and sweepings from the houses of people who had removed. There lay ***fragments*** of plates, pieces of plaster, rags, old hats, and other rubbish not pleasant to see. Amidst all this confusion, the angel pointed to the pieces of a broken flower-pot, and to a lump of earth which had fallen out of it. The earth had been kept from falling to pieces by the roots of a withered field-flower, which had been thrown amongst the rubbish.

"We will take this with us," said the angel, "I will tell you why as we fly along."

And as they flew the angel related the history.

"Down in that narrow lane, in a low cellar, lived a poor sick boy; he had been afflicted from his childhood, and even in his best days he could just manage to walk up and down the room on crutches once or twice, but no more. During some days in summer, the sunbeams would lie on the floor of the cellar for about half an hour. In this spot the poor sick boy would sit warming himself in the sunshine, and watching the red blood through his delicate fingers as he held them before his face. Then he would say he had been out, yet he knew nothing of the green forest in its spring verdure, till a neighbor's son brought him a green bough from a beech-tree. This he would place over his head, and fancy that he was in the beech-wood while the sun shone, and the birds carolled gayly. One spring day the neighbor's boy brought him some field-flowers, and among them was one to which the root still adhered. This he carefully planted in a flower-pot, and placed in a window-seat near his bed. And the flower had been planted by a fortunate hand, for it grew, put forth fresh shoots, and blossomed every year. It became a splendid flower-garden to the sick boy, and his little treasure upon earth. He watered it, and cherished it, and took care it should have the benefit of every sunbeam that found its way into the cellar, from the earliest morning ray to the evening sunset. The flower entwined itself even in his dreams—for him it bloomed, for him spread its perfume. And it gladdened his eyes, and to the flower he turned, even in death, when the Lord called him. He has been one year with God. During that time the flower has stood in the window, withered and forgotten, till at length cast out among the sweepings into the street, on the day of the lodgers' removal. And this poor flower, withered and faded as it is, we have added to our nosegay, because it gave more real joy than the most beautiful flower in the garden of a queen."

"But how do you know all this?" asked the child whom the angel was carrying to heaven.

"I know it," said the angel, "because I myself was the poor sick boy who walked upon crutches, and I know my own flower well."

Then the child opened his eyes and looked into the glorious happy face of the angel, and at the same moment they found themselves in that heavenly home where all is happiness and joy. And God pressed the dead child to His heart, and wings were given him so that he could fly with the angel, hand in hand. Then the

---

fragments: pieces

Almighty pressed all the flowers to His heart; but He kissed the withered field-flower, and it received a voice. Then it joined in the song of the angels, who surrounded the throne, some near, and others in a distant circle, but all equally happy. They all joined in the chorus of praise, both great and small,—the good, happy child, and the poor field-flower, that once lay withered and cast away on a heap of rubbish in a narrow, dark street.

The Nightingale

IN China, you know, the emperor is a Chinese, and all those about him are Chinamen also. The story I am going to tell you happened a great many years ago, so it is well to hear it now before it is forgotten. The emperor's palace was the most beautiful in the world. It was built ***entirely*** of porcelain, and very costly, but so delicate and brittle that whoever touched it was obliged to be careful. In the garden could be seen the most singular flowers, with pretty silver bells tied to them, which tinkled so that everyone who passed could not help noticing the flowers. Indeed, everything in the emperor's garden was remarkable, and it extended so far that the gardener himself did not know where it ended. Those who travelled beyond its limits knew that there was a noble forest, with lofty trees, sloping down to the deep blue sea, and the great ships sailed under the shadow of its branches. In one of these trees lived a nightingale, who sang so beautifully that even the poor fishermen, who had so many other things to do, would stop and listen. Sometimes, when they went at night to spread their nets, they would hear her sing, and say, "Oh, is not that beautiful?" But when they returned to their fishing, they forgot the bird until the next night. Then they would hear it again, and exclaim "Oh, how beautiful is the nightingale's song!"

Travellers from every country in the world came to the city of the emperor, which they admired very much, as well as the palace and gardens; but when they heard the nightingale, they all declared it to be the best of all. And the travellers, on their return home, related what they had seen; and learned men wrote books, containing descriptions of the town, the palace, and the gardens; but they did not forget the nightingale, which was really the greatest wonder. And those who could write poetry composed beautiful verses about the nightingale, who lived in a forest near the deep sea. The books travelled all over the world, and some of them came into the hands of the emperor; and he sat in his golden chair, and, as he read, he nodded his ***approval*** every moment, for it pleased him to find such a beautiful description of his city, his palace, and his gardens. But when he came to the words, "the nightingale is the most beautiful of all," he exclaimed, "What is this? I know nothing of any nightingale. Is there such a bird in my empire? And even in my garden? I have never heard of it. Something, it appears, may be

---

entirely: completely
approval: appreciation

learnt from books."

Then he called one of his lords-in-waiting, who was so high-bred, that when any in an inferior rank to himself spoke to him, or asked him a question, he would answer, "Pooh," which means nothing.

"There is a very wonderful bird mentioned here, called a nightingale," said the emperor; "they say it is the best thing in my large kingdom. Why have I not been told of it?"

"I have never heard the name," replied the cavalier; "she has not been presented at court."

"It is my pleasure that she shall appear this evening." said the emperor; "the whole world knows what I possess better than I do myself."

"I have never heard of her," said the cavalier; "yet I will ***endeavor*** to find her."

But where was the nightingale to be found? The nobleman went up stairs and down, through halls and passages; yet none of those whom he met had heard of the bird. So he returned to the emperor, and said that it must be a fable, invented by those who had written the book. "Your imperial majesty," said he, "cannot believe everything contained in books; sometimes they are only fiction, or what is called the black art."

"But the book in which I have read this account," said the emperor, "was sent to me by the great and mighty emperor of Japan, and therefore it cannot contain a falsehood. I will hear the nightingale, she must be here this evening; she has my highest favor; and if she does not come, the whole court shall be ***trampled*** upon after supper is ended."

"Tsing-pe!" cried the lord-in-waiting, and again he ran up and down stairs, through all the halls and corridors; and half the court ran with him, for they did not like the idea of being trampled upon. There was a great inquiry about this wonderful nightingale, whom all the world knew, but who was unknown to the court.

At last they met with a poor little girl in the kitchen, who said, "Oh, yes, I know the nightingale quite well; indeed, she can sing. Every evening I have permission to take home to my poor sick mother the scraps from the table; she lives down by the sea-shore, and as I come back I feel tired, and I sit down in the wood to rest, and listen to the nightingale's song. Then the tears come into my eyes, and it is just as if my mother kissed me."

"Little maiden," said the lord-in-waiting, "I will obtain for you constant employment in the kitchen, and you shall have permission to see the emperor dine, if you will lead us to the nightingale; for she is invited for this evening to the palace." So she went into the wood where the nightingale sang, and half the court followed her. As they went along, a cow began lowing.

"Oh," said a young courtier, "now we have found her; what wonderful power for such a small creature; I have certainly heard it before."

"No, that is only a cow lowing," said the little girl; "we are a long way from

---

endeavor: try
trampled: crushed

the place yet."

Then some frogs began to croak in the marsh.

"Beautiful," said the young courtier again. "Now I hear it, tinkling like little church bells."

"No, those are frogs," said the little maiden; "but I think we shall soon hear her now:" and presently the nightingale began to sing.

"Hark, hark! There she is," said the girl, "and there she sits," she added, pointing to a little gray bird who was perched on a bough.

"Is it possible?" said the lord-in-waiting, "I never imagined it would be a little, plain, simple thing like that. She has certainly changed color at seeing so many grand people around her."

"Little nightingale," cried the girl, raising her voice, "our most gracious emperor wishes you to sing before him."

"With the greatest pleasure," said the nightingale, and began to sing most delightfully.

"It sounds like tiny glass bells," said the lord-in-waiting, "and see how her little throat works. It is surprising that we have never heard this before; she will be a great success at court."

"Shall I sing once more before the emperor?" asked the nightingale, who thought he was present.

"My excellent little nightingale," said the courtier, "I have the great pleasure of inviting you to a court festival this evening, where you will gain imperial favor by your charming song."

"My song sounds best in the green wood," said the bird; but still she came willingly when she heard the emperor's wish.

The palace was elegantly decorated for the occasion. The walls and floors of porcelain glittered in the light of a thousand lamps. Beautiful flowers, round which little bells were tied, stood in the corridors: what with the running to and fro and the draught, these bells tinkled so loudly that no one could speak to be heard. In the centre of the great hall, a golden perch had been fixed for the nightingale to sit on. The whole court was present, and the little kitchen-maid had received permission to stand by the door. She was not installed as a real court cook. All were in full dress, and every eye was turned to the little gray bird when the emperor nodded to her to begin. The nightingale sang so sweetly that the tears came into the emperor's eyes, and then rolled down his cheeks, as her song became still more touching and went to every one's heart. The emperor was so delighted that he declared the nightingale should have his gold slipper to wear round her neck, but she ***declined*** the honor with thanks: she had been sufficiently rewarded already. "I have seen tears in an emperor's eyes," she said, "that is my richest reward. An emperor's tears have wonderful power, and are quite sufficient honor for me;" and then she sang again more enchantingly than ever.

"That singing is a lovely gift;" said the ladies of the court to each other; and then they took water in their mouths to make them utter the gurgling sounds of

---

declined: refused

the nightingale when they spoke to any one so that they might fancy themselves nightingales. And the footmen and chambermaids also expressed their satisfaction, which is saying a great deal, for they are very difficult to please. In fact the nightingale's visit was most successful. She was now to remain at court, to have her own cage, with liberty to go out twice a day, and once during the night. Twelve servants were ***appointed*** to attend her on these occasions, who each held her by a silken string fastened to her leg. There was certainly not much pleasure in this kind of flying.

The whole city spoke of the wonderful bird, and when two people met, one said "nightin," and the other said "gale," and they understood what was meant, for nothing else was talked of. Eleven peddlers' children were named after her, but not of them could sing a note.

One day the emperor received a large packet on which was written "The Nightingale." "Here is no doubt a new book about our celebrated bird," said the emperor. But instead of a book, it was a work of art contained in a casket, an artificial nightingale made to look like a living one, and covered all over with diamonds, rubies, and sapphires. As soon as the artificial bird was wound up, it could sing like the real one, and could move its tail up and down, which sparkled with silver and gold. Round its neck hung a piece of ribbon, on which was written "The Emperor of Japan's nightingale is poor compared with that of the Emperor of China's."

"This is very beautiful," exclaimed all who saw it, and he who had brought the artificial bird received the title of "Imperial nightingale-bringer-in-chief."

"Now they must sing together," said the court, "and what a duet it will be." But they did not get on well, for the real nightingale sang in its own natural way, but the artificial bird sang only waltzes.

"That is not a fault," said the music-master, "it is quite perfect to my taste," so then it had to sing alone, and was as successful as the real bird; besides, it was so much prettier to look at, for it sparkled like bracelets and breast-pins. Three and thirty times did it sing the same tunes without being tired; the people would gladly have heard it again, but the emperor said the living nightingale ought to sing something. But where was she? No one had noticed her when she flew out at the open window, back to her own green woods.

"What strange conduct," said the emperor, when her flight had been discovered; and all the courtiers blamed her, and said she was a very ungrateful creature.

"But we have the best bird after all," said one, and then they would have the bird sing again, although it was the thirty-fourth time they had listened to the same piece, and even then they had not learnt it, for it was rather difficult. But the music-master praised the bird in the highest degree, and even asserted that it was better than a real nightingale, not only in its dress and the beautiful diamonds, but also in its musical power. "For you must perceive, my chief lord and emperor, that with a real nightingale we can never tell what is going to be sung, but with this bird everything is settled. It can be opened and explained, so

---

appointed: employed

that people may understand how the waltzes are formed, and why one note follows upon another."

"This is exactly what we think," they all replied, and then the music-master received permission to ***exhibit*** the bird to the people on the following Sunday, and the emperor commanded that they should be present to hear it sing. When they heard it they were like people ***intoxicated***; however it must have been with drinking tea, which is quite a Chinese custom. They all said "Oh!" and held up their forefingers and nodded, but a poor fisherman, who had heard the real nightingale, said, "it sounds prettily enough, and the melodies are all alike; yet there seems something ***wanting***, I cannot exactly tell what."

And after this the real nightingale was banished from the empire, and the artificial bird placed on a silk cushion close to the emperor's bed. The presents of gold and precious stones which had been received with it were round the bird, and it was now advanced to the title of "Little Imperial Toilet Singer," and to the rank of No. 1 on the left hand; for the emperor considered the left side, on which the heart lies, as the most noble, and the heart of an emperor is in the same place as that of other people.

The music-master wrote a work, in twenty-five volumes, about the artificial bird, which was very learned and very long, and full of the most difficult Chinese words; yet all the people said they had read it, and understood it, for fear of being thought stupid and having their bodies trampled upon.

So a year passed, and the emperor, the court, and all the other Chinese knew every little turn in the artificial bird's song; and for that same reason it pleased them better. They could sing with the bird, which they often did. The street-boys sang, "Zi-zi-zi, cluck, cluck, cluck," and the emperor himself could sing it also. It was really most amusing.

One evening, when the artificial bird was singing its best, and the emperor lay in bed listening to it, something inside the bird sounded "whizz." Then a spring cracked. "Whir-r-r-r" went all the wheels, running round, and then the music stopped. The emperor immediately sprang out of bed, and called for his physician; but what could he do? Then they sent for a watchmaker; and, after a great deal of talking and examination, the bird was put into something like order; but he said that it must be used very carefully, as the barrels were worn, and it would be impossible to put in new ones without injuring the music. Now there was great sorrow, as the bird could only be allowed to play once a year; and even that was dangerous for the works inside it. Then the music-master made a little speech, full of hard words, and declared that the bird was as good as ever; and, of course no one ***contradicted*** him.

Five years passed, and then a real grief came upon the land. The Chinese really were fond of their emperor, and he now lay so ill that he was not expected to live. Already a new emperor had been chosen and the people who stood in the

---

exhibit: show; put on display
intoxicated: drunk
wanting: missing
contradicted: disagreed with

street asked the lord-in-waiting how the old emperor was; but he only said, "Pooh!" and shook his head.

Cold and pale lay the emperor in his royal bed; the whole court thought he was dead, and everyone ran away to pay ***homage*** to his successor. The chamberlains went out to have a talk on the matter, and the ladies'-maids invited company to take coffee. Cloth had been laid down on the halls and passages, so that not a footstep should be heard, and all was silent and still. But the emperor was not yet dead, although he lay white and stiff on his gorgeous bed, with the long velvet curtains and heavy gold tassels. A window stood open, and the moon shone in upon the emperor and the artificial bird. The poor emperor, finding he could scarcely breathe with a strange weight on his chest, opened his eyes, and saw Death sitting there. He had put on the emperor's golden crown, and held in one hand his sword of state, and in the other his beautiful banner. All around the bed and peeping through the long velvet curtains, were a number of strange heads, some very ugly, and others lovely and gentle-looking. These were the emperor's good and bad deeds, which stared him in the face now Death sat at his heart.

"Do you remember this?" "Do you recollect that?" they asked one after another, thus bringing to his remembrance circumstances that made the perspiration stand on his brow.

"I know nothing about it," said the emperor. "Music! Music!" he cried; "the large Chinese drum that I may not hear what they say." But they still went on, and Death nodded like a Chinaman to all they said. "Music! Music!" shouted the emperor. "You little precious golden bird, sing, pray sing! I have given you gold and costly presents; I have even hung my golden slipper round your neck. Sing! Sing!" But the bird remained silent. There was no one to wind it up, and therefore it could not sing a note.

Death continued to stare at the emperor with his cold, hollow eyes, and the room was fearfully still. Suddenly there came through the open window the sound of sweet music. Outside, on the bough of a tree, sat the living nightingale. She had heard of the emperor's illness, and was therefore come to sing to him of hope and trust. And as she sung, the shadows grew paler and paler; the blood in the emperor's veins flowed more rapidly, and gave life to his weak limbs; and even Death himself listened, and said, "Go on, little nightingale, go on."

"Then will you give me the beautiful golden sword and that rich banner? And will you give me the emperor's crown?" said the bird.

So Death gave up each of these treasures for a song; and the nightingale continued her singing. She sung of the quiet churchyard, where the white roses grow, where the elder-tree wafts its perfume on the breeze, and the fresh, sweet grass is moistened by the mourners' tears. Then Death longed to go and see his garden, and floated out through the window in the form of a cold, white mist.

"Thanks, thanks, you heavenly little bird. I know you well. I banished you from my kingdom once, and yet you have charmed away the evil faces from my bed, and banished Death from my heart, with your sweet song. How can I

---

homage: respect

reward you?"

"You have already rewarded me," said the nightingale. "I shall never forget that I drew tears from your eyes the first time I sang to you. These are the jewels that rejoice a singer's heart. But now sleep, and grow strong and well again. I will sing to you again."

And as she sung, the emperor fell into a sweet sleep; and how mild and refreshing that slumber was! When he awoke, strengthened and restored, the sun shone brightly through the window; but not one of his servants had returned—they all believed he was dead; only the nightingale still sat beside him, and sang.

"You must always remain with me," said the emperor. "You shall sing only when it pleases you; and I will break the artificial bird into a thousand pieces."

"No; do not do that," replied the nightingale; "the bird did very well as long as it could. Keep it here still. I cannot live in the palace, and build my nest; but let me come when I like. I will sit on a bough outside your window, in the evening, and sing to you, so that you may be happy, and have thoughts full of joy. I will sing to you of those who are happy, and those who suffer; of the good and the evil, who are hidden around you. The little singing bird flies far from you and your court to the home of the fisherman and the peasant's cot. I love your heart better than your crown; and yet something holy lingers round that also. I will come, I will sing to you; but you must promise me one thing."

"Everything," said the emperor, who, having dressed himself in his imperial robes, stood with the hand that held the heavy golden sword pressed to his heart.

"I only ask one thing," she replied; "let no one know that you have a little bird who tells you everything. It will be best to ***conceal*** it." So saying, the nightingale flew away.

The servants now came in to look after the dead emperor; when, lo! there he stood, and, to their astonishment, said, "Good morning."

The Ugly Duckling

IT was lovely summer weather in the country, and the golden corn, the green oats, and the haystacks piled up in the meadows looked beautiful. The stork walking about on his long red legs chattered in the Egyptian language, which he had learnt from his mother. The corn-fields and meadows were surrounded by large forests, in the midst of which were deep pools. It was, indeed, delightful to walk about in the country. In a sunny spot stood a pleasant old farm-house close by a deep river, and from the house down to the water side grew great burdock leaves, so high that under the tallest of them a little child could stand upright. The spot was as wild as the centre of a thick wood. In this snug retreat sat a duck on her nest, watching for her young brood to hatch; she was beginning to get tired of her task, for the little ones were a long time coming out of their shells, and she seldom had any visitors. The other ducks liked much better to swim

---

conceal: hide

about in the river than to climb the slippery banks, and sit under a burdock leaf, to have a gossip with her. At length one shell cracked, and then another, and from each egg came a living creature that lifted its head and cried, "Peep, peep." "Quack, quack," said the mother, and then they all quacked as well as they could, and looked about them on every side at the large green leaves. Their mother allowed them to look as much as they liked, because green is good for the eyes. "How large the world is," said the young ducks, when they found how much more room they now had than while they were inside the egg-shell. "Do you imagine this is the whole world?" asked the mother; "Wait till you have seen the garden; it stretches far beyond that to the parson's field, but I have never ventured to such a distance. Are you all out?" she continued, rising; "No, I declare, the largest egg lies there still. I wonder how long this is to last, I am quite tired of it;" and she seated herself again on the nest.

"Well, how are you getting on?" asked an old duck, who paid her a visit.

"One egg is not hatched yet," said the duck, "it will not break. But just look at all the others. Are they not the prettiest little ducklings you ever saw? They are the image of their father, who is so unkind, he never comes to see."

"Let me see the egg that will not break," said the duck; "I have no doubt it is a turkey's egg. I was persuaded to hatch some once, and after all my care and trouble with the young ones, they were afraid of the water. I quacked and clucked, but all to no purpose. I could not get them to venture in. Let me look at the egg. Yes, that is a turkey's egg; take my advice, leave it where it is and teach the other children to swim."

"I think I will sit on it a little while longer," said the duck; "as I have sat so long already, a few days will be nothing."

"Please yourself," said the old duck, and she went away.

At last the large egg broke, and a young one crept forth crying, "Peep, peep." It was very large and ugly. The duck stared at it and exclaimed, "It is very large and not at all like the others. I wonder if it really is a turkey. We shall soon find it out, however when we go to the water. It must go in, if I have to push it myself."

On the next day the weather was delightful, and the sun shone brightly on the green burdock leaves, so the mother duck took her young brood down to the water, and jumped in with a splash. "Quack, quack," cried she, and one after another the little ducklings jumped in. The water closed over their heads, but they came up again in an instant, and swam about quite prettily with their legs paddling under them as easily as possible, and the ugly duckling was also in the water swimming with them.

"Oh," said the mother, "that is not a turkey; how well he uses his legs, and how upright he holds himself! He is my own child, and he is not so very ugly after all if you look at him properly. Quack, quack! Come with me now, I will take you into grand society, and introduce you to the farmyard, but you must keep close to me or you may be trodden upon; and, above all, beware of the cat."

When they reached the farmyard, there was a great disturbance; two families were fighting for an eel's head, which, after all, was carried off by the cat. "See, children, that is the way of the world," said the mother duck, whetting her beak, for she would have liked the eel's head herself. "Come, now, use your legs, and let me see how well you can behave. You must bow your heads prettily to that old duck ***yonder***; she is the highest born of them all, and has Spanish blood, therefore, she is well off. Don't you see she has a red flag tied to her leg, which is something very grand, and a great honor for a duck; it shows that everyone is anxious not to lose her, as she can be recognized both by man and beast. Come, now, don't turn your toes, a well-bred duckling spreads his feet wide apart, just like his father and mother, in this way; now bend your neck, and say 'quack.'"

The ducklings did as they were bid, but the other duck stared, and said, "Look, here comes another brood, as if there were not enough of us already! And what a queer looking object one of them is; we don't want him here," and then one flew out and bit him in the neck.

"Let him alone," said the mother; "he is not doing any harm."

"Yes, but he is so big and ugly," said the ***spiteful*** duck "and therefore he must be turned out."

"The others are very pretty children," said the old duck, with the rag on her leg, "all but that one; I wish his mother could improve him a little."

"That is impossible, your grace," replied the mother; "he is not pretty; but he has a very good ***disposition***, and swims as well or even better than the others. I think he will grow up pretty, and perhaps be smaller; he has remained too long in the egg, and therefore his figure is not properly formed;" and then she stroked his neck and smoothed the feathers, saying, "It is a drake, and therefore not of so much consequence. I think he will grow up strong, and able to take care of himself."

"The other ducklings are graceful enough," said the old duck. "Now make yourself at home, and if you can find an eel's head, you can bring it to me."

And so they made themselves comfortable; but the poor duckling, who had crept out of his shell last of all, and looked so ugly, was bitten and pushed and made fun of, not only by the ducks, but by all the poultry. "He is too big," they all said, and the turkey cock, who had been born into the world with spurs, and fancied himself really an emperor, puffed himself out like a vessel in full sail, and flew at the duckling, and became quite red in the head with passion, so that the poor little thing did not know where to go, and was quite miserable because he was so ugly and laughed at by the whole farmyard. So it went on from day to day till it got worse and worse. The poor duckling was driven about by everyone; even his brothers and sisters were unkind to him, and would say, "Ah, you ugly creature, I wish the cat would get you," and his mother said she wished he had never been born. The ducks pecked him, the chickens beat him, and the girl who fed the poultry kicked him with her feet. So at last he ran away, frightening the little birds in the hedge as he flew over the palings.

"They are afraid of me because I am ugly," he said. So he closed his eyes,

---

yonder: over there
spiteful: mean: hurtful
disposition: temperament

and flew still farther, until he came out on a large moor, inhabited by wild ducks. Here he remained the whole night, feeling very tired and sorrowful.

In the morning, when the wild ducks rose in the air, they stared at their new comrade. "What sort of a duck are you?" they all said, coming round him.

He bowed to them, and was as polite as he could be, but he did not reply to their question. "You are exceedingly ugly," said the wild ducks, "but that will not matter if you do not want to marry one of our family."

Poor thing! He had no thoughts of marriage; all he wanted was permission to lie among the rushes, and drink some of the water on the moor. After he had been on the moor two days, there came two wild geese, or rather goslings, for they had not been out of the egg long, and were very ***saucy***. "Listen, friend," said one of them to the duckling, "you are so ugly, that we like you very well. Will you go with us, and become a bird of passage? Not far from here is another moor, in which there are some pretty wild geese, all unmarried. It is a chance for you to get a wife; you may be lucky, ugly as you are."

"Pop, pop," sounded in the air, and the two wild geese fell dead among the rushes, and the water was tinged with blood. "Pop, pop," echoed far and wide in the distance, and whole flocks of wild geese rose up from the rushes. The sound continued from every direction, for the sportsmen surrounded the moor, and some were even seated on branches of trees, overlooking the rushes. The blue smoke from the guns rose like clouds over the dark trees, and as it floated away across the water, a number of sporting dogs bounded in among the rushes, which bent beneath them wherever they went. How they terrified the poor duckling! He turned away his head to hide it under his wing, and at the same moment a large terrible dog passed quite near him. His jaws were open, his tongue hung from his mouth, and his eyes glared fearfully. He thrust his nose close to the duckling, showing his sharp teeth, and then, "splash, splash," he went into the water without touching him, "Oh," sighed the duckling, "how thankful I am for being so ugly; even a dog will not bite me." And so he lay quite still, while the shot rattled through the rushes, and gun after gun was fired over him. It was late in the day before all became quiet, but even then the poor young thing did not dare to move. He waited quietly for several hours, and then, after looking carefully around him, hastened away from the moor as fast as he could. He ran over field and meadow till a storm arose, and he could hardly struggle against it. Towards evening, he reached a poor little cottage that seemed ready to fall, and only remained standing because it could not decide on which side to fall first. The storm continued so violent, that the duckling could go no farther; he sat down by the cottage, and then he noticed that the door was not quite closed in consequence of one of the hinges having given way. There was therefore a narrow opening near the bottom large enough for him to slip through, which he did very quietly, and got a shelter for the night. A woman, a tom cat, and a hen lived in this cottage. The tom cat, whom the mistress called, "My little son," was a great favorite; he could raise his back, and purr, and could even throw out sparks from his fur if it were stroked the wrong way. The hen had very short

---

saucy: rude

legs, so she was called "Chickie short legs." She laid good eggs, and her mistress loved her as if she had been her own child. In the morning, the strange visitor was discovered, and the tom cat began to purr, and the hen to cluck.

"What is that noise about?" said the old woman, looking round the room, but her sight was not very good; therefore, when she saw the duckling she thought it must be a fat duck, that had ***strayed*** from home. "Oh what a prize!" she exclaimed, "I hope it is not a drake, for then I shall have some duck's eggs. I must wait and see." So the duckling was allowed to remain on trial for three weeks, but there were no eggs. Now the tom cat was the master of the house, and the hen was mistress, and they always said, "We and the world," for they believed themselves to be half the world, and the better half too. The duckling thought that others might hold a different opinion on the subject, but the hen would not listen to such doubts. "Can you lay eggs?" she asked. "No." "Then have the goodness to hold your tongue." "Can you raise your back, or purr, or throw out sparks?" said the tom cat. "No." "Then you have no right to express an opinion when sensible people are speaking." So the duckling sat in a corner, feeling very low spirited, till the sunshine and the fresh air came into the room through the open door, and then he began to feel such a great longing for a swim on the water, that he could not help telling the hen.

"What an absurd idea," said the hen. "You have nothing else to do, therefore you have foolish fancies. If you could purr or lay eggs, they would pass away."

"But it is so delightful to swim about on the water," said the duckling, "and so refreshing to feel it close over your head, while you dive down to the bottom."

"Delightful, indeed!" said the hen, "why you must be crazy! Ask the cat, he is the cleverest animal I know, ask him how he would like to swim about on the water, or to dive under it, for I will not speak of my own opinion; ask our mistress, the old woman—there is no one in the world more clever than she is. Do you think she would like to swim, or to let the water close over her head?"

"You don't understand me," said the duckling.

"We don't understand you? Who can understand you, I wonder? Do you consider yourself more clever than the cat, or the old woman? I will say nothing of myself. Don't imagine such nonsense, child, and thank your good fortune that you have been received here. Are you not in a warm room, and in society from which you may learn something. But you are a chatterer, and your company is not very agreeable. Believe me, I speak only for your own good. I may tell you unpleasant truths, but that is a proof of my friendship. I advise you, therefore, to lay eggs, and learn to purr as quickly as possible."

"I believe I must go out into the world again," said the duckling.

"Yes, do," said the hen. So the duckling left the cottage, and soon found water on which it could swim and dive, but was avoided by all other animals, because of its ugly appearance. Autumn came, and the leaves in the forest turned to orange and gold. Then, as winter approached, the wind caught them as they fell and whirled them in the cold air. The clouds, heavy with hail and snow-

---

strayed: wandered away

flakes, hung low in the sky, and the raven stood on the ferns crying, "Croak, croak." It made one shiver with cold to look at him. All this was very sad for the poor little duckling. One evening, just as the sun set ***amid*** radiant clouds, there came a large flock of beautiful birds out of the bushes. The duckling had never seen any like them before. They were swans, and they curved their graceful necks, while their soft plumage shown with dazzling whiteness. They uttered a singular cry, as they spread their glorious wings and flew away from those cold regions to warmer countries across the sea. As they mounted higher and higher in the air, the ugly little duckling felt quite a strange ***sensation*** as he watched them. He whirled himself in the water like a wheel, stretched out his neck towards them, and uttered a cry so strange that it frightened himself. Could he ever forget those beautiful, happy birds; and when at last they were out of his sight, he dived under the water, and rose again almost beside himself with excitement. He knew not the names of these birds, nor where they had flown, but he felt towards them as he had never felt for any other bird in the world. He was not ***envious*** of these beautiful creatures, but wished to be as lovely as they. Poor ugly creature, how gladly he would have lived even with the ducks had they only given him encouragement. The winter grew colder and colder; he was obliged to swim about on the water to keep it from freezing, but every night the space on which he swam became smaller and smaller. At length it froze so hard that the ice in the water crackled as he moved, and the duckling had to paddle with his legs as well as he could, to keep the space from closing up. He became ***exhausted*** at last, and lay still and helpless, frozen fast in the ice.

Early in the morning, a peasant, who was passing by, saw what had happened. He broke the ice in pieces with his wooden shoe, and carried the duckling home to his wife. The warmth revived the poor little creature; but when the children wanted to play with him, the duckling thought they would do him some harm; so he started up in terror, fluttered into the milk-pan, and splashed the milk about the room. Then the woman clapped her hands, which frightened him still more. He flew first into the butter-cask, then into the meal-tub, and out again. What a condition he was in! The woman screamed, and struck at him with the tongs; the children laughed and screamed, and tumbled over each other, in their efforts to catch him; but luckily he escaped. The door stood open; the poor creature could just manage to slip out among the bushes, and lie down quite exhausted in the newly fallen snow.

It would be very sad, were I to relate all the misery and privations which the poor little duckling ***endured*** during the hard winter; but when it had passed, he found himself lying one morning in a moor, amongst the rushes. He felt the warm sun shining, and heard the lark singing, and saw that all around was beautiful spring. Then the young bird felt that his wings were strong, as he

---

amid: among
sensation: feeling
envious: jealous
exhausted: very tired
endured: suffered; tolerated

flapped them against his sides, and rose high into the air. They bore him onwards, until he found himself in a large garden, before he well knew how it had happened. The apple-trees were in full blossom, and the fragrant elders bent their long green branches down to the stream which wound round a smooth lawn. Everything looked beautiful, in the freshness of early spring. From a thicket close by came three beautiful white swans, rustling their feathers, and swimming lightly over the smooth water. The duckling remembered the lovely birds, and felt more strangely unhappy than ever.

"I will fly to those royal birds," he exclaimed, "and they will kill me, because I am so ugly, and dare to approach them; but it does not matter: better be killed by them than pecked by the ducks, beaten by the hens, pushed about by the maiden who feeds the poultry, or starved with hunger in the winter."

Then he flew to the water, and swam towards the beautiful swans. The moment they espied the stranger, they rushed to meet him with outstretched wings.

"Kill me," said the poor bird; and he bent his head down to the surface of the water, and awaited death.

But what did he see in the clear stream below? His own image; no longer a dark, gray bird, ugly and disagreeable to look at, but a graceful and beautiful swan. To be born in a duck's nest, in a farmyard, is of no consequence to a bird, if it is hatched from a swan's egg. He now felt glad at having suffered sorrow and trouble, because it enabled him to enjoy so much better all the pleasure and happiness around him; for the great swans swam round the new-comer, and stroked his neck with their beaks, as a welcome.

Into the garden presently came some little children, and threw bread and cake into the water.

"See," cried the youngest, "there is a new one;" and the rest were delighted, and ran to their father and mother, dancing and clapping their hands, and shouting joyously, "There is another swan come; a new one has arrived."

Then they threw more bread and cake into the water, and said, "The new one is the most beautiful of all; he is so young and pretty." And the old swans bowed their heads before him.

Then he felt quite ashamed, and hid his head under his wing; for he did not know what to do, he was so happy, and yet not at all proud. He had been ***persecuted*** and despised for his ugliness, and now he heard them say he was the most beautiful of all the birds. Even the elder-tree bent down its bows into the water before him, and the sun shone warm and bright. Then he rustled his feathers, curved his slender neck, and cried joyfully, from the depths of his heart, "I never dreamed of such happiness as this, while I was an ugly duckling."

---

persecuted: treated cruelly

The Fir Tree

FAR down in the forest, where the warm sun and the fresh air made a sweet resting-place, grew a pretty little fir-tree; and yet it was not happy, it wished so much to be tall like its companions— the pines and firs which grew around it. The sun shone, and the soft air fluttered its leaves, and the little peasant children passed by, prattling merrily, but the fir-tree ***heeded*** them not. Sometimes the children would bring a large basket of raspberries or strawberries, wreathed on a straw, and seat themselves near the fir-tree, and say, "Is it not a pretty little tree?" which made it feel more unhappy than before. And yet all this while the tree grew a notch or joint taller every year; for by the number of joints in the stem of a fir-tree we can discover its age. Still, as it grew, it complained, "Oh! How I wish I were as tall as the other trees! Then I would spread out my branches on every side, and my top would over-look the wide world. I should have the birds building their nests on my boughs, and when the wind blew, I should bow with stately dignity like my tall companions." The tree was so discontented, that it took no pleasure in the warm sunshine, the birds, or the rosy clouds that floated over it morning and evening. Sometimes, in winter, when the snow lay white and glittering on the ground, a hare would come springing along, and jump right over the little tree; and then how ***mortified*** it would feel! Two winters passed, and when the third arrived, the tree had grown so tall that the hare was obliged to run round it. Yet it remained unsatisfied, and would exclaim, "Oh, if I could but keep on growing tall and old! There is nothing else worth caring for in the world!" In the autumn, as usual, the wood-cutters came and cut down several of the tallest trees, and the young fir-tree, which was now grown to its full height, ***shuddered*** as the noble trees fell to the earth with a crash. After the branches were lopped off, the trunks looked so slender and bare, that they could scarcely be recognized. Then they were placed upon wagons, and drawn by horses out of the forest. "Where were they going? What would become of them?" The young fir-tree wished very much to know; so in the spring, when the swallows and the storks came, it asked, "Do you know where those trees were taken? Did you meet them?"

The swallows knew nothing, but the stork, after a little reflection, nodded his head, and said, "Yes, I think I do. I met several new ships when I flew from Egypt, and they had fine masts that smelt like fir. I think these must have been the trees; I assure you they were stately, very stately."

"Oh, how I wish I were tall enough to go on the sea," said the fir-tree. "What is the sea, and what does it look like?"

"It would take too much time to explain," said the stork, flying quickly away.

"Rejoice in thy youth," said the sunbeam; "rejoice in thy fresh growth, and

---

heeded: paid attention to
mortified: humiliated
shuddered: trembled

the young life that is in thee."

And the wind kissed the tree, and the dew watered it with tears; but the fir-tree regarded them not.

Christmas-time drew near, and many young trees were cut down, some even smaller and younger than the fir-tree who enjoyed neither rest nor peace with longing to leave its forest home. These young trees, which were chosen for their beauty, kept their branches, and were also laid on wagons and drawn by horses out of the forest.

"Where are they going?" asked the fir-tree. "They are not taller than I am: indeed, one is much less; and why are the branches not cut off? Where are they going?"

"We know, we know," sang the sparrows; "we have looked in at the windows of the houses in the town, and we know what is done with them. They are dressed up in the most splendid manner. We have seen them standing in the middle of a warm room, and ***adorned*** with all sorts of beautiful things,—honey cakes, gilded apples, playthings, and many hundreds of wax tapers."

"And then," asked the fir-tree, trembling through all its branches, "and then what happens?"

"We did not see any more," said the sparrows; "but this was enough for us."

"I wonder whether anything so brilliant will ever happen to me," thought the fir-tree. "It would be much better than crossing the sea. I long for it almost with pain. Oh! When will Christmas be here? I am now as tall and well grown as those which were taken away last year. Oh! That I were now laid on the wagon, or standing in the warm room, with all that brightness and splendor around me! Something better and more beautiful is to come after, or the trees would not be so decked out. Yes, what follows will be grander and more splendid. What can it be? I am ***weary*** with longing. I scarcely know how I feel."

"Rejoice with us," said the air and the sunlight. "Enjoy thine own bright life in the fresh air."

But the tree would not rejoice, though it grew taller every day; and, winter and summer, its dark-green foliage might be seen in the forest, while passersby would say, "What a beautiful tree!"

A short time before Christmas, the discontented fir-tree was the first to fall. As the axe cut through the stem, and divided the pith, the tree fell with a groan to the earth, conscious of pain and faintness, and forgetting all its ***anticipations*** of happiness, in sorrow at leaving its home in the forest. It knew that it should never again see its dear old companions, the trees, nor the little bushes and many-colored flowers that had grown by its side; perhaps not even the birds. Neither was the journey at all pleasant. The tree first recovered itself while being unpacked in the courtyard of a house, with several other trees; and it heard a man say, "We only want one, and this is the prettiest."

Then came two servants in grand livery, and carried the fir-tree into a large

---

adorned: decorated
weary: tired
anticipations: expectations

and beautiful apartment. On the walls hung pictures, and near the great stove stood great china vases, with lions on the lids. There were rocking chairs, silken sofas, large tables, covered with pictures, books, and playthings, worth a great deal of money,—at least, the children said so. Then the fir-tree was placed in a large tub, full of sand; but green baize hung all around it, so that no one could see it was a tub, and it stood on a very handsome carpet. How the fir-tree trembled! "What was going to happen to him now?" Some young ladies came, and the servants helped them to adorn the tree. On one branch they hung little bags cut out of colored paper, and each bag was filled with sweetmeats; from other branches hung gilded apples and walnuts, as if they had grown there; and above, and all round, were hundreds of red, blue, and white tapers, which were fastened on the branches. Dolls, exactly like real babies were placed under the green leaves,—the tree had never seen such things before,—and at the very top was fastened a glittering star, made of tinsel. Oh, it was very beautiful!

"This evening," they all exclaimed, "how bright it will be!" "Oh, that the evening were come," thought the tree, "and the tapers lighted! Then I shall know what else is going to happen. Will the trees of the forest come to see me? I wonder if the sparrows will peep in at the windows as they fly. Shall I grow faster here, and keep on all these ornaments summer and winter?" But guessing was of very little use; it made his bark ache, and this pain is as bad for a slender fir-tree, as headache is for us. At last the tapers were lighted, and then what a glistening blaze of light the tree presented! It trembled so with joy in all its branches that one of the candles fell among the green leaves and burnt some of them. "Help! Help!" exclaimed the young ladies, but there was no danger, for they quickly extinguished the fire. After this, the tree tried not to tremble at all, though the fire frightened him; he was so anxious not to hurt any of the beautiful ornaments, even while their brilliancy dazzled him. And now the folding doors were thrown open, and a troop of children rushed in as if they intended to upset the tree; they were followed more silently by their elders. For a moment the little ones stood silent with ***astonishment***, and then they shouted for joy, till the room rang, and they danced merrily round the tree, while one present after another was taken from it.

"What are they doing? What will happen next?" thought the fir. At last the candles burnt down to the branches and were put out. Then the children received permission to plunder the tree.

Oh, how they rushed upon it, till the branches cracked, and had it not been fastened with the glistening star to the ceiling, it must have been thrown down. The children then danced about with their pretty toys, and no one noticed the tree, except the children's maid who came and peeped among the branches to see if an apple or a fig had been forgotten.

"A story, a story," cried the children, pulling a little fat man towards the tree.

"Now we shall be in the green shade," said the man, as he seated himself under it, "and the tree will have the pleasure of hearing also, but I shall only relate one story; what shall it be? Ivede-Avede, or Humpty Dumpty, who fell

---

astonishment: surprise; amazement

down stairs, but soon got up again, and at last married a princess."

"Ivede-Avede," cried some. "Humpty Dumpty," cried others, and there was a fine shouting and crying out. But the fir-tree remained quite still, and thought to himself, "Shall I have anything to do with all this?" but he had already amused them as much as they wished. Then the old man told them the story of Humpty Dumpty, how he fell down stairs, and was raised up again, and married a princess. And the children clapped their hands and cried, "Tell another, tell another," for they wanted to hear the story of "Ivede-Avede;" but they only had "Humpty Dumpty." After this the fir-tree became quite silent and thoughtful; never had the birds in the forest told such tales as "Humpty Dumpty," who fell down stairs, and yet married a princess.

"Ah! Yes, so it happens in the world," thought the fir-tree; he believed it all, because it was related by such a nice man. "Ah! Well," he thought, "who knows? Perhaps I may fall down too, and marry a princess;" and he looked forward joyfully to the next evening, expecting to be again decked out with lights and playthings, gold and fruit. "To-morrow I will not tremble," thought he; "I will enjoy all my splendor, and I shall hear the story of Humpty Dumpty again, and perhaps Ivede-Avede." And the tree remained quiet and thoughtful all night. In the morning the servants and the housemaid came in. "Now," thought the fir, "all my splendor is going to begin again." But they dragged him out of the room and up stairs to the garret, and threw him on the floor, in a dark corner, where no daylight shone, and there they left him. "What does this mean?" thought the tree, "what am I to do here? I can hear nothing in a place like this," and he had time enough to think, for days and nights passed and no one came near him, and when at last somebody did come, it was only to put away large boxes in a corner. So the tree was completely hidden from sight as if it had never existed. "It is winter now," thought the tree, "the ground is hard and covered with snow, so that people cannot plant me. I shall be sheltered here, I dare say, until spring comes. How thoughtful and kind everybody is to me! Still I wish this place were not so dark, as well as lonely, with not even a little hare to look at. How pleasant it was out in the forest while the snow lay on the ground, when the hare would run by, yes, and jump over me too, although I did not like it then. Oh! It is terrible lonely here."

"Squeak, squeak," said a little mouse, creeping cautiously towards the tree; then came another; and they both sniffed at the fir-tree and crept between the branches.

"Oh, it is very cold," said the little mouse, "or else we should be so comfortable here, shouldn't we, you old fir-tree?"

"I am not old," said the fir-tree, "there are many who are older than I am."

"Where do you come from? And what do you know?" asked the mice, who were full of curiosity. "Have you seen the most beautiful places in the world, and can you tell us all about them? And have you been in the storeroom, where cheeses lie on the shelf, and hams hang from the ceiling? One can run about on tallow candles there, and go in thin and come out fat."

"I know nothing of that place," said the fir-tree, "but I know the wood where the sun shines and the birds sing." And then the tree told the little mice all about its youth. They had never heard such an account in their lives; and after they had listened to it ***attentively***, they said, "What a number of things you have seen? You must have been very happy."

"Happy!" exclaimed the fir-tree, and then as he reflected upon what he had been telling them, he said, "Ah, yes! After all, those were happy days." But when he went on and related all about Christmas-eve, and how he had been dressed up with cakes and lights, the mice said, "How happy you must have been, you old fir-tree."

"I am not old at all," replied the tree, "I only came from the forest this winter. I am now checked in my growth."

"What splendid stories you can relate," said the little mice. And the next night four other mice came with them to hear what the tree had to tell. The more he talked the more he remembered, and then he thought to himself, "Those were happy days, but they may come again. Humpty Dumpty fell down stairs, and yet he married the princess; perhaps I may marry a princess too." And the fir-tree thought of the pretty little birch-tree that grew in the forest, which was to him a real beautiful princess.

"Who is Humpty Dumpty?" asked the little mice. And then the tree related the whole story; he could remember every single word, and the little mice were so delighted with it that they were ready to jump to the top of the tree. The next night a great many more mice made their appearance, and on Sunday two rats came with them; but they said it was not a pretty story at all, and the little mice were very sorry for it made them also think less of it.

"Do you know only one story?" asked the rats.

"Only one," replied the fir-tree; "I heard it on the happiest evening of my life; but I did not know I was so happy at the time."

"We think it is a very miserable story," said the rats. "Don't you know any story about bacon, or tallow in the storeroom?"

"No," replied the tree.

"Many thanks to you then," replied the rats, and they marched off.

The little mice also kept away after this, and the tree sighed, and said, "It was very pleasant when the merry little mice sat round me and listened while I talked. Now that is all passed too. However, I shall consider myself happy when someone comes to take me out of this place." But would this ever happen? Yes; one morning people came to clear out the garret, the boxes were packed away, and the tree was pulled out of the corner and thrown roughly on the garret floor; then the servant dragged it out upon the staircase where the daylight shone. "Now life is beginning again," said the tree, rejoicing in the sunshine and fresh air. Then it was carried down stairs and taken into the courtyard so quickly that it forgot to think of itself and could only look about; there was so much to be seen. The court was close to a garden, where everything looked blooming. Fresh and fragrant roses hung over the little palings. The linden-trees were in blossom; while the swallows flew here and there, crying, "Twit, twit, twit, my mate is coming,"—but it was not the fir-tree they meant. "Now I shall live," cried the

---

attentively: carefully; with interest

tree, joyfully spreading out its branches; but alas! They were all withered and yellow, and it lay in a corner amongst weeds and nettles. The star of gold paper still stuck in the top of the tree and glittered in the sunshine. In the same courtyard two of the merry children were playing who had danced round the tree at Christmas, and had been so happy. The youngest saw the gilded star, and ran and pulled it off the tree. "Look what is sticking to the ugly old fir-tree," said the child, treading on the branches till they crackled under his boots. And the tree saw all the fresh bright flowers in the garden, and then looked at itself, and wished it had remained in the dark corner of the garret. It thought of its fresh youth in the forest, of the merry Christmas evening, and of the little mice who had listened to the story of "Humpty Dumpty." "Past! Past!" said the old tree; "Oh, had I but enjoyed myself while I could have done so! But now it is too late." Then a lad came and chopped the tree into small pieces, till a large bundle lay in a heap on the ground. The pieces were placed in a fire under the copper, and they quickly blazed up brightly, while the tree sighed so deeply that each sigh was like a pistol-shot. Then the children, who were at play, came and seated themselves in front of the fire, and looked at it and cried, "Pop, pop." But at each "pop," which was a deep sigh, the tree was thinking of a summer day in the forest; and of Christmas evening, and of "Humpty Dumpty," the only story it had ever heard or knew how to relate, till at last it was consumed. The boys still played in the garden, and the youngest wore the golden star on his breast, with which the tree had been adorned during the happiest evening of its existence. Now all was past; the tree's life was past and the story also—for all stories must come to an end at last.

The Snow Queen

In Seven Stories

Story the First, Which Describes a Looking-Glass and the Broken Fragments

YOU must attend to the ***commencement*** of this story, for when we get to the end we shall know more than we do now about a very wicked hobgoblin; he was one of the very worst, for he was a real demon. One day, when he was in a merry mood, he made a looking-glass which had the power of making everything good or beautiful that was reflected in it almost shrink to nothing, while everything that was worthless and bad looked increased in size and worse than ever. The most lovely landscapes appeared like boiled spinach, and the people became hideous, and looked as if they stood on their heads and had no bodies. Their countenances were so ***distorted*** that no one could recognize them,

---

commencement: beginning
distorted: changed the shape, appearance

and even one freckle on the face appeared to spread over the whole of the nose and mouth. The demon said this was very amusing. When a good or pious thought passed through the mind of any one it was misrepresented in the glass; and then how the demon laughed at his ***cunning*** invention. All who went to the demon's school—for he kept a school—talked everywhere of the wonders they had seen, and declared that people could now, for the first time, see what the world and mankind were really like. They carried the glass about everywhere, till at last there was not a land nor a people who had not been looked at through this distorted mirror. They wanted even to fly with it up to heaven to see the angels, but the higher they flew the more slippery the glass became, and they could scarcely hold it, till at last it slipped from their hands, fell to the earth, and was broken into millions of pieces. But now the looking-glass caused more unhappiness than ever, for some of the fragments were not so large as a grain of sand, and they flew about the world into every country. When one of these tiny atoms flew into a person's eye, it stuck there unknown to him, and from that moment he saw everything through a distorted medium, or could see only the worst side of what he looked at, for even the smallest fragment retained the same power which had belonged to the whole mirror. Some few persons even got a fragment of the looking-glass in their hearts, and this was very terrible for their hearts became cold like a lump of ice. A few of the pieces were so large that they could be used as window-panes; it would have been a sad thing to look at our friends through them. Other pieces were made into spectacles; this was dreadful for those who wore them for they could see nothing either rightly or justly. At all this the wicked demon laughed till his sides shook—it tickled him so to see the mischief he had done. There were still a number of these little fragments of glass floating about in the air, and now you shall hear what happened with one of them.

Second Story: A Little Boy and a Little Girl

IN a large town, full of houses and people, there is not room for everybody to have even a little garden, therefore they are obliged to be satisfied with a few flowers in flower-pots. In one of these large towns lived two poor children who had a garden something larger and better than a few flower-pots. They were not brother and sister, but they loved each other almost as much as if they had been. Their parents lived opposite to each other in two garrets, where the roofs of neighboring houses projected out towards each other and the water-pipe ran between them. In each house was a little window, so that anyone could step across the gutter from one window to the other. The parents of these children had each a large wooden box in which they cultivated kitchen herbs for their own use, and a little rose-bush in each box, which grew splendidly. Now after a while the parents decided to place these two boxes across the water-pipe, so that they reached from one window to the other and looked like two banks of

---

cunning: clever and skilful

flowers. Sweet-peas drooped over the boxes, and the rose-bushes shot forth long branches, which were trained round the windows and clustered together almost like a triumphal arch of leaves and flowers. The boxes were very high, and the children knew they must not climb upon them, without permission, but they were often, however, allowed to step out together and sit upon their little stools under the rose-bushes, or play quietly. In winter all this pleasure came to an end, for the windows were sometimes quite frozen over. But then they would warm copper pennies on the stove, and hold the warm pennies against the frozen pane; there would be very soon a little round hole through which they could peep, and the soft bright eyes of the little boy and girl would beam through the hole at each window as they looked at each other. Their names were Kay and Gerda. In summer they could be together with one jump from the window, but in winter they had to go up and down the long staircase, and out through the snow before they could meet.

"See there are the white bees swarming," said Kay's old grandmother one day when it was snowing.

"Have they a queen bee?" asked the little boy, for he knew that the real bees had a queen.

"To be sure they have," said the grandmother. "She is flying there where the swarm is thickest. She is the largest of them all, and never remains on the earth, but flies up to the dark clouds. Often at midnight she flies through the streets of the town, and looks in at the windows, then the ice freezes on the panes into wonderful shapes, that look like flowers and castles."

"Yes, I have seen them," said both the children, and they knew it must be true.

"Can the Snow Queen come in here?" asked the little girl.

"Only let her come," said the boy, "I'll set her on the stove and then she'll melt."

Then the grandmother smoothed his hair and told him some more tales. One evening, when little Kay was at home, half undressed, he climbed on a chair by the window and peeped out through the little hole. A few flakes of snow were falling, and one of them, rather larger than the rest, alighted on the edge of one of the flower boxes. This snow-flake grew larger and larger, till at last it became the figure of a woman, dressed in garments of white gauze, which looked like millions of starry snow-flakes linked together. She was fair and beautiful, but made of ice—shining and glittering ice. Still she was alive and her eyes sparkled like bright stars, but there was neither peace nor rest in their glance. She nodded towards the window and waved her hand. The little boy was frightened and sprang from the chair; at the same moment it seemed as if a large bird flew by the window. On the following day there was a clear frost, and very soon came the spring. The sun shone; the young green leaves burst forth; the swallows built their nests; windows were opened, and the children sat once more in the garden on the roof, high above all the other rooms. How beautiful the roses blossomed this summer. The little girl had learnt a hymn in which roses were spoken of, and then she thought of their own roses, and she sang the hymn to the little boy, and he sang too:—

"Roses bloom and cease to be,
But we shall the Christ-child see."

Then the little ones held each other by the hand, and kissed the roses, and looked at the bright sunshine, and spoke to it as if the Christ-child were there. Those were splendid summer days. How beautiful and fresh it was out among the rose-bushes, which seemed as if they would never leave off blooming. One day Kay and Gerda sat looking at a book full of pictures of animals and birds, and then just as the clock in the church tower struck twelve, Kay said, "Oh, something has struck my heart!" and soon after, "There is something in my eye."

The little girl put her arm round his neck, and looked into his eye, but she could see nothing.

"I think it is gone," he said. But it was not gone; it was one of those bits of the looking-glass—that magic mirror, of which we have spoken—the ugly glass which made everything great and good appear small and ugly, while all that was wicked and bad became more visible, and every little fault could be ***plainly*** seen. Poor little Kay had also received a small grain in his heart, which very quickly turned to a lump of ice. He felt no more pain, but the glass was there still. "Why do you cry?" said he at last; "it makes you look ugly. There is nothing the matter with me now. Oh, see!" he cried suddenly, "that rose is worm-eaten, and this one is quite crooked. After all they are ugly roses, just like the box in which they stand," and then he kicked the boxes with his foot, and pulled off the two roses.

"Kay, what are you doing?" cried the little girl; and then, when he saw how frightened she was, he tore off another rose, and jumped through his own window away from little Gerda.

When she afterwards brought out the picture book, he said, "It was only fit for babies in long clothes," and when grandmother told any stories, he would interrupt her with "but;" or, when he could manage it, he would get behind her chair, put on a pair of spectacles, and imitate her very cleverly, to make people laugh. By-and-by he began to mimic the speech and ***gait*** of persons in the street. All that was peculiar or disagreeable in a person he would imitate directly, and people said, "That boy will be very clever; he has a remarkable genius." But it was the piece of glass in his eye, and the coldness in his heart, that made him act like this. He would even tease little Gerda, who loved him with all her heart. His games, too, were quite different; they were not so childish. One winter's day, when it snowed, he brought out a burning-glass. Then he held out the tail of his blue coat, and let the snow-flakes fall upon it. "Look in this glass, Gerda," said he; and she saw how every flake of snow was magnified, and looked like a beautiful flower or a glittering star. "Is it not clever?" said Kay, "and much more interesting than looking at real flowers. There is not a single fault in it, and the snow-flakes are quite perfect till they begin to melt."

Soon after Kay made his appearance in large thick gloves, and with his

---

plainly: clearly
gait: way of walking

sledge at his back. He called up stairs to Gerda, "I've got to leave to go into the great square, where the other boys play and ride." And away he went.

In the great square, the boldest among the boys would often tie their sledges to the country people's carts, and go with them a good way. This was capital. But while they were all amusing themselves, and Kay with them, a great sledge came by; it was painted white, and in it sat someone wrapped in a rough white fur, and wearing a white cap. The sledge drove twice round the square, and Kay fastened his own little sledge to it, so that when it went away, he followed with it. It went faster and faster right through the next street, and then the person who drove turned round and nodded pleasantly to Kay, just as if they were acquainted with each other, but whenever Kay wished to loosen his little sledge the driver nodded again, so Kay sat still, and they drove out through the town gate. Then the snow began to fall so heavily that the little boy could not see a hand's breadth before him, but still they drove on; then he suddenly loosened the cord so that the large sled might go on without him, but it was of no use, his little carriage held fast, and away they went like the wind. Then he called out loudly, but nobody heard him, while the snow beat upon him, and the sledge flew onwards. Every now and then it gave a jump as if it were going over hedges and ditches. The boy was frightened, and tried to say a prayer, but he could remember nothing but the multiplication table.

The snow-flakes became larger and larger, till they appeared like great white chickens. All at once they sprang on one side, the great sledge stopped, and the person who had driven it rose up. The fur and the cap, which were made entirely of snow, fell off, and he saw a lady, tall and white, it was the Snow Queen.

"We have driven well," said she, "but why do you tremble? Here, creep into my warm fur." Then she seated him beside her in the sledge, and as she wrapped the fur round him he felt as if he were sinking into a snow drift.

"Are you still cold," she asked, as she kissed him on the forehead. The kiss was colder than ice; it went quite through to his heart, which was already almost a lump of ice; he felt as if he were going to die, but only for a moment; he soon seemed quite well again, and did not notice the cold around him.

"My sledge! Don't forget my sledge," was his first thought, and then he looked and saw that it was bound fast to one of the white chickens, which flew behind him with the sledge at its back. The Snow Queen kissed little Kay again, and by this time he had forgotten little Gerda, his grandmother, and all at home.

"Now you must have no more kisses," she said, "or I should kiss you to death."

Kay looked at her and saw that she was so beautiful he could not imagine a more lovely and intelligent face; she did not now seem to be made of ice, as when he had seen her through his window, and she had nodded to him. In his eyes she was perfect, and she did not feel at all afraid. He told her he could do mental arithmetic, as far as fractions, and that he knew the number of square miles and the number of inhabitants in the country. And she always smiled so that he thought he did not know enough yet, and she looked round the vast expanse as she flew higher and higher with him upon a black cloud, while the storm blew and howled as if it were singing old songs. They flew over woods and lakes, over sea and land; below them roared the wild wind; the wolves howled and the snow crackled; over them flew the black screaming crows, and above all shone the moon, clear and bright,—and so Kay passed through the long winter's night, and by day he slept at the feet of the Snow Queen.

Third Story: The Flower Garden of the Woman Who Could Conjure

BUT how fared little Gerda during Kay's absence? What had become of him, no one knew, nor could anyone give the slightest information, excepting the boys, who said that he had tied his sledge to another very large one, which had driven through the street, and out at the town gate. Nobody knew where it went; many tears were shed for him, and little Gerda wept bitterly for a long time. She said she knew he must be dead; that he was drowned in the river which flowed close by the school. Oh, indeed those long winter days were very dreary. But at last spring came, with warm sunshine. "Kay is dead and gone," said little Gerda.

"I don't believe it," said the sunshine.

"He is dead and gone," she said to the sparrows.

"We don't believe it," they replied; and at last little Gerda began to doubt it herself. "I will put on my new red shoes," she said one morning, "those that Kay has never seen, and then I will go down to the river, and ask for him." It was quite early when she kissed her old grandmother, who was still asleep; then she put on her red shoes, and went quite alone out of the town gates toward the river. "Is it true that you have taken my little playmate away from me?" said she to the river. "I will give you my red shoes if you will give him back to me." And it seemed as if the waves nodded to her in a strange manner. Then she took off her red shoes, which she liked better than anything else, and threw them both into the river, but they fell near the bank, and the little waves carried them back to the land, just as if the river would not take from her what she loved best, because they could not give her back little Kay. But she thought the shoes had not been thrown out far enough. Then she crept into a boat that lay among the reeds, and threw the shoes again from the farther end of the boat into the water, but it was not fastened. And her movement sent it gliding away from the land. When she saw this she hastened to reach the end of the boat, but before she could so it was more than a yard from the bank, and drifting away faster than ever. Then little Gerda was very much frightened, and began to cry, but no one heard her except the sparrows, and they could not carry her to land, but they flew along by the shore, and sang, as if to comfort her, "Here we are! Here we are!" The boat floated with the stream; little Gerda sat quite still with only her stockings on her feet; the red shoes floated after her, but she could not reach them because the boat kept so much in advance. The banks on each side of the river were very pretty. There were beautiful flowers, old trees, sloping fields, in which cows and sheep were grazing, but not a man to be seen. Perhaps the river will carry me to little Kay, thought Gerda, and then she became more cheerful, and raised her head, and looked at the beautiful green banks; and so the boat sailed on for hours. At length she came to a large cherry orchard, in which stood a small red house with strange red and blue windows. It had also a thatched roof, and outside were two wooden soldiers, that presented arms to her as she sailed past. Gerda called out to them, for she thought they were alive, but of course they did not answer; and as the boat drifted nearer to the shore, she saw what they really were. Then Gerda called still louder, and there came a very old woman out of the house, leaning on a crutch. She wore a large hat to shade her from the sun, and on it were painted all sorts of pretty flowers. "You poor little child," said the old woman, "how did you manage to come all this distance into the wide world on such a rapid rolling stream?" And then the old woman walked in the water, seized the boat with her crutch, drew it to land, and lifted Gerda out. And Gerda was glad to feel herself on dry ground, although she was rather afraid of the strange old woman. "Come and tell me who you are," said she, "and how came you here."

Then Gerda told her everything, while the old woman shook her head, and said, "Hem-hem;" and when she had finished, Gerda asked if she had not seen little Kay, and the old woman told her he had not passed by that way, but he very likely would come. So she told Gerda not to be sorrowful, but to taste the cherries and look at the flowers; they were better than any picture-book, for each of them could tell a story. Then she took Gerda by the hand and led her into the little house, and the old woman closed the door. The windows were very high, and as the panes were red, blue, and yellow, the daylight shone through them in all sorts of singular colors. On the table stood beautiful cherries, and Gerda had permission to eat as many as she would. While she was eating them the old woman combed out her long flaxen ringlets with a golden comb, and the glossy curls hung down on each side of the little round pleasant face, which looked fresh and blooming as a rose. "I have long been wishing for a dear little maiden like you," said the old woman, "and now you must stay with me, and see how happily we shall live together." And while she went on combing little Gerda's hair, she thought less and less about her adopted brother Kay, for the old woman could ***conjure***, although she was not a wicked witch; she conjured only a little for her own amusement, and now, because she wanted to keep Gerda. Therefore she went into the garden, and stretched out her crutch towards all the rose-trees, beautiful though they were; and they immediately sunk into the dark earth, so that no one could tell where they had once stood. The old woman was afraid that if little Gerda saw roses she would think of those at home, and then remember little Kay, and run away. Then she took Gerda into the flower-garden. How fragrant and beautiful it was! Every flower that could be thought of for every season of the year was here in full bloom; no picture-book could have more beautiful colors. Gerda jumped for joy, and played till the sun went down behind the tall cherry-trees; then she slept in an elegant bed with red silk pillows, embroidered with colored violets; and then she dreamed as pleasantly as a queen on her wedding day. The next day, and for many days after, Gerda played with the flowers in the warm sunshine. She knew every flower, and yet, although

---

conjure: do magic tricks

there were so many of them, it seemed as if one were missing, but which it was she could not tell. One day, however, as she sat looking at the old woman's hat with the painted flowers on it, she saw that the prettiest of them all was a rose. The old woman had forgotten to take it from her hat when she made all the roses sink into the earth. But it is difficult to keep the thoughts together in everything; one little mistake upsets all our arrangements.

"What, are there no roses here?" cried Gerda; and she ran out into the garden, and examined all the beds, and searched and searched. There was not one to be found. Then she sat down and wept, and her tears fell just on the place where one of the rose-trees had sunk down. The warm tears moistened the earth, and the rose-tree sprouted up at once, as blooming as when it had sunk; and Gerda embraced it and kissed the roses, and thought of the beautiful roses at home, and, with them, of little Kay.

"Oh, how I have been detained!" said the little maiden, "I wanted to seek for little Kay. Do you know where he is?" she asked the roses; "do you think he is dead?"

And the roses answered, "No, he is not dead. We have been in the ground where all the dead lie; but Kay is not there."

"Thank you," said little Gerda, and then she went to the other flowers, and looked into their little cups, and asked, "Do you know where little Kay is?" But each flower, as it stood in the sunshine, dreamed only of its own little fairy tale of history. Not one knew anything of Kay. Gerda heard many stories from the flowers, as she asked them one after another about him.

And what, said the tiger-lily? "Hark, do you hear the drum? — 'turn, turn,'—there are only two notes, always, 'turn, turn.' Listen to the women's song of mourning! Hear the cry of the priest! In her long red robe stands the Hindoo widow by the funeral pile. The flames rise around her as she places herself on the dead body of her husband; but the Hindoo woman is thinking of the living one in that circle; of him, her son, who lighted those flames. Those shining eyes trouble her heart more painfully than the flames which will soon consume her body to ashes. Can the fire of the heart be extinguished in the flames of the funeral pile?"

"I don't understand that at all," said little Gerda.

"That is my story," said the tiger-lily.

What says the convolvulus? "Near yonder narrow road stands an old knight's castle; thick ivy creeps over the old ruined walls, leaf over leaf, even to the balcony, in which stands a beautiful maiden. She bends over the balustrades, and looks up the road. No rose on its stem is fresher than she; no apple-blossom, wafted by the wind, floats more lightly than she moves. Her rich silk rustles as she bends over and exclaims, 'Will he not come?'

"Is it Kay you mean?" asked Gerda.

"I am only speaking of a story of my dream," replied the flower.

What said the little snow-drop? "Between two trees a rope is hanging; there is a piece of board upon it; it is a swing. Two pretty little girls, in dresses white as snow, and with long green ribbons fluttering from their hats, are sitting upon it swinging. Their brother, who is taller than they are, stands in the swing; he has one arm round the rope, to steady himself; in one hand he holds a little bowl, and in the other a clay pipe; he is blowing bubbles. As the swing goes on, the bubbles fly upward, reflecting the most beautiful varying colors. The last still hangs from the bowl of the pipe, and sways in the wind. On goes the swing; and then a little black dog comes running up. He is almost as light as the bubble, and he raises himself on his hind legs, and wants to be taken into the swing; but it does not stop, and the dog falls; then he barks and gets angry. The children stoop towards him, and the bubble bursts. A swinging plank, a light sparkling foam picture,—that is my story."

"It may be all very pretty what you are telling me," said little Gerda, "but you speak so mournfully, and you do not mention little Kay at all."

What do the hyacinths say? "There were three beautiful sisters, fair and delicate. The dress of one was red, of the second blue, and of the third pure white. Hand in hand they danced in the bright moonlight, by the calm lake; but they were human beings, not fairy elves. The sweet fragrance attracted them, and they disappeared in the wood; here the fragrance became stronger. Three coffins, in which lay the three beautiful maidens, glided from the thickest part of the forest across the lake. The fire-flies flew lightly over them, like little floating torches. Do the dancing maidens sleep, or are they dead? The scent of the flower says that they are corpses. The evening bell tolls their knell."

"You make me quite sorrowful," said little Gerda; "your perfume is so strong, you make me think of the dead maidens. Ah! Is little Kay really dead then? The roses have been in the earth, and they say no."

"Cling, clang," tolled the hyacinth bells. "We are not tolling for little Kay; we do not know him. We sing our song, the only one we know."

Then Gerda went to the buttercups that were glittering amongst the bright green leaves.

"You are little bright suns," said Gerda; "tell me if you know where I can find my play-fellow."

And the buttercups sparkled gayly, and looked again at Gerda. What song could the buttercups sing? It was not about Kay.

"The bright warm sun shone on a little court, on the first warm day of spring. His bright beams rested on the white walls of the neighboring house; and close by bloomed the first yellow flower of the season, glittering like gold in the sun's warm ray. An old woman sat in her arm chair at the house door, and her granddaughter, a poor and pretty servant-maid came to see her for a short visit. When she kissed her grandmother there was gold everywhere: the gold of the heart in that holy kiss; it was a golden morning; there was gold in the beaming sunlight, gold in the leaves of the lowly flower, and on the lips of the maiden. There, that is my story," said the buttercup.

"My poor old grandmother!" sighed Gerda; "she is longing to see me, and grieving for me as she did for little Kay; but I shall soon go home now, and take little Kay with me. It is no use asking the flowers; they know only their own songs and can give me no information."

And then she tucked up her little dress, that she might run faster, but the narcissus caught her by the leg as she was jumping over it; so she stopped and looked at the tall yellow flower, and said, "Perhaps you may know something."

Then she stooped down quite close to the flower, and listened; and what did he say?

"I can see myself, I can see myself," said the narcissus. "Oh, how sweet is my perfume! Up in a little room with a bow window, stands a little dancing girl, half undressed; she stands sometimes on one leg, and sometimes on both, and looks as if she would tread the whole world under her feet. She is nothing but a delusion. She is pouring water out of a tea-pot on a piece of stuff which she holds in her hand; it is her bodice. 'Cleanliness is a good thing,' she says. Her white dress hangs on a peg; it has also been washed in the tea-pot, and dried on the roof. She puts it on, and ties a saffron-colored handkerchief round her neck, which makes the dress look whiter. See how she stretches out her legs, as if she were showing off on a stem. I can see myself, I can see myself."

"What do I care for all that," said Gerda, "you need not tell me such stuff." And then she ran to the other end of the garden. The door was fastened, but she pressed against the rusty latch, and it gave way. The door sprang open, and little Gerda ran out with bare feet into the wide world. She looked back three times, but no one seemed to be following her. At last she could run no longer, so she sat down to rest on a great stone, and when she looked round she saw that the summer was over, and autumn very far advanced. She had known nothing of this in the beautiful garden, where the sun shone and the flowers grew all the year round.

"Oh, how I have wasted my time?" said little Gerda; "it is autumn. I must not rest any longer," and she rose up to go on. But her little feet were wounded and sore, and everything around her looked so cold and ***bleak***. The long willow-leaves were quite yellow. The dew-drops fell like water, leaf after leaf dropped from the trees, the sloe-thorn alone still bore fruit, but the sloes were sour, and set the teeth on edge. Oh, how dark and weary the whole world appeared!

Fourth Story: The Prince and Princess

GERDA was obliged to rest again, and just opposite the place where she sat, she saw a great crow come hopping across the snow toward her. He stood looking at her for some time, and then he wagged his head and said, "Caw, caw; good-day, good-day." He pronounced the words as plainly as he could, because he meant to be kind to the little girl; and then he asked her where she was going all alone in the wide world.

The word alone Gerda understood very well, and knew how much it expressed. So then she told the crow the whole story of her life and adventures, and asked him if he had seen little Kay.

The crow nodded his head very gravely, and said, "Perhaps I have—it may

---

bleak: miserable; depressing

be."

"No! Do you think you have?" cried little Gerda, and she kissed the crow, and hugged him almost to death with joy.

"Gently, gently," said the crow. "I believe I know. I think it may be little Kay; but he has certainly forgotten you by this time for the princess."

"Does he live with a princess?" asked Gerda.

"Yes, listen," replied the crow, "but it is so difficult to speak your language. If you understand the crows' language then I can explain it better. Do you?"

"No, I have never learnt it," said Gerda, "but my grandmother understands it, and used to speak it to me. I wish I had learnt it."

"It does not matter," answered the crow; "I will explain as well as I can, although it will be very badly done;" and he told her what he had heard. "In this kingdom where we now are," said he, "there lives a princess, who is so wonderfully clever that she has read all the newspapers in the world, and forgotten them too, although she is so clever. A short time ago, as she was sitting on her throne, which people say is not such an agreeable seat as is often supposed, she began to sing a song which commences in these words:

'Why should I not be married?'

'Why not indeed?' said she, and so she determined to marry if she could find a husband who knew what to say when he was spoken to, and not one who could only look grand, for that was so tiresome. Then she assembled all her court ladies together at the beat of the drum, and when they heard of her intentions they were very much pleased. 'We are so glad to hear it,' said they, 'we were talking about it ourselves the other day.' You may believe that every word I tell you is true," said the crow, "for I have a tame sweetheart who goes freely about the palace, and she told me all this."

Of course his sweetheart was a crow, for "birds of a feather flock together," and one crow always chooses another crow.

"Newspapers were published immediately, with a border of hearts, and the initials of the princess among them. They gave notice that every young man who was handsome was free to visit the castle and speak with the princess; and those who could reply loud enough to be heard when spoken to, were to make themselves quite at home at the palace; but the one who spoke best would be chosen as a husband for the princess. Yes, yes, you may believe me, it is all as true as I sit here," said the crow. "The people came in crowds. There was a great deal of crushing and running about, but no one succeeded either on the first or second day. They could all speak very well while they were outside in the streets, but when they entered the palace gates, and saw the guards in silver uniforms, and the footmen in their golden livery on the staircase, and the great halls lighted up, they became quite confused. And when they stood before the throne on which the princess sat, they could do nothing but repeat the last words she had said; and she had no particular wish to hear her own words over again. It was just as if they had all taken something to make them sleepy while they were in the palace, for they did not recover themselves nor speak till they got back again into the street. There was quite a long line of them reaching from the town-gate to the palace. I went myself to see them," said the crow. "They were hungry and thirsty, for at the palace they did not get even a glass of water. Some of the wisest had taken a few slices of bread and butter with them, but they did not share it with their neighbors; they thought if they went in to the princess looking hungry, there would be a better chance for themselves."

"But Kay! Tell me about little Kay!" said Gerda, "was he amongst the crowd?"

"Stop a bit; we are just coming to him. It was on the third day, there came marching cheerfully along to the palace a little personage, without horses or carriage, his eyes sparkling like yours; he had beautiful long hair, but his clothes were very poor."

"That was Kay!" said Gerda joyfully. "Oh, then I have found him;" and she clapped her hands.

"He had a little knapsack on his back," added the crow.

"No, it must have been his sledge," said Gerda; "for he went away with it."

"It may have been so," said the crow; "I did not look at it very closely. But I know from my tame sweetheart that he passed through the palace gates, saw the guards in their silver uniform, and the servants in their liveries of gold on the stairs, but he was not in the least embarrassed. 'It must be very tiresome to stand on the stairs,' he said. 'I prefer to go in.' The rooms were blazing with light. Councillors and ambassadors walked about with bare feet, carrying golden vessels; it was enough to make any one feel serious. His boots creaked loudly as he walked, and yet he was not at all uneasy."

"It must be Kay," said Gerda, "I know he had new boots on, I have heard them creak in grandmother's room."

"They really did creak," said the crow, "yet he went boldly up to the princess herself, who was sitting on a pearl as large as a spinning wheel, and all the ladies of the court were present with their maids, and all the cavaliers with their servants; and each of the maids had another maid to wait upon her, and the cavaliers' servants had their own servants, as well as a page each. They all stood in circles round the princess, and the nearer they stood to the door, the prouder they looked. The servants' pages, who always wore slippers, could hardly be looked at; they held themselves up so proudly by the door."

"It must be quite awful," said little Gerda, "but did Kay win the princess?"

"If I had not been a crow," said he, "I would have married her myself, although I am engaged. He spoke just as well as I do, when I speak the crows' language, so I heard from my tame sweetheart. He was quite free and agreeable and said he had not come to woo the princess, but to hear her wisdom; and he was as pleased with her as she was with him."

"Oh, certainly that was Kay," said Gerda, "he was so clever; he could work mental arithmetic and fractions. Oh, will you take me to the palace?"

"It is very easy to ask that," replied the crow, "but how are we to manage it? However, I will speak about it to my tame sweetheart, and ask her advice; for I must tell you it will be very difficult to gain permission for a little girl like you to enter the palace."

"Oh, yes; but I shall gain permission easily," said Gerda, "for when Kay hears that I am here, he will come out and fetch me in immediately."

“Wait for me here by the palings,” said the crow, wagging his head as he flew away.

It was late in the evening before the crow returned. “Caw, caw,” he said, “she sends you greeting, and here is a little roll which she took from the kitchen for you; there is plenty of bread there, and she thinks you must be hungry. It is not possible for you to enter the palace by the front entrance. The guards in silver uniform and the servants in gold livery would not allow it. But do not cry, we will manage to get you in; my sweetheart knows a little back-staircase that leads to the sleeping apartments, and she knows where to find the key.”

Then they went into the garden through the great avenue, where the leaves were falling one after another, and they could see the light in the palace being put out in the same manner. And the crow led little Gerda to the back door, which stood ajar. Oh! How little Gerda’s heart beat with anxiety and longing; it was just as if she were going to do something wrong, and yet she only wanted to know where little Kay was. “It must be he,” she thought, “with those clear eyes, and that long hair.” She could fancy she saw him smiling at her, as he used to at home, when they sat among the roses. He would certainly be glad to see her, and to hear what a long distance she had come for his sake, and to know how sorry they had been at home because he did not come back. Oh what joy and yet fear she felt! They were now on the stairs, and in a small closet at the top a lamp was burning. In the middle of the floor stood the tame crow, turning her head from side to side, and gazing at Gerda, who curtseyed as her grandmother had taught her to do.

“My betrothed has spoken so very highly of you, my little lady,” said the tame crow. “Your life-history, Vita, as it may be called, is very touching. If you will take the lamp I will walk before you. We will go straight along this way; then we shall meet no one.”

“It seems to me as if somebody were behind us,” said Gerda, as something rushed by her like a shadow on the wall, and then horses with flying manes and thin legs, hunters, ladies and gentlemen on horseback, glided by her, like shadows on the wall.

“They are only dreams,” said the crow, “they are coming to fetch the thoughts of the great people out hunting.”

“All the better, for we shall be able to look at them in their beds more safely. I hope that when you rise to honor and favor, you will show a grateful heart.”

“You may be quite sure of that,” said the crow from the forest.

They now came into the first hall, the walls of which were hung with rose-colored satin, embroidered with artificial flowers. Here the dreams again flitted by them but so quickly that Gerda could not distinguish the royal persons. Each hall appeared more splendid than the last; it was enough to bewilder any one. At length they reached a bedroom. The ceiling was like a great palm-tree, with glass leaves of the most costly crystal, and over the centre of the floor two beds, each resembling a lily, hung from a stem of gold. One, in which the princess lay, was white, the other was red; and in this Gerda had to seek for little Kay. She pushed one of the red leaves aside, and saw a little brown neck. Oh, that must be Kay! She called his name out quite loud, and held the lamp over him. The dreams rushed back into the room on horseback. He woke, and turned his head round, it was not little Kay! The prince was only like him in the neck; still he was young and pretty. Then the princess peeped out of her white-lily bed, and asked what was the matter. Then little Gerda wept and told her story, and all that the crows had done to help her.

"You poor child," said the prince and princess; then they praised the crows, and said they were not angry for what they had done, but that it must not happen again, and this time they should be rewarded.

"Would you like to have your freedom?" asked the princess, "or would you prefer to be raised to the position of court crows, with all that is left in the kitchen for yourselves?"

Then both the crows bowed, and begged to have a fixed appointment, for they thought of their old age, and said it would be so comfortable to feel that they had provision for their old days, as they called it. And then the prince got out of his bed, and gave it up to Gerda,—he could do no more; and she lay down. She folded her little hands, and thought, "How good everyone is to me, men and animals too;" then she closed her eyes and fell into a sweet sleep. All the dreams came flying back again to her, and they looked like angels, and one of them drew a little sledge, on which sat Kay, and nodded to her. But all this was only a dream, and vanished as soon as she awoke.

The following day she was dressed from head to foot in silk and velvet, and they invited her to stay at the palace for a few days, and enjoy herself, but she only begged for a pair of boots, and a little carriage, and a horse to draw it, so that she might go into the wide world to seek for Kay. And she obtained, not only boots, but also a muff, and she was neatly dressed; and when she was ready to go, there, at the door, she found a coach made of pure gold, with the coat-of-arms of the prince and princess shining upon it like a star, and the coachman, footman, and outriders all wearing golden crowns on their heads. The prince and princess themselves helped her into the coach, and wished her success. The forest crow, who was now married, accompanied her for the first three miles; he sat by Gerda's side, as he could not bear riding backwards. The tame crow stood in the door-way flapping her wings. She could not go with them, because she had been suffering from headache ever since the new appointment, no doubt from eating too much. The coach was well stored with sweet cakes, and under the seat were fruit and gingerbread nuts. "Farewell, farewell," cried the prince and princess, and little Gerda wept, and the crow wept; and then, after a few miles, the crow also said "Farewell," and this was the saddest parting. However, he flew to a tree, and stood flapping his black wings as long as he could see the coach, which glittered in the bright sunshine.

Fifth Story: Little Robber-Girl

THE coach drove on through a thick forest, where it lighted up the way like a torch, and dazzled the eyes of some robbers, who could not bear to let it pass them unmolested.

"It is gold! It is gold!" cried they, rushing forward, and seizing the horses. Then they struck the little jockeys, the coachman, and the footman dead, and pulled little Gerda out of the carriage.

"She is fat and pretty, and she has been fed with the kernels of nuts," said the old robber-woman, who had a long beard and eyebrows that hung over her eyes. "She is as good as a little lamb; how nice she will taste!" and as she said this, she drew forth a shining knife, that glittered horribly. "Oh!" screamed the old woman the same moment; for her own daughter, who held her back, had bitten her in the ear. She was a wild and naughty girl, and the mother called her an ugly thing, and had not time to kill Gerda.

"She shall play with me," said the little robber-girl; "she shall give me her muff and her pretty dress, and sleep with me in my bed." And then she bit her mother again, and made her spring in the air, and jump about; and all the robbers laughed, and said, "See how she is dancing with her young cub."

"I will have a ride in the coach," said the little robber-girl; and she would have her own way; for she was so self-willed and obstinate.

She and Gerda seated themselves in the coach, and drove away, over stumps and stones, into the depths of the forest. The little robber-girl was about the same size as Gerda, but stronger; she had broader shoulders and a darker skin; her eyes were quite black, and she had a mournful look. She clasped little Gerda round the waist, and said,—

"They shall not kill you as long as you don't make us ***vexed*** with you. I suppose you are a princess."

"No," said Gerda; and then she told her all her history, and how fond she was of little Kay.

The robber-girl looked earnestly at her, nodded her head slightly, and said, "They shan't kill you, even if I do get angry with you; for I will do it myself." And then she wiped Gerda's eyes, and stuck her own hands in the beautiful muff which was so soft and warm.

The coach stopped in the courtyard of a robber's castle, the walls of which were cracked from top to bottom. Ravens and crows flew in and out of the holes and crevices, while great bulldogs, either of which looked as if it could swallow a man, were jumping about; but they were not allowed to bark. In the large and smoky hall a bright fire was burning on the stone floor. There was no chimney; so the smoke went up to the ceiling, and found a way out for itself. Soup was boiling in a large cauldron, and hares and rabbits were roasting on the spit.

"You shall sleep with me and all my little animals to-night," said the robber-girl, after they had had something to eat and drink. So she took Gerda to a corner of the hall, where some straw and carpets were laid down. Above them, on laths and perches, were more than a hundred pigeons, who all seemed to be asleep, although they moved slightly when the two little girls came near them. "These all belong to me," said the robber-girl; and she seized the nearest to her, held it by the feet, and shook it till it flapped its wings. "Kiss it," cried she, flapping it in Gerda's face. "There sit the wood-pigeons," continued she, pointing to a

---

vexed: displeased

number of laths and a cage which had been fixed into the walls, near one of the openings. "Both rascals would fly away directly, if they were not closely locked up. And here is my old sweetheart 'Ba;'" and she dragged out a reindeer by the horn; he wore a bright copper ring round his neck, and was tied up. "We are obliged to hold him tight too, or else he would run away from us also. I tickle his neck every evening with my sharp knife, which frightens him very much." And then the robber-girl drew a long knife from a chink in the wall, and let it slide gently over the reindeer's neck. The poor animal began to kick, and the little robber-girl laughed, and pulled down Gerda into bed with her.

"Will you have that knife with you while you are asleep?" asked Gerda, looking at it in great fright.

"I always sleep with the knife by me," said the robber-girl. "No one knows what may happen. But now tell me again all about little Kay, and why you went out into the world."

Then Gerda repeated her story over again, while the wood-pigeons in the cage over her cooed, and the other pigeons slept. The little robber-girl put one arm across Gerda's neck, and held the knife in the other, and was soon fast asleep and snoring. But Gerda could not close her eyes at all; she knew not whether she was to live or die. The robbers sat round the fire, singing and drinking, and the old woman stumbled about. It was a terrible sight for a little girl to witness.

Then the wood-pigeons said, "Coo, coo; we have seen little Kay. A white fowl carried his sledge, and he sat in the carriage of the Snow Queen, which drove through the wood while we were lying in our nest. She blew upon us, and all the young ones died excepting us two. Coo, coo."

"What are you saying up there?" cried Gerda. "Where was the Snow Queen going? Do you know anything about it?"

"She was most likely travelling to Lapland, where there is always snow and ice. Ask the reindeer that is fastened up there with a rope."

"Yes, there is always snow and ice," said the reindeer; "and it is a glorious place; you can leap and run about freely on the sparkling ice plains. The Snow Queen has her summer tent there, but her strong castle is at the North Pole, on an island called Spitzbergen."

"Oh, Kay, little Kay!" sighed Gerda.

"Lie still," said the robber-girl, "or I shall run my knife into your body."

In the morning Gerda told her all that the wood-pigeons had said; and the little robber-girl looked quite serious, and nodded her head, and said, "That is all talk, that is all talk. Do you know where Lapland is?" she asked the reindeer.

"Who should know better than I do?" said the animal, while his eyes sparkled. "I was born and brought up there, and used to run about the snow-covered plains."

"Now listen," said the robber-girl; "all our men are gone away, — only mother is here, and here she will stay; but at noon she always drinks out of a great bottle, and afterwards sleeps for a little while; and then, I'll do something for you." Then she jumped out of bed, clasped her mother round the neck, and pulled her by the beard, crying, "My own little nanny goat, good morning." Then her mother filliped her nose till it was quite red; yet she did it all for love.

When the mother had drunk out of the bottle, and was gone to sleep, the little robber-maiden went to the reindeer, and said, "I should like very much to tickle your neck a few times more with my knife, for it makes you look so funny; but never mind,—I will untie your cord, and set you free, so that you may run away to Lapland; but you must make good use of your legs, and carry this little maiden to the castle of the Snow Queen, where her play-fellow is. You have heard what she told me, for she spoke loud enough, and you were listening."

Then the reindeer jumped for joy; and the little robber-girl lifted Gerda on his back, and had the forethought to tie her on, and even to give her her own little cushion to sit on.

"Here are your fur boots for you," said she; "for it will be very cold; but I must keep the muff; it is so pretty. However, you shall not be frozen for the want of it; here are my mother's large warm mittens; they will reach up to your elbows. Let me put them on. There, now your hands look just like my mother's."

But Gerda wept for joy.

"I don't like to see you fret," said the little robber-girl; "you ought to look quite happy now; and here are two loaves and a ham, so that you need not starve." These were fastened on the reindeer, and then the little robber-maiden opened the door, coaxed in all the great dogs, and then cut the string with which the reindeer was fastened, with her sharp knife, and said, "Now run, but mind you take good care of the little girl." And then Gerda stretched out her hand, with the great mitten on it, towards the little robber-girl, and said, "Farewell," and away flew the reindeer, over stumps and stones, through the great forest, over marshes and plains, as quickly as he could. The wolves howled, and the ravens screamed; while up in the sky quivered red lights like flames of fire. "There are my old northern lights," said the reindeer; "see how they flash." And he ran on day and night still faster and faster, but the loaves and the ham were all eaten by the time they reached Lapland.

Sixth Story: The Lapland Woman and the Finland Woman

THEY stopped at a little hut; it was very mean looking; the roof sloped nearly down to the ground, and the door was so low that the family had to creep in on their hands and knees, when they went in and out. There was no one at home but an old Lapland woman, who was cooking fish by the light of a train-oil lamp. The reindeer told her all about Gerda's story, after having first told his own, which seemed to him the most important, but Gerda was so pinched with the cold that she could not speak. "Oh, you poor things," said the Lapland woman, "you have a long way to go yet. You must travel more than a hundred miles farther, to Finland. The Snow Queen lives there now, and she burns Bengal lights every evening. I will write a few words on a dried stock-fish, for I have no paper, and you can take it from me to the Finland woman who lives there; she can give you better information than I can." So when Gerda was warmed, and had taken something to eat and drink, the woman wrote a few words on the dried fish, and told Gerda to take great care of it. Then she tied her again on the reindeer, and he set off at full speed. Flash, flash, went the beautiful blue northern lights in the air the whole night long. And at length they reached Finland, and knocked at the chimney of the Finland woman's hut, for it had no door above the ground. They crept in, but it was so terribly hot inside that that woman wore scarcely any clothes; she was small and very dirty looking. She loosened little Gerda's dress, and took off the fur boots and the mittens, or Gerda would have been unable to bear the heat; and then she placed a piece of ice on the reindeer's head, and read what was written on the dried fish. After she had read it three times, she knew it by heart, so she popped the fish into the soup saucepan, as she knew it was good to eat, and she never wasted anything. The reindeer told his own story first, and then little Gerda's, and the Finlander twinkled with her clever eyes, but she said nothing. "You are so clever," said the reindeer; "I know you can tie all the winds of the world with a piece of twine. If a sailor unties one knot, he has a fair wind; when he unties the second, it blows hard; but if the third and fourth are loosened, then comes a storm, which will root up whole forests. Cannot you give this little maiden something which will make her as strong as twelve men, to overcome the Snow Queen?"

"The Power of twelve men!" said the Finland woman; "that would be of very little use." But she went to a shelf and took down and unrolled a large skin, on which were inscribed wonderful characters, and she read till the perspiration ran down from her forehead. But the reindeer begged so hard for little Gerda, and Gerda looked at the Finland woman with such ***beseeching*** tearful eyes that her own eyes began to twinkle again; so she drew the reindeer into a corner, and whispered to him while she laid a fresh piece of ice on his head, "Little Kay is really with the Snow Queen, but he finds everything there so much to his taste and his liking, that he believes it is the finest place in the world; but this is because he has a piece of broken glass in his heart, and a little piece of glass in his eye. These must be taken out, or he will never be a human being again, and the Snow Queen will retain her power over him."

"But can you not give little Gerda something to help her to conquer this power?"

"I can give her no greater power than she has already," said the woman; "don't you see how strong that is? How men and animals are obliged to serve her, and how well she has got through the world, barefooted as she is. She cannot receive any power from me greater than she now has, which consists in her own purity and innocence of heart. If she cannot herself obtain access to the Snow Queen, and remove the glass fragments from little Kay, we can do nothing to help her. Two miles from here the Snow Queen's garden begins; you can carry the little girl so far, and set her down by the large bush which stands in the snow, covered with red berries. Do not stay gossiping, but come back here as quickly as you can." Then the Finland woman lifted little Gerda upon the reindeer, and he ran away with her as quickly as he could.

---

beseeching: pleading; wanting very much

"Oh, I have forgotten my boots and my mittens," cried little Gerda, as soon as she felt the cutting cold, but the reindeer dared not stop, so he ran on till he reached the bush with the red berries; here he set Gerda down, and he kissed her, and the great bright tears trickled over the animal's cheeks; then he left her and ran back as fast as he could.

There stood poor Gerda, without shoes, without gloves, in the midst of cold, dreary, ice-bound Finland. She ran forwards as quickly as she could, when a whole regiment of snow-flakes came round her; they did not, however, fall from the sky, which was quite clear and glittering with the northern lights. The snow-flakes ran along the ground, and the nearer they came to her, the larger they appeared. Gerda remembered how large and beautiful they looked through the burning-glass. But these were really larger, and much more terrible, for they were alive, and were the guards of the Snow Queen, and had the strangest shapes. Some were like great porcupines, others like twisted serpents with their heads stretching out, and some few were like little fat bears with their hair bristled; but all were dazzlingly white, and all were living snow-flakes. Then little Gerda repeated the Lord's Prayer, and the cold was so great that she could see her own breath come out of her mouth like steam as she uttered the words. The steam appeared to increase, as she continued her prayer, till it took the shape of little angels who grew larger the moment they touched the earth. They all wore helmets on their heads, and carried spears and shields. Their number continued to increase more and more; and by the time Gerda had finished her prayers, a whole legion stood round her. They thrust their spears into the terrible snow-flakes, so that they shivered into a hundred pieces, and little Gerda could go forward with courage and safety. The angels stroked her hands and feet, so that she felt the cold less, and she hastened on to the Snow Queen's castle.

But now we must see what Kay is doing. In truth he thought not of little Gerda, and never supposed she could be standing in the front of the palace.

Seventh Story: Of the Palace of the Snow Queen and What Happened There At Last

THE walls of the palace were formed of drifted snow, and the windows and doors of the cutting winds. There were more than a hundred rooms in it, all as if they had been formed with snow blown together. The largest of them extended for several miles; they were all lighted up by the vivid light of the aurora, and they were so large and empty, so icy cold and glittering! There were no amusements here, not even a little bear's ball, when the storm might have been the music, and the bears could have danced on their hind legs, and shown their good manners. There were no pleasant games of snap-dragon, or touch, or even a gossip over the tea-table, for the young-lady foxes. Empty, vast, and cold were the halls of the Snow Queen. The flickering flame of the northern lights could be plainly seen, whether they rose high or low in the heavens, from every part of the castle. In the midst of its empty, endless hall of snow was a frozen lake,

© Inga Dudkina/Dreamstime.com

broken on its surface into a thousand forms; each piece resembled another, from being in itself perfect as a work of art, and in the centre of this lake sat the Snow Queen, when she was at home. She called the lake "The Mirror of Reason," and said that it was the best and indeed the only one in the world.

Little Kay was quite blue with cold, indeed almost black, but he did not feel it; for the Snow Queen had kissed away the icy shiverings, and his heart was already a lump of ice. He dragged some sharp, flat pieces of ice to and fro, and placed them together in all kinds of positions, as if he wished to make something out of them; just as we try to form various figures with little tablets of wood which we call "a Chinese puzzle." Kay's fingers were very artistic; it was the icy game of reason at which he played, and in his eyes the figures were very remarkable, and of the highest importance; this opinion was owing to the piece of glass still sticking in his eye. He composed many complete figures, forming different words, but there was one word he never could manage to form, although he wished it very much. It was the word "***Eternity***." The Snow Queen had said to him, "When you can find out this, you shall be your own master, and I will give you the whole world and a new pair of skates." But he could not ***accomplish*** it.

"Now I must hasten away to warmer countries," said the Snow Queen. "I will go and look into the black craters of the tops of the burning mountains, Etna and Vesuvius, as they are called,—I shall make them look white, which will be good for them, and for the lemons and the grapes." And away flew the Snow Queen, leaving little Kay quite alone in the great hall which was so many miles in length; so he sat and looked at his pieces of ice, and was thinking so deeply, and sat so still, that anyone might have supposed he was frozen.

Just at this moment it happened that little Gerda came through the great door of the castle. Cutting winds were raging around her, but she offered up a prayer and the winds sank down as if they were going to sleep; and she went on till she came to the large empty hall, and caught sight of Kay; she knew him directly; she flew to him and threw her arms round his neck, and held him fast, while she exclaimed, "Kay, dear little Kay, I have found you at last."

But he sat quite still, stiff and cold.

Then little Gerda wept hot tears, which fell on his breast, and penetrated into his heart, and thawed the lump of ice, and washed away the little piece of glass which had stuck there. Then he looked at her, and she sang—

"Roses bloom and cease to be,
But we shall the Christ-child see."

Then Kay burst into tears, and he wept so that the splinter of glass swam out of his eye. Then he recognized Gerda, and said, joyfully, "Gerda, dear little Gerda, where have you been all this time, and where have I been?" And he looked all around him, and said, "How cold it is, and how large and empty it all looks," and he clung to Gerda, and she laughed and wept for joy. It was so pleasing to see them that the pieces of ice even danced about; and when they

---

eternity: time without end
accomplish: achieve

were tired and went to lie down, they formed themselves into the letters of the word which the Snow Queen had said he must find out before he could be his own master, and have the whole world and a pair of new skates. Then Gerda kissed his cheeks, and they became blooming; and she kissed his eyes, and they shone like her own; she kissed his hands and his feet, and then he became quite healthy and cheerful. The Snow Queen might come home now when she pleased, for there stood his certainty of freedom, in the word she wanted, written in shining letters of ice.

Then they took each other by the hand, and went forth from the great palace of ice. They spoke of the grandmother, and of the roses on the roof, and as they went on the winds were at rest, and the sun burst forth. When they arrived at the bush with red berries, there stood the reindeer waiting for them, and he had brought another young reindeer with him, whose udders were full, and the children drank her warm milk and kissed her on the mouth. Then they carried Kay and Gerda first to the Finland woman, where they warmed themselves thoroughly in the hot room, and she gave them directions about their journey home. Next they went to the Lapland woman, who had made some new clothes for them, and put their sleighs in order. Both the reindeer ran by their side, and followed them as far as the boundaries of the country, where the first green leaves were budding. And here they took leave of the two reindeer and the Lapland woman, and all said—Farewell. Then the birds began to twitter, and the forest too was full of green young leaves; and out of it came a beautiful horse, which Gerda remembered, for it was one which had drawn the golden coach. A young girl was riding upon it, with a shining red cap on her head, and pistols in her belt. It was the little robber-maiden, who had got tired of staying at home; she was going first to the north, and if that did not suit her, she meant to try some other part of the world. She knew Gerda directly, and Gerda remembered her: it was a joyful meeting.

"You are a fine fellow to go gadding about in this way," said she to little Kay, "I should like to know whether you deserve that anyone should go to the end of the world to find you."

But Gerda patted her cheeks, and asked after the prince and princess.

"They are gone to foreign countries," said the robber-girl.

"And the crow?" asked Gerda.

"Oh, the crow is dead," she replied; "his tame sweetheart is now a widow, and wears a bit of black worsted round her leg. She mourns very pitifully, but it is all stuff. But now tell me how you managed to get him back."

Then Gerda and Kay told her all about it.

"Snip, snap, snare! It's all right at last," said the robber-girl.

Then she took both their hands, and promised that if ever she should pass through the town, she would call and pay them a visit. And then she rode away into the wide world. But Gerda and Kay went hand-in-hand towards home; and as they advanced, spring appeared more lovely with its green verdure and its beautiful flowers. Very soon they recognized the large town where they lived, and the tall steeples of the churches, in which the sweet bells were ringing a merry peal as they entered it, and found their way to their grandmother's door.

They went upstairs into the little room, where all looked just as it used to do. The old clock was going "tick, tick," and the hands pointed to the time of day, but as they passed through the door into the room they perceived that they were both grown up, and become a man and woman. The roses out on the roof were in full bloom, and peeped in at the window; and there stood the little chairs, on which they had sat when children; and Kay and Gerda seated themselves each on their own chair, and held each other by the hand, while the cold empty grandeur of the Snow Queen's palace vanished from their memories like a painful dream. The grandmother sat in God's bright sunshine, and she read aloud from the Bible, "Except ye become as little children, ye shall in no wise enter into the kingdom of God." And Kay and Gerda looked into each other's eyes, and all at once understood the words of the old song,

"Roses bloom and cease to be,
But we shall the Christ-child see."

And they both sat there, grown up, yet children at heart; and it was summer,—warm, beautiful summer.

The Red Shoes

ONCE upon a time there was little girl, pretty and dainty. But in summer time she was obliged to go barefooted because she was poor, and in winter she had to wear large wooden shoes, so that her little instep grew quite red.

In the middle of the village lived an old shoemaker's wife; she sat down and made, as well as she could, a pair of little shoes out of some old pieces of red cloth. They were clumsy, but she meant well, for they were intended for the little girl, whose name was Karen.

Karen received the shoes and wore them for the first time on the day of her mother's funeral. They were certainly not suitable for mourning; but she had no others, and so she put her bare feet into them and walked behind the humble coffin.

Just then a large old carriage came by, and in it sat an old lady; she looked at the little girl, and taking pity on her, said to the clergyman, "Look here, if you will give me the little girl, I will take care of her."

Karen believed that this was all ***on account of*** the red shoes, but the old lady thought them hideous, and so they were burnt. Karen herself was dressed very neatly and cleanly; she was taught to read and to sew, and people said that she was pretty. But the mirror told her, "You are more than pretty—you are beautiful."

One day the Queen was travelling through that part of the country, and had her little daughter, who was a princess, with her. All the people, amongst them Karen too, streamed towards the castle, where the little princess, in fine white clothes, stood before the window and allowed herself to be stared at. She

---

on account of: because of; owing to

wore neither a train nor a golden crown, but beautiful red morocco shoes; they were indeed much finer than those which the shoemaker's wife had sewn for little Karen. There is really nothing in the world that can be compared to red shoes!

Karen was now old enough to be ***confirmed***; she received some new clothes, and she was also to have some new shoes. The rich shoemaker in the town took the measure of her little foot in his own room, in which there stood great glass cases full of pretty shoes and white slippers. It all looked very lovely, but the old lady could not see very well, and therefore did not get much pleasure out of it. Amongst the shoes stood a pair of red ones, like those which the princess had worn. How beautiful they were! And the shoemaker said that they had been made for a count's daughter, but that they had not fitted her.

"I suppose they are of shiny leather?" asked the old lady. "They shine so."

"Yes, they do shine," said Karen. They fitted her, and were bought. But the old lady knew nothing of their being red, for she would never have allowed Karen to be confirmed in red shoes, as she was now to be.

Everybody looked at her feet, and the whole of the way from the church door to the choir it seemed to her as if even the ancient figures on the monuments, in their stiff collars and long black robes, had their eyes fixed on her red shoes. It was only of these that she thought when the clergyman laid his hand upon her head and spoke of the holy baptism, of the covenant with God, and told her that she was now to be a grown-up Christian. The organ pealed forth solemnly, and the sweet children's voices mingled with that of their old leader; but Karen thought only of her red shoes. In the afternoon the old lady heard from everybody that Karen had worn red shoes. She said that it was a shocking thing to do, that it was very improper, and that Karen was always to go to church in future in black shoes, even if they were old.

On the following Sunday there was Communion. Karen looked first at the black shoes, then at the red ones—looked at the red ones again, and put them on.

The sun was shining gloriously, so Karen and the old lady went along the footpath through the corn, where it was rather dusty.

At the church door stood an old crippled soldier leaning on a crutch; he had a wonderfully long beard, more red than white, and he bowed down to the ground and asked the old lady whether he might wipe her shoes. Then Karen put out her little foot too. "Dear me, what pretty dancing-shoes!" said the soldier. "Sit fast, when you dance," said he, addressing the shoes, and slapping the soles with his hand.

The old lady gave the soldier some money and then went with Karen into the church.

And all the people inside looked at Karen's red shoes, and all the figures gazed at them; when Karen knelt before the altar and put the golden goblet to her mouth, she thought only of the red shoes. It seemed to her as though they were swimming about in the goblet, and she forgot to sing the psalm, forgot to say the "Lord's Prayer."

---

be confirmed: become a full member of the Christian Church

Now everyone came out of church, and the old lady stepped into her carriage. But just as Karen was lifting up her foot to get in too, the old soldier said: "Dear me, what pretty dancing shoes!" and Karen could not help it, she was obliged to dance a few steps; and when she had once begun, her legs continued to dance. It seemed as if the shoes had got power over them. She danced round the church corner, for she could not stop; the coachman had to run after her and seize her. He lifted her into the carriage, but her feet continued to dance, so that she kicked the good old lady violently. At last they took off her shoes, and her legs were at rest.

At home the shoes were put into the cupboard, but Karen could not help looking at them.

Now the old lady fell ill, and it was said that she would not rise from her bed again. She had to be nursed and waited upon, and this was no one's duty more than Karen's. But there was a grand ball in the town, and Karen was invited. She looked at the red shoes, saying to herself that there was no sin in doing that; she put the red shoes on, thinking there was no harm in that either; and then she went to the ball; and commenced to dance.

But when she wanted to go to the right, the shoes danced to the left, and when she wanted to dance up the room, the shoes danced down the room, down the stairs through the street, and out through the gates of the town. She danced, and was obliged to dance, far out into the dark wood. Suddenly something shone up among the trees, and she believed it was the moon, for it was a face. But it was the old soldier with the red beard; he sat there nodding his head and said: "Dear me, what pretty dancing shoes!"

She was frightened, and wanted to throw the red shoes away; but they stuck fast. She tore off her stockings, but the shoes had grown fast to her feet. She danced and was obliged to go on dancing over field and meadow, in rain and sunshine, by night and by day—but by night it was most horrible.

She danced out into the open churchyard; but the dead there did not dance. They had something better to do than that. She wanted to sit down on the pauper's grave where the bitter fern grows; but for her there was neither peace nor rest. And as she danced past the open church door she saw an angel there in long white robes, with wings reaching from his shoulders down to the earth; his face was stern and grave, and in his hand he held a broad shining sword.

"Dance you shall," said he, "dance in your red shoes till you are pale and cold, till your skin shrivels up and you are a skeleton! Dance you shall, from door to door, and where proud and wicked children live you shall knock, so that they may hear you and fear you! Dance you shall, dance—!"

"Mercy!" cried Karen. But she did not hear what the angel answered, for the shoes carried her through the gate into the fields, along highways and byways, and unceasingly she had to dance.

One morning she danced past a door that she knew well; they were singing a psalm inside, and a coffin was being carried out covered with flowers. Then she knew that she was ***forsaken*** by everyone and damned by the angel of God.

---

forsaken: abandoned

She danced, and was obliged to go on dancing through the dark night. The shoes bore her away over thorns and stumps till she was all torn and bleeding; she danced away over the heath to a lonely little house. Here, she knew, lived the executioner; and she tapped with her finger at the window and said:

"Come out, come out! I cannot come in, for I must dance."

And the executioner said: "I don't suppose you know who I am. I strike off the heads of the wicked, and I notice that my axe is tingling to do so."

"Don't cut off my head!" said Karen, "for then I could not ***repent*** of my sin. But cut off my feet with the red shoes."

And then she confessed all her sin, and the executioner struck off her feet with the red shoes; but the shoes danced away with the little feet across the field into the deep forest.

And he carved her a pair of wooden feet and some crutches, and taught her a psalm which is always sung by sinners; she kissed the hand that guided the axe, and went away over the heath.

"Now, I have suffered enough for the red shoes," she said; "I will go to church, so that people can see me." And she went quickly up to the church-door; but when she came there, the red shoes were dancing before her, and she was frightened, and turned back.

During the whole week she was sad and wept many bitter tears, but when Sunday came again she said: "Now I have suffered and striven enough. I believe I am quite as good as many of those who sit in church and give themselves airs." And so she went boldly on; but she had not got farther than the churchyard gate when she saw the red shoes dancing along before her. Then she became terrified, and turned back and repented right heartily of her sin.

She went to the parsonage, and begged that she might be taken into service there. She would be ***industrious***, she said, and do everything that she could; she did not mind about the wages as long as she had a roof over her, and was with good people. The pastor's wife had pity on her, and took her into service. And she was industrious and thoughtful. She sat quiet and listened when the pastor read aloud from the Bible in the evening. All the children liked her very much, but when they spoke about dress and grandeur and beauty she would shake her head.

On the following Sunday they all went to church, and she was asked whether she wished to go too; but, with tears in her eyes, she looked sadly at her crutches. And then the others went to hear God's Word, but she went alone into her little room; this was only large enough to hold the bed and a chair. Here she sat down with her hymn-book, and as she was reading it with a pious mind, the wind carried the notes of the organ over to her from the church, and in tears she lifted up her face and said: "O God! Help me!"

Then the sun shone so brightly, and right before her stood an angel of God in white robes; it was the same one whom she had seen that night at the church-door. He no longer carried the sharp sword, but a beautiful green branch, full of

---

repent: be sorry; be penitent
industrious: hard-working

roses; with this he touched the ceiling, which rose up very high, and where he had touched it there shone a golden star. He touched the walls, which opened wide apart, and she saw the organ which was pealing forth; she saw the pictures of the old pastors and their wives, and the ***congregation*** sitting in the polished chairs and singing from their hymn-books. The church itself had come to the poor girl in her narrow room, or the room had gone to the church. She sat in the pew with the rest of the pastor's household, and when they had finished the hymn and looked up, they nodded and said, "It was right of you to come, Karen."

"It was mercy," said she.

The organ played and the children's voices in the choir sounded soft and lovely. The bright warm sunshine streamed through the window into the pew where Karen sat, and her heart became so filled with it, so filled with peace and joy, that it broke. Her soul flew on the sunbeams to Heaven, and no one was there who asked after the *Red Shoes.*

THE ARABIAN NIGHTS ENTERTAINMENTS

Andrew Lang

The Seven Voyages of Sindbad the Sailor

In the times of the Caliph Haroun-al-Raschid there lived in Bagdad a poor porter named Hindbad, who on a very hot day was sent to carry a heavy load from one end of the city to the other. Before he had accomplished half the distance he was so tired that, finding himself in a quiet street where the pavement was sprinkled with rose water, and a cool breeze was blowing, he set his ***burden*** upon the ground, and sat down to rest in the shade of a grand house. Very soon he decided that he could not have chosen a pleasanter place; a delicious perfume of aloes wood and pastilles came from the open windows and ***mingled*** with the scent of the rose water which steamed up from the hot pavement. Within the palace he heard some music, as of many instruments cunningly played, and the melodious warble of nightingales and other birds, and by this, and the appetising smell of many dainty dishes of which he presently became aware, he judged that feasting and merry making were going on. He wondered who lived in this magnificent house which he had never seen before, the street in which it stood being one which he seldom had occasion to pass. To satisfy his curiosity he went up to some splendidly dressed servants who stood at

---

congregation: people attending worship
burden: load
mingled: mixed

the door, and asked one of them the name of the master of the mansion.

"What," replied he, "do you live in Bagdad, and not know that here lives the noble Sindbad the Sailor, that famous traveller who sailed over every sea upon which the sun shines?"

The porter, who had often heard people speak of the immense wealth of Sindbad, could not help feeling envious of one whose lot seemed to be as happy as his own was miserable. Casting his eyes up to the sky he exclaimed aloud,

"Consider, Mighty Creator of all things, the differences between Sindbad's life and mine. Every day I suffer a thousand hardships and misfortunes, and have hard work to get even enough bad barley bread to keep myself and my family alive, while the lucky Sindbad spends money right and left and lives upon the fat of the land! What has he done that you should give him this pleasant life--what have I done to deserve so hard a fate?"

So saying he stamped upon the ground like one beside himself with misery and despair. Just at this moment a servant came out of the palace, and taking him by the arm said, "Come with me, the noble Sindbad, my master, wishes to speak to you."

Hindbad was not a little surprised at this summons, and feared that his unguarded words might have drawn upon him the displeasure of Sindbad, so he tried to excuse himself upon the ***pretext*** that he could not leave the burden which had been entrusted to him in the street. However the lackey promised him that it should be taken care of, and urged him to obey the call so pressingly that at last the porter was obliged to yield.

He followed the servant into a vast room, where a great company was seated round a table covered with all sorts of delicacies. In the place of honour sat a tall, ***grave*** man whose long white beard gave him a ***venerable*** air. Behind his chair stood a crowd of attendants eager to minister to his wants. This was the famous Sindbad himself. The porter, more than ever alarmed at the sight of so much magnificence, tremblingly saluted the noble company. Sindbad, making a sign to him to approach, caused him to be seated at his right hand, and himself heaped choice morsels upon his plate, and poured out for him a draught of excellent wine, and presently, when the banquet drew to a close, spoke to him familiarly, asking his name and occupation.

"My lord," replied the porter, "I am called Hindbad."

"I am glad to see you here," continued Sindbad. "And I will answer for the rest of the company that they are equally pleased, but I wish you to tell me what it was that you said just now in the street." For Sindbad, passing by the open window before the feast began, had heard his complaint and therefore had sent for him.

At this question Hindbad was covered with confusion, and hanging down his head, replied, "My lord, I confess that, overcome by ***weariness*** and ill-humour, I

---

pretext: excuse
grave: serious
venerable: respected
weariness: tiredness

uttered indiscreet words, which I pray you to pardon me."

"Oh!" replied Sindbad, "do not imagine that I am so unjust as to blame you. On the contrary, I understand your situation and can pity you. Only you appear to be mistaken about me, and I wish to set you right. You doubtless imagine that I have acquired all the wealth and luxury that you see me enjoy without difficulty or danger, but this is far indeed from being the case. I have only reached this happy state after having for years suffered every possible kind of toil and danger.

"Yes, my noble friends," he continued, addressing the company, "I assure you that my adventures have been strange enough to ***deter*** even the most ***avaricious*** men from seeking wealth by traversing the seas. Since you have, perhaps, heard but confused accounts of my seven voyages, and the dangers and wonders that I have met with by sea and land, I will now give you a full and true account of them, which I think you will be well pleased to hear."

As Sindbad was relating his adventures chiefly on account of the porter, he ordered, before beginning his tale, that the burden which had been left in the street should be carried by some of his own servants to the place for which Hindbad had set out at first, while he remained to listen to the story.

First Voyage

I had inherited considerable wealth from my parents, and being young and foolish I at first ***squandered*** it ***recklessly*** upon every kind of pleasure, but presently, finding that riches speedily take to themselves wings if managed as badly as I was managing mine, and remembering also that to be old and poor is misery indeed, I began to bethink me of how I could make the best of what still remained to me. I sold all my household goods by public auction, and joined a company of merchants who traded by sea, embarking with them at Balsora in a ship which we had fitted out between us.

We set sail and took our course towards the East Indies by the Persian Gulf, having the coast of Persia upon our left hand and upon our right the shores of Arabia Felix. I was at first much troubled by the uneasy motion of the vessel, but speedily recovered my health, and since that hour have been no more plagued by sea-sickness.

From time to time we landed at various islands, where we sold or exchanged our merchandise, and one day, when the wind dropped suddenly, we found ourselves becalmed close to a small island like a green meadow, which only rose slightly above the surface of the water. Our sails were furled, and the captain gave permission to all who wished to land for a while and amuse themselves. I was among the number, but when after strolling about for some time we lighted

---

deter: discourage
avaricious: greedy
squandered: wasted
recklessly: irresponsibly

a fire and sat down to enjoy the repast which we had brought with us, we were startled by a sudden and violent trembling of the island, while at the same moment those left upon the ship set up an outcry bidding us come on board for our lives, since what we had taken for an island was nothing but the back of a sleeping whale. Those who were nearest to the boat threw themselves into it, others sprang into the sea, but before I could save myself the whale plunged suddenly into the depths of the ocean, leaving me clinging to a piece of the wood which we had brought to make our fire. Meanwhile a breeze had sprung up, and in the confusion that ***ensued*** on board our vessel in hoisting the sails and taking up those who were in the boat and clinging to its sides, no one missed me and I was left at the mercy of the waves. All that day I floated up and down, now beaten this way, now that, and when night fell I despaired for my life; but, weary and spent as I was, I clung to my frail support, and great was my joy when the morning light showed me that I had drifted against an island.

The cliffs were high and steep, but luckily for me some tree-roots protruded in places, and by their aid I climbed up at last, and stretched myself upon the turf at the top, where I lay, more dead than alive, till the sun was high in the heavens. By that time I was very hungry, but after some searching I came upon some eatable herbs, and a spring of clear water, and much refreshed I set out to explore the island. Presently I reached a great plain where a grazing horse was tethered, and as I stood looking at it I heard voices talking apparently underground, and in a moment a man appeared who asked me how I came upon the island. I told him my adventures, and heard in return that he was one of the grooms of Mihrage, the king of the island, and that each year they came to feed their master's horses in this plain. He took me to a cave where his companions were assembled, and when I had eaten of the food they set before me, they bade me think myself fortunate to have come upon them when I did, since they were going back to their master on the morrow, and without their aid I could certainly never have found my way to the inhabited part of the island.

Early the next morning we accordingly set out, and when we reached the capital I was graciously received by the king, to whom I related my adventures, upon which he ordered that I should be well cared for and provided with such things as I needed. Being a merchant I sought out men of my own profession, and particularly those who came from foreign countries, as I hoped in this way to hear news from Bagdad, and find out some means of returning thither, for the capital was situated upon the sea-shore, and visited by vessels from all parts of the world. In the meantime I heard many curious things, and answered many questions concerning my own country, for I talked willingly with all who came to me. Also to while away the time of waiting I explored a little island named Cassel, which belonged to King Mihrage, and which was supposed to be inhabited by a spirit named Deggial. Indeed, the sailors assured me that often at night the playing of timbals could be heard upon it. However, I saw nothing strange upon my voyage, saving some fish that were full two hundred cubits long, but were fortunately more in dread of us than even we were of them, and

---

ensued: resulted

fled from us if we did but strike upon a board to frighten them. Other fishes there were only a cubit long which had heads like owls.

One day after my return, as I went down to the quay, I saw a ship which had just cast anchor, and was discharging her cargo, while the merchants to whom it belonged were busily directing the removal of it to their warehouses. Drawing nearer I presently noticed that my own name was marked upon some of the packages, and after having carefully examined them, I felt sure that they were indeed those which I had put on board our ship at Balsora. I then recognised the captain of the vessel, but as I was certain that he believed me to be dead, I went up to him and asked who owned the packages that I was looking at.

"There was on board my ship," he replied, "a merchant of Bagdad named Sindbad. One day he and several of my other passengers landed upon what we supposed to be an island, but which was really an enormous whale floating asleep upon the waves. No sooner did it feel upon its back the heat of the fire which had been kindled, than it plunged into the depths of the sea. Several of the people who were upon it perished in the waters, and among others this unlucky Sindbad. This merchandise is his, but I have ***resolved*** to dispose of it for the benefit of his family if I should ever chance to meet with them."

"Captain," said I, "I am that Sindbad whom you believe to be dead, and these are my possessions!"

When the captain heard these words he cried out in amazement, "Lackaday! and what is the world coming to? In these days there is not an honest man to be met with. Did I not with my own eyes see Sindbad drown, and now you have the ***audacity*** to tell me that you are he! I should have taken you to be a just man, and yet for the sake of obtaining that which does not belong to you, you are ready to invent this horrible falsehood."

"Have patience, and do me the favour to hear my story," said I.

"Speak then," replied the captain, "I'm all attention."

So I told him of my escape and of my fortunate meeting with the king's grooms, and how kindly I had been received at the palace. Very soon I began to see that I had made some impression upon him, and after the arrival of some of the other merchants, who showed great joy at once more seeing me alive, he declared that he also recognised me.

Throwing himself upon my neck he exclaimed, "Heaven be praised that you have escaped from so great a danger. As to your goods, I pray you take them, and dispose of them as you please." I thanked him, and praised his honesty, begging him to accept several bales of merchandise in token of my gratitude, but he would take nothing. Of the choicest of my goods I prepared a present for King Mihrage, who was at first amazed, having known that I had lost my all. However, when I had explained to him how my bales had been miraculously restored to me, he graciously accepted my gifts, and in return gave me many valuable things. I then took leave of him, and exchanging my merchandise for sandal and aloes wood, camphor, nutmegs, cloves, pepper, and ginger, I

---

resolved: decided
audacity: nerve; cheek

embarked upon the same vessel and traded so successfully upon our homeward voyage that I arrived in Balsora with about one hundred thousand sequins. My family received me with as much joy as I felt upon seeing them once more. I bought land and slaves, and built a great house in which I resolved to live happily, and in the enjoyment of all the pleasures of life to forget my past sufferings.

Here Sindbad paused, and commanded the musicians to play again, while the feasting continued until evening. When the time came for the porter to depart, Sindbad gave him a purse containing one hundred sequins, saying, "Take this, Hindbad, and go home, but to-morrow come again and you shall hear more of my adventures."

The porter retired quite overcome by so much generosity, and you may imagine that he was well received at home, where his wife and children thanked their lucky stars that he had found such a benefactor.

The next day Hindbad, dressed in his best, returned to the voyager's house, and was received with open arms. As soon as all the guests had arrived the banquet began as before, and when they had feasted long and merrily, Sindbad addressed them thus:

"My friends, I beg that you will give me your attention while I relate the adventures of my second voyage, which you will find even more astonishing than the first."

Second Voyage

I had resolved, as you know, on my return from my first voyage, to spend the rest of my days quietly in Bagdad, but very soon I grew tired of such an idle life and longed once more to find myself upon the sea.

I procured, therefore, such goods as were suitable for the places I intended to visit, and embarked for the second time in a good ship with other merchants whom I knew to be honourable men. We went from island to island, often making excellent bargains, until one day we landed at a spot which, though covered with fruit trees and abounding in springs of excellent water, appeared to possess neither houses nor people. While my companions wandered here and there gathering flowers and fruit I sat down in a shady place, and, having heartily enjoyed the provisions and the wine I had brought with me, I fell asleep, lulled by the murmur of a clear brook which flowed close by.

How long I slept I know not, but when I opened my eyes and started to my feet I perceived with horror that I was alone and that the ship was gone. I rushed to and fro like one distracted, uttering cries of despair, and when from the shore I saw the vessel under full sail just disappearing upon the horizon, I wished bitterly enough that I had been content to stay at home in safety. But since wishes could do me no good, I presently took courage and looked about me for a means of escape. When I had climbed a tall tree I first of all directed my

---

embarked: went on board

anxious glances towards the sea; but, finding nothing hopeful there, I turned landward, and my curiosity was excited by a huge dazzling white object, so far off that I could not make out what it might be.

Descending from the tree I hastily collected what remained of my provisions and set off as fast as I could go towards it. As I drew near it seemed to me to be a white ball of immense size and height, and when I could touch it, I found it marvellously smooth and soft. As it was impossible to climb it--for it presented no foot-hold--I walked round about it seeking some opening, but there was none. I counted, however, that it was at least fifty paces round. By this time the sun was near setting, but quite suddenly it fell dark, something like a huge black cloud came swiftly over me, and I saw with amazement that it was a bird of extraordinary size which was hovering near. Then I remembered that I had often heard the sailors speak of a wonderful bird called a roc, and it occurred to me that the white object which had so puzzled me must be its egg.

Sure enough the bird settled slowly down upon it, covering it with its wings to keep it warm, and I cowered close beside the egg in such a position that one of the bird's feet, which was as large as the trunk of a tree, was just in front of me. Taking off my turban I bound myself securely to it with the linen in the hope that the roc, when it took flight next morning, would bear me away with it from the desolate island. And this was precisely what did happen. As soon as the dawn appeared the bird rose into the air carrying me up and up till I could no longer see the earth, and then suddenly it descended so swiftly that I almost lost consciousness. When I became aware that the roc had settled and that I was once again upon solid ground, I hastily unbound my turban from its foot and freed myself, and that not a moment too soon; for the bird, pouncing upon a huge snake, killed it with a few blows from its powerful beak, and seizing it up rose into the air once more and soon disappeared from my view. When I had looked about me I began to doubt if I had gained anything by quitting the desolate island.

The valley in which I found myself was deep and narrow, and surrounded by mountains which towered into the clouds, and were so steep and rocky that there was no way of climbing up their sides. As I wandered about, seeking anxiously for some means of escaping from this trap, I observed that the ground was strewed with diamonds, some of them of an astonishing size. This sight gave me great pleasure, but my delight was speedily damped when I saw also numbers of horrible snakes so long and so large that the smallest of them could have swallowed an elephant with ease. Fortunately for me they seemed to hide in caverns of the rocks by day, and only came out by night, probably because of their enemy the roc.

All day long I wandered up and down the valley, and when it grew dusk I crept into a little cave, and having blocked up the entrance to it with a stone, I ate part of my little store of food and lay down to sleep, but all through the night the serpents crawled to and fro, hissing horribly, so that I could scarcely close my eyes for terror. I was thankful when the morning light appeared, and when I judged by the silence that the serpents had retreated to their dens I came tremblingly out of my cave and wandered up and down the valley once more, kicking the diamonds ***contemptuously*** out of my path, for I felt that they were indeed vain things to a man in my situation. At last, overcome with weariness, I sat down upon a rock, but I had hardly closed my eyes when I was startled by something which fell to the ground with a thud close beside me.

It was a huge piece of fresh meat, and as I stared at it several more pieces rolled over the cliffs in different places. I had always thought that the stories the sailors told of the famous valley of diamonds, and of the cunning way which some merchants had devised for getting at the precious stones, were mere travellers' tales invented to give pleasure to the hearers, but now I perceived that they were surely true. These merchants came to the valley at the time when the eagles, which keep their eyries in the rocks, had hatched their young. The merchants then threw great lumps of meat into the valley. These, falling with so much force upon the diamonds, were sure to take up some of the precious stones with them, when the eagles pounced upon the meat and carried it off to their nests to feed their hungry broods. Then the merchants, scaring away the parent birds with shouts and outcries, would secure their treasures. Until this moment I had looked upon the valley as my grave, for I had seen no possibility of getting out of it alive, but now I took courage and began to devise a means of escape. I began by picking up all the largest diamonds I could find and storing them carefully in the leathern wallet which had held my provisions; this I tied securely to my belt. I then chose the piece of meat which seemed most suited to my purpose, and with the aid of my turban bound it firmly to my back; this done I laid down upon my face and awaited the coming of the eagles. I soon heard the flapping of their mighty wings above me, and had the satisfaction of feeling one of them seize upon my piece of meat, and me with it, and rise slowly towards his nest, into which he presently dropped me. Luckily for me the merchants were on the watch, and setting up their usual outcries they rushed to the nest scaring away the eagle. Their amazement was great when they discovered me, and also their disappointment, and with one accord they fell to abusing me for having robbed them of their usual profit. Addressing myself to the one who seemed most aggrieved, I said: "I am sure, if you knew all that I have suffered, you would show more kindness towards me, and as for diamonds, I have enough here of the very best for you and me and all your company." So saying I showed them to him. The others all crowded round me, wondering at my adventures and admiring the device by which I had escaped from the valley, and when they had led me to their camp and examined my diamonds, they assured me that in all the years that they had carried on their trade they had seen no stones to be compared with them for size and beauty.

I found that each merchant chose a particular nest, and took his chance of what he might find in it. So I begged the one who owned the nest to which I had been carried to take as much as he would of my treasure, but he contented himself with one stone, and that by no means the largest, assuring me that with such a gem his fortune was made, and he need toil no more. I stayed with the merchants several days, and then as they were journeying homewards I gladly

---

contemptuously: scornfully

accompanied them. Our way lay across high mountains infested with frightful serpents, but we had the good luck to escape them and came at last to the seashore. Thence we sailed to the isle of Rohat where the camphor trees grow to such a size that a hundred men could shelter under one of them with ease. The sap flows from an incision made high up in the tree into a vessel hung there to receive it, and soon hardens into the substance called camphor, but the tree itself withers up and dies when it has been so treated.

In this same island we saw the rhinoceros, an animal which is smaller than the elephant and larger than the buffalo. It has one horn about a cubit long which is solid, but has a furrow from the base to the tip. Upon it is traced in white lines the figure of a man. The rhinoceros fights with the elephant, and transfixing him with his horn carries him off upon his head, but becoming blinded with the blood of his enemy, he falls helpless to the ground, and then comes the roc, and clutches them both up in his talons and takes them to feed his young. This doubtless astonishes you, but if you do not believe my tale go to Rohat and see for yourself. For fear of wearying you I pass over in silence many other wonderful things which we saw in this island. Before we left I exchanged one of my diamonds for much goodly merchandise by which I profited greatly on our homeward way. At last we reached Balsora, whence I hastened to Bagdad, where my first action was to ***bestow*** large sums of money upon the poor, after which I settled down to enjoy tranquilly the riches I had gained with so much toil and pain.

Having thus related the adventures of his second voyage, Sindbad again bestowed a hundred sequins upon Hindbad, inviting him to come again on the following day and hear how he fared upon his third voyage. The other guests also departed to their homes, but all returned at the same hour next day, including the porter, whose former life of hard work and poverty had already begun to seem to him like a bad dream. Again after the feast was over did Sindbad claim the attention of his guests and began the account of his third voyage.

Third Voyage

After a very short time the pleasant easy life I led made me quite forget the ***perils*** of my two voyages. Moreover, as I was still in the prime of life, it pleased me better to be up and doing. So once more providing myself with the rarest and choicest merchandise of Bagdad, I conveyed it to Balsora, and set sail with other merchants of my acquaintance for distant lands. We had touched at many ports and made much profit, when one day upon the open sea we were caught by a terrible wind which blew us completely out of our reckoning, and lasting for several days finally drove us into harbour on a strange island.

"I would rather have come to anchor anywhere than here," quoth our captain.

---

bestow: give
peril: danger

"This island and all adjoining it are inhabited by hairy savages, who are certain to attack us, and whatever these dwarfs may do we dare not resist, since they ***swarm*** like locusts, and if one of them is killed the rest will fall upon us, and speedily make an end of us."

These words caused great ***consternation*** among all the ship's company, and only too soon we were to find out that the captain spoke truly. There appeared a vast multitude of hideous savages, not more than two feet high and covered with reddish fur. Throwing themselves into the waves they surrounded our vessel. Chattering meanwhile in a language we could not understand, and clutching at ropes and gangways, they swarmed up the ship's side with such speed and agility that they almost seemed to fly.

You may imagine the rage and terror that seized us as we watched them, neither daring to hinder them nor able to speak a word to ***deter*** them from their purpose, whatever it might be. Of this we were not left long in doubt. Hoisting the sails, and cutting the cable of the anchor, they sailed our vessel to an island which lay a little further off, where they drove us ashore; then taking possession of her, they made off to the place from which they had come, leaving us helpless upon a shore avoided with horror by all mariners for a reason which you will soon learn.

Turning away from the sea we wandered miserably inland, finding as we went various herbs and fruits which we ate, feeling that we might as well live as long as possible though we had no hope of escape. Presently we saw in the far distance what seemed to us to be a splendid palace, towards which we turned our weary steps, but when we reached it we saw that it was a castle, lofty, and strongly built. Pushing back the heavy ebony doors we entered the courtyard, but upon the threshold of the great hall beyond it we paused, frozen with horror, at the sight which greeted us. On one side lay a huge pile of bones--human bones, and on the other numberless spits for roasting! Overcome with ***despair*** we sank trembling to the ground, and lay there without speech or motion. The sun was setting when a loud noise aroused us, the door of the hall was violently burst open and a horrible giant entered. He was as tall as a palm tree, and perfectly black, and had one eye, which flamed like a burning coal in the middle of his forehead. His teeth were long and sharp and grinned horribly, while his lower lip hung down upon his chest, and he had ears like elephant's ears, which covered his shoulders, and nails like the claws of some fierce bird.

At this terrible sight our senses left us and we lay like dead men. When at last we came to ourselves the giant sat examining us attentively with his fearful eye. Presently when he had looked at us enough he came towards us, and stretching out his hand took me by the back of the neck, turning me this way and that, but feeling that I was mere skin and bone he set me down again and went on to the next, whom he treated in the same fashion; at last he came to the

---

swarm: group; flock
consternation: alarm; anxiety
deter: prevent; discourage
despair: hopelessness

captain, and finding him the fattest of us all, he took him up in one hand and stuck him upon a spit and proceeded to kindle a huge fire at which he presently roasted him. After the giant had supped he lay down to sleep, snoring like the loudest thunder, while we lay shivering with horror the whole night through, and when day broke he awoke and went out, leaving us in the castle.

When we believed him to be really gone we started up bemoaning our horrible fate, until the hall echoed with our despairing cries. Though we were many and our enemy was alone it did not occur to us to kill him, and indeed we should have found that a hard task, even if we had thought of it, and no plan could we ***devise*** to deliver ourselves. So at last, submitting to our sad fate, we spent the day in wandering up and down the island eating such fruits as we could find, and when night came we returned to the castle, having sought in vain for any other place of shelter. At sunset the giant returned, supped upon one of our unhappy comrades, slept and snored till dawn, and then left us as before. Our condition seemed to us so frightful that several of my companions thought it would be better to leap from the cliffs and perish in the waves at once, rather than await so miserable an end; but I had a plan of escape which I now unfolded to them, and which they at once agreed to attempt.

"Listen, my brothers," I added. "You know that plenty of driftwood lies along the shore. Let us make several rafts, and carry them to a suitable place. If our plot succeeds, we can wait patiently for the chance of some passing ship which would rescue us from this fatal island. If it fails, we must quickly take to our rafts; frail as they are, we have more chance of saving our lives with them than we have if we remain here."

All agreed with me, and we spent the day in building rafts, each capable of carrying three persons. At nightfall we returned to the castle, and very soon in came the giant, and one more of our number was sacrificed. But the time of our vengeance was at hand! As soon as he had finished his horrible repast he lay down to sleep as before, and when we heard him begin to snore I, and nine of the boldest of my comrades, rose softly, and took each a spit, which we made red-hot in the fire, and then at a given signal we plunged it with one accord into the giant's eye, completely blinding him. Uttering a terrible cry, he sprang to his feet clutching in all directions to try to seize one of us, but we had all fled different ways as soon as the deed was done, and thrown ourselves flat upon the ground in corners where he was not likely to touch us with his feet.

After a vain search he fumbled about till he found the door, and fled out of it howling frightfully. As for us, when he was gone we made haste to leave the fatal castle, and, stationing ourselves beside our rafts, we waited to see what would happen. Our idea was that if, when the sun rose, we saw nothing of the giant, and no longer heard his howls, which still came faintly through the darkness, growing more and more distant, we should conclude that he was dead, and that we might safely stay upon the island and need not risk our lives upon the frail rafts. But alas! morning light showed us our enemy approaching us, supported on either hand by two giants nearly as large and fearful as himself,

---

devise: think up

while a crowd of others followed close upon their heels. Hesitating no longer we clambered upon our rafts and rowed with all our might out to sea. The giants, seeing their prey escaping them, seized up huge pieces of rock, and wading into the water hurled them after us with such good aim that all the rafts except the one I was upon were swamped, and their luckless crews drowned, without our being able to do anything to help them. Indeed I and my two companions had all we could do to keep our own raft beyond the reach of the giants, but by dint of hard rowing we at last gained the open sea. Here we were at the mercy of the winds and waves, which tossed us to and fro all that day and night, but the next morning we found ourselves near an island, upon which we gladly landed.

There we found delicious fruits, and having satisfied our hunger we presently lay down to rest upon the shore. Suddenly we were aroused by a loud rustling noise, and starting up, saw that it was caused by an immense snake which was gliding towards us over the sand. So swiftly it came that it had seized one of my comrades before he had time to fly, and in spite of his cries and struggles speedily crushed the life out of him in its mighty coils and proceeded to swallow him. By this time my other companion and I were running for our lives to some place where we might hope to be safe from this new horror, and seeing a tall tree we climbed up into it, having first provided ourselves with a store of fruit off the surrounding bushes. When night came I fell asleep, but only to be awakened once more by the terrible snake, which after hissing horribly round the tree at last reared itself up against it, and finding my sleeping comrade who was perched just below me, it swallowed him also, and crawled away leaving me half dead with terror.

When the sun rose I crept down from the tree with hardly a hope of escaping the dreadful fate which had over-taken my comrades; but life is sweet, and I determined to do all I could to save myself. All day long I ***toiled*** with frantic haste and collected quantities of dry brushwood, reeds and thorns, which I bound with faggots, and making a circle of them under my tree I piled them firmly one upon another until I had a kind of tent in which I crouched like a mouse in a hole when she sees the cat coming. You may imagine what a fearful night I passed, for the snake returned eager to devour me, and glided round and round my frail shelter seeking an entrance. Every moment I feared that it would succeed in pushing aside some of the faggots, but happily for me they held together, and when it grew light my enemy retired, baffled and hungry, to his den. As for me I was more dead than alive! Shaking with fright and half suffocated by the poisonous breath of the monster, I came out of my tent and crawled down to the sea, feeling that it would be better to plunge from the cliffs and end my life at once than pass such another night of horror. But to my joy and relief I saw a ship sailing by, and by shouting wildly and waving my turban I managed to attract the attention of her crew.

A boat was sent to rescue me, and very soon I found myself on board surrounded by a wondering crowd of sailors and merchants eager to know by what chance I found myself in that desolate island. After I had told my story

---

toiled: worked

they regaled me with the choicest food the ship afforded, and the captain, seeing that I was in rags, generously bestowed upon me one of his own coats. After sailing about for some time and touching at many ports we came at last to the island of Salahat, where sandal wood grows in great abundance. Here we anchored, and as I stood watching the merchants disembarking their goods and preparing to sell or exchange them, the captain came up to me and said,

"I have here, brother, some merchandise belonging to a passenger of mine who is dead. Will you do me the favour to trade with it, and when I meet with his heirs I shall be able to give them the money, though it will be only just that you shall have a portion for your trouble."

I consented gladly, for I did not like standing by idle. Whereupon he pointed the bales out to me, and sent for the person whose duty it was to keep a list of the goods that were upon the ship. When this man came he asked in what name the merchandise was to be registered.

"In the name of Sindbad the Sailor," replied the captain.

At this I was greatly surprised, but looking carefully at him I recognised him to be the captain of the ship upon which I had made my second voyage, though he had altered much since that time. As for him, believing me to be dead it was no wonder that he had not recognised me.

"So, captain," said I, "the merchant who owned those bales was called Sindbad?"

"Yes," he replied. "He was so named. He belonged to Bagdad, and joined my ship at Balsora, but by mischance he was left behind upon a desert island where we had landed to fill up our water-casks, and it was not until four hours later that he was missed. By that time the wind had freshened, and it was impossible to put back for him."

"You suppose him to have perished then?" said I.

"Alas! yes," he answered.

"Why, captain!" I cried, "look well at me. I am that Sindbad who fell asleep upon the island and awoke to find himself abandoned!"

The captain stared at me in amazement, but was presently convinced that I was indeed speaking the truth, and rejoiced greatly at my escape.

"I am glad to have that piece of carelessness off my conscience at any rate," said he. "Now take your goods, and the profit I have made for you upon them, and may you prosper in future."

I took them gratefully, and as we went from one island to another I laid in stores of cloves, cinnamon, and other spices. In one place I saw a tortoise which was twenty cubits long and as many broad, also a fish that was like a cow and had skin so thick that it was used to make shields. Another I saw that was like a camel in shape and colour. So by degrees we came back to Balsora, and I returned to Bagdad with so much money that I could not myself count it, besides treasures without end. I gave largely to the poor, and bought much land to add to what I already possessed, and thus ended my third voyage.

When Sindbad had finished his story he gave another hundred sequins to Hindbad, who then departed with the other guests, but next day when they had all reassembled, and the banquet was ended, their host continued his adventures.

Fourth Voyage

Rich and happy as I was after my third voyage, I could not make up my mind to stay at home altogether. My love of trading, and the pleasure I took in anything that was new and strange, made me set my affairs in order, and begin my journey through some of the Persian provinces, having first sent off stores of goods to await my coming in the different places I intended to visit. I took ship at a distant seaport, and for some time all went well, but at last, being caught in a violent hurricane, our vessel became a total wreck in spite of all our worthy captain could do to save her, and many of our company perished in the waves. I, with a few others, had the good fortune to be washed ashore clinging to pieces of the wreck, for the storm had driven us near an island, and scrambling up beyond the reach of the waves we threw ourselves down quite exhausted, to wait for morning.

At daylight we wandered inland, and soon saw some huts, to which we directed our steps. As we drew near their black inhabitants swarmed out in great numbers and surrounded us, and we were led to their houses, and as it were divided among our captors. I with five others was taken into a hut, where we were made to sit upon the ground, and certain herbs were given to us, which the blacks made signs to us to eat. Observing that they themselves did not touch them, I was careful only to pretend to taste my portion; but my companions, being very hungry, rashly ate up all that was set before them, and very soon I had the horror of seeing them become perfectly mad. Though they chattered incessantly I could not understand a word they said, nor did they heed when I spoke to them. The savages now produced large bowls full of rice prepared with cocoanut oil, of which my crazy comrades ate eagerly, but I only tasted a few grains, understanding clearly that the object of our captors was to fatten us speedily for their own eating, and this was exactly what happened. My unlucky companions having lost their reason, felt neither anxiety nor fear, and ate greedily all that was offered them. So they were soon fat and there was an end of them, but I grew leaner day by day, for I ate but little, and even that little did me no good by reason of my fear of what lay before me. However, as I was so far from being a tempting morsel, I was allowed to wander about freely, and one day, when all the blacks had gone off upon some expedition leaving only an old man to guard me, I managed to escape from him and plunged into the forest, running faster the more he cried to me to come back, until I had completely distanced him.

For seven days I hurried on, resting only when the darkness stopped me, and living chiefly upon cocoanuts, which afforded me both meat and drink, and on the eighth day I reached the seashore and saw a party of white men gathering pepper, which grew abundantly all about. Reassured by the nature of their occupation, I advanced towards them and they greeted me in Arabic, asking who I was and whence I came. My delight was great on hearing this familiar speech, and I willingly satisfied their curiosity, telling them how I had been shipwrecked, and captured by the blacks. "But these savages devour men!" said they. "How did you escape?" I repeated to them what I have just told you, at which they were mightily astonished. I stayed with them until they had collected as much pepper as they wished, and then they took me back to their own country and presented me to their king, by whom I was hospitably received. To him also I had to relate my adventures, which surprised him much, and when I had finished he ordered that I should be supplied with food and ***raiment*** and treated with consideration.

The island on which I found myself was full of people, and abounded in all sorts of desirable things, and a great deal of traffic went on in the capital, where I soon began to feel at home and contented. Moreover, the king treated me with special favour, and in consequence of this everyone, whether at the court or in the town, sought to make life pleasant to me. One thing I remarked which I thought very strange; this was that, from the greatest to the least, all men rode their horses without bridle or stirrups. I one day presumed to ask his majesty why he did not use them, to which he replied, "You speak to me of things of which I have never before heard!" This gave me an idea. I found a clever workman, and made him cut out under my direction the foundation of a saddle, which I wadded and covered with choice leather, adorning it with rich gold embroidery. I then got a lock-smith to make me a bit and a pair of spurs after a pattern that I drew for him, and when all these things were completed I presented them to the king and showed him how to use them. When I had saddled one of his horses he mounted it and rode about quite delighted with the novelty, and to show his gratitude he rewarded me with large gifts. After this I had to make saddles for all the principal officers of the king's household, and as they all gave me rich presents I soon became very wealthy and quite an important person in the city.

One day the king sent for me and said, "Sindbad, I am going to ask a favour of you. Both I and my subjects ***esteem*** you, and wish you to end your days amongst us. Therefore I desire that you will marry a rich and beautiful lady whom I will find for you, and think no more of your own country."

As the king's will was law I accepted the charming bride he presented to me, and lived happily with her. Nevertheless I had every intention of escaping at the first opportunity, and going back to Bagdad. Things were thus going prosperously with me when it happened that the wife of one of my neighbours, with whom I had struck up quite a friendship, fell ill, and presently died. I went to his house to offer my consolations, and found him in the depths of woe.

"Heaven preserve you," said I, "and send you a long life!"

"Alas!" he replied, "what is the good of saying that when I have but an hour left to live!"

"Come, come!" said I, "surely it is not so bad as all that. I trust that you may be spared to me for many years."

"I hope," answered he, "that your life may be long, but as for me, all is finished. I have set my house in order, and to-day I shall be buried with my

---

raiment: clothing
esteem: respect

wife. This has been the law upon our island from the earliest ages--the living husband goes to the grave with his dead wife, the living wife with her dead husband. So did our fathers, and so must we do. The law changes not, and all must submit to it!"

As he spoke the friends and relations of the unhappy pair began to assemble. The body, decked in rich robes and sparkling with jewels, was laid upon an open bier, and the procession started, taking its way to a high mountain at some distance from the city, the wretched husband, clothed from head to foot in a black mantle, following mournfully.

When the place of ***interment*** was reached the corpse was lowered, just as it was, into a deep pit. Then the husband, bidding farewell to all his friends, stretched himself upon another bier, upon which were laid seven little loaves of bread and a pitcher of water, and he also was let down-down-down to the depths of the horrible cavern, and then a stone was laid over the opening, and the melancholy company wended its way back to the city.

You may imagine that I was no unmoved spectator of these proceedings; to all the others it was a thing to which they had been accustomed from their youth up; but I was so horrified that I could not help telling the king how it struck me.

"Sire," I said, "I am more astonished than I can express to you at the strange custom which exists in your dominions of burying the living with the dead. In all my travels I have never before met with so cruel and horrible a law."

"What would you have, Sindbad?" he replied. "It is the law for everybody. I myself should be buried with the Queen if she were the first to die."

"But, your Majesty," said I, "dare I ask if this law applies to foreigners also?"

"Why, yes," replied the king smiling, in what I could but consider a very heartless manner, "they are no exception to the rule if they have married in the country."

When I heard this I went home much cast down, and from that time forward my mind was never easy. If only my wife's little finger ached I fancied she was going to die, and sure enough before very long she fell really ill and in a few days breathed her last. My dismay was great, for it seemed to me that to be buried alive was even a worse fate than to be devoured by cannibals, nevertheless there was no escape. The body of my wife, arrayed in her richest robes and decked with all her jewels, was laid upon the bier. I followed it, and after me came a great procession, headed by the king and all his nobles, and in this order we reached the fatal mountain, which was one of a lofty chain bordering the sea.

Here I made one more frantic effort to excite the pity of the king and those who stood by, hoping to save myself even at this last moment, but it was of no avail. No one spoke to me, they even appeared to hasten over their dreadful task, and I speedily found myself descending into the gloomy pit, with my seven loaves and pitcher of water beside me. Almost before I reached the bottom the stone was rolled into its place above my head, and I was left to my fate. A feeble ray of light shone into the cavern through some chink, and when I had the

---

interment: burial

courage to look about me I could see that I was in a vast vault, bestrewn with bones and bodies of the dead. I even fancied that I heard the expiring sighs of those who, like myself, had come into this dismal place alive. All in vain did I shriek aloud with rage and despair, reproaching myself for the love of gain and adventure which had brought me to such a pass, but at length, growing calmer, I took up my bread and water, and wrapping my face in my mantle I groped my way towards the end of the cavern, where the air was fresher.

Here I lived in darkness and misery until my provisions were exhausted, but just as I was nearly dead from starvation the rock was rolled away overhead and I saw that a bier was being lowered into the cavern, and that the corpse upon it was a man. In a moment my mind was made up, the woman who followed had nothing to expect but a lingering death; I should be doing her a service if I shortened her misery. Therefore when she descended, already insensible from terror, I was ready armed with a huge bone, one blow from which left her dead, and I secured the bread and water which gave me a hope of life. Several times did I have recourse to this desperate expedient, and I know not how long I had been a prisoner when one day I fancied that I heard something near me, which breathed loudly. Turning to the place from which the sound came I dimly saw a shadowy form which fled at my movement, squeezing itself through a cranny in the wall. I pursued it as fast as I could, and found myself in a narrow crack among the rocks, along which I was just able to force my way. I followed it for what seemed to me many miles, and at last saw before me a glimmer of light which grew clearer every moment until I emerged upon the sea shore with a joy which I cannot describe. When I was sure that I was not dreaming, I realised that it was doubtless some little animal which had found its way into the cavern from the sea, and when disturbed had fled, showing me a means of escape which I could never have discovered for myself. I hastily surveyed my surroundings, and saw that I was safe from all pursuit from the town.

The mountains sloped sheer down to the sea, and there was no road across them. Being assured of this I returned to the cavern, and amassed a rich treasure of diamonds, rubies, emeralds, and jewels of all kinds which strewed the ground. These I made up into bales, and stored them into a safe place upon the beach, and then waited hopefully for the passing of a ship. I had looked out for two days, however, before a single sail appeared, so it was with much delight that I at last saw a vessel not very far from the shore, and by waving my arms and uttering loud cries succeeded in attracting the attention of her crew. A boat was sent off to me, and in answer to the questions of the sailors as to how I came to be in such a plight, I replied that I had been shipwrecked two days before, but had managed to scramble ashore with the bales which I pointed out to them. Luckily for me they believed my story, and without even looking at the place where they found me, took up my bundles, and rowed me back to the ship. Once on board, I soon saw that the captain was too much occupied with the difficulties of navigation to pay much heed to me, though he generously made me welcome, and would not even accept the jewels with which I offered to pay my passage. Our voyage was prosperous, and after visiting many lands, and collecting in each place great store of goodly merchandise, I found myself at last in Bagdad once more with unheard of riches of every description. Again I gave large sums of money to the poor, and enriched all the mosques in the city, after which I gave myself up to my friends and relations, with whom I passed my time in feasting and merriment.

Here Sindbad paused, and all his hearers declared that the adventures of his fourth voyage had pleased them better than anything they had heard before. They then took their leave, followed by Hindbad, who had once more received a hundred sequins, and with the rest had been bidden to return next day for the story of the fifth voyage.

When the time came all were in their places, and when they had eaten and drunk of all that was set before them Sindbad began his tale.

Fifth Voyage

Not even all that I had gone through could make me contented with a quiet life. I soon wearied of its pleasures, and longed for change and adventure. Therefore I set out once more, but this time in a ship of my own, which I built and fitted out at the nearest seaport. I wished to be able to call at whatever port I chose, taking my own time; but as I did not intend carrying enough goods for a full cargo, I invited several merchants of different nations to join me. We set sail with the first favourable wind, and after a long voyage upon the open seas we landed upon an unknown island which proved to be uninhabited. We determined, however, to explore it, but had not gone far when we found a roc's egg, as large as the one I had seen before and evidently very nearly hatched, for the beak of the young bird had already pierced the shell. In spite of all I could say to deter them, the merchants who were with me fell upon it with their hatchets, breaking the shell, and killing the young roc. Then lighting a fire upon the ground they hacked morsels from the bird, and proceeded to roast them while I stood by ***aghast***.

Scarcely had they finished their ill-omened repast, when the air above us was darkened by two mighty shadows. The captain of my ship, knowing by experience what this meant, cried out to us that the parent birds were coming, and urged us to get on board with all speed. This we did, and the sails were hoisted, but before we had made any way the rocs reached their despoiled nest and hovered about it, uttering frightful cries when they discovered the mangled remains of their young one. For a moment we lost sight of them, and were flattering ourselves that we had escaped, when they reappeared and soared into the air directly over our vessel, and we saw that each held in its claws an immense rock ready to crush us. There was a moment of breathless suspense, then one bird loosed its hold and the huge block of stone hurtled through the air, but thanks to the presence of mind of the helmsman, who turned our ship violently in another direction, it fell into the sea close beside us, cleaving it asunder till we could nearly see the bottom. We had hardly time to draw a breath

---

aghast: horrified

of relief before the other rock fell with a mighty crash right in the midst of our luckless vessel, smashing it into a thousand fragments, and crushing, or hurling into the sea, passengers and crew. I myself went down with the rest, but had the good fortune to rise unhurt, and by holding on to a piece of driftwood with one hand and swimming with the other I kept myself afloat and was presently washed up by the tide on to an island. Its shores were steep and rocky, but I scrambled up safely and threw myself down to rest upon the green turf.

When I had somewhat recovered I began to examine the spot in which I found myself, and truly it seemed to me that I had reached a garden of delights. There were trees everywhere, and they were laden with flowers and fruit, while a crystal stream wandered in and out under their shadow. When night came I slept sweetly in a cosy nook, though the remembrance that I was alone in a strange land made me sometimes start up and look around me in alarm, and then I wished heartily that I had stayed at home at ease. However, the morning sunlight restored my courage, and I once more wandered among the trees, but always with some anxiety as to what I might see next. I had penetrated some distance into the island when I saw an old man bent and ***feeble*** sitting upon the river bank, and at first I took him to be some ship-wrecked mariner like myself. Going up to him I greeted him in a friendly way, but he only nodded his head at me in reply. I then asked what he did there, and he made signs to me that he wished to get across the river to gather some fruit, and seemed to beg me to carry him on my back. Pitying his age and feebleness, I took him up, and wading across the stream I bent down that he might more easily reach the bank, and bade him get down. But instead of allowing himself to be set upon his feet (even now it makes me laugh to think of it!), this creature who had seemed to me so ***decrepit*** leaped ***nimbly*** upon my shoulders, and hooking his legs round my neck gripped me so tightly that I was well-nigh choked, and so overcome with terror that I fell insensible to the ground. When I recovered my enemy was still in his place, though he had released his hold enough to allow me breathing space, and seeing me revive he prodded me adroitly first with one foot and then with the other, until I was forced to get up and stagger about with him under the trees while he gathered and ate the choicest fruits. This went on all day, and even at night, when I threw myself down half dead with weariness, the terrible old man held on tight to my neck, nor did he fail to greet the first glimmer of morning light by drumming upon me with his heels, until I perforce awoke and resumed my dreary march with rage and bitterness in my heart.

It happened one day that I passed a tree under which lay several dry gourds, and catching one up I amused myself with scooping out its contents and pressing into it the juice of several bunches of grapes which hung from every bush. When it was full I left it propped in the fork of a tree, and a few days later, carrying the hateful old man that way, I snatched at my gourd as I passed it and had the satisfaction of a draught of excellent wine so good and refreshing that I even

---

feeble: weak
decrepit: feeble
nimbly: agilely; quickly

forgot my detestable burden, and began to sing and caper.

The old monster was not slow to perceive the effect which my draught had produced and that I carried him more lightly than usual, so he stretched out his skinny hand and seizing the gourd first tasted its contents cautiously, then drained them to the very last drop. The wine was strong and the gourd capacious, so he also began to sing after a fashion, and soon I had the delight of feeling the iron grip of his goblin legs unclasp, and with one vigorous effort I threw him to the ground, from which he never moved again. I was so rejoiced to have at last got rid of this uncanny old man that I ran leaping and bounding down to the sea shore, where, by the greatest good luck, I met with some mariners who had anchored off the island to enjoy the delicious fruits, and to renew their supply of water.

They heard the story of my escape with amazement, saying, "You fell into the hands of the Old Man of the Sea, and it is a mercy that he did not strangle you as he has everyone else upon whose shoulders he has managed to perch himself. This island is well known as the scene of his evil deeds, and no merchant or sailor who lands upon it cares to stray far away from his comrades." After we had talked for a while they took me back with them on board their ship, where the captain received me kindly, and we soon set sail, and after several days reached a large and prosperous-looking town where all the houses were built of stone. Here we anchored, and one of the merchants, who had been very friendly to me on the way, took me ashore with him and showed me a lodging set apart for strange merchants. He then provided me with a large sack, and pointed out to me a party of others equipped in like manner.

"Go with them," said he, "and do as they do, but beware of losing sight of them, for if you strayed your life would be in danger."

With that he supplied me with provisions, and bade me farewell, and I set out with my new companions. I soon learnt that the object of our expedition was to fill our sacks with cocoanuts, but when at length I saw the trees and noted their immense height and the slippery smoothness of their slender trunks, I did not at all understand how we were to do it. The crowns of the cocoa-palms were all alive with monkeys, big and little, which skipped from one to the other with surprising agility, seeming to be curious about us and disturbed at our appearance, and I was at first surprised when my companions after collecting stones began to throw them at the lively creatures, which seemed to me quite harmless. But very soon I saw the reason of it and joined them heartily, for the monkeys, annoyed and wishing to pay us back in our own coin, began to tear the nuts from the trees and cast them at us with angry and spiteful gestures, so that after very little labour our sacks were filled with the fruit which we could not otherwise have obtained.

As soon as we had as many as we could carry we went back to the town, where my friend bought my share and advised me to continue the same occupation until I had earned money enough to carry me to my own country. This I did, and before long had amassed a considerable sum. Just then I heard that there was a trading ship ready to sail, and taking leave of my friend I went on board, carrying with me a goodly store of cocoanuts; and we sailed first to the islands where pepper grows, then to Comari where the best aloes wood is found, and where men drink no wine by an unalterable law. Here I exchanged my nuts for pepper and good aloes wood, and went a-fishing for pearls with some of the other merchants, and my divers were so lucky that very soon I had an immense number, and those very large and perfect. With all these treasures I came joyfully back to Bagdad, where I disposed of them for large sums of money, of which I did not fail as before to give the tenth part to the poor, and after that I rested from my labours and comforted myself with all the pleasures that my riches could give me.

Having thus ended his story, Sindbad ordered that one hundred sequins should be given to Hindbad, and the guests then withdrew; but after the next day's feast he began the account of his sixth voyage as follows.

Sixth Voyage

It must be a marvel to you how, after having five times met with shipwreck and unheard of perils, I could again tempt fortune and risk fresh trouble. I am even surprised myself when I look back, but evidently it was my fate to rove, and after a year of repose I prepared to make a sixth voyage, regardless of the entreaties of my friends and relations, who did all they could to keep me at home. Instead of going by the Persian Gulf, I travelled a considerable way overland, and finally embarked from a distant Indian port with a captain who meant to make a long voyage. And truly he did so, for we fell in with stormy weather which drove us completely out of our course, so that for many days neither captain nor pilot knew where we were, nor where we were going. When they did at last discover our position we had small ground for rejoicing, for the captain, casting his turban upon the deck and tearing his beard, declared that we were in the most dangerous spot upon the whole wide sea, and had been caught by a current which was at that minute sweeping us to destruction. It was too true! In spite of all the sailors could do we were driven with frightful rapidity towards the foot of a mountain, which rose sheer out of the sea, and our vessel was dashed to pieces upon the rocks at its base, not, however, until we had managed to scramble on shore, carrying with us the most precious of our possessions. When we had done this the captain said to us:

"Now we are here we may as well begin to dig our graves at once, since from this fatal spot no shipwrecked mariner has ever returned."

This speech discouraged us much, and we began to ***lament*** over our sad fate.

The mountain formed the seaward boundary of a large island, and the narrow strip of rocky shore upon which we stood was strewn with the wreckage of a thousand gallant ships, while the bones of the luckless mariners shone white in the sunshine, and we shuddered to think how soon our own would be added to the heap. All around, too, lay vast quantities of the costliest merchandise, and treasures were heaped in every cranny of the rocks, but all these things only

---

lament: grieve

added to the desolation of the scene. It struck me as a very strange thing that a river of clear fresh water, which gushed out from the mountain not far from where we stood, instead of flowing into the sea as rivers generally do, turned off sharply, and flowed out of sight under a natural archway of rock, and when I went to examine it more closely I found that inside the cave the walls were thick with diamonds, and rubies, and masses of crystal, and the floor was strewn with ambergris. Here, then, upon this desolate shore we abandoned ourselves to our fate, for there was no possibility of scaling the mountain, and if a ship had appeared it could only have shared our doom. The first thing our captain did was to divide equally amongst us all the food we possessed, and then the length of each man's life depended on the time he could make his portion last. I myself could live upon very little.

Nevertheless, by the time I had buried the last of my companions my stock of provisions was so small that I hardly thought I should live long enough to dig my own grave, which I set about doing, while I regretted bitterly the roving disposition which was always bringing me into such straits, and thought longingly of all the comfort and luxury that I had left. But luckily for me the fancy took me to stand once more beside the river where it plunged out of sight in the depths of the cavern, and as I did so an idea struck me. This river which hid itself underground doubtless emerged again at some distant spot. Why should I not build a raft and trust myself to its swiftly flowing waters? If I perished before I could reach the light of day once more I should be no worse off than I was now, for death stared me in the face, while there was always the possibility that, as I was born under a lucky star, I might find myself safe and sound in some desirable land. I decided at any rate to risk it, and speedily built myself a stout raft of drift-wood with strong cords, of which enough and to spare lay strewn upon the beach. I then made up many packages of rubies, emeralds, rock crystal, ambergris, and precious stuffs, and bound them upon my raft, being careful to preserve the balance, and then I seated myself upon it, having two small oars that I had fashioned laid ready to my hand, and loosed the cord which held it to the bank. Once out in the current my raft flew swiftly under the gloomy archway, and I found myself in total darkness, carried smoothly forward by the rapid river. On I went as it seemed to me for many nights and days. Once the channel became so small that I had a narrow escape of being crushed against the rocky roof, and after that I took the precaution of lying flat upon my precious bales. Though I only ate what was absolutely necessary to keep myself alive, the inevitable moment came when, after swallowing my last morsel of food, I began to wonder if I must after all die of hunger. Then, worn out with anxiety and fatigue, I fell into a deep sleep, and when I again opened my eyes I was once more in the light of day; a beautiful country lay before me, and my raft, which was tied to the river bank, was surrounded by friendly looking black men. I rose and saluted them, and they spoke to me in return, but I could not understand a word of their language. Feeling perfectly bewildered by my sudden return to life and light, I murmured to myself in Arabic, "Close thine eyes, and while thou sleepest Heaven will change thy fortune from evil to good."

One of the natives, who understood this tongue, then came forward saying:

"My brother, be not surprised to see us; this is our land, and as we came to get water from the river we noticed your raft floating down it, and one of us swam out and brought you to the shore. We have waited for your awakening; tell us now whence you come and where you were going by that dangerous way?"

I replied that nothing would please me better than to tell them, but that I was starving, and would fain eat something first. I was soon supplied with all I needed, and having satisfied my hunger I told them faithfully all that had befallen me. They were lost in wonder at my tale when it was interpreted to them, and said that adventures so surprising must be related to their king only by the man to whom they had happened. So, procuring a horse, they mounted me upon it, and we set out, followed by several strong men carrying my raft just as it was upon their shoulders. In this order we marched into the city of Serendib, where the natives presented me to their king, whom I saluted in the Indian fashion, prostrating myself at his feet and kissing the ground; but the monarch bade me rise and sit beside him, asking first what was my name.

"I am Sindbad," I replied, "whom men call `the Sailor,' for I have voyaged much upon many seas."

"And how come you here?" asked the king.

I told my story, ***concealing*** nothing, and his surprise and delight were so great that he ordered my adventures to be written in letters of gold and laid up in the archives of his kingdom.

Presently my raft was brought in and the bales opened in his presence, and the king declared that in all his treasury there were no such rubies and emeralds as those which lay in great heaps before him. Seeing that he looked at them with interest, I ventured to say that I myself and all that I had were at his disposal, but he answered me smiling:

"Nay, Sindbad. Heaven forbid that I should ***covet*** your riches; I will rather add to them, for I desire that you shall not leave my kingdom without some tokens of my good will." He then commanded his officers to provide me with a suitable lodging at his expense, and sent slaves to wait upon me and carry my raft and my bales to my new dwelling place. You may imagine that I praised his generosity and gave him grateful thanks, nor did I fail to present myself daily in his audience chamber, and for the rest of my time I amused myself in seeing all that was most worthy of attention in the city. The island of Serendib being situated on the equinoctial line, the days and nights there are of equal length. The chief city is placed at the end of a beautiful valley, formed by the highest mountain in the world, which is in the middle of the island. I had the curiosity to ascend to its very summit, for this was the place to which Adam was banished out of Paradise. Here are found rubies and many precious things, and rare plants grow abundantly, with cedar trees and cocoa palms. On the seashore and at the mouths of the rivers the divers seek for pearls, and in some valleys diamonds are plentiful. After many days I petitioned the king that I might return to my own

---

concealing: hiding
covet: desire

country, to which he graciously consented. Moreover, he loaded me with rich gifts, and when I went to take leave of him he entrusted me with a royal present and a letter to the Commander of the Faithful, our sovereign lord, saying, "I pray you give these to the Caliph Haroun al Raschid, and assure him of my friendship."

I accepted the charge respectfully, and soon embarked upon the vessel which the king himself had chosen for me. The king's letter was written in blue characters upon a rare and precious skin of yellowish colour, and these were the words of it: "The King of the Indies, before whom walk a thousand elephants, who lives in a palace, of which the roof blazes with a hundred thousand rubies, and whose treasure house contains twenty thousand diamond crowns, to the Caliph Haroun al Raschid sends greeting. Though the offering we present to you is unworthy of your notice, we pray you to accept it as a mark of the esteem and friendship which we cherish for you, and of which we gladly send you this token, and we ask of you a like regard if you deem us worthy of it. Adieu, brother."

The present consisted of a vase carved from a single ruby, six inches high and as thick as my finger; this was filled with the choicest pearls, large, and of perfect shape and lustre; secondly, a huge snake skin, with scales as large as a sequin, which would preserve from sickness those who slept upon it. Then quantities of aloes wood, camphor, and pistachio-nuts; and lastly, a beautiful slave girl, whose robes glittered with precious stones.

After a long and prosperous voyage we landed at Balsora, and I made haste to reach Bagdad, and taking the king's letter I presented myself at the palace gate, followed by the beautiful slave, and various members of my own family, bearing the treasure.

As soon as I had declared my ***errand*** I was conducted into the presence of the Caliph, to whom, after I had made my obeisance, I gave the letter and the king's gift, and when he had examined them he demanded of me whether the Prince of Serendib was really as rich and powerful as he claimed to be.

"Commander of the Faithful," I replied, again bowing humbly before him, "I can assure your Majesty that he has in no way exaggerated his wealth and grandeur. Nothing can equal the magnificence of his palace. When he goes abroad his throne is prepared upon the back of an elephant, and on either side of him ride his ministers, his favourites, and courtiers. On his elephant's neck sits an officer, his golden lance in his hand, and behind him stands another bearing a pillar of gold, at the top of which is an emerald as long as my hand. A thousand men in cloth of gold, mounted upon richly caparisoned elephants, go before him, and as the procession moves onward the officer who guides his elephant cries aloud, `Behold the mighty monarch, the powerful and valiant Sultan of the Indies, whose palace is covered with a hundred thousand rubies, who possesses twenty thousand diamond crowns. Behold a monarch greater than Solomon and Mihrage in all their glory!'"

"Then the one who stands behind the throne answers: 'This king, so great and

---

errand: task

powerful, must die, must die, must die!'"

"And the first takes up the chant again, `All praise to Him who lives for evermore.'"

"Further, my lord, in Serendib no judge is needed, for to the king himself his people come for justice."

The Caliph was well satisfied with my report.

"From the king's letter," said he, "I judged that he was a wise man. It seems that he is worthy of his people, and his people of him."

So saying he dismissed me with rich presents, and I returned in peace to my own house.

When Sindbad had done speaking his guests withdrew, Hindbad having first received a hundred sequins, but all returned next day to hear the story of the seventh voyage, Sindbad thus began.

Seventh and Last Voyage

After my sixth voyage I was quite determined that I would go to sea no more. I was now of an age to appreciate a quiet life, and I had run risks enough. I only wished to end my days in peace. One day, however, when I was entertaining a number of my friends, I was told that an officer of the Caliph wished to speak to me, and when he was admitted he bade me follow him into the presence of Haroun al Raschid, which I accordingly did. After I had saluted him, the Caliph said:

"I have sent for you, Sindbad, because I need your services. I have chosen you to bear a letter and a gift to the King of Serendib in return for his message of friendship."

The Caliph's commandment fell upon me like a thunderbolt.

"Commander of the Faithful," I answered, "I am ready to do all that your Majesty commands, but I humbly pray you to remember that I am utterly disheartened by the unheard of sufferings I have undergone. Indeed, I have made a vow never again to leave Bagdad."

With this I gave him a long account of some of my strangest adventures, to which he listened patiently.

"I admit," said he, "that you have indeed had some extraordinary experiences, but I do not see why they should ***hinder*** you from doing as I wish. You have only to go straight to Serendib and give my message, then you are free to come back and do as you will. But go you must; my honour and dignity demand it."

Seeing that there was no help for it, I declared myself willing to obey; and the Caliph, delighted at having got his own way, gave me a thousand sequins for the expenses of the voyage. I was soon ready to start, and taking the letter

---

hinder: deter

and the present I embarked at Balsora, and sailed quickly and safely to Serendib. Here, when I had disclosed my errand, I was well received, and brought into the presence of the king, who greeted me with joy.

"Welcome, Sindbad," he cried. "I have thought of you often, and rejoice to see you once more."

After thanking him for the honour that he did me, I displayed the Caliph's gifts. First a bed with complete hangings all cloth of gold, which cost a thousand sequins, and another like to it of crimson stuff. Fifty robes of rich embroidery, a hundred of the finest white linen from Cairo, Suez, Cufa, and Alexandria. Then more beds of different fashion, and an agate vase carved with the figure of a man aiming an arrow at a lion, and finally a costly table, which had once belonged to King Solomon. The King of Serendib received with satisfaction the assurance of the Caliph's friendliness toward him, and now my task being accomplished I was anxious to depart, but it was some time before the king would think of letting me go. At last, however, he dismissed me with many presents, and I lost no time in going on board a ship, which sailed at once, and for four days all went well. On the fifth day we had the misfortune to fall in with pirates, who seized our vessel, killing all who resisted, and making prisoners of those who were ***prudent*** enough to ***submit*** at once, of whom I was one. When they had despoiled us of all we possessed, they forced us to put on vile raiment, and sailing to a distant island there sold us for slaves. I fell into the hands of a rich merchant, who took me home with him, and clothed and fed me well, and after some days sent for me and questioned me as to what I could do.

I answered that I was a rich merchant who had been captured by pirates, and therefore I knew no trade.

"Tell me," said he, "can you shoot with a bow?"

I replied that this had been one of the pastimes of my youth, and that doubtless with practice my skill would come back to me.

Upon this he provided me with a bow and arrows, and mounting me with him upon his own elephant took the way to a vast forest which lay far from the town. When we had reached the wildest part of it we stopped, and my master said to me: "This forest swarms with elephants. Hide yourself in this great tree, and shoot at all that pass you. When you have succeeded in killing one come and tell me."

So saying he gave me a supply of food, and returned to the town, and I perched myself high up in the tree and kept watch. That night I saw nothing, but just after sunrise the next morning a large herd of elephants came crashing and trampling by. I lost no time in letting fly several arrows, and at last one of the great animals fell to the ground dead, and the others retreated, leaving me free to come down from my hiding place and run back to tell my master of my success, for which I was praised and regaled with good things. Then we went back to the forest together and dug a mighty trench in which we buried the elephant I had killed, in order that when it became a skeleton my master might return and

---

prudent: sensible
submit: surrender

secure its tusks.

For two months I hunted thus, and no day passed without my securing, an elephant. Of course I did not always station myself in the same tree, but sometimes in one place, sometimes in another. One morning as I watched the coming of the elephants I was surprised to see that, instead of passing the tree I was in, as they usually did, they paused, and completely surrounded it, trumpeting horribly, and shaking the very ground with their heavy tread, and when I saw that their eyes were fixed upon me I was terrified, and my arrows dropped from my trembling hand. I had indeed good reason for my terror when, an instant later, the largest of the animals wound his trunk round the stem of my tree, and with one mighty effort tore it up by the roots, bringing me to the ground entangled in its branches. I thought now that my last hour was surely come; but the huge creature, picking me up gently enough, set me upon its back, where I clung more dead than alive, and followed by the whole herd turned and crashed off into the dense forest. It seemed to me a long time before I was once more set upon my feet by the elephant, and I stood as if in a dream watching the herd, which turned and trampled off in another direction, and were soon hidden in the dense underwood. Then, recovering myself, I looked about me, and found that I was standing upon the side of a great hill, strewn as far as I could see on either hand with bones and tusks of elephants. "This then must be the elephants' burying place," I said to myself, "and they must have brought me here that I might cease to persecute them, seeing that I want nothing but their tusks, and here lie more than I could carry away in a lifetime."

Whereupon I turned and made for the city as fast as I could go, not seeing a single elephant by the way, which convinced me that they had retired deeper into the forest to leave the way open to the Ivory Hill, and I did not know how sufficiently to admire their ***sagacity***. After a day and a night I reached my master's house, and was received by him with joyful surprise.

"Ah! poor Sindbad," he cried, "I was wondering what could have become of you. When I went to the forest I found the tree newly uprooted, and the arrows lying beside it, and I feared I should never see you again. Pray tell me how you escaped death."

I soon satisfied his curiosity, and the next day we went together to the Ivory Hill, and he was overjoyed to find that I had told him nothing but the truth. When we had loaded our elephant with as many tusks as it could carry and were on our way back to the city, he said:

"My brother--since I can no longer treat as a slave one who has enriched me thus--take your liberty and may Heaven prosper you. I will no longer conceal from you that these wild elephants have killed numbers of our slaves every year. No matter what good advice we gave them, they were caught sooner or later. You alone have escaped the wiles of these animals, therefore you must be under the special protection of Heaven. Now through you the whole town will be enriched without further loss of life, therefore you shall not only receive your liberty, but I will also bestow a fortune upon you."

---

sagacity: wisdom

To which I replied, "Master, I thank you, and wish you all prosperity. For myself I only ask liberty to return to my own country."

"It is well," he answered, "the monsoon will soon bring the ivory ships hither, then I will send you on your way with somewhat to pay your passage."

So I stayed with him till the time of the monsoon, and every day we added to our store of ivory till all his ware-houses were overflowing with it. By this time the other merchants knew the secret, but there was enough and to spare for all. When the ships at last arrived my master himself chose the one in which I was to sail, and put on board for me a great store of choice provisions, also ivory in abundance, and all the costliest curiosities of the country, for which I could not thank him enough, and so we parted. I left the ship at the first port we came to, not feeling at ease upon the sea after all that had happened to me by reason of it, and having disposed of my ivory for much gold, and bought many rare and costly presents, I loaded my pack animals, and joined a caravan of merchants. Our journey was long and tedious, but I bore it patiently, reflecting that at least I had not to fear tempests, nor pirates, nor serpents, nor any of the other perils from which I had suffered before, and at length we reached Bagdad. My first care was to present myself before the Caliph, and give him an account of my embassy. He assured me that my long absence had disquieted him much, but he had nevertheless hoped for the best. As to my adventure among the elephants he heard it with amazement, declaring that he could not have believed it had not my truthfulness been well known to him.

By his orders this story and the others I had told him were written by his scribes in letters of gold, and laid up among his treasures. I took my leave of him, well satisfied with the honours and rewards he bestowed upon me; and since that time I have rested from my labours, and given myself up wholly to my family and my friends.

Thus Sindbad ended the story of his seventh and last voyage, and turning to Hindbad he added:

"Well, my friend, and what do you think now? Have you ever heard of anyone who has suffered more, or had more narrow escapes than I have? Is it not just that I should now enjoy a life of ease and tranquillity?"

Hindbad drew near, and kissing his hand respectfully, replied, "Sir, you have indeed known fearful perils; my troubles have been nothing compared to yours. Moreover, the generous use you make of your wealth proves that you deserve it. May you live long and happily in the enjoyment in it."

Sindbad then gave him a hundred sequins, and hence-forward counted him among his friends; also he caused him to give up his profession as a porter, and to eat daily at his table that he might all his life remember Sindbad the Sailor.

Aladdin and the Wonderful Lamp

There once lived a poor tailor, who had a son called Aladdin, a careless, idle boy who would do nothing but play all day long in the streets with little idle boys like himself. This so grieved the father that he died; yet, in spite of his

mother's tears and prayers, Aladdin did not mend his ways. One day, when he was playing in the streets as usual, a stranger asked him his age, and if he were not the son of Mustapha the tailor.

"I am, sir," replied Aladdin; "but he died a long while ago."

On this the stranger, who was a famous African magician, fell on his neck and kissed him, saying: "I am your uncle, and knew you from your likeness to my brother. Go to your mother and tell her I am coming."

Aladdin ran home, and told his mother of his newly found uncle.

"Indeed, child," she said, "your father had a brother, but I always thought he was dead."

However, she prepared supper, and bade Aladdin seek his uncle, who came laden with wine and fruit. He presently fell down and kissed the place where Mustapha used to sit, bidding Aladdin's mother not to be surprised at not having seen him before, as he had been forty years out of the country. He then turned to Aladdin, and asked him his trade, at which the boy hung his head, while his mother burst into tears. On learning that Aladdin was idle and would learn no trade, he offered to take a shop for him and stock it with merchandise. Next day he bought Aladdin a fine suit of clothes, and took him all over the city, showing him the sights, and brought him home at nightfall to his mother, who was overjoyed to see her son so fine.

Next day the magician led Aladdin into some beautiful gardens a long way outside the city gates. They sat down by a fountain, and the magician pulled a cake from his girdle, which he divided between them. They then journeyed onwards till they almost reached the mountains. Aladdin was so tired that he begged to go back, but the magician beguiled him with pleasant stories, and led him on in spite of himself.

At last they came to two mountains divided by a narrow valley.

"We will go no farther," said the false uncle. "I will show you something wonderful; only do you gather up sticks while I kindle a fire."

When it was lit the magician threw on it a powder he had about him, at the same time saying some magical words. The earth trembled a little and opened in front of them, disclosing a square flat stone with a brass ring in the middle to raise it by. Aladdin tried to run away, but the magician caught him and gave him a blow that knocked him down.

"What have I done, uncle?" he said piteously; whereupon the magician said more kindly: "Fear nothing, but obey me. Beneath this stone lies a treasure which is to be yours, and no one else may touch it, so you must do exactly as I tell you."

At the word treasure, Aladdin forgot his fears, and grasped the ring as he was told, saying the names of his father and grandfather. The stone came up quite easily and some steps appeared.

"Go down," said the magician; "at the foot of those steps you will find an open door leading into three large halls. Tuck up your gown and go through them without touching anything, or you will die instantly. These halls lead into a garden of fine fruit trees. Walk on till you come to a niche in a terrace where stands a lighted lamp. Pour out the oil it contains and bring it to me."

He drew a ring from his finger and gave it to Aladdin, bidding him prosper.

Aladdin found everything as the magician had said, gathered some fruit off the trees, and, having got the lamp, arrived at the mouth of the cave. The magician cried out in a great hurry:

"Make haste and give me the lamp." This Aladdin refused to do until he was out of the cave. The magician flew into a terrible passion, and throwing some more powder on the fire, he said something, and the stone rolled back into its place.

The magician left Persia for ever, which plainly showed that he was no uncle of Aladdin's, but a cunning magician who had read in his magic books of a wonderful lamp, which would make him the most powerful man in the world. Though he alone knew where to find it, he could only receive it from the hand of another. He had picked out the foolish Aladdin for this purpose, intending to get the lamp and kill him afterwards.

For two days Aladdin remained in the dark, crying and lamenting. At last he clasped his hands in prayer, and in so doing rubbed the ring, which the magician had forgotten to take from him. Immediately an enormous and frightful genie rose out of the earth, saying:

"What wouldst thou with me? I am the Slave of the Ring, and will obey thee in all things."

Aladdin fearlessly replied: "Deliver me from this place!" whereupon the earth opened, and he found himself outside. As soon as his eyes could bear the light he went home, but fainted on the threshold. When he came to himself he told his mother what had passed, and showed her the lamp and the fruits he had gathered in the garden, which were in reality precious stones. He then asked for some food.

"Alas! child," she said, "I have nothing in the house, but I have spun a little cotton and will go and sell it."

Aladdin bade her keep her cotton, for he would sell the lamp instead. As it was very dirty she began to rub it, that it might fetch a higher price. Instantly a hideous genie appeared, and asked what she would have. She fainted away, but Aladdin, snatching the lamp, said boldly:

"Fetch me something to eat!"

The genie returned with a silver bowl, twelve silver plates containing rich meats, two silver cups, and two bottles of wine. Aladdin's mother, when she came to herself, said:

"Whence comes this splendid feast?"

"Ask not, but eat," replied Aladdin.

So they sat at breakfast till it was dinner-time, and Aladdin told his mother about the lamp. She begged him to sell it, and have nothing to do with devils.

"No," said Aladdin, "since chance has made us aware of its virtues, we will use it and the ring likewise, which I shall always wear on my finger." When they had eaten all the genie had brought, Aladdin sold one of the silver plates, and so on till none were left. He then had recourse to the genie, who gave him another set of plates, and thus they lived for many years.

One day Aladdin heard an order from the Sultan ***proclaimed*** that everyone was to stay at home and close his shutters while the princess, his daughter, went to and from the bath. Aladdin was seized by a desire to see her face, which was very difficult, as she always went veiled. He hid himself behind the door of the bath, and peeped through a chink. The princess lifted her veil as she went in, and looked so beautiful that Aladdin fell in love with her at first sight. He went home so changed that his mother was frightened. He told her he loved the princess so deeply that he could not live without her, and meant to ask her in marriage of her father. His mother, on hearing this, burst out laughing, but Aladdin at last prevailed upon her to go before the Sultan and carry his request. She fetched a napkin and laid in it the magic fruits from the enchanted garden, which sparkled and shone like the most beautiful jewels. She took these with her to please the Sultan, and set out, trusting in the lamp. The grand-vizir and the lords of council had just gone in as she entered the hall and placed herself in front of the Sultan. He, however, took no notice of her. She went every day for a week, and stood in the same place.

When the council broke up on the sixth day the Sultan said to his vizir: "I see a certain woman in the audience-chamber every day carrying something in a napkin. Call her next time, that I may find out what she wants."

Next day, at a sign from the vizir, she went up to the foot of the throne, and remained kneeling till the Sultan said to her: "Rise, good woman, and tell me what you want."

She hesitated, so the Sultan sent away all but the vizir, and bade her speak freely, promising to forgive her beforehand for anything she might say. She then told him of her son's violent love for the princess.

"I prayed him to forget her," she said, "but in vain; he threatened to do some desperate deed if I refused to go and ask your Majesty for the hand of the princess. Now I pray you to forgive not me alone, but my son Aladdin."

The Sultan asked her kindly what she had in the napkin, whereupon she unfolded the jewels and presented them.

He was thunderstruck, and turning to the vizir said: "What sayest thou? Ought I not to bestow the princess on one who values her at such a price?"

The vizir, who wanted her for his own son, begged the Sultan to withhold her for three months, in the course of which he hoped his son would contrive to make him a richer present. The Sultan granted this, and told Aladdin's mother that, though he consented to the marriage, she must not appear before him again for three months.

Aladdin waited patiently for nearly three months, but after two had elapsed his mother, going into the city to buy oil, found everyone rejoicing, and asked what was going on.

"Do you not know," was the answer, "that the son of the grand-vizir is to marry the Sultan's daughter to-night?"

Breathless, she ran and told Aladdin, who was overwhelmed at first, but presently bethought him of the lamp. He rubbed it, and the genie appeared,

---

proclaimed: announced

saying: "What is thy will?"

Aladdin replied: "The Sultan, as thou knowest, has broken his promise to me, and the vizir's son is to have the princess. My command is that to-night you bring hither the bride and bridegroom."

"Master, I obey," said the genie.

Aladdin then went to his chamber, where, sure enough at midnight the genie transported the bed containing the vizir's son and the princess.

"Take this new-married man," he said, "and put him outside in the cold, and return at daybreak."

Whereupon the genie took the vizir's son out of bed, leaving Aladdin with the princess.

"Fear nothing," Aladdin said to her; "you are my wife, promised to me by your unjust father, and no harm shall come to you."

The princess was too frightened to speak, and passed the most miserable night of her life, while Aladdin lay down beside her and slept soundly. At the appointed hour the genie fetched in the shivering bridegroom, laid him in his place, and transported the bed back to the palace.

Presently the Sultan came to wish his daughter good-morning. The unhappy vizir's son jumped up and hid himself, while the princess would not say a word, and was very sorrowful.

The Sultan sent her mother to her, who said: "How comes it, child, that you will not speak to your father? What has happened?"

The princess sighed deeply, and at last told her mother how, during the night, the bed had been carried into some strange house, and what had passed there. Her mother did not believe her in the least, but bade her rise and consider it an idle dream.

The following night exactly the same thing happened, and next morning, on the princess's refusing to speak, the Sultan threatened to cut off her head. She then confessed all, bidding him ask the vizir's son if it were not so. The Sultan told the vizir to ask his son, who owned the truth, adding that, dearly as he loved the princess, he had rather die than go through another such fearful night, and wished to be separated from her. His wish was granted, and there was an end of feasting and rejoicing.

When the three months were over, Aladdin sent his mother to remind the Sultan of his promise. She stood in the same place as before, and the Sultan, who had forgotten Aladdin, at once remembered him, and sent for her. On seeing her poverty the Sultan felt less inclined than ever to keep his word, and asked the vizir's advice, who counselled him to set so high a value on the princess that no man living could come up to it.

The Sultan then turned to Aladdin's mother, saying: "Good woman, a Sultan must remember his promises, and I will remember mine, but your son must first send me forty basins of gold brimful of jewels, carried by forty black slaves, led by as many white ones, splendidly dressed. Tell him that I await his answer." The mother of Aladdin bowed low and went home, thinking all was lost.

She gave Aladdin the message, adding: "He may wait long enough for your answer!"

"Not so long, mother, as you think," her son replied "I would do a great deal more than that for the princess."

He summoned the genie, and in a few moments the eighty slaves arrived, and filled up the small house and garden.

Aladdin made them set out to the palace, two and two, followed by his mother. They were so richly dressed, with such splendid jewels in their girdles, that everyone crowded to see them and the basins of gold they carried on their heads.

They entered the palace, and, after kneeling before the Sultan, stood in a half-circle round the throne with their arms crossed, while Aladdin's mother presented them to the Sultan.

He hesitated no longer, but said: "Good woman, return and tell your son that I wait for him with open arms."

She lost no time in telling Aladdin, bidding him make haste. But Aladdin first called the genie.

"I want a scented bath," he said, "a richly embroidered habit, a horse surpassing the Sultan's, and twenty slaves to attend me. Besides this, six slaves, beautifully dressed, to wait on my mother; and lastly, ten thousand pieces of gold in ten purses."

No sooner said than done. Aladdin mounted his horse and passed through the streets, the slaves strewing gold as they went. Those who had played with him in his childhood knew him not, he had grown so handsome.

When the Sultan saw him he came down from his throne, embraced him, and led him into a hall where a feast was spread, intending to marry him to the princess that very day.

But Aladdin refused, saying, "I must build a palace fit for her," and took his leave.

Once home he said to the genie: "Build me a palace of the finest marble, set with jasper, agate, and other precious stones. In the middle you shall build me a large hall with a dome, its four walls of massy gold and silver, each side having six windows, whose lattices, all except one, which is to be left unfinished, must be set with diamonds and rubies. There must be stables and horses and grooms and slaves; go and see about it!"

The palace was finished by next day, and the genie carried him there and showed him all his orders faithfully carried out, even to the laying of a velvet carpet from Aladdin's palace to the Sultan's. Aladdin's mother then dressed herself carefully, and walked to the palace with her slaves, while he followed her on horseback. The Sultan sent musicians with trumpets and cymbals to meet them, so that the air resounded with music and cheers. She was taken to the princess, who saluted her and treated her with great honour. At night the princess said good-bye to her father, and set out on the carpet for Aladdin's palace, with his mother at her side, and followed by the hundred slaves. She was charmed at the sight of Aladdin, who ran to receive her.

"Princess," he said, "blame your beauty for my boldness if I have displeased you."

She told him that, having seen him, she willingly obeyed her father in this matter. After the wedding had taken place Aladdin led her into the hall, where a feast was spread, and she supped with him, after which they danced till midnight.

Next day Aladdin invited the Sultan to see the palace. On entering the hall with the four-and-twenty windows, with their rubies, diamonds, and emeralds, he cried:

"It is a world's wonder! There is only one thing that surprises me. Was it by accident that one window was left unfinished?"

"No, sir, by design," returned Aladdin. "I wished your Majesty to have the glory of finishing this palace."

The Sultan was pleased, and sent for the best jewelers in the city. He showed them the unfinished window, and bade them fit it up like the others.

"Sir," replied their spokesman, "we cannot find jewels enough."

The Sultan had his own fetched, which they soon used, but to no purpose, for in a month's time the work was not half done. Aladdin, knowing that their task was vain, bade them undo their work and carry the jewels back, and the genie finished the window at his command. The Sultan was surprised to receive his jewels again and visited Aladdin, who showed him the window finished. The Sultan embraced him, the envious vizir meanwhile hinting that it was the work of enchantment.

Aladdin had won the hearts of the people by his gentle bearing. He was made captain of the Sultan's armies, and won several battles for him, but remained modest and courteous as before, and lived thus in peace and content for several years.

But far away in Africa the magician remembered Aladdin, and by his magic arts discovered that Aladdin, instead of perishing miserably in the cave, had escaped, and had married a princess, with whom he was living in great honour and wealth. He knew that the poor tailor's son could only have accomplished this by means of the lamp, and travelled night and day till he reached the capital of China, bent on Aladdin's ruin. As he passed through the town he heard people talking everywhere about a marvellous palace.

"Forgive my ignorance," he asked, "what is this palace you speak of?"

"Have you not heard of Prince Aladdin's palace," was the reply, "the greatest wonder of the world? I will direct you if you have a mind to see it."

The magician thanked him who spoke, and having seen the palace knew that it had been raised by the genie of the lamp, and became half mad with rage. He determined to get hold of the lamp, and again plunge Aladdin into the deepest poverty.

Unluckily, Aladdin had gone a-hunting for eight days, which gave the magician plenty of time. He bought a dozen copper lamps, put them into a basket, and went to the palace, crying: "New lamps for old!" followed by a jeering crowd.

The princess, sitting in the hall of four-and-twenty windows, sent a slave to find out what the noise was about, who came back laughing, so that the princess scolded her.

"Madam," replied the slave, "who can help laughing to see an old fool offering to exchange fine new lamps for old ones?"

Another slave, hearing this, said: "There is an old one on the cornice there which he can have."

Now this was the magic lamp, which Aladdin had left there, as he could not take it out hunting with him. The princess, not knowing its value, laughingly bade the slave take it and make the exchange.

She went and said to the magician: "Give me a new lamp for this."

He snatched it and bade the slave take her choice, amid the jeers of the crowd. Little he cared, but left off crying his lamps, and went out of the city gates to a lonely place, where he remained till nightfall, when he pulled out the lamp and rubbed it. The genie appeared, and at the magician's command carried him, together with the palace and the princess in it, to a lonely place in Africa.

Next morning the Sultan looked out of the window towards Aladdin's palace and rubbed his eyes, for it was gone. He sent for the vizir, and asked what had become of the palace. The vizir looked out too, and was lost in astonishment. He again put it down to enchantment, and this time the Sultan believed him, and sent thirty men on horseback to fetch Aladdin in chains. They met him riding home, bound him, and forced him to go with them on foot. The people, however, who loved him, followed, armed, to see that he came to no harm. He was carried before the Sultan, who ordered the executioner to cut off his head. The executioner made Aladdin kneel down, bandaged his eyes, and raised his scimitar to strike.

At that instant the vizir, who saw that the crowd had forced their way into the courtyard and were scaling the walls to rescue Aladdin, called to the executioner to stay his hand. The people, indeed, looked so threatening that the Sultan gave way and ordered Aladdin to be unbound, and pardoned him in the sight of the crowd.

Aladdin now begged to know what he had done.

"False wretch!" said the Sultan, "come hither," and showed him from the window the place where his palace had stood.

Aladdin was so amazed that he could not say a word.

"Where is my palace and my daughter?" demanded the Sultan. "For the first I am not so deeply concerned, but my daughter I must have, and you must find her or lose your head."

Aladdin begged for forty days in which to find her, promising if he failed to return and suffer death at the Sultan's pleasure. His prayer was granted, and he went forth sadly from the Sultan's presence. For three days he wandered about like a madman, asking everyone what had become of his palace, but they only laughed and pitied him. He came to the banks of a river, and knelt down to say his prayers before throwing himself in. In so doing he rubbed the magic ring he still wore.

The genie he had seen in the cave appeared, and asked his will.

"Save my life, genie," said Aladdin, "and bring my palace back."

"That is not in my power," said the genie; "I am only the slave of the ring; you must ask the slave of the lamp."

"Even so," said Aladdin "but thou canst take me to the palace, and set me down under my dear wife's window." He at once found himself in Africa, under the window of the princess, and fell asleep out of sheer weariness.

He was awakened by the singing of the birds, and his heart was lighter. He saw plainly that all his misfortunes were owing to the loss of the lamp, and vainly wondered who had robbed him of it.

That morning the princess rose earlier than she had done since she had been carried into Africa by the magician, whose company she was forced to endure once a day. She, however, treated him so harshly that he dared not live there altogether. As she was dressing, one of her women looked out and saw Aladdin. The princess ran and opened the window, and at the noise she made Aladdin looked up. She called to him to come to her, and great was the joy of these lovers at seeing each other again.

After he had kissed her Aladdin said: "I beg of you, Princess, in God's name, before we speak of anything else, for your own sake and mine, tell me what has become of an old lamp I left on the cornice in the hall of four-and-twenty windows, when I went a-hunting."

"Alas!" she said "I am the innocent cause of our sorrows," and told him of the exchange of the lamp.

"Now I know," cried Aladdin, "that we have to thank the African magician for this! Where is the lamp?"

"He carries it about with him," said the princess, "I know, for he pulled it out of his breast to show me. He wishes me to break my faith with you and marry him, saying that you were beheaded by my father's command. He is forever speaking ill of you, but I only reply by my tears. If I persist, I doubt not that he will use violence."

Aladdin comforted her, and left her for a while. He changed clothes with the first person he met in the town, and having bought a certain powder returned to the princess, who let him in by a little side door.

"Put on your most beautiful dress," he said to her, "and receive the magician with smiles, leading him to believe that you have forgotten me. Invite him to sup with you, and say you wish to taste the wine of his country. He will go for some, and while he is gone I will tell you what to do."

She listened carefully to Aladdin, and when he left her arrayed herself gaily for the first time since she left China. She put on a girdle and head-dress of diamonds, and seeing in a glass that she looked more beautiful than ever, received the magician, saying to his great amazement: "I have made up my mind that Aladdin is dead, and that all my tears will not bring him back to me, so I am resolved to mourn no more, and have therefore invited you to sup with me; but I am tired of the wines of China, and would fain taste those of Africa."

The magician flew to his cellar, and the princess put the powder Aladdin had given her in her cup. When he returned she asked him to drink her health in the wine of Africa, handing him her cup in exchange for his as a sign she was reconciled to him.

Before drinking the magician made her a speech in praise of her beauty, but the princess cut him short saying:

"Let me drink first, and you shall say what you will afterwards." She set her cup to her lips and kept it there, while the magician drained his to the dregs and fell back lifeless.

The princess then opened the door to Aladdin, and flung her arms round his neck, but Aladdin put her away, bidding her to leave him, as he had more to do. He then went to the dead magician, took the lamp out of his vest, and bade the genie carry the palace and all in it back to China. This was done, and the princess in her chamber only felt two little shocks, and little thought she was at home again.

The Sultan, who was sitting in his closet, mourning for his lost daughter, happened to look up, and rubbed his eyes, for there stood the palace as before! He hastened thither, and Aladdin received him in the hall of the four-and-twenty windows, with the princess at his side. Aladdin told him what had happened, and showed him the dead body of the magician, that he might believe. A ten days' feast was proclaimed, and it seemed as if Aladdin might now live the rest of his life in peace; but it was not to be.

The African magician had a younger brother, who was, if possible, more wicked and more cunning than himself. He travelled to China to avenge his brother's death, and went to visit a pious woman called Fatima, thinking she might be of use to him. He entered her cell and clapped a dagger to her breast, telling her to rise and do his bidding on pain of death. He changed clothes with her, coloured his face like hers, put on her veil and murdered her, that she might tell no tales. Then he went towards the palace of Aladdin, and all the people thinking he was the holy woman, gathered round him, kissing his hands and begging his blessing. When he got to the palace there was such a noise going on round him that the princess bade her slave look out of the window and ask what was the matter. The slave said it was the holy woman, curing people by her touch of their ailments, whereupon the princess, who had long desired to see Fatima, sent for her. On coming to the princess the magician offered up a prayer for her health and prosperity. When he had done the princess made him sit by her, and begged him to stay with her always. The false Fatima, who wished for nothing better, ***consented***, but kept his veil down for fear of discovery. The princess showed him the hall, and asked him what he thought of it.

"It is truly beautiful," said the false Fatima. "In my mind it wants but one thing."

"And what is that?" said the princess.

"If only a roc's egg," replied he, "were hung up from the middle of this dome, it would be the wonder of the world."

After this the princess could think of nothing but a roc's egg, and when Aladdin returned from hunting he found her in a very ill humour. He begged to know what was amiss, and she told him that all her pleasure in the hall was spoilt for the want of a roc's egg hanging from the dome.

"It that is all," replied Aladdin, "you shall soon be happy."

---

consented: agreed

He left her and rubbed the lamp, and when the genie appeared commanded him to bring a roc's egg. The genie gave such a loud and terrible shriek that the hall shook.

"Wretch!" he cried, "is it not enough that I have done everything for you, but you must command me to bring my master and hang him up in the midst of this dome? You and your wife and your palace deserve to be burnt to ashes; but this request does not come from you, but from the brother of the African magician whom you destroyed. He is now in your palace disguised as the holy woman--whom he murdered. He it was who put that wish into your wife's head. Take care of yourself, for he means to kill you." So saying the genie disappeared.

Aladdin went back to the princess, saying his head ached, and requesting that the holy Fatima should be fetched to lay her hands on it. But when the magician came near, Aladdin, seizing his dagger, pierced him to the heart.

"What have you done?" cried the princess. "You have killed the holy woman!"

"Not so," replied Aladdin, "but a wicked magician," and told her of how she had been deceived.

After this Aladdin and his wife lived in peace. He succeeded the Sultan when he died, and reigned for many years, leaving behind him a long line of kings.

The Enchanted Horse

It was the Feast of the New Year, the oldest and most splendid of all the feasts in the Kingdom of Persia, and the day had been spent by the king in the city of Schiraz, taking part in the magnificent spectacles prepared by his subjects to do honour to the festival. The sun was setting, and the monarch was about to give his court the signal to retire, when suddenly an Indian appeared before his throne, leading a horse richly harnessed, and looking in every respect exactly like a real one.

"Sire," said he, prostrating himself as he spoke, "although I make my appearance so late before your Highness, I can confidently assure you that none of the wonders you have seen during the day can be compared to this horse, if you will deign to cast your eyes upon him."

"I see nothing in it," replied the king, "except a clever imitation of a real one; and any skilled workman might do as much."

"Sire," returned the Indian, "it is not of his outward form that I would speak, but of the use that I can make of him. I have only to mount him, and to wish myself in some special place, and no matter how distant it may be, in a very few moments I shall find myself there. It is this, Sire, that makes the horse so marvellous, and if your Highness will allow me, you can prove it for yourself."

The King of Persia, who was interested in everything out of the common, and had never before come across a horse with such qualities, bade the Indian mount the animal, and show what he could do. In an instant the man had vaulted on his back, and inquired where the monarch wished to send him.

"Do you see that mountain?" asked the king, pointing to a huge mass that towered into the sky about three leagues from Schiraz; "go and bring me the leaf of a palm that grows at the foot."

The words were hardly out of the king's mouth when the Indian turned a screw placed in the horse's neck, close to the saddle, and the animal bounded like lightning up into the air, and was soon beyond the sight even of the sharpest eyes. In a quarter of an hour the Indian was seen returning, bearing in his hand the palm, and, guiding his horse to the foot of the throne, he dismounted, and laid the leaf before the king.

Now the monarch had no sooner proved the astonishing speed of which the horse was capable than he longed to possess it himself, and indeed, so sure was he that the Indian would be quite ready to sell it, that he looked upon it as his own already.

"I never guessed from his mere outside how valuable an animal he was," he remarked to the Indian, "and I am grateful to you for having shown me my error," said he. "If you will sell it, name your own price."

"Sire," replied the Indian, "I never doubted that a sovereign so wise and accomplished as your Highness would do justice to my horse, when he once knew its power; and I even went so far as to think it probable that you might wish to possess it. Greatly as I prize it, I will yield it up to your Highness on one condition. The horse was not constructed by me, but it was given me by the inventor, in exchange for my only daughter, who made me take a solemn oath that I would never part with it, except for some object of equal value."

"Name anything you like," cried the monarch, interrupting him. "My kingdom is large, and filled with fair cities. You have only to choose which you would prefer, to become its ruler to the end of your life."

"Sire," answered the Indian, to whom the proposal did not seem nearly so generous as it appeared to the king, "I am most grateful to your Highness for your princely offer, and beseech you not to be offended with me if I say that I can only deliver up my horse in exchange for the hand of the princess your daughter."

A shout of laughter burst from the courtiers as they heard these words, and Prince Firouz Schah, the heir apparent, was filled with anger at the Indian's presumption. The king, however, thought that it would not cost him much to part from the princess in order to gain such a delightful toy, and while he was hesitating as to his answer the prince broke in.

"Sire," he said, "it is not possible that you can doubt for an instant what reply you should give to such an insolent bargain. Consider what you owe to yourself, and to the blood of your ancestors."

"My son," replied the king, "you speak nobly, but you do not realise either the value of the horse, or the fact that if I reject the proposal of the Indian, he will only make the same to some other monarch, and I should be filled with despair at the thought that anyone but myself should own this Seventh Wonder of the World. Of course I do not say that I shall accept his conditions, and perhaps he may be brought to reason, but meanwhile I should like you to examine the horse, and, with the owner's permission, to make trial of its powers."

The Indian, who had overheard the king's speech, thought that he saw in it signs of yielding to his proposal, so he joyfully agreed to the monarch's wishes, and came forward to help the prince to mount the horse, and show him how to guide it: but, before he had finished, the young man turned the screw, and was soon out of sight.

They waited some time, expecting that every moment he might be seen returning in the distance, but at length the Indian grew frightened, and prostrating himself before the throne, he said to the king, "Sire, your Highness must have noticed that the prince, in his impatience, did not allow me to tell him what it was necessary to do in order to return to the place from which he started. I implore you not to punish me for what was not my fault, and not to visit on me any misfortune that may occur."

"But why," cried the king in a burst of fear and anger, "why did you not call him back when you saw him disappearing?"

"Sire," replied the Indian, "the rapidity of his movements took me so by surprise that he was out of hearing before I recovered my speech. But we must hope that he will perceive and turn a second screw, which will have the effect of bringing the horse back to earth."

"But supposing he does!" answered the king, "what is to hinder the horse from descending straight into the sea, or dashing him to pieces on the rocks?"

"Have no fears, your Highness," said the Indian; "the horse has the gift of passing over seas, and of carrying his rider wherever he wishes to go."

"Well, your head shall answer for it," returned the monarch, "and if in three months he is not safe back with me, or at any rate does not send me news of his safety, your life shall pay the penalty." So saying, he ordered his guards to seize the Indian and throw him into prison.

Meanwhile, Prince Firouz Schah had gone gaily up into the air, and for the space of an hour continued to ascend higher and higher, till the very mountains were not ***distinguishable*** from the plains. Then he began to think it was time to come down, and ***took for granted*** that, in order to do this, it was only needful to turn the screw the reverse way; but, to his surprise and horror, he found that, turn as he might, he did not make the smallest impression. He then remembered that he had never waited to ask how he was to get back to earth again, and understood the danger in which he stood. Luckily, he did not lose his head, and set about examining the horse's neck with great care, till at last, to his intense joy, he discovered a tiny little peg, much smaller than the other, close to the right ear. This he turned, and found himself dropping to the earth, though more slowly than he had left it.

It was now dark, and as the prince could see nothing, he was obliged, not without some feeling of disquiet, to allow the horse to direct his own course, and midnight was already passed before Prince Firouz Schah again touched the

---

distinguishable: noticeable
took for granted: assumed

ground, faint and weary from his long ride, and from the fact that he had eaten nothing since early morning.

The first thing he did on dismounting was to try to find out where he was, and, as far as he could discover in the thick darkness, he found himself on the terraced roof of a huge palace, with a balustrade of marble running round. In one corner of the terrace stood a small door, opening on to a staircase which led down into the palace.

Some people might have hesitated before exploring further, but not so the prince. "I am doing no harm," he said, "and whoever the owner may be, he will not touch me when he sees I am unarmed," and in dread of making a false step, he went cautiously down the staircase. On a landing, he noticed an open door, beyond which was a faintly lighted hall.

Before entering, the prince paused and listened, but he heard nothing except the sound of men snoring. By the light of a lantern suspended from the roof, he perceived a row of black guards sleeping, each with a naked sword lying by him, and he understood that the hall must form the ante-room to the chamber of some queen or princess.

Standing quite still, Prince Firouz Schah looked about him, till his eyes grew ***accustomed*** to the gloom, and he noticed a bright light shining through a curtain in one corner. He then made his way softly towards it, and, drawing aside its folds, passed into a magnificent chamber full of sleeping women, all lying on low couches, except one, who was on a sofa; and this one, he knew, must be the princess.

Gently stealing up to the side of her bed he looked at her, and saw that she was more beautiful than any woman he had ever beheld. But, fascinated though he was, he was well aware of the danger of his position, as one cry of surprise would awake the guards, and cause his certain death.

So sinking quietly on his knees, he took hold of the sleeve of the princess and drew her arm lightly towards him. The princess opened her eyes, and seeing before her a handsome well-dressed man, she remained speechless with astonishment.

This favourable moment was seized by the prince, who bowing low while he knelt, thus addressed her:

"You behold, madame, a prince in distress, son to the King of Persia, who, owing to an adventure so strange that you will scarcely believe it, finds himself here, a suppliant for your protection. But yesterday, I was in my father's court, engaged in the celebration of our most solemn festival; to-day, I am in an unknown land, in danger of my life."

Now the princess whose mercy Prince Firouz Schah implored was the eldest daughter of the King of Bengal, who was enjoying rest and change in the palace her father had built her, at a little distance from the capital. She listened kindly to what he had to say, and then answered:

"Prince, be not uneasy; hospitality and humanity are practised as widely in Bengal as they are in Persia. The protection you ask will be given you by all.

---

accustomed: used to

You have my word for it." And as the prince was about to thank her for her goodness, she added quickly, "However great may be my curiosity to learn by what means you have travelled here so speedily, I know that you must be faint for want of food, so I shall give orders to my women to take you to one of my chambers, where you will be provided with supper, and left to repose."

By this time the princess's attendants were all awake, and listening to the conversation. At a sign from their mistress they rose, dressed themselves hastily, and snatching up some of the tapers which lighted the room, conducted the prince to a large and lofty room, where two of the number prepared his bed, and the rest went down to the kitchen, from which they soon returned with all sorts of dishes. Then, showing him cupboards filled with dresses and linen, they quitted the room.

During their absence the Princess of Bengal, who had been greatly struck by the beauty of the prince, tried in vain to go to sleep again. It was of no use: she felt broad awake, and when her women entered the room, she inquired eagerly if the prince had all he wanted, and what they thought of him.

"Madame," they replied, "it is of course impossible for us to tell what impression this young man has made on you. For ourselves, we think you would be fortunate if the king your father should allow you to marry anyone so amiable. Certainly there is no one in the Court of Bengal who can be compared with him."

These flattering observations were by no means displeasing to the princess, but as she did not wish to betray her own feelings she merely said, "You are all a set of chatterboxes; go back to bed, and let me sleep."

When she dressed the following morning, her maids noticed that, contrary to her usual habit, the princess was very particular about her toilette, and insisted on her hair being dressed two or three times over. "For," she said to herself, "if my appearance was not displeasing to the prince when he saw me in the condition I was, how much more will he be struck with me when he beholds me with all my charms."

Then she placed in her hair the largest and most brilliant diamonds she could find, with a necklace, bracelets and girdle, all of precious stones. And over her shoulders her ladies put a robe of the richest stuff in all the Indies, that no one was allowed to wear except members of the royal family. When she was fully dressed according to her wishes, she sent to know if the Prince of Persia was awake and ready to receive her, as she desired to present herself before him.

When the princess's messenger entered his room, Prince Firouz Schah was in the act of leaving it, to inquire if he might be allowed to pay his homage to her mistress: but on hearing the princess's wishes, he at once gave way. "Her will is my law," he said, "I am only here to obey her orders."

In a few moments the princess herself appeared, and after the usual compliments had passed between them, the princess sat down on a sofa, and began to explain to the prince her reasons for not giving him an audience in her own apartments. "Had I done so," she said, "we might have been interrupted at any hour by the chief of the eunuchs, who has the right to enter whenever it pleases him, whereas this is forbidden ground. I am all impatience to learn the wonderful accident which has procured the pleasure of your arrival, and that is why I have come to you here, where no one can intrude upon us. Begin then, I entreat you, without delay."

So the prince began at the beginning, and told all the story of the festival of Nedrouz held yearly in Persia, and of the splendid spectacles celebrated in its honour. But when he came to the enchanted horse, the princess declared that she could never have imagined anything half so surprising. "Well then," continued the prince, "you can easily understand how the King my father, who has a passion for all curious things, was seized with a violent desire to possess this horse, and asked the Indian what sum he would take for it.

"The man's answer was absolutely absurd, as you will agree, when I tell you that it was nothing less than the hand of the princess my sister; but though all the bystanders laughed and ***mocked***, and I was beside myself with rage, I saw to my despair that my father could not make up his mind to treat the insolent proposal as it deserved. I tried to argue with him, but in vain. He only begged me to examine the horse with a view (as I quite understood) of making me more sensible of its value."

"To please my father, I mounted the horse, and, without waiting for any instructions from the Indian, turned the peg as I had seen him do. In an instant I was soaring upwards, much quicker than an arrow could fly, and I felt as if I must be getting so near the sky that I should soon hit my head against it! I could see nothing beneath me, and for some time was so confused that I did not even know in what direction I was travelling. At last, when it was growing dark, I found another screw, and on turning it, the horse began slowly to sink towards the earth. I was forced to trust to chance, and to see what fate had in store, and it was already past midnight when I found myself on the roof of this palace. I crept down the little staircase, and made directly for a light which I perceived through an open door--I peeped cautiously in, and saw, as you will guess, the eunuchs lying asleep on the floor. I knew the risks I ran, but my need was so great that I paid no attention to them, and stole safely past your guards, to the curtain which concealed your doorway.

"The rest, Princess, you know; and it only remains for me to thank you for the kindness you have shown me, and to assure you of my gratitude. By the law of nations, I am already your slave, and I have only my heart, that is my own, to offer you. But what am I saying? My own? Alas, madame, it was yours from the first moment I beheld you!"

The air with which he said these words could have left no doubt on the mind of the princess as to the effect of her charms, and the blush which mounted to her face only increased her beauty.

"Prince," returned she as soon as her confusion permitted her to speak, "you have given me the greatest pleasure, and I have followed you closely in all your adventures, and though you are positively sitting before me, I even trembled at your danger in the upper regions of the air! Let me say what a debt I owe to the chance that has led you to my house; you could have entered none which would

---

mocked: made fun of

have given you a warmer welcome. As to your being a slave, of course that is merely a joke, and my reception must itself have assured you that you are as free here as at your father's court. As to your heart," continued she in tones of encouragement, "I am quite sure that must have been disposed of long ago, to some princess who is well worthy of it, and I could not think of being the cause of your unfaithfulness to her."

Prince Firouz Schah was about to protest that there was no lady with any prior claims, but he was stopped by the entrance of one of the princess's attendants, who announced that dinner was served, and, after all, neither was sorry for the interruption.

Dinner was laid in a magnificent apartment, and the table was covered with delicious fruits; while during the repast richly dressed girls sang softly and sweetly to stringed instruments. After the prince and princess had finished, they passed into a small room hung with blue and gold, looking out into a garden stocked with flowers and arbutus trees, quite different from any that were to be found in Persia.

"Princess," observed the young man, "till now I had always believed that Persia could boast finer palaces and more lovely gardens than any kingdom upon earth. But my eyes have been opened, and I begin to perceive that, wherever there is a great king he will surround himself with buildings worthy of him."

"Prince," replied the Princess of Bengal, "I have no idea what a Persian palace is like, so I am unable to make comparisons. I do not wish to depreciate my own palace, but I can assure you that it is very poor beside that of the King my father, as you will agree when you have been there to greet him, as I hope you will shortly do."

Now the princess hoped that, by bringing about a meeting between the prince and her father, the King would be so struck with the young man's distinguished air and fine manners, that he would offer him his daughter to wife. But the reply of the Prince of Persia to her suggestion was not quite what she wished.

"Madame," he said, "by taking advantage of your proposal to visit the palace of the King of Bengal, I should satisfy not merely my curiosity, but also the sentiments of respect with which I regard him. But, Princess, I am persuaded that you will feel with me, that I cannot possibly present myself before so great a sovereign without the attendants suitable to my rank. He would think me an adventurer."

"If that is all," she answered, "you can get as many attendants here as you please. There are plenty of Persian merchants, and as for money, my treasury is always open to you. Take what you please."

Prince Firouz Schah guessed what prompted so much kindness on the part of the princess, and was much touched by it. Still his passion, which increased every moment, did not make him forget his duty. So he replied without hesitation:

"I do not know, Princess, how to express my gratitude for your obliging offer, which I would accept at once if it were not for the recollection of all the uneasiness the King my father must be suffering on my account. I should be unworthy indeed of all the love he showers upon me, if I did not return to him at the first possible moment. For, while I am enjoying the society of the most amiable of all princesses, he is, I am quite convinced, plunged in the deepest grief, having lost all hope of seeing me again. I am sure you will understand my position, and will feel that to remain away one instant longer than is necessary would not only be ungrateful on my part, but perhaps even a crime, for how do I know if my absence may not break his heart?

"But," continued the prince, "having obeyed the voice of my conscience, I shall count the moments when, with your gracious permission, I may present myself before the King of Bengal, not as a wanderer, but as a prince, to ***implore*** the favour of your hand. My father has always informed me that in my marriage I shall be left quite free, but I am persuaded that I have only to describe your generosity, for my wishes to become his own."

The Princess of Bengal was too reasonable not to accept the explanation offered by Prince Firouz Schah, but she was much disturbed at his intention of departing at once, for she feared that, no sooner had he left her, than the impression she had made on him would fade away. So she made one more effort to keep him, and after assuring him that she entirely approved of his anxiety to see his father, begged him to give her a day or two more of his company.

In common politeness the prince could hardly refuse this request, and the princess set about inventing every kind of amusement for him, and succeeded so well that two months slipped by almost unnoticed, in balls, spectacles and in hunting, of which, when unattended by danger, the princess was passionately fond. But at last, one day, he declared seriously that he could neglect his duty no longer, and entreated her to put no further obstacles in his way, promising at the same time to return, as soon as he could, with all the magnificence due both to her and to himself.

"Princess," he added, "it may be that in your heart you class me with those false lovers whose devotion cannot stand the test of absence. If you do, you wrong me; and were it not for fear of offending you, I would beseech you to come with me, for my life can only be happy when passed with you. As for your reception at the Persian Court, it will be as warm as your merits deserve; and as for what concerns the King of Bengal, he must be much more indifferent to your welfare than you have led me to believe if he does not give his consent to our marriage."

The princess could not find words in which to reply to the arguments of the Prince of Persia, but her silence and her downcast eyes spoke for her, and declared that she had no objection to accompanying him on his travels.

The only difficulty that occurred to her was that Prince Firouz Schah did not know how to manage the horse, and she dreaded lest they might find themselves in the same plight as before. But the prince soothed her fears so successfully, that she soon had no other thought than to arrange for their flight so secretly, that no one in the palace should suspect it.

---

implore: beseech; request

This was done, and early the following morning, when the whole palace was wrapped in sleep, she stole up on to the roof, where the prince was already awaiting her, with his horse's head towards Persia. He mounted first and helped the princess up behind; then, when she was firmly seated, with her hands holding tightly to his belt, he touched the screw, and the horse began to leave the earth quickly behind him.

He travelled with his accustomed speed, and Prince Firouz Schah guided him so well that in two hours and a half from the time of starting, he saw the capital of Persia lying beneath him. He determined to alight neither in the great square from which he had started, nor in the Sultan's palace, but in a country house at a little distance from the town. Here he showed the princess a beautiful suite of rooms, and begged her to rest, while he informed his father of their arrival, and prepared a public reception worthy of her rank. Then he ordered a horse to be saddled, and set out.

All the way through the streets he was welcomed with shouts of joy by the people, who had long lost all hope of seeing him again. On reaching the palace, he found the Sultan surrounded by his ministers, all clad in the deepest mourning, and his father almost went out of his mind with surprise and delight at the mere sound of his son's voice. When he had calmed down a little, he begged the prince to relate his adventures.

The prince at once seized the opening thus given him, and told the whole story of his treatment by the Princess of Bengal, not even concealing the fact that she had fallen in love with him. "And, Sire," ended the prince, "having given my royal word that you would not refuse your consent to our marriage, I persuaded her to return with me on the Indian's horse. I have left her in one of your Highness's country houses, where she is waiting anxiously to be assured that I have not promised in vain."

As he said this the prince was about to throw himself at the feet of the Sultan, but his father prevented him, and embracing him again, said eagerly:

"My son, not only do I gladly consent to your marriage with the Princess of Bengal, but I will hasten to pay my respects to her, and to thank her in my own person for the benefits she has conferred on you. I will then bring her back with me, and make all arrangements for the wedding to be celebrated to-day."

So the Sultan gave orders that the habits of mourning worn by the people should be thrown off and that there should be a concert of drums, trumpets and cymbals. Also that the Indian should be taken from prison, and brought before him.

His commands were obeyed, and the Indian was led into his presence, surrounded by guards. "I have kept you locked up," said the Sultan, "so that in case my son was lost, your life should pay the penalty. He has now returned; so take your horse, and begone for ever."

The Indian hastily quitted the presence of the Sultan, and when he was outside, he inquired of the man who had taken him out of prison where the prince had really been all this time, and what he had been doing. They told him the whole story, and how the Princess of Bengal was even then awaiting in the country palace the consent of the Sultan, which at once put into the Indian's head a plan of revenge for the treatment he had experienced. Going straight to the country house, he informed the doorkeeper who was left in charge that he had been sent by the Sultan and by the Prince of Persia to fetch the princess on the enchanted horse, and to bring her to the palace.

The doorkeeper knew the Indian by sight, and was of course aware that nearly three months before he had been thrown into prison by the Sultan; and seeing him at liberty, the man took for granted that he was speaking the truth, and made no difficulty about leading him before the Princess of Bengal; while on her side, hearing that he had come from the prince, the lady gladly consented to do what he wished.

The Indian, delighted with the success of his scheme, mounted the horse, assisted the princess to mount behind him, and turned the peg at the very moment that the prince was leaving the palace in Schiraz for the country house, followed closely by the Sultan and all the court. Knowing this, the Indian deliberately steered the horse right above the city, in order that his revenge for his unjust imprisonment might be all the quicker and sweeter.

When the Sultan of Persia saw the horse and its riders, he stopped short with astonishment and horror, and broke out into oaths and curses, which the Indian heard quite unmoved, knowing that he was perfectly safe from pursuit. But mortified and furious as the Sultan was, his feelings were nothing to those of Prince Firouz Schah, when he saw the object of his passionate devotion being borne rapidly away. And while he was struck speechless with grief and remorse at not having guarded her better, she vanished swiftly out of his sight. What was he to do? Should he follow his father into the palace, and there give reins to his despair? Both his love and his courage alike forbade it; and he continued his way to the palace.

The sight of the prince showed the doorkeeper of what folly he had been guilty, and flinging himself at his master's feet, implored his pardon. "Rise," said the prince, "I am the cause of this misfortune, and not you. Go and find me the dress of a dervish, but beware of saying it is for me."

At a short distance from the country house, a convent of dervishes was situated, and the superior, or scheih, was the doorkeeper's friend. So by means of a false story made up ***on the spur of the moment***, it was easy enough to get hold of a dervish's dress, which the prince at once put on, instead of his own. Disguised like this and concealing about him a box of pearls and diamonds he had intended as a present to the princess, he left the house at nightfall, uncertain where he should go, but firmly resolved not to return without her.

Meanwhile the Indian had turned the horse in such a direction that, before many hours had passed, it had entered a wood close to the capital of the kingdom of Cashmere. Feeling very hungry, and supposing that the princess also might be in want of food, he brought his steed down to the earth, and left the princess in a shady place, on the banks of a clear stream.

At first, when the princess had found herself alone, the idea had occurred to her of trying to escape and hide herself. But as she had eaten scarcely anything

---

on the spur of the moment: impulsively; suddenly

since she had left Bengal, she felt she was too weak to venture far, and was obliged to abandon her design. On the return of the Indian with meats of various kinds, she began to eat voraciously, and soon had regained sufficient courage to reply with spirit to his insolent remarks. Goaded by his threats she sprang to her feet, calling loudly for help, and luckily her cries were heard by a troop of horsemen, who rode up to inquire what was the matter.

Now the leader of these horsemen was the Sultan of Cashmere, returning from the chase, and he instantly turned to the Indian to inquire who he was, and whom he had with him. The Indian rudely answered that it was his wife, and there was no occasion for anyone else to interfere between them.

The princess, who, of course, was ignorant of the rank of her deliverer, denied altogether the Indian's story. "My lord," she cried, "whoever you may be, put no faith in this impostor. He is an abominable magician, who has this day torn me from the Prince of Persia, my destined husband, and has brought me here on this enchanted horse." She would have continued, but her tears choked her, and the Sultan of Cashmere, convinced by her beauty and her distinguished air of the truth of her tale, ordered his followers to cut off the Indian's head, which was done immediately.

But rescued though she was from one peril, it seemed as if she had only fallen into another. The Sultan commanded a horse to be given her, and conducted her to his own palace, where he led her to a beautiful apartment, and selected female slaves to wait on her, and eunuchs to be her guard. Then, without allowing her time to thank him for all he had done, he bade her repose, saying she should tell him her adventures on the following day.

The princess fell asleep, flattering herself that she had only to relate her story for the Sultan to be touched by ***compassion***, and to restore her to the prince without delay. But a few hours were to undeceive her.

When the King of Cashmere had quitted her presence the evening before, he had resolved that the sun should not set again without the princess becoming his wife, and at daybreak proclamation of his intention was made throughout the town, by the sound of drums, trumpets, cymbals, and other instruments calculated to fill the heart with joy. The Princess of Bengal was early awakened by the noise, but she did not for one moment imagine that it had anything to do with her, till the Sultan, arriving as soon as she was dressed to inquire after her health, informed her that the trumpet blasts she heard were part of the solemn marriage ceremonies, for which he begged her to prepare. This unexpected announcement caused the princess such terror that she sank down in a dead faint.

The slaves that were in waiting ran to her aid, and the Sultan himself did his best to bring her back to consciousness, but for a long while it was all to no purpose. At length her senses began slowly to come back to her, and then, rather than break faith with the Prince of Persia by consenting to such a marriage, she determined to ***feign*** madness. So she began by saying all sorts of absurdities,

---

compassion: sympathy
feign: pretend: fake

and using all kinds of strange gestures, while the Sultan stood watching her with sorrow and surprise. But as this sudden seizure showed no sign of abating, he left her to her women, ordering them to take the greatest care of her. Still, as the day went on, the malady seemed to become worse, and by night it was almost violent.

Days passed in this manner, till at last the Sultan of Cashmere decided to summon all the doctors of his court to consult together over her sad state. Their answer was that madness is of so many different kinds that it was impossible to give an opinion on the case without seeing the princess, so the Sultan gave orders that they were to be introduced into her chamber, one by one, every man according to his rank.

This decision had been foreseen by the princess, who knew quite well that if once she allowed the physicians to feel her pulse, the most ignorant of them would discover that she was in perfectly good health, and that her madness was feigned, so as each man approached, she broke out into such violent paroxysms, that not one dared to lay a finger on her. A few, who pretended to be cleverer than the rest, declared that they could diagnose sick people only from sight, ordered her certain potions, which she made no difficulty about taking, as she was persuaded they were all harmless.

When the Sultan of Cashmere saw that the court doctors could do nothing towards curing the princess, he called in those of the city, who fared no better. Then he had recourse to the most celebrated physicians in the other large towns, but finding that the task was beyond their science, he finally sent messengers into the other neighbouring states, with a memorandum containing full particulars of the princess's madness, offering at the same time to pay the expenses of any physician who would come and see for himself, and a handsome reward to the one who should cure her. In answer to this proclamation many foreign professors flocked into Cashmere, but they naturally were not more successful than the rest had been, as the cure depended neither on them nor their skill, but only on the princess herself.

It was during this time that Prince Firouz Schah, wandering sadly and hopelessly from place to place, arrived in a large city of India, where he heard a great deal of talk about the Princess of Bengal who had gone out of her senses, on the very day that she was to have been married to the Sultan of Cashmere. This was quite enough to induce him to take the road to Cashmere, and to inquire at the first inn at which he lodged in the capital the full particulars of the story. When he knew that he had at last found the princess whom he had so long lost, he set about devising a plan for her rescue.

The first thing he did was to procure a doctor's robe, so that his dress, added to the long beard he had allowed to grow on his travels, might unmistakably proclaim his profession. He then lost no time in going to the palace, where he obtained an audience of the chief usher, and while apologizing for his boldness in presuming to think that he could cure the princess, where so many others had failed, declared that he had the secret of certain remedies, which had hitherto never failed of their effect.

The chief usher assured him that he was heartily welcome, and that the Sultan would receive him with pleasure; and in case of success, he would gain a magnificent reward.

When the Prince of Persia, in the disguise of a physician, was brought before him, the Sultan wasted no time in talking, beyond remarking that the mere sight of a doctor threw the princess into transports of rage. He then led the prince up to a room under the roof, which had an opening through which he might observe the princess, without himself being seen.

The prince looked, and beheld the princess reclining on a sofa with tears in her eyes, singing softly to herself a song bewailing her sad destiny, which had deprived her, perhaps for ever, of a being she so tenderly loved. The young man's heart beat fast as he listened, for he needed no further proof that her madness was feigned, and that it was love of him which had caused her to resort to this species of trick. He softly left his hiding-place, and returned to the Sultan, to whom he reported that he was sure from certain signs that the princess's malady was not incurable, but that he must see her and speak with her alone.

The Sultan made no difficulty in consenting to this, and commanded that he should be ushered in to the princess's apartment. The moment she caught sight of his physician's robe, she sprang from her seat in a fury, and heaped insults upon him. The prince took no notice of her behaviour, and approaching quite close, so that his words might be heard by her alone, he said in a low whisper, "Look at me, princess, and you will see that I am no doctor, but the Prince of Persia, who has come to set you free."

At the sound of his voice, the Princess of Bengal suddenly grew calm, and an expression of joy overspread her face, such as only comes when what we wish for most and expect the least suddenly happens to us. For some time she was too enchanted to speak, and Prince Firouz Schah took advantage of her silence to explain to her all that had occurred, his despair at watching her disappear before his very eyes, the oath he had sworn to follow her over the world, and his ***rapture*** at finally discovering her in the palace at Cashmere. When he had finished, he begged in his turn that the princess would tell him how she had come there, so that he might the better devise some means of rescuing her from the tyranny of the Sultan.

It needed but a few words from the princess to make him acquainted with the whole situation, and how she had been forced to play the part of a mad woman in order to escape from a marriage with the Sultan, who had not had sufficient politeness even to ask her consent. If necessary, she added, she had resolved to die sooner than permit herself to be forced into such a union, and break faith with a prince whom she loved.

The prince then inquired if she knew what had become of the enchanted horse since the Indian's death, but the princess could only reply that she had heard nothing about it. Still she did not suppose that the horse could have been forgotten by the Sultan, after all she had told him of its value.

To this the prince agreed, and they consulted together over a plan by which

---

rapture: delight

she might be able to make her escape and return with him into Persia. And as the first step, she was to dress herself with care, and receive the Sultan with civility when he visited her next morning.

The Sultan was transported with delight on learning the result of the interview, and his opinion of the doctor's skill was raised still higher when, on the following day, the princess behaved towards him in such a way as to persuade him that her complete cure would not be long delayed. However he contented himself with assuring her how happy he was to see her health so much improved, and exhorted her to make every use of so clever a physician, and to repose entire confidence in him. Then he retired, without awaiting any reply from the princess.

The Prince of Persia left the room at the same time, and asked if he might be allowed humbly to inquire by what means the Princess of Bengal had reached Cashmere, which was so far distant from her father's kingdom, and how she came to be there alone. The Sultan thought the question very natural, and told him the same story that the Princess of Bengal had done, adding that he had ordered the enchanted horse to be taken to his treasury as a curiosity, though he was quite ignorant how it could be used.

"Sire," replied the physician, "your Highness's tale has supplied me with the clue I needed to complete the recovery of the princess. During her voyage hither on an enchanted horse, a portion of its enchantment has by some means been communicated to her person, and it can only be dissipated by certain perfumes of which I possess the secret. If your Highness will deign to consent, and to give the court and the people one of the most astonishing spectacles they have ever witnessed, command the horse to be brought into the big square outside the palace, and leave the rest to me. I promise that in a very few moments, in presence of all the assembled multitude, you shall see the princess as healthy both in mind and body as ever she was in her life. And in order to make the spectacle as impressive as possible, I would suggest that she should be richly dressed and covered with the noblest jewels of the crown."

The Sultan readily agreed to all that the prince proposed, and the following morning he desired that the enchanted horse should be taken from the treasury, and brought into the great square of the palace. Soon the rumour began to spread through the town, that something extraordinary was about to happen, and such a crowd began to collect that the guards had to be called out to keep order, and to make a way for the enchanted horse.

When all was ready, the Sultan appeared, and took his place on a platform, surrounded by the chief nobles and officers of his court. When they were seated, the Princess of Bengal was seen leaving the palace, accompanied by the ladies who had been assigned to her by the Sultan. She slowly approached the enchanted horse, and with the help of her ladies, she mounted on its back. Directly she was in the saddle, with her feet in the stirrups and the bridle in her hand, the physician placed around the horse some large braziers full of burning coals, into each of which he threw a perfume composed of all sorts of delicious scents. Then he crossed his hands over his breast, and with lowered eyes walked three times round the horse, muttering the while certain words. Soon there arose from the burning braziers a thick smoke which almost concealed both the horse and princess, and this was the moment for which he had been waiting. Springing lightly up behind the lady, he leaned forward and turned the peg, and as the horse darted up into the air, he cried aloud so that his words were heard by all present, "Sultan of Cashmere, when you wish to marry princesses who have sought your protection, learn first to gain their consent."

It was in this way that the Prince of Persia rescued the Princess of Bengal, and returned with her to Persia, where they descended this time before the palace of the King himself. The marriage was only delayed just long enough to make the ceremony as brilliant as possible, and, as soon as the rejoicings were over, an ambassador was sent to the King of Bengal, to inform him of what had passed, and to ask his approbation of the alliance between the two countries, which he heartily gave.

THE BLUE FAIRY BOOK

Andrew Lang

The Forty Thieves

In a town in Persia there dwelt two brothers, one named Cassim, the other Ali Baba. Cassim was married to a rich wife and lived in plenty, while Ali Baba had to maintain his wife and children by cutting wood in a neighboring forest and selling it in the town. One day, when Ali Baba was in the forest, he saw a troop of men on horseback, coming toward him in a cloud of dust. He was afraid they were robbers, and climbed into a tree for safety. When they came up to him and dismounted, he counted forty of them. They unbridled their horses and tied them to trees. The finest man among them, whom Ali Baba took to be their captain, went a little way among some bushes, and said, "Open, Sesame!" so plainly that Ali Baba heard him. A door opened in the rocks, and having made the troop go in, he followed them, and the door shut again of itself. They stayed some time inside, and Ali Baba, fearing they might come out and catch him, was forced to sit patiently in the tree. At last the door opened again, and the Forty Thieves came out. As the Captain went in last he came out first, and made them all pass by him; he then closed the door, saying, "Shut, Sesame!" Every man bridled his horse and mounted, the Captain put himself at their head, and they returned as they came.

Then Ali Baba climbed down and went to the door concealed among the bushes, and said, "Open, Sesame!" and it flew open. Ali Baba, who expected a dull, dismal place, was greatly surprised to find it large and well lighted, hollowed by the hand of man in the form of a vault, which received the light from an opening in the ceiling. He saw rich bales of merchandise -- silk, stuff-brocades, all piled together, and gold and silver in heaps, and money in leather purses. He went in and the door shut behind him. He did not look at the silver, but brought out as many bags of gold as he thought his asses, which were browsing outside, could carry, loaded them with the bags, and hid it all with fagots. Using the words, "Shut, Sesame!" he closed the door and went home.

Then he drove his asses into the yard, shut the gates, carried the money-bags to his wife, and emptied them out before her. He bade her keep the secret, and he would go and bury the gold. "Let me first measure it," said his wife. "I will go borrow a measure of someone, while you dig the hole." So she ran to the wife of Cassim and borrowed a measure. Knowing Ali Baba's poverty, the sister was curious to find out what sort of grain his wife wished to measure, and artfully put some suet at the bottom of the measure. Ali Baba's wife went home and set the measure on the heap of gold, and filled it and emptied it often, to her great content. She then carried it back to her sister, without noticing that a piece of gold was sticking to it, which Cassim's wife perceived directly her back was turned. She grew very curious, and said to Cassim when he came home, "Cassim, your brother is richer than you. He does not count his money, he measures it." He begged her to explain this riddle, which she did by showing him the piece of money and telling him where she found it. Then Cassim grew so envious that he could not sleep, and went to his brother in the morning before sunrise. "Ali Baba," he said, showing him the gold piece, "you pretend to be poor and yet you measure gold." By this Ali Baba perceived that through his wife's folly Cassim and his wife knew their secret, so he confessed all and offered Cassim a share. "That I expect," said Cassim; "but I must know where to find the treasure, otherwise I will discover all, and you will lose all." Ali Baba, more out of kindness than fear, told him of the cave, and the very words to use. Cassim left Ali Baba, meaning to be beforehand with him and get the treasure for himself. He rose early next morning, and set out with ten mules loaded with great chests. He soon found the place, and the door in the rock. He said, "Open, Sesame!" and the door opened and shut behind him. He could have feasted his eyes all day on the treasures, but he now hastened to gather together as much of it as possible; but when he was ready to go he could not remember what to say for thinking of his great riches. Instead of "Sesame," he said, "Open, Barley!" and the door remained fast. He named several different sorts of grain, all but the right one, and the door still stuck fast. He was so frightened at the danger he was in that he had as much forgotten the word as if he had never heard it.

About noon the robbers returned to their cave, and saw Cassim's mules roving about with great chests on their backs. This gave them the alarm; they drew their sabers, and went to the door, which opened on their Captain's saying, "Open, Sesame!" Cassim, who had heard the trampling of their horses' feet, resolved to sell his life dearly, so when the door opened he leaped out and threw the Captain down. In vain, however, for the robbers with their sabers soon killed him. On entering the cave they saw all the bags laid ready, and could not imagine how anyone had got in without knowing their secret. They cut Cassim's body into four quarters, and nailed them up inside the cave, in order to frighten anyone who should venture in, and went away in search of more treasure.

As night drew on Cassim's wife grew very uneasy, and ran to her brother-in-law, and told him where her husband had gone. Ali Baba did his best to comfort her, and set out to the forest in search of Cassim. The first thing he saw on entering the cave was his dead brother. Full of horror, he put the body on one of his asses, and bags of gold on the other two, and, covering all with some fagots, returned home. He drove the two asses laden with gold into his own yard, and led the other to Cassim's house. The door was opened by the slave Morgiana, whom he knew to be both brave and cunning. Unloading the ass, he said to her, "This is the body of your master, who has been murdered, but whom we must bury as though he had died in his bed. I will speak with you again, but now tell your mistress I am come." The wife of Cassim, on learning the fate of her husband, broke out into cries and tears, but Ali Baba offered to take her to live with him and his wife if she would promise to keep his counsel and leave everything to Morgiana; whereupon she agreed, and dried her eyes.

Morgiana, meanwhile, sought an apothecary and asked him for some lozenges. "My poor master," she said, "can neither eat nor speak, and no one knows what his distemper is." She carried home the lozenges and returned next day weeping, and asked for an essence only given to those just about to die. Thus, in the evening, no one was surprised to hear the wretched shrieks and cries of Cassim's wife and Morgiana, telling everyone that Cassim was dead. The day after Morgiana went to an old cobbler near the gates of the town who opened his stall early, put a piece of gold in his hand, and bade him follow her with his needle and thread. Having bound his eyes with a handkerchief, she took him to the room where the body lay, pulled off the bandage, and bade him sew the quarters together, after which she covered his eyes again and led him home. Then they buried Cassim, and Morgiana his slave followed him to the grave, weeping and tearing her hair, while Cassim's wife stayed at home uttering lamentable cries. Next day she went to live with Ali Baba, who gave Cassim's shop to his eldest son.

The Forty Thieves, on their return to the cave, were much astonished to find Cassim's body gone and some of their money-bags. "We are certainly discovered," said the Captain, "and shall be undone if we cannot find out who it is that knows our secret. Two men must have known it; we have killed one, we must now find the other. To this end one of you who is bold and artful must go into the city dressed as a traveler, and discover whom we have killed, and whether men talk of the strange manner of his death. If the messenger fails he must lose his life, lest we be betrayed." One of the thieves started up and offered to do this, and after the rest had highly commended him for his bravery he disguised himself, and happened to enter the town at daybreak, just by Baba Mustapha's stall. The thief bade him good-day, saying, "Honest man, how can you possibly see to stitch at your age?" "Old as I am," replied the cobbler, "I have very good eyes, and will you believe me when I tell you that I sewed a dead body together in a place where I had less light than I have now." The robber was overjoyed at his good fortune, and, giving him a piece of gold, desired to be shown the house where he stitched up the dead body. At first Mustapha refused, saying that he had been blindfolded; but when the robber gave him another piece of gold he began to think he might remember the turnings if blindfolded as before. This means succeeded; the robber partly led him, and was partly guided by him, right in front of Cassim's house, the door of which the robber marked with a piece of chalk. Then, well pleased, he bade farewell to Baba Mustapha and returned to the forest. By and by Morgiana, going out, saw the mark the robber had made, quickly guessed that some mischief was brewing, and fetching a piece of chalk marked two or three doors on each side, without saying anything to her master or mistress.

The thief, meantime, told his comrades of his discovery. The Captain thanked him, and bade him show him the house he had marked. But when they came to it they saw that five or six of the houses were chalked in the same manner. The guide was so ***confounded*** that he knew not what answer to make, and when they returned he was at once beheaded for having failed. Another robber was dispatched, and, having won over Baba Mustapha, marked the house in red chalk; but Morgiana being again too clever for them, the second messenger was put to death also. The Captain now resolved to go himself, but, wiser than the others, he did not mark the house, but looked at it so closely that he could not fail to remember it. He returned, and ordered his men to go into the neighboring villages and buy nineteen mules, and thirty-eight leather jars, all empty except one, which was full of oil. The Captain put one of his men, fully armed, into each, rubbing the outside of the jars with oil from the full vessel. Then the nineteen mules were loaded with thirty-seven robbers in jars, and the jar of oil, and reached the town by dusk. The Captain stopped his mules in front of Ali Baba's house, and said to Ali Baba, who was sitting outside for coolness, "I have brought some oil from a distance to sell at tomorrow's market, but it is now so late that I know not where to pass the night, unless you will do me the favor to take me in." Though Ali Baba had seen the Captain of the robbers in the forest, he did not recognize him in the disguise of an oil merchant. He bade him welcome, opened his gates for the mules to enter, and went to Morgiana to bid her prepare a bed and supper for his guest. He brought the stranger into his hall, and after they had supped went again to speak to Morgiana in the kitchen, while the Captain went into the yard under pretense of seeing after his mules, but really to tell his men what to do. Beginning at the first jar and ending at the last, he said to each man, "As soon as I throw some stones from the window of the chamber where I lie, cut the jars open with your knives and come out, and I will be with you in a trice." He returned to the house, and Morgiana led him to his chamber. She then told Abdallah, her fellow slave, to set on the pot to make some broth for her master, who had gone to bed. Meanwhile her lamp went out, and she had no more oil in the house. "Do not be uneasy," said Abdallah; "go into the yard and take some out of one of those jars." Morgiana thanked him for his advice, took the oil pot, and went into the yard. When she came to the first jar the robber inside said softly, "Is it time?"

Any other slave but Morgiana, on finding a man in the jar instead of the oil she wanted, would have screamed and made a noise; but she, knowing the danger her master was in, bethought herself of a plan, and answered quietly, "Not yet, but presently." She went to all the jars, giving the same answer, till she came to the jar of oil. She now saw that her master, thinking to entertain an oil

---

confounded: confused

merchant, had let thirty-eight robbers into his house. She filled her oil pot, went back to the kitchen, and, having lit her lamp, went again to the oil jar and filled a large kettle full of oil. When it boiled she went and poured enough oil into every jar to stifle and kill the robber inside. When this brave deed was done she went back to the kitchen, put out the fire and the lamp, and waited to see what would happen.

In a quarter of an hour the Captain of the robbers awoke, got up, and opened the window. As all seemed quiet, he threw down some little pebbles which hit the jars. He listened, and as none of his men seemed to stir he grew uneasy, and went down into the yard. On going to the first jar and saying, "Are you asleep?" he smelt the hot boiled oil, and knew at once that his plot to murder Ali Baba and his household had been discovered. He found all the gang was dead, and, missing the oil out of the last jar, became aware of the manner of their death. He then forced the lock of a door leading into a garden, and climbing over several walls made his escape. Morgiana heard and saw all this, and, rejoicing at her success, went to bed and fell asleep.

At daybreak Ali Baba arose, and, seeing the oil jars still there, asked why the merchant had not gone with his mules. Morgiana bade him look in the first jar and see if there was any oil. Seeing a man, he started back in terror. "Have no fear," said Morgiana; "the man cannot harm you; he is dead." Ali Baba, when he had recovered somewhat from his astonishment, asked what had become of the merchant. "Merchant!" said she, "he is no more a merchant than I am!" and she told him the whole story, assuring him that it was a plot of the robbers of the forest, of whom only three were left, and that the white and red chalk marks had something to do with it. Ali Baba at once gave Morgiana her freedom, saying that he owed her his life. They then buried the bodies in Ali Baba's garden, while the mules were sold in the market by his slaves.

The Captain returned to his lonely cave, which seemed frightful to him without his lost companions, and firmly resolved to avenge them by killing Ali Baba. He dressed himself carefully, and went into the town, where he took lodgings in an inn. In the course of a great many journeys to the forest he carried away many rich stuffs and much fine linen, and set up a shop opposite that of Ali Baba's son. He called himself Cogia Hassan, and as he was both civil and well dressed he soon made friends with Ali Baba's son, and through him with Ali Baba, whom he was continually asking to sup with him. Ali Baba, wishing to return his kindness, invited him into his house and received him smiling, thanking him for his kindness to his son. When the merchant was about to take his leave Ali Baba stopped him, saying, "Where are you going, sir, in such haste? Will you not stay and sup with me?" The merchant refused, saying that he had a reason; and, on Ali Baba's asking him what that was, he replied, "It is, sir, that I can eat no victuals that have any salt in them." "If that is all," said Ali Baba, "let me tell you that there shall be no salt in either the meat or the bread that we eat to-night." He went to give this order to Morgiana, who was much surprised. "Who is this man," she said, "who eats no salt with his meat?" "He is an honest man, Morgiana," returned her master; "therefore do as I bid you." But she could not withstand a desire to see this strange man, so she helped Abdallah to carry up the dishes, and saw in a moment that Cogia Hassan was the robber Captain, and carried a dagger under his garment. "I am not surprised," she said to herself, "that this wicked man, who intends to kill my master, will eat no salt with him; but I will hinder his plans."

She sent up the supper by Abdallah, while she made ready for one of the boldest acts that could be thought on. When the dessert had been served, Cogia Hassan was left alone with Ali Baba and his son, whom he thought to make drunk and then to murder them. Morgiana, meanwhile, put on a headdress like a dancing-girl's, and clasped a girdle round her waist, from which hung a dagger with a silver hilt, and said to Abdallah, "Take your tabor, and let us go and ***divert*** our master and his guest." Abdallah took his tabor and played before Morgiana until they came to the door, where Abdallah stopped playing and Morgiana made a low courtesy. "Come in, Morgiana," said Ali Baba, "and let Cogia Hassan see what you can do"; and, turning to Cogia Hassan, he said, "She's my slave and my housekeeper." Cogia Hassan was by no means pleased, for he feared that his chance of killing Ali Baba was gone for the present; but he pretended great eagerness to see Morgiana, and Abdallah began to play and Morgiana to dance. After she had performed several dances she drew her dagger and made passes with it, sometimes pointing it at her own breast, sometimes at her master's, as if it were part of the dance. Suddenly, out of breath, she snatched the tabor from Abdallah with her left hand, and, holding the dagger in her right hand, held out the tabor to her master. Ali Baba and his son put a piece of gold into it, and Cogia Hassan, seeing that she was coming to him, pulled out his purse to make her a present, but while he was putting his hand into it Morgiana plunged the dagger into his heart.

"Unhappy girl!" cried Ali Baba and his son, "what have you done to ruin us?"

"It was to preserve you, master, not to ruin you," answered Morgiana. "See here," opening the false merchant's garment and showing the dagger; "see what an enemy you have entertained! Remember, he would eat no salt with you, and what more would you have? Look at him! He is both the false oil merchant and the Captain of the Forty Thieves."

Ali Baba was so grateful to Morgiana for thus saving his life that he offered her to his son in marriage, who readily consented, and a few days after the wedding was celebrated with greatest splendor.

At the end of a year Ali Baba, hearing nothing of the two remaining robbers, judged they were dead, and set out to the cave. The door opened on his saying, "Open Sesame!" He went in, and saw that nobody had been there since the Captain left it. He brought away as much gold as he could carry, and returned to town. He told his son the secret of the cave, which his son handed down in his turn, so the children and grandchildren of Ali Baba were rich to the end of their lives.

---

divert: distract

HOUSEHOLD TALES BY BROTHERS GRIMM

Jacob Grimm and Wilhelm Grimm (Translated by Margaret Hunt-1884)

The Frog-King, or Iron Henry

In old times when wishing still helped one, there lived a king whose daughters were all beautiful, but the youngest was so beautiful that the sun itself, which has seen so much, was astonished whenever it shone in her face. Close by the King's castle lay a great dark forest, and under an old lime-tree in the forest was a well, and when the day was very warm, the King's child went out into the forest and sat down by the side of the cool fountain, and when she was dull she took a golden ball, and threw it up on high and caught it, and this ball was her favorite plaything.

Now it so happened that on one occasion the princess's golden ball did not fall into the little hand which she was holding up for it, but on to the ground beyond, and rolled straight into the water. The King's daughter followed it with her eyes, but it vanished, and the well was deep, so deep that the bottom could not be seen. On this she began to cry, and cried louder and louder, and could not be comforted. And as she thus lamented some one said to her, "What ails thee, King's daughter? Thou weepest so that even a stone would show pity." She looked round to the side from whence the voice came, and saw a frog stretching forth its thick, ugly head from the water. "Ah! old water-splasher, is it thou?" said she; "I am weeping for my golden ball, which has fallen into the well."

"Be quiet, and do not weep," answered the frog, "I can help thee, but what wilt thou give me if I bring thy plaything up again?" "Whatever thou wilt have, dear frog," said she—"My clothes, my pearls and jewels, and even the golden crown which I am wearing."

The frog answered, "I do not care for thy clothes, thy pearls and jewels, or thy golden crown, but if thou wilt love me and let me be thy companion and play-fellow, and sit by thee at thy little table, and eat off thy little golden plate, and drink out of thy little cup, and sleep in thy little bed—-if thou wilt promise me this I will go down below, and bring thee thy golden ball up again."

"Oh yes," said she, "I promise thee all thou wishest, if thou wilt but bring me my ball back again." She, however, thought, "How the silly frog does talk! He lives in the water with the other frogs, and croaks, and can be no companion to any human being!"

But the frog when he had received this promise, put his head into the water and sank down, and in a short while came swimming up again with the ball in his mouth, and threw it on the grass. The King's daughter was delighted to see her pretty plaything once more, and picked it up, and ran away with it. "Wait, wait," said the frog. "Take me with thee. I can't run as thou canst." But what did

it ***avail*** him to scream his croak, croak, after her, as loudly as he could? She did not listen to it, but ran home and soon forgot the poor frog, who was forced to go back into his well again.

The next day when she had seated herself at table with the King and all the courtiers, and was eating from her little golden plate, something came creeping splish splash, splish splash, up the marble staircase, and when it had got to the top, it knocked at the door and cried, "Princess, youngest princess, open the door for me." She ran to see who was outside, but when she opened the door, there sat the frog in front of it. Then she slammed the door to, in great haste, sat down to dinner again, and was quite frightened. The King saw plainly that her heart was beating violently, and said, "My child, what art thou so afraid of? Is there perchance a giant outside who wants to carry thee away?" "Ah, no," replied she. "It is no giant but a disgusting frog."

"What does a frog want with thee?" "Ah, dear father, yesterday as I was in the forest sitting by the well, playing, my golden ball fell into the water. And because I cried so, the frog brought it out again for me, and because he so insisted, I promised him he should be my companion, but I never thought he would be able to come out of his water! And now he is outside there, and wants to come in to me."

In the meantime it knocked a second time, and cried,

"Princess! youngest princess!
Open the door for me!
Dost thou not know what thou saidst to me
Yesterday by the cool waters of the fountain?
Princess, youngest princess!
Open the door for me!"

Then said the King, "That which thou hast promised must thou perform. Go and let him in." She went and opened the door, and the frog hopped in and followed her, step by step, to her chair. There he sat and cried, "Lift me up beside thee." She delayed, until at last the King commanded her to do it. When the frog was once on the chair he wanted to be on the table, and when he was on the table he said, "Now, push thy little golden plate nearer to me that we may eat together." She did this, but it was easy to see that she did not do it willingly. The frog enjoyed what he ate, but almost every mouthful she took choked her. At length he said, "I have eaten and am satisfied; now I am tired, carry me into thy little room and make thy little silken bed ready, and we will both lie down and go to sleep."

The King's daughter began to cry, for she was afraid of the cold frog which she did not like to touch, and which was now to sleep in her pretty, clean little bed. But the King grew angry and said, "He who helped thee when thou wert in trouble ought not afterwards to be despised by thee." So she took hold of the frog with two fingers, carried him upstairs, and put him in a corner. But when she was in bed he crept to her and said, "I am tired, I want to sleep as well as thou, lift me up or I will tell thy father." Then she was terribly angry, and took

---

avail: gain

him up and threw him with all her might against the wall. "Now, thou wilt be quiet, ***odious*** frog," said she. But when he fell down he was no frog but a King's son with beautiful kind eyes. He by her father's will was now her dear companion and husband. Then he told her how he had been bewitched by a wicked witch, and how no one could have delivered him from the well but herself, and that to-morrow they would go together into his kingdom. Then they went to sleep, and next morning when the sun awoke them, a carriage came driving up with eight white horses, which had white ostrich feathers on their heads, and were harnessed with golden chains, and behind stood the young King's servant Faithful Henry. Faithful Henry had been so unhappy when his master was changed into a frog, that he had caused three iron bands to be laid round his heart, lest it should burst with grief and sadness. The carriage was to conduct the young King into his Kingdom. Faithful Henry helped them both in, and placed himself behind again, and was full of joy because of this deliverance. And when they had driven a part of the way the King's son heard a cracking behind him as if something had broken. So he turned round and cried, "Henry, the carriage is breaking."

"No, master, it is not the carriage. It is a band from my heart, which was put there in my great pain when you were a frog and imprisoned in the well." Again and once again while they were on their way something cracked, and each time the King's son thought the carriage was breaking; but it was only the bands which were springing from the heart of faithful Henry because his master was set free and was happy.

Rapunzel

There were once a man and a woman who had long in vain wished for a child. At length the woman hoped that God was about to grant her desire. These people had a little window at the back of their house from which a splendid garden could be seen, which was full of the most beautiful flowers and herbs. It was, however, surrounded by a high wall, and no one dared to go into it because it belonged to an enchantress, who had great power and was dreaded by all the world. One day the woman was standing by this window and looking down into the garden, when she saw a bed which was planted with the most beautiful rampion (rapunzel), and it looked so fresh and green that she longed for it, and had the greatest desire to eat some. This desire increased every day, and as she knew that she could not get any of it, she quite pined away, and looked pale and miserable. Then her husband was alarmed, and asked, "What aileth thee, dear wife?" "Ah," she replied, "if I can't get some of the rampion, which is in the garden behind our house, to eat, I shall die." The man, who loved her, thought, "Sooner than let thy wife die, bring her some of the rampion thyself, let it cost thee what it will." In the twilight of the evening, he clambered down over the wall into the garden of the enchantress, hastily clutched a handful of rampion,

---

odious: repulsive

and took it to his wife. She at once made herself a salad of it, and ate it with much relish. She, however, liked it so much—-so very much, that the next day she longed for it three times as much as before. If he was to have any rest, her husband must once more descend into the garden. In the gloom of evening, therefore, he let himself down again; but when he had clambered down the wall he was terribly afraid, for he saw the enchantress standing before him. "How canst thou dare," said she with angry look, "to descend into my garden and steal my rampion like a thief? Thou shalt suffer for it!" "Ah," answered he, "let mercy take the place of justice, I only made up my mind to do it out of necessity. My wife saw your rampion from the window, and felt such a longing for it that she would have died if she had not got some to eat." Then the enchantress allowed her anger to be softened, and said to him, "If the case be as thou sayest, I will allow thee to take away with thee as much rampion as thou wilt, only I make one condition, thou must give me the child which thy wife will bring into the world; it shall be well treated, and I will care for it like a mother." The man in his terror consented to everything, and when the woman was brought to bed, the enchantress appeared at once, gave the child the name of Rapunzel, and took it away with her.

Rapunzel grew into the most beautiful child beneath the sun. When she was twelve years old, the enchantress shut her into a tower, which lay in a forest, and had neither stairs nor door, but quite at the top was a little window. When the enchantress wanted to go in, she placed herself beneath it and cried,

"Rapunzel, Rapunzel,
Let down thy hair to me."

Rapunzel had magnificent long hair, fine as spun gold, and when she heard the voice of the enchantress she unfastened her braided tresses, wound them round one of the hooks of the window above, and then the hair fell twenty ells down, and the enchantress climbed up by it.

After a year or two, it came to pass that the King's son rode through the forest and went by the tower. Then he heard a song, which was so charming that he stood still and listened. This was Rapunzel, who in her solitude passed her time in letting her sweet voice resound. The King's son wanted to climb up to her, and looked for the door of the tower, but none was to be found. He rode home, but the singing had so deeply touched his heart, that every day he went out into the forest and listened to it. Once when he was thus standing behind a tree, he saw that an enchantress came there, and he heard how she cried,

"Rapunzel, Rapunzel,
Let down thy hair."

Then Rapunzel let down the braids of her hair, and the enchantress climbed up to her. "If that is the ladder by which one mounts, I will for once try my fortune," said he, and the next day when it began to grow dark, he went to the tower and cried,

"Rapunzel, Rapunzel,
Let down thy hair."

Immediately the hair fell down and the King's son climbed up.

At first Rapunzel was terribly frightened when a man such as her eyes had never yet beheld, came to her; but the King's son began to talk to her quite like a friend, and told her that his heart had been so stirred that it had let him have no rest, and he had been forced to see her. Then Rapunzel lost her fear, and when he asked her if she would take him for her husband, and she saw that he was young and handsome, she thought, "He will love me more than old Dame Gothel does;" and she said yes, and laid her hand in his. She said, "I will willingly go away with thee, but I do not know how to get down. Bring with thee a skein of silk every time that thou comest, and I will weave a ladder with it, and when that is ready I will descend, and thou wilt take me on thy horse." They agreed that until that time he should come to her every evening, for the old woman came by day. The enchantress remarked nothing of this, until once Rapunzel said to her, "Tell me, Dame Gothel, how it happens that you are so much heavier for me to draw up than the young King's son—-he is with me in a moment." "Ah! thou wicked child," cried the enchantress "What do I hear thee say! I thought I had separated thee from all the world, and yet thou hast deceived me." In her anger she clutched Rapunzel's beautiful tresses, wrapped them twice round her left hand, seized a pair of scissors with the right, and snip, snap, they were cut off, and the lovely braids lay on the ground. And she was so pitiless that she took poor Rapunzel into a desert where she had to live in great grief and misery.

On the same day, however, that she cast out Rapunzel, the enchantress in the evening fastened the braids of hair which she had cut off, to the hook of the window, and when the King's son came and cried,

"Rapunzel, Rapunzel,
Let down thy hair,"

she let the hair down. The King's son ascended, but he did not find his dearest Rapunzel above, but the enchantress, who gazed at him with wicked and venomous looks. "Aha!" she cried mockingly, "Thou wouldst fetch thy dearest, but the beautiful bird sits no longer singing in the nest; the cat has got it, and will scratch out thy eyes as well. Rapunzel is lost to thee; thou wilt never see her more." The King's son was beside himself with pain, and in his despair he leapt down from the tower. He escaped with his life, but the thorns into which he fell, pierced his eyes. Then he wandered quite blind about the forest, ate nothing but roots and berries, and did nothing but lament and weep over the loss of his dearest wife. Thus he roamed about in misery for some years, and at length came to the desert where Rapunzel, with the twins to which she had given birth, a boy and a girl, lived in wretchedness. He heard a voice, and it seemed so familiar to him that he went towards it, and when he approached, Rapunzel knew him and fell on his neck and wept. Two of her tears wetted his eyes and they grew clear again, and he could see with them as before. He led her to his kingdom where he was joyfully received, and they lived for a long time afterwards, happy and contented.

Hansel and Grethel

Hard by a great forest dwelt a poor wood-cutter with his wife and his two children. The boy was called Hansel and the girl Grethel. He had little to bite and to break, and once when great scarcity fell on the land, he could no longer procure daily bread. Now when he thought over this by night in his bed, and tossed about in his anxiety, he groaned and said to his wife, "What is to become of us? How are we to feed our poor children, when we no longer have anything even for ourselves?" "I'll tell you what, husband," answered the woman, "Early to-morrow morning we will take the children out into the forest to where it is the thickest, there we will light a fire for them, and give each of them one piece of bread more, and then we will go to our work and leave them alone. They will not find the way home again, and we shall be rid of them." "No, wife," said the man, "I will not do that; how can I bear to leave my children alone in the forest?--the wild animals would soon come and tear them to pieces." "O, thou fool!" said she, "Then we must all four die of hunger, thou mayest as well plane the planks for our coffins," and she left him no peace until he consented. "But I feel very sorry for the poor children, all the same," said the man.

The two children had also not been able to sleep for hunger, and had heard what their step-mother had said to their father. Grethel wept bitter tears, and said to Hansel, "Now all is over with us." "Be quiet, Grethel," said Hansel, "do not distress thyself, I will soon find a way to help us." And when the old folks had fallen asleep, he got up, put on his little coat, opened the door below, and crept outside. The moon shone brightly, and the white pebbles which lay in front of the house glittered like real silver pennies. Hansel stooped and put as many of them in the little pocket of his coat as he could possibly get in. Then he went back and said to Grethel, "Be comforted, dear little sister, and sleep in peace, God will not forsake us," and he lay down again in his bed. When day dawned, but before the sun had risen, the woman came and awoke the two children, saying "Get up, you sluggards! We are going into the forest to fetch wood." She gave each a little piece of bread, and said, "There is something for your dinner, but do not eat it up before then, for you will get nothing else." Grethel took the bread under her apron, as Hansel had the stones in his pocket. Then they all set out together on the way to the forest. When they had walked a short time, Hansel stood still and peeped back at the house, and did so again and again. His father said, "Hansel, what art thou looking at there and staying behind for? Mind what thou art about, and do not forget how to use thy legs." "Ah, father," said Hansel, "I am looking at my little white cat, which is sitting up on the roof, and wants to say good-bye to me." The wife said, "Fool, that is not thy little cat, that is the morning sun which is shining on the chimneys." Hansel, however, had not been looking back at the cat, but had been constantly throwing one of the white pebble-stones out of his pocket on the road.

When they had reached the middle of the forest, the father said, "Now, children, pile up some wood, and I will light a fire that you may not be cold." Hansel and Grethel gathered brushwood together, as high as a little hill. The

©Scusi/Dreamstime.com

brushwood was lighted, and when the flames were burning very high, the woman said, "Now, children, lay yourselves down by the fire and rest, we will go into the forest and cut some wood. When we have done, we will come back and fetch you away."

Hansel and Grethel sat by the fire, and when noon came, each ate a little piece of bread, and as they heard the strokes of the wood-axe they believed that their father was near. It was not, however, the axe, it was a branch which he had fastened to a withered tree which the wind was blowing backwards and forwards. And as they had been sitting such a long time, their eyes shut with fatigue, and they fell fast asleep. When at last they awoke, it was already dark night. Grethel began to cry and said, "How are we to get out of the forest now?" But Hansel comforted her and said, "Just wait a little, until the moon has risen, and then we will soon find the way." And when the full moon had risen, Hansel took his little sister by the hand, and followed the pebbles which shone like newly-coined silver pieces, and showed them the way.

They walked the whole night long, and by break of day came once more to their father's house. They knocked at the door, and when the woman opened it and saw that it was Hansel and Grethel, she said, "You naughty children, why have you slept so long in the forest?--we thought you were never coming back at all!" The father, however, rejoiced, for it had cut him to the heart to leave them behind alone.

Not long afterwards, there was once more great scarcity in all parts, and the children heard their mother saying at night to their father, "Everything is eaten again, we have one half loaf left, and after that there is an end. The children must go, we will take them farther into the wood, so that they will not find their way out again; there is no other means of saving ourselves!" The man's heart was heavy, and he thought "it would be better for thee to share the last mouthful with thy children." The woman, however, would listen to nothing that he had to say, but scolded and reproached him. He who says A must say B, likewise, and as he had yielded the first time, he had to do so a second time also.

The children were, however, still awake and had heard the conversation. When the old folks were asleep, Hansel again got up, and wanted to go out and pick up pebbles as he had done before, but the woman had locked the door, and Hansel could not get out. Nevertheless he comforted his little sister, and said, "Do not cry, Grethel, go to sleep quietly, the good God will help us."

Early in the morning came the woman, and took the children out of their beds. Their bit of bread was given to them, but it was still smaller than the time before. On the way into the forest Hansel crumbled his in his pocket, and often stood still and threw a morsel on the ground. "Hansel, why dost thou stop and look round?" said the father, "go on." "I am looking back at my little pigeon which is sitting on the roof, and wants to say good-bye to me," answered Hansel. "Simpleton!" said the woman, "that is not thy little pigeon, that is the morning sun that is shining on the chimney." Hansel, however, little by little, threw all the crumbs on the path.

The woman led the children still deeper into the forest, where they had never in their lives been before. Then a great fire was again made, and the mother said,

"Just sit there, you children, and when you are tired you may sleep a little; we are going into the forest to cut wood, and in the evening when we are done, we will come and fetch you away." When it was noon, Grethel shared her piece of bread with Hansel, who had scattered his by the way. Then they fell asleep and evening came and went, but no one came to the poor children. They did not awake until it was dark night, and Hansel comforted his little sister and said, "Just wait, Grethel, until the moon rises, and then we shall see the crumbs of bread which I have strewn about, they will show us our way home again." When the moon came they set out, but they found no crumbs, for the many thousands of birds which fly about in the woods and fields had picked them all up. Hansel said to Grethel, "We shall soon find the way," but they did not find it. They walked the whole night and all the next day too from morning till evening, but they did not get out of the forest, and were very hungry, for they had nothing to eat but two or three berries, which grew on the ground. And as they were so weary that their legs would carry them no longer, they lay down beneath a tree and fell asleep.

It was now three mornings since they had left their father's house. They began to walk again, but they always got deeper into the forest, and if help did not come soon, they must die of hunger and weariness. When it was mid-day, they saw a beautiful snow-white bird sitting on a bough, which sang so delightfully that they stood still and listened to it. And when it had finished its song, it spread its wings and flew away before them, and they followed it until they reached a little house, on the roof of which it alighted; and when they came quite up to little house they saw that it was built of bread and covered with cakes, but that the windows were of clear sugar. "We will set to work on that," said Hansel, "and have a good meal. I will eat a bit of the roof, and thou, Grethel, canst eat some of the window, it will taste sweet." Hansel reached up above, and broke off a little of the roof to try how it tasted, and Grethel leant against the window and nibbled at the panes. Then a soft voice cried from the room,

"Nibble, nibble, gnaw,
Who is nibbling at my little house?"

The children answered,

"The wind, the wind,
The heaven-born wind,"

and went on eating without disturbing themselves. Hansel, who thought the roof tasted very nice, tore down a great piece of it, and Grethel pushed out the whole of one round window-pane, sat down, and enjoyed herself with it. Suddenly the door opened, and a very, very old woman, who supported herself on crutches, came creeping out. Hansel and Grethel were so terribly frightened that they let fall what they had in their hands. The old woman, however, nodded her head, and said, "Oh, you dear children, who has brought you here? Do come in, and stay with me. No harm shall happen to you." She took them both by the hand, and led them into her little house. Then good food was set before them, milk and pancakes, with sugar, apples, and nuts. Afterwards two pretty little beds were covered with clean white linen, and Hansel and Grethel lay down in them, and thought they were in heaven.

The old woman had only pretended to be so kind; she was in reality a wicked witch, who lay in wait for children, and had only built the little house of bread in order to entice them there. When a child fell into her power, she killed it, cooked and ate it, and that was a feast day with her. Witches have red eyes, and cannot see far, but they have a keen scent like the beasts, and are aware when human beings draw near. When Hansel and Grethel came into her neighborhood, she laughed maliciously, and said mockingly, "I have them, they shall not escape me again!" Early in the morning before the children were awake, she was already up, and when she saw both of them sleeping and looking so pretty, with their plump red cheeks, she muttered to herself, "That will be a dainty mouthful!" Then she seized Hansel with her shrivelled hand, carried him into a little stable, and shut him in with a grated door. He might scream as he liked, that was of no use. Then she went to Grethel, shook her till she awoke, and cried, "Get up, lazy thing, fetch some water, and cook something good for thy brother, he is in the stable outside, and is to be made fat. When he is fat, I will eat him." Grethel began to weep bitterly, but it was all in vain, she was forced to do what the wicked witch ordered her.

And now the best food was cooked for poor Hansel, but Grethel got nothing but crab-shells. Every morning the woman crept to the little stable, and cried, "Hansel, stretch out thy finger that I may feel if thou wilt soon be fat." Hansel, however, stretched out a little bone to her, and the old woman, who had dim eyes, could not see it, and thought it was Hansel's finger, and was astonished that there was no way of fattening him. When four weeks had gone by, and Hansel still continued thin, she was seized with impatience and would not wait any longer. "Hola, Grethel," she cried to the girl, "be active, and bring some water. Let Hansel be fat or lean, to-morrow I will kill him, and cook him." Ah, how the poor little sister did lament when she had to fetch the water, and how her tears did flow down over her cheeks! "Dear God, do help us," she cried. "If the wild beasts in the forest had but devoured us, we should at any rate have died together." "Just keep thy noise to thyself," said the old woman, "all that won't help thee at all."

Early in the morning, Grethel had to go out and hang up the cauldron with the water, and light the fire. "We will bake first," said the old woman, "I have already heated the oven, and kneaded the dough." She pushed poor Grethel out to the oven, from which flames of fire were already darting. "Creep in," said the witch, "and see if it is properly heated, so that we can shut the bread in." And when once Grethel was inside, she intended to shut the oven and let her bake in it, and then she would eat her, too. But Grethel saw what she had in her mind, and said, "I do not know how I am to do it; how do you get in?" "Silly goose," said the old woman, "The door is big enough; just look, I can get in myself!" and she crept up and thrust her head into the oven. Then Grethel gave her a push that drove her far into it, and shut the iron door, and fastened the bolt. Oh! then she began to howl quite horribly, but Grethel ran away, and the godless witch was miserably burnt to death.

Grethel, however, ran like lightning to Hansel, opened his little stable, and cried, "Hansel, we are saved! The old witch is dead!" Then Hansel sprang out like a bird from its cage when the door is opened for it. How they did rejoice and embrace each other, and dance about and kiss each other! And as they had no longer any need to fear her, they went into the witch's house, and in every corner there stood chests full of pearls and jewels. "These are far better than pebbles!" said Hansel, and thrust into his pockets whatever could be got in, and Grethel said, "I, too, will take something home with me," and filled her pinafore full. "But now we will go away." said Hansel, "that we may get out of the witch's forest."

When they had walked for two hours, they came to a great piece of water. "We cannot get over," said Hansel, "I see no foot-plank, and no bridge." "And no boat crosses either," answered Grethel, "but a white duck is swimming there; if I ask her, she will help us over." Then she cried,

"Little duck, little duck, dost thou see,
Hansel and Grethel are waiting for thee?
There's never a plank, or bridge in sight,
Take us across on thy back so white."

The duck came to them, and Hansel seated himself on its back, and told his sister to sit by him. "No," replied Grethel, "that will be too heavy for the little duck; she shall take us across, one after the other." The good little duck did so, and when they were once safely across and had walked for a short time, the forest seemed to be more and more familiar to them, and at length they saw from afar their father's house. Then they began to run, rushed into the parlour, and threw themselves into their father's arms. The man had not known one happy hour since he had left the children in the forest; the woman, however, was dead. Grethel emptied her pinafore until pearls and precious stones ran about the room, and Hansel threw one handful after another out of his pocket to add to them. Then all anxiety was at an end, and they lived together in perfect happiness. My tale is done, there runs a mouse, whosoever catches it, may make himself a big fur cap out of it.

Cinderella

The wife of a rich man fell sick, and as she felt that her end was drawing near, she called her only daughter to her bedside and said, "Dear child, be good and pious, and then the good God will always protect thee, and I will look down on thee from heaven and be near thee." Thereupon she closed her eyes and departed. Every day the maiden went out to her mother's grave, and wept, and she remained pious and good. When winter came the snow spread a white sheet over the grave, and when the spring sun had drawn it off again, the man had taken another wife.

The woman had brought two daughters into the house with her, who were beautiful and fair of face, but ***vile*** and black of heart. Now began a bad time for

---

vile: wicked

the poor step-child. "Is the stupid goose to sit in the parlour with us?" said they. "He who wants to eat bread must earn it; out with the kitchen-wench." They took her pretty clothes away from her, put an old grey bedgown on her, and gave her wooden shoes. "Just look at the proud princess, how decked out she is!" they cried, and laughed, and led her into the kitchen. There she had to do hard work from morning till night, get up before daybreak, carry water, light fires, cook and wash. Besides this, the sisters did her every imaginable injury — they mocked her and emptied her peas and lentils into the ashes, so that she was forced to sit and pick them out again. In the evening when she had worked till she was weary she had no bed to go to, but had to sleep by the fireside in the ashes. And as on that account she always looked dusty and dirty, they called her Cinderella. It happened that the father was once going to the fair, and he asked his two step-daughters what he should bring back for them. "Beautiful dresses," said one, "Pearls and jewels," said the second. "And thou, Cinderella," said he, "what wilt thou have?" "Father, break off for me the first branch which knocks against your hat on your way home." So he bought beautiful dresses, pearls and jewels for his two step-daughters, and on his way home, as he was riding through a green thicket, a hazel twig brushed against him and knocked off his hat. Then he broke off the branch and took it with him. When he reached home he gave his step-daughters the things which they had wished for, and to Cinderella he gave the branch from the hazel-bush. Cinderella thanked him, went to her mother's grave and planted the branch on it, and wept so much that the tears fell down on it and watered it. And it grew, however, and became a handsome tree. Thrice a day Cinderella went and sat beneath it, and wept and prayed, and a little white bird always came on the tree, and if Cinderella expressed a wish, the bird threw down to her what she had wished for.

It happened, however, that the King appointed a festival which was to last three days, and to which all the beautiful young girls in the country were invited, in order that his son might choose himself a bride. When the two step-sisters heard that they too were to appear among the number, they were delighted, called Cinderella and said, "Comb our hair for us, brush our shoes and fasten our buckles, for we are going to the festival at the King's palace." Cinderella obeyed, but wept, because she too would have liked to go with them to the dance, and begged her step-mother to allow her to do so. "Thou go, Cinderella!" said she; "Thou art dusty and dirty and wouldst go to the festival? Thou hast no clothes and shoes, and yet wouldst dance!" As, however, Cinderella went on asking, the step-mother at last said, "I have emptied a dish of lentils into the ashes for thee, if thou hast picked them out again in two hours, thou shalt go with us." The maiden went through the back-door into the garden, and called, "You tame pigeons, you turtle-doves, and all you birds beneath the sky, come and help me to pick

"The good into the pot,
The bad into the crop."

Then two white pigeons came in by the kitchen-window, and afterwards the turtle-doves, and at last all the birds beneath the sky, came whirring and crowding in, and alighted amongst the ashes. And the pigeons nodded with their

heads and began pick, pick, pick, pick, and the rest began also pick, pick, pick, pick, and gathered all the good grains into the dish. Hardly had one hour passed before they had finished, and all flew out again. Then the girl took the dish to her step-mother, and was glad, and believed that now she would be allowed to go with them to the festival. But the step-mother said, "No, Cinderella, thou hast no clothes and thou canst not dance; thou wouldst only be laughed at." And as Cinderella wept at this, the step-mother said, "If thou canst pick two dishes of lentils out of the ashes for me in one hour, thou shalt go with us." And she thought to herself, "That she most certainly cannot do." When the step-mother had emptied the two dishes of lentils amongst the ashes, the maiden went through the back-door into the garden and cried, You tame pigeons, you turtle-doves, and all you birds under heaven, come and help me to pick

"The good into the pot,
The bad into the crop."

Then two white pigeons came in by the kitchen-window, and afterwards the turtle-doves, and at length all the birds beneath the sky, came whirring and crowding in, and alighted amongst the ashes. And the doves nodded with their heads and began pick, pick, pick, pick, and the others began also pick, pick, pick, pick, and gathered all the good seeds into the dishes, and before half an hour was over they had already finished, and all flew out again. Then the maiden carried the dishes to the step-mother and was delighted, and believed that she might now go with them to the festival. But the step-mother said, "All this will not help thee; thou goest not with us, for thou hast no clothes and canst not dance; we should be ashamed of thee!" On this she turned her back on Cinderella, and hurried away with her two proud daughters.

As no one was now at home, Cinderella went to her mother's grave beneath the hazel-tree, and cried,

"Shiver and quiver, little tree,
Silver and gold throw down over me."

Then the bird threw a gold and silver dress down to her, and slippers embroidered with silk and silver. She put on the dress with all speed, and went to the festival. Her step-sisters and the step-mother however did not know her, and thought she must be a foreign princess, for she looked so beautiful in the golden dress. They never once thought of Cinderella, and believed that she was sitting at home in the dirt, picking lentils out of the ashes. The prince went to meet her, took her by the hand and danced with her. He would dance with no other maiden, and never left loose of her hand, and if anyone else came to invite her, he said, "This is my partner."

She danced till it was evening, and then she wanted to go home. But the King's son said, "I will go with thee and bear thee company," for he wished to see to whom the beautiful maiden belonged. She escaped from him, however, and sprang into the pigeon-house. The King's son waited until her father came, and then he told him that the stranger maiden had leapt into the pigeon-house. The old man thought, "Can it be Cinderella?" and they had to bring him an axe and a pickaxe that he might hew the pigeon-house to pieces, but no one was inside it. And when they got home Cinderella lay in her dirty clothes among the ashes, and a dim little oil-lamp was burning on the mantle-piece, for Cinderella had jumped quickly down from the back of the pigeon-house and had run to the little hazel-tree, and there she had taken off her beautiful clothes and laid them on the grave, and the bird had taken them away again, and then she had placed herself in the kitchen amongst the ashes in her grey gown.

Next day when the festival began afresh, and her parents and the step-sisters had gone once more, Cinderella went to the hazel-tree and said—-

"Shiver and quiver, my little tree,
Silver and gold throw down over me."

Then the bird threw down a much more beautiful dress than on the preceding day. And when Cinderella appeared at the festival in this dress, everyone was astonished at her beauty. The King's son had waited until she came, and instantly took her by the hand and danced with no one but her. When others came and invited her, he said, "She is my partner." When evening came she wished to leave, and the King's son followed her and wanted to see into which house she went. But she sprang away from him, and into the garden behind the house. Therein stood a beautiful tall tree on which hung the most magnificent pears. She clambered so nimbly between the branches like a squirrel that the King's son did not know where she was gone. He waited until her father came, and said to him, "The stranger-maiden has escaped from me, and I believe she has climbed up the pear-tree." The father thought, "Can it be Cinderella?" and had an axe brought and cut the tree down, but no one was on it. And when they got into the kitchen, Cinderella lay there amongst the ashes, as usual, for she had jumped down on the other side of the tree, had taken the beautiful dress to the bird on the little hazel-tree, and put on her grey gown.

On the third day, when the parents and sisters had gone away, Cinderella went once more to her mother's grave and said to the little tree—-

"Shiver and quiver, my little tree,
Silver and gold throw down over me."

And now the bird threw down to her a dress which was more splendid and magnificent than any she had yet had, and the slippers were golden. And when she went to the festival in the dress, no one knew how to speak for astonishment. The King's son danced with her only, and if any one invited her to dance, he said, "She is my partner."

When evening came, Cinderella wished to leave, and the King's son was anxious to go with her, but she escaped from him so quickly that he could not follow her. The King's son had, however, used a ***stratagem***, and had caused the whole staircase to be smeared with pitch, and there, when she ran down, had the maiden's left slipper remained sticking. The King's son picked it up, and it was small and dainty, and all golden. Next morning, he went with it to the father, and said to him, "No one shall be my wife but she whose foot this golden slipper fits." Then were the two sisters glad, for they had pretty feet. The eldest went with the shoe into her room and wanted to try it on, and her mother stood by. But she could not get her big toe into it, and the shoe was too small for her. Then

---

stratagem: scheme

© Ginosphotos /Dreamstime.com

her mother gave her a knife and said, "Cut the toe off; when thou art Queen thou wilt have no more need to go on foot." The maiden cut the toe off, forced the foot into the shoe, swallowed the pain, and went out to the King's son. Then he took her on his horse as his bride and rode away with her. They were, however, obliged to pass the grave, and there, on the hazel-tree, sat the two pigeons and cried,

"Turn and peep, turn and peep,
There's blood within the shoe,
The shoe it is too small for her,
The true bride waits for you."

Then he looked at her foot and saw how the blood was streaming from it. He turned his horse round and took the false bride home again, and said she was not the true one, and that the other sister was to put the shoe on. Then this one went into her chamber and got her toes safely into the shoe, but her heel was too large. So her mother gave her a knife and said, "Cut a bit off thy heel; when thou art Queen thou wilt have no more need to go on foot." The maiden cut a bit off her heel, forced her foot into the shoe, swallowed the pain, and went out to the King's son. He took her on his horse as his bride, and rode away with her, but when they passed by the hazel-tree, two little pigeons sat on it and cried,

"Turn and peep, turn and peep,
There's blood within the shoe
The shoe it is too small for her,
The true bride waits for you."

He looked down at her foot and saw how the blood was running out of her shoe, and how it had stained her white stocking. Then he turned his horse and took the false bride home again. "This also is not the right one," said he, "have you no other daughter?" "No," said the man, "There is still a little stunted kitchen-wench which my late wife left behind her, but she cannot possibly be the bride." The King's son said he was to send her up to him; but the mother answered, "Oh, no, she is much too dirty, she cannot show herself!" He absolutely insisted on it, and Cinderella had to be called. She first washed her hands and face clean, and then went and bowed down before the King's son, who gave her the golden shoe. Then she seated herself on a stool, drew her foot out of the heavy wooden shoe, and put it into the slipper, which fitted like a glove. And when she rose up and the King's son looked at her face he recognized the beautiful maiden who had danced with him and cried, "That is the true bride!" The step-mother and the two sisters were terrified and became pale with rage; he, however, took Cinderella on his horse and rode away with her. As they passed by the hazel-tree, the two white doves cried,

"Turn and peep, turn and peep,
No blood is in the shoe,
The shoe is not too small for her,
The true bride rides with you,"

and when they had cried that, the two came flying down and placed themselves on Cinderella's shoulders, one on the right, the other on the left, and remained sitting there.

When the wedding with the King's son had to be celebrated, the two false sisters came and wanted to get into favour with Cinderella and share her good fortune. When the betrothed couple went to church, the elder was at the right side and the younger at the left, and the pigeons pecked out one eye of each of them. Afterwards as they came back, the elder was at the left, and the younger at the right, and then the pigeons pecked out the other eye of each. And thus, for their wickedness and falsehood, they were punished with blindness as long as they lived.

Mother Holle

There was once a widow who had two daughters—-one of whom was pretty and industrious, whilst the other was ugly and idle. But she was much fonder of the ugly and idle one, because she was her own daughter; and the other, who was a step-daughter, was obliged to do all the work, and be the Cinderella of the house. Every day the poor girl had to sit by a well, in the highway, and spin and spin till her fingers bled.

Now it happened that one day the shuttle was marked with her blood, so she dipped it in the well, to wash the mark off; but it dropped out of her hand and fell to the bottom. She began to weep, and ran to her step-mother and told her of the mishap. But she scolded her sharply, and was so merciless as to say, "Since you have let the shuttle fall in, you must fetch it out again."

So the girl went back to the well, and did not know what to do; and in the sorrow of her heart she jumped into the well to get the shuttle. She lost her senses; and when she awoke and came to herself again, she was in a lovely meadow where the sun was shining and many thousands of flowers were growing. Along this meadow she went, and at last came to a baker's oven full of bread, and the bread cried out, "Oh, take me out! Take me out! Or I shall burn; I have been baked a long time!" So she went up to it, and took out all the loaves one after another with the bread-shovel. After that she went on till she came to a tree covered with apples, which called out to her, "Oh, shake me! Shake me! We apples are all ripe!" So she shook the tree till the apples fell like rain, and went on shaking till they were all down, and when she had gathered them into a heap, she went on her way.

At last she came to a little house, out of which an old woman peeped; but she had such large teeth that the girl was frightened, and was about to run away.

But the old woman called out to her, "What are you afraid of, dear child? Stay with me; if you will do all the work in the house properly, you shall be the better for it. Only you must take care to make my bed well, and shake it thoroughly till the feathers fly--for then there is snow on the earth. I am Mother Holle.

As the old woman spoke so kindly to her, the girl took courage and agreed to enter her service. She attended to everything to the satisfaction of her mistress, and always shook her bed so vigorously that the feathers flew about like snow-flakes. So she had a pleasant life with her; never an angry word; and boiled or roast meat every day.

She stayed some time with Mother Holle, and then she became sad. At first she did not know what was the matter with her, but found at length that it was home-sickness: although she was many thousand times better off here than at home, still she had a longing to be there. At last she said to the old woman, "I have a longing for home; and however well off I am down here, I cannot stay any longer; I must go up again to my own people." Mother Holle said, "I am pleased that you long for your home again, and as you have served me so truly, I myself will take you up again." Thereupon she took her by the hand, and led her to a large door. The door was opened, and just as the maiden was standing beneath the doorway, a heavy shower of golden rain fell, and all the gold remained sticking to her, so that she was completely covered over with it.

"You shall have that because you have been so industrious," said Mother Holle, and at the same time she gave her back the shuttle which she had let fall into the well. Thereupon the door closed, and the maiden found herself up above upon the earth, not far from her mother's house.

And as she went into the yard the cock was standing by the well-side, and cried--

"Cock-a-doodle-doo!

Your golden girl's come back to you!"

So she went in to her mother, and as she arrived thus covered with gold, she was well received, both by her and her sister.

The girl told all that had happened to her; and as soon as the mother heard how she had come by so much wealth, she was very anxious to obtain the same good luck for the ugly and lazy daughter. She had to seat herself by the well and spin; and in order that her shuttle might be stained with blood, she stuck her hand into a thorn bush and pricked her finger. Then she threw her shuttle into the well, and jumped in after it.

She came, like the other, to the beautiful meadow and walked along the very same path. When she got to the oven the bread again cried, "Oh, take me out! Take me out! Or I shall burn; I have been baked a long time!" But the lazy thing answered, "As if I had any wish to make myself dirty?" and on she went. Soon she came to the apple-tree, which cried, "Oh, shake me! Shake me! We apples are all ripe!" But she answered, "I like that! One of you might fall on my head," and so went on.

When she came to Mother Holle's house she was not afraid, for she had already heard of her big teeth, and she hired herself to her immediately.

The first day she forced herself to work diligently, and obeyed Mother Holle when she told her to do anything, for she was thinking of all the gold that she would give her. But on the second day she began to be lazy, and on the third day still more so, and then she would not get up in the morning at all. Neither did she make Mother Holle's bed as she ought, and did not shake it so as to make the feathers fly up. Mother Holle was soon tired of this, and gave her notice to leave. The lazy girl was willing enough to go, and thought that now the golden rain would come. Mother Holle led her also to the great door; but while she was standing beneath it, instead of the gold a big kettleful of pitch was emptied over her. "That is the reward for your service," said Mother Holle, and shut the door.

So the lazy girl went home; but she was quite covered with pitch, and the cock by the well-side, as soon as he saw her, cried out--

"Cock-a-doodle-doo!
Your pitchy girl's come back to you!"

But the pitch stuck fast to her, and could not be got off as long as she lived.

Little Red-Cap

Once upon a time there was a dear little girl who was loved by every one who looked at her, but most of all by her grandmother, and there was nothing that she would not have given to the child. Once she gave her a little cap of red velvet, which suited her so well that she would never wear anything else; so she was always called "Little Red-Cap."

One day her mother said to her, "Come, Little Red-Cap, here is a piece of cake and a bottle of wine; take them to your grandmother, she is ill and weak, and they will do her good. Set out before it gets hot, and when you are going, walk nicely and quietly and do not run off the path, or you may fall and break the bottle, and then your grandmother will get nothing; and when you go into her room, don't forget to say, 'Good-morning,' and don't peep into every corner before you do it."

"I will take great care," said Little Red-Cap to her mother, and gave her hand on it.

The grandmother lived out in the wood, half a league from the village, and just as Little Red-Cap entered the wood, a wolf met her. Red-Cap did not know what a wicked creature he was, and was not at all afraid of him.

"Good-day, Little Red-Cap," said he.

"Thank you kindly, wolf."

"Whither away so early, Little Red-Cap?"

"To my grandmother's."

"What have you got in your apron?"

"Cake and wine; yesterday was baking-day, so poor sick grandmother is to have something good, to make her stronger."

"Where does your grandmother live, Little Red-Cap?"

"A good quarter of a league farther on in the wood; her house stands under the three large oak-trees, the nut-trees are just below; you surely must know it," replied Little Red-Cap.

The wolf thought to himself, "What a tender young creature! What a nice plump mouthful--she will be better to eat than the old woman. I must act ***craftily***, so as to catch both." So he walked for a short time by the side of Little Red-Cap, and then he said, "See Little Red-Cap, how pretty the flowers are about here--why do you not look round? I believe, too, that you do not hear how

---

craftily: cunningly

sweetly the little birds are singing; you walk gravely along as if you were going to school, while everything else out here in the wood is merry."

Little Red-Cap raised her eyes, and when she saw the sunbeams dancing here and there through the trees, and pretty flowers growing everywhere, she thought, "Suppose I take grandmother a fresh nosegay; that would please her too. It is so early in the day that I shall still get there in good time;" and so she ran from the path into the wood to look for flowers. And whenever she had picked one, she fancied that she saw a still prettier one farther on, and ran after it, and so got deeper and deeper into the wood.

Meanwhile the wolf ran straight to the grandmother's house and knocked at the door.

"Who is there?"

"Little Red-Cap," replied the wolf. "She is bringing cake and wine; open the door."

"Lift the latch," called out the grandmother, "I am too weak, and cannot get up."

The wolf lifted the latch, the door flew open, and without saying a word he went straight to the grandmother's bed, and devoured her. Then he put on her clothes, dressed himself in her cap, laid himself in bed and drew the curtains.

Little Red-Cap, however, had been running about picking flowers, and when she had gathered so many that she could carry no more, she remembered her grandmother, and set out on the way to her.

She was surprised to find the cottage-door standing open, and when she went into the room, she had such a strange feeling that she said to herself, "Oh dear! how uneasy I feel to-day, and at other times I like being with grandmother so much." She called out, "Good morning," but received no answer; so she went to the bed and drew back the curtains. There lay her grandmother with her cap pulled far over her face, and looking very strange.

"Oh! grandmother," she said, "what big ears you have!"

"The better to hear you with, my child," was the reply.

"But, grandmother, what big eyes you have!" she said.

"The better to see you with, my dear."

"But, grandmother, what large hands you have!"

"The better to hug you with."

"Oh! but, grandmother, what a terrible big mouth you have!"

"The better to eat you with!"

And scarcely had the wolf said this, than with one bound he was out of bed and swallowed up Red-Cap.

When the wolf had appeased his appetite, he lay down again in the bed, fell asleep and began to snore very loud. The huntsman was just passing the house, and thought to himself, "How the old woman is snoring! I must just see if she wants anything." So he went into the room, and when he came to the bed, he saw that the wolf was lying in it. "Do I find thee here, thou old sinner!" said he. "I have long sought thee!" Then just as he was going to fire at him, it occurred to him that the wolf might have devoured the grandmother, and that she might still be saved, so he did not fire, but took a pair of scissors, and began to cut open the stomach of the sleeping wolf. When he had made two snips, he saw the little Red-Cap shining, and then he made two snips more, and the little girl sprang out, crying, "Ah, how frightened I have been! How dark it was inside the wolf;" and after that the aged grandmother came out alive also, but scarcely able to breathe. Red-Cap, however, quickly fetched great stones with which they filled the wolf's body, and when he awoke, he wanted to run away, but the stones were so heavy that he fell down at once, and fell dead.

Then all three were delighted. The huntsman drew off the wolf's skin and went home with it; the grandmother ate the cake and drank the wine which Red-Cap had brought, and revived, but Red-Cap thought to herself, "As long as I live, I will never by myself leave the path, to run into the wood, when my mother has forbidden me to do so."

* * * * * * *

It is also related that once when Red-Cap was again taking cakes to the old grandmother, another wolf spoke to her, and tried to ***entice*** her from the path. Red-Cap, however, was on her guard, and went straight forward on her way, and told her grandmother that she had met the wolf, and that he had said "good-morning" to her, but with such a wicked look in his eyes, that if they had not been on the public road she was certain he would have eaten her up. "Well," said the grandmother, "we will shut the door, that he may not come in." Soon afterwards the wolf knocked, and cried, "Open the door, grandmother, I am little Red-Cap, and am fetching you some cakes." But they did not speak, or open the door, so the grey-beard stole twice or thrice round the house, and at last jumped on the roof, intending to wait until Red-Cap went home in the evening, and then to steal after her and devour her in the darkness. But the grandmother saw what was in his thoughts. In front of the house was a great stone trough, so she said to the child, "Take the pail, Red-Cap; I made some sausages yesterday, so carry the water in which I boiled them to the trough." Red-Cap carried until the great trough was quite full. Then the smell of the sausages reached the wolf, and he sniffed and peeped down, and at last stretched out his neck so far that he could no longer keep his footing and began to slip, and slipped down from the roof straight into the great trough, and was drowned. But Red-Cap went joyously home, and never did anything to harm anyone.

The Fisherman and His Wife

There was once on a time a Fisherman who lived with his wife in a miserable hovel close by the sea, and every day he went out fishing. And once as he was sitting with his rod, looking at the clear water, his line suddenly went down, far down below, and when he drew it up again he brought out a large

---

entice: lure

Flounder. Then the Flounder said to him, "Hark, you Fisherman, I pray you, let me live, I am no Flounder really, but an enchanted prince. What good will it do you to kill me? I should not be good to eat. Put me in the water again, and let me go." "Come," said the Fisherman, "there is no need for so many words about it--a fish that can talk I should certainly let go, anyhow," with that he put him back again into the clear water, and the Flounder went to the bottom, leaving a long streak of blood behind him. Then the Fisherman got up and went home to his wife in the hovel.

"Husband," said the woman, "have you caught nothing to-day?" "No," said the man, "I did catch a Flounder, who said he was an enchanted prince, so I let him go again." "Did you not wish for anything first?" said the woman. "No," said the man; "what should I wish for?" "Ah," said the woman, "it is surely hard to have to live always in this dirty hovel; you might have wished for a small cottage for us. Go back and call him. Tell him we want to have a small cottage; he will certainly give us that." "Ah," said the man, "why should I go there again?" "Why," said the woman, "you did catch him, and you let him go again; he is sure to do it. Go at once." The man still did not quite like to go, but did not like to oppose his wife, and went to the sea.

When he got there the sea was all green and yellow, and no longer so smooth; so he stood still and said,

"Flounder, flounder in the sea,
Come, I pray thee, here to me;
For my wife, good Ilsabil,
Wills not as I'd have her will."

Then the Flounder came swimming to him and said, "Well what does she want, then?" "Ah," said the man, "I did catch you, and my wife says I really ought to have wished for something. She does not like to live in a wretched hovel any longer. She would like to have a cottage." "Go, then," said the Flounder, "she has it already."

When the man went home, his wife was no longer in the hovel, but instead of it there stood a small cottage, and she was sitting on a bench before the door. Then she took him by the hand and said to him, "Just come inside, look, now isn't this a great deal better?" So they went in, and there was a small porch, and a pretty little parlor and bedroom, and a kitchen and pantry, with the best of furniture, and fitted up with the most beautiful things made of tin and brass, whatsoever was wanted. And behind the cottage there was a small yard, with hens and ducks, and a little garden with flowers and fruit. "Look," said the wife, "is not that nice!" "Yes," said the husband, "and so we must always think it, — now we will live quite contented." "We will think about that," said the wife. With that they ate something and went to bed.

Everything went well for a week or a fortnight, and then the woman said, "Hark you, husband, this cottage is far too small for us, and the garden and yard are little; the Flounder might just as well have given us a larger house. I should like to live in a great stone castle; go to the Flounder, and tell him to give us a castle." "Ah, wife," said the man, "the cottage is quite good enough; why should we live in a castle?" "What!" said the woman; "just go there, the Flounder can always do that." "No, wife," said the man, "the Flounder has just given us the cottage, I do not like to go back so soon, it might make him angry." "Go," said the woman, "he can do it quite easily, and will be glad to do it; just you go to him."

The man's heart grew heavy, and he would not go. He said to himself, "It is not right," and yet he went. And when he came to the sea the water was quite purple and dark-blue, and grey and thick, and no longer so green and yellow, but it was still quiet. And he stood there and said--

"Flounder, flounder in the sea,
Come, I pray thee, here to me;
For my wife, good Ilsabil,
Wills not as I'd have her will."

"Well, what does she want, then?" said the Flounder. "Alas," said the man, half scared, "she wants to live in a great stone castle." "Go to it, then, she is standing before the door," said the Flounder.

Then the man went away, intending to go home, but when he got there, he found a great stone palace, and his wife was just standing on the steps going in, and she took him by the hand and said, "Come in." So he went in with her, and in the castle was a great hall paved with marble, and many servants, who flung wide the doors; And the walls were all bright with beautiful hangings, and in the rooms were chairs and tables of pure gold, and crystal chandeliers hung from the ceiling, and all the rooms and bedrooms had carpets, and food and wine of the very best were standing on all the tables, so that they nearly broke down beneath it. Behind the house, too, there was a great court-yard, with stables for horses and cows, and the very best of carriages; there was a magnificent large garden, too, with the most beautiful flowers and fruit-trees, and a park quite half a mile long, in which were stags, deer, and hares, and everything that could be desired. "Come," said the woman, "isn't that beautiful?" "Yes, indeed," said the man, "now let it be; and we will live in this beautiful castle and be content." "We will consider about that," said the woman, "and sleep upon it;" thereupon they went to bed.

Next morning the wife awoke first, and it was just daybreak, and from her bed she saw the beautiful country lying before her. Her husband was still stretching himself, so she poked him in the side with her elbow, and said, "Get up, husband, and just peep out of the window. Look you, couldn't we be the King over all that land? Go to the Flounder, we will be the King." "Ah, wife," said the man, "why should we be King? I do not want to be King." "Well," said the wife, "if you won't be King, I will; go to the Flounder, for I will be King." "Ah, wife," said the man, "why do you want to be King? I do not like to say that to him." "Why not?" said the woman; "go to him this instant; I must be King!" So the man went, and was quite unhappy because his wife wished to be King. "It is not right; it is not right," thought he. He did not wish to go, but yet he went.

And when he came to the sea, it was quite dark-grey, and the water heaved up from below, and smelt putrid. Then he went and stood by it, and said,

"Flounder, flounder in the sea,
Come, I pray thee, here to me;

For my wife, good Ilsabil,
Wills not as I'd have her will"

"Well, what does she want, then?" said the Flounder. "Alas," said the man, "she wants to be King." "Go to her; she is King already."

So the man went, and when he came to the palace, the castle had become much larger, and had a great tower and magnificent ornaments, and the sentinel was standing before the door, and there were numbers of soldiers with kettle-drums and trumpets. And when he went inside the house, everything was of real marble and gold, with velvet covers and great golden tassels. Then the doors of the hall were opened, and there was the court in all its splendour, and his wife was sitting on a high throne of gold and diamonds, with a great crown of gold on her head, and a sceptre of pure gold and jewels in her hand, and on both sides of her stood her maids-in-waiting in a row, each of them always one head shorter than the last.

Then he went and stood before her, and said, "Ah, wife, and now you are King." "Yes," said the woman, "now I am King." So he stood and looked at her, and when he had looked at her thus for some time, he said, "And now that you are King, let all else be, now we will wish for nothing more." "Nay, husband," said the woman, quite anxiously, "I find time pass very heavily, I can bear it no longer; go to the Flounder--I am King, but I must be Emperor, too." "Alas, wife, why do you wish to be Emperor?" "Husband," said she, "go to the Flounder. I will be Emperor." "Alas, wife," said the man, "he cannot make you Emperor; I may not say that to the fish. There is only one Emperor in the land. An Emperor the Flounder cannot make you! I assure you he cannot."

"What!" said the woman, "I am the King, and you are nothing but my husband; will you go this moment? Go at once! If he can make a King he can make an emperor. I will be Emperor; go instantly." So he was forced to go. As the man went, however, he was troubled in mind, and thought to himself, "It will not end well; it will not end well! Emperor is too shameless! The Flounder will at last be tired out."

With that he reached the sea, and the sea was quite black and thick, and began to boil up from below, so that it threw up bubbles, and such a sharp wind blew over it that it curdled, and the man was afraid. Then he went and stood by it, and said,

"Flounder, flounder in the sea,
Come, I pray thee, here to me;
For my wife, good Ilsabil,
Wills not as I'd have her will."

"Well, what does she want, then?" said the Flounder. "Alas, Flounder," said he, "my wife wants to be Emperor." "Go to her," said the Flounder; "she is Emperor already."

So the man went, and when he got there the whole palace was made of polished marble with alabaster figures and golden ornaments, and soldiers were marching before the door blowing trumpets, and beating cymbals and drums; and in the house, barons, and counts, and dukes were going about as servants. Then they opened the doors to him, which were of pure gold. And when he entered, there sat his wife on a throne, which was made of one piece of gold, and was quite two miles high; and she wore a great golden crown that was three yards high, and set with diamonds and carbuncles, and in one hand she had the sceptre, and in the other the imperial orb; and on both sides of her stood the yeomen of the guard in two rows, each being smaller than the one before him, from the biggest giant, who was two miles high, to the very smallest dwarf, just as big as my little finger. And before it stood a number of princes and dukes.

Then the man went and stood among them, and said, "Wife, are you Emperor now?" "Yes," said she, "now I am Emperor." Then he stood and looked at her well, and when he had looked at her thus for some time, he said, "Ah, wife, be content, now that you are Emperor." "Husband," said she, "why are you standing there? Now, I am Emperor, but I will be Pope too; go to the Flounder." "Alas, wife," said the man, "what will you not wish for? You cannot be Pope. There is but one in Christendom. He cannot make you Pope." "Husband," said she, "I will be Pope; go immediately, I must be Pope this very day." "No, wife," said the man, "I do not like to say that to him; that would not do, it is too much; the Flounder can't make you Pope." "Husband," said she, "what nonsense! If he can make an emperor he can make a pope. Go to him directly. I am Emperor, and you are nothing but my husband; will you go at once?"

Then he was afraid and went; but he was quite faint and shivered and shook, and his knees and legs trembled. And a high wind blew over the land, and the clouds flew, and towards evening all grew dark, and the leaves fell from the trees, and the water rose and roared as if it were boiling, and splashed upon the shore. And in the distance he saw ships which were firing guns in their sore need, pitching and tossing on the waves. And yet in the midst of the sky there was still a small bit of blue, though on every side it was as red as in a heavy storm. So, full of despair, he went and stood in much fear and said,

"Flounder, flounder in the sea, Come, I pray thee, here to me;" For my wife, good Ilsabil, Wills not as I'd have her will.

"Well, what does she want, then?" said the Flounder. "Alas," said the man, "she wants to be Pope." "Go to her then," said the Flounder; "she is Pope already."

So he went, and when he got there, he saw what seemed to be a large church surrounded by palaces. He pushed his way through the crowd. Inside, however, everything was lighted up with thousands and thousands of candles, and his wife was clad in gold, and she was sitting on a much higher throne, and had three great golden crowns on, and round about her there was much ecclesiastical splendour; and on both sides of her was a row of candles the largest of which was as tall as the very tallest tower, down to the very smallest kitchen candle, and all the emperors and kings were on their knees before her, kissing her shoe. "Wife," said the man, and looked attentively at her, "are you now Pope?" "Yes," said she, "I am Pope." So he stood and looked at her, and it was just as if he was looking at the bright sun. When he had stood looking at her thus for a short time, he said, "Ah, wife, if you are Pope, do let well alone!" But she looked as stiff as a post, and did not move or show any signs of life. Then said he, "Wife, now that you are Pope, be satisfied, you cannot become anything greater now." "I will consider about that," said the woman. Thereupon they both went to bed, but she was not satisfied, and greediness let her have no sleep, for she was continually thinking what there was left for her to be.

The man slept well and soundly, for he had run about a great deal during the day; but the woman could not fall asleep at all, and flung herself from one side to the other the whole night through, thinking always what more was left for her to be, but unable to call to mind anything else. At length the sun began to rise, and when the woman saw the red of dawn, she sat up in bed and looked at it. And when, through the window, she saw the sun thus rising, she said, "Cannot I, too, order the sun and moon to rise?" "Husband," she said, poking him in the ribs with her elbows, "wake up! Go to the Flounder, for I wish to be even as God is." The man was still half asleep, but he was so horrified that he fell out of bed. He thought he must have heard ***amiss***, and rubbed his eyes, and said, "Alas, wife, what are you saying?" "Husband," said she, "if I can't order the sun and moon to rise, and have to look on and see the sun and moon rising, I can't bear it. I shall not know what it is to have another happy hour, unless I can make them rise myself." Then she looked at him so terribly that a shudder ran over him, and said, "Go at once; I wish to be like unto God." "Alas, wife," said the man, falling on his knees before her, "the Flounder cannot do that; he can make an emperor and a pope; I beseech you, go on as you are, and be Pope." Then she fell into a rage, and her hair flew wildly about her head, and she cried, "I will not endure this, I'll not bear it any longer; wilt thou go?" Then he put on his trousers and ran away like a madman. But outside a great storm was raging, and blowing so hard that he could scarcely keep his feet; houses and trees toppled over, the mountains trembled, rocks rolled into the sea, the sky was pitch black, and it thundered and lightened, and the sea came in with black waves as high as church-towers and mountains, and all with crests of white foam at the top. Then he cried, but could not hear his own words,

"Flounder, flounder in the sea,
Come, I pray thee, here to me;
For my wife, good Ilsabil,
Wills not as I'd have her will."

"Well, what does she want, then?" said the Flounder. "Alas," said he, "she wants to be like unto God." "Go to her, and you will find her back again in the dirty hovel." And there they are living still at this very time.

The Bremen Town-Musicians

A certain man had a donkey, which had carried the corn-sacks to the mill ***indefatigably*** for many a long year; but his strength was going, and he was growing more and more unfit for work. Then his master began to consider how

---

amiss: wrong
indefatigably: tirelessly

he might best save his keep; but the donkey, seeing that no good wind was blowing, ran away and set out on the road to Bremen. "There," he thought, "I can surely be town-musician." When he had walked some distance, he found a hound lying on the road, gasping like one who had run till he was tired. "What are you gasping so for, you big fellow?" asked the donkey.

"Ah," replied the hound, "as I am old, and daily grow weaker, and no longer can hunt, my master wanted to kill me, so I took to flight; but now how am I to earn my bread?"

"I tell you what," said the donkey, "I am going to Bremen, and shall be town-musician there; go with me and engage yourself also as a musician. I will play the lute, and you shall beat the kettledrum."

The hound agreed, and on they went.

Before long they came to a cat, sitting on the path, with a face like three rainy days! "Now then, old shaver, what has gone askew with you?" asked the donkey.

"Who can be merry when his neck is in danger?" answered the cat. "Because I am now getting old, and my teeth are worn to stumps, and I prefer to sit by the fire and spin, rather than hunt about after mice, my mistress wanted to drown me, so I ran away. But now good advice is scarce. Where am I to go?"

"Go with us to Bremen. You understand night-music; you can be a town-musician."

The cat thought well of it, and went with them. After this the three fugitives came to a farm-yard, where the cock was sitting upon the gate, crowing with all his might. "Your crow goes through and through one," said the donkey. "What is the matter?"

"I have been foretelling fine weather, because it is the day on which Our Lady washes the Christ-child's little shirts, and wants to dry them," said the cock; "but guests are coming for Sunday, so the housewife has no pity, and has told the cook that she intends to eat me in the soup to-morrow, and this evening I am to have my head cut off. Now I am crowing at full pitch while I can."

"Ah, but red-comb," said the donkey, "you had better come away with us. We are going to Bremen; you can find something better than death everywhere: you have a good voice, and if we make music together it must have some quality!"

The cock agreed to this plan, and all four went on together. They could not, however, reach the city of Bremen in one day, and in the evening they came to a forest where they meant to pass the night. The donkey and the hound laid themselves down under a large tree, the cat and the cock settled themselves in the branches; but the cock flew right to the top, where he was most safe. Before he went to sleep he looked round on all four sides, and thought he saw in the distance a little spark burning; so he called out to his companions that there must be a house not far off, for he saw a light. The donkey said, "If so, we had better get up and go on, for the shelter here is bad." The hound thought that a few bones with some meat on would do him good too!

So they made their way to the place where the light was, and soon saw it shine brighter and grow larger, until they came to a well-lighted robber's house. The donkey, as the biggest, went to the window and looked in.

"What do you see, my grey-horse?" asked the cock. "What do I see?" answered the donkey; "a table covered with good things to eat and drink, and robbers sitting at it enjoying themselves." "That would be the sort of thing for us," said the cock. "Yes, yes; ah, how I wish we were there!" said the donkey.

Then the animals took counsel together how they should manage to drive away the robbers, and at last they thought of a plan. The donkey was to place himself with his fore-feet upon the window-ledge, the hound was to jump on the donkey's back, the cat was to climb upon the dog, and lastly the cock was to fly up and perch upon the head of the cat.

When this was done, at a given signal, they began to perform their music together: the donkey brayed, the hound barked, the cat mewed, and the cock crowed; then they burst through the window into the room, so that the glass clattered! At this horrible din, the robbers sprang up, thinking no otherwise than that a ghost had come in, and fled in a great fright out into the forest. The four companions now sat down at the table, well content with what was left, and ate as if they were going to fast for a month.

As soon as the four minstrels had done, they put out the light, and each sought for himself a sleeping-place according to his nature and to what suited him. The donkey laid himself down upon some straw in the yard, the hound behind the door, the cat upon the hearth near the warm ashes, and the cock perched himself upon a beam of the roof; and being tired from their long walk, they soon went to sleep.

When it was past midnight, and the robbers saw from afar that the light was no longer burning in their house, and all appeared quiet, the captain said, "We ought not to have let ourselves be frightened out of our wits;" and ordered one of them to go and examine the house.

The messenger finding all still, went into the kitchen to light a candle, and, taking the glistening fiery eyes of the cat for live coals, he held a lucifer-match to them to light it. But the cat did not understand the joke, and flew in his face, spitting and scratching. He was dreadfully frightened, and ran to the back-door, but the dog, who lay there sprang up and bit his leg; and as he ran across the yard by the straw-heap, the donkey gave him a smart kick with its hind foot. The cock, too, who had been awakened by the noise, and had become lively, cried down from the beam, "Cock-a-doodle-doo!"

Then the robber ran back as fast as he could to his captain, and said, "Ah, there is a horrible witch sitting in the house, who spat on me and scratched my face with her long claws; and by the door stands a man with a knife, who stabbed me in the leg; and in the yard there lies a black monster, who beat me with a wooden club; and above, upon the roof, sits the judge, who called out, 'Bring the rogue here to me!' so I got away as well as I could."

After this the robbers did not trust themselves in the house again; but it suited the four musicians of Bremen so well that they did not care to leave it any more. And the mouth of him who last told this story is still warm.

Briar-Rose

A long time ago there were a King and Queen who said every day, "Ah, if only we had a child!" but they never had one. But it happened that once when the Queen was bathing, a frog crept out of the water on to the land, and said to her, "Your wish shall be fulfilled; before a year has gone by, you shall have a daughter."

What the frog had said came true, and the Queen had a little girl who was so pretty that the King could not contain himself for joy, and ordered a great feast. He invited not only his kindred, friends and acquaintance, but also the Wise Women, in order that they might be kind and well-disposed towards the child. There were thirteen of them in his kingdom, but, as he had only twelve golden plates for them to eat out of, one of them had to be left at home.

The feast was held with all manner of splendour and when it came to an end the Wise Women bestowed their magic gifts upon the baby: one gave virtue, another beauty, a third riches, and so on with everything in the world that one can wish for.

When eleven of them had made their promises, suddenly the thirteenth came in. She wished to avenge herself for not having been invited, and without greeting, or even looking at any one, she cried with a loud voice, "The King's daughter shall in her fifteenth year prick herself with a spindle, and fall down dead." And, without saying a word more, she turned round and left the room.

They were all shocked; but the twelfth, whose good wish still remained unspoken, came forward, and as she could not undo the evil sentence, but only soften it, she said, "It shall not be death, but a deep sleep of a hundred years, into which the princess shall fall."

The King, who would fain keep his dear child from the misfortune, gave orders that every spindle in the whole kingdom should be burnt. Meanwhile the gifts of the Wise Women were plenteously fulfilled on the young girl, for she was so beautiful, modest, good-natured, and wise, that everyone who saw her was bound to love her.

It happened that on the very day when she was fifteen years old, the King and Queen were not at home, and the maiden was left in the palace quite alone. So she went round into all sorts of places, looked into rooms and bed-chambers just as she liked, and at last came to an old tower. She climbed up the narrow winding-staircase, and reached a little door. A rusty key was in the lock, and when she turned it the door sprang open, and there in a little room sat an old woman with a spindle, busily spinning her flax.

"Good day, old dame," said the King's daughter; "what are you doing there?" "I am spinning," said the old woman, and nodded her head. "What sort of thing is that, that rattles round so merrily?" said the girl, and she took the spindle and wanted to spin too. But scarcely had she touched the spindle when the magic decree was fulfilled, and she pricked her finger with it.

And, in the very moment when she felt the prick, she fell down upon the bed that stood there, and lay in a deep sleep. And this sleep extended over the whole palace; the King and Queen who had just come home, and had entered the great hall, began to go to sleep, and the whole of the court with them. The horses, too, went to sleep in the stable, the dogs in the yard, the pigeons upon the roof, the flies on the wall; even the fire that was flaming on the hearth became quiet and slept, the roast meat left off frizzling, and the cook, who was just going to pull the hair of the scullery boy, because he had forgotten something, let him go, and went to sleep. And the wind fell, and on the trees before the castle not a leaf moved again.

But round about the castle there began to grow a hedge of thorns, which every year became higher, and at last grew close up round the castle and all over it, so that there was nothing of it to be seen, not even the flag upon the roof. But the story of the beautiful sleeping "Briar-rose," for so the princess was named, went about the country, so that from time to time kings' sons came and tried to get through the thorny hedge into the castle.

But they found it impossible, for the thorns held fast together, as if they had hands, and the youths were caught in them, could not get loose again, and died a miserable death.

After long, long years a King's son came again to that country, and heard an old man talking about the thorn-hedge, and that a castle was said to stand behind it in which a wonderfully beautiful princess, named Briar-rose, had been asleep for a hundred years; and that the King and Queen and the whole court were asleep likewise. He had heard, too, from his grandfather, that many kings' sons had already come, and had tried to get through the thorny hedge, but they had remained sticking fast in it, and had died a pitiful death. Then the youth said, "I am not afraid, I will go and see the beautiful Briar-rose." The good old man might dissuade him as he would, he did not listen to his words.

But by this time the hundred years had just passed, and the day had come when Briar-rose was to awake again. When the King's son came near to the thorn-hedge, it was nothing but large and beautiful flowers, which parted from each other of their own accord, and let him pass unhurt. Then they closed again behind him like a hedge. In the castle-yard he saw the horses and the spotted hounds lying asleep; on the roof sat the pigeons with their heads under their wings. And when he entered the house, the flies were asleep upon the wall, the cook in the kitchen was still holding out his hand to seize the boy, and the maid was sitting by the black hen which she was going to pluck.

He went on farther, and in the great hall he saw the whole of the court lying asleep, and up by the throne lay the King and Queen.

Then he went on still farther, and all was so quiet that a breath could be heard, and at last he came to the tower, and opened the door into the little room where Briar-rose was sleeping. There she lay, so beautiful that he could not turn his eyes away; and he stooped down and gave her a kiss. But as soon as he kissed her, Briar-rose opened her eyes and awoke, and looked at him quite sweetly.

Then they went down together, and the King awoke, and the Queen, and the whole court, and looked at each other in great astonishment. And the horses in the court-yard stood up and shook themselves; the hounds jumped up and wagged their tails; the pigeons upon the roof pulled out their heads from under their wings, looked round, and flew into the open country; the flies on the wall crept again; the fire in the kitchen burned up and flickered and cooked the meat; the joint began to turn and frizzle again, and the cook gave the boy such a box on the ear that he screamed, and the maid plucked the fowl ready for the spit.

And then the marriage of the King's son with Briar-rose was celebrated with all splendour, and they lived contented to the end of their days.

Little Snow-White

Once upon a time in the middle of winter, when the flakes of snow were falling like feathers from the sky, a queen sat at a window sewing, and the frame of the window was made of black ebony. And whilst she was sewing and looking out of the window at the snow, she pricked her finger with the needle, and three drops of blood fell upon the snow. And the red looked pretty upon the white snow, and she thought to herself, "Would that I had a child as white as snow, as red as blood, and as black as the wood of the window-frame."

Soon after that she had a little daughter, who was as white as snow, and as red as blood, and her hair was as black as ebony; and she was therefore called Little Snow-white. And when the child was born, the Queen died.

After a year had passed the King took to himself another wife. She was a beautiful woman, but proud and haughty, and she could not bear that anyone else should surpass her in beauty. She had a wonderful looking-glass, and when she stood in front of it and looked at herself in it, and said--

"Looking-glass, Looking-glass, on the wall,
Who in this land is the fairest of all?"

The looking-glass answered,

"Thou, O Queen, art the fairest of all!"

Then she was satisfied, for she knew that the looking-glass spoke the truth.

But Snow-white was growing up, and grew more and more beautiful; and when she was seven years old she was as beautiful as the day, and more beautiful than the Queen herself. And once when the Queen asked her looking-glass,

"Looking-glass, Looking-glass, on the wall,
Who in this land is the fairest of all?"

It answered,

"Thou art fairer than all who are here, Lady Queen."
But more beautiful still is Snow-white, as I ween."

Then the Queen was shocked, and turned yellow and green with envy. From that hour, whenever she looked at Snow-white, her heart heaved in her breast; she hated the girl so much.

And envy and pride grew higher and higher in her heart like a weed, so that she had no peace day or night. She called a huntsman, and said, "Take the child away into the forest; I will no longer have her in my sight. Kill her, and bring me back her heart as a token." The huntsman obeyed, and took her away; but when he had drawn his knife, and was about to pierce Snow-white's innocent heart, she began to weep, and said, "Ah dear huntsman, leave me my life! I will run away into the wild forest, and never come home again."

And as she was so beautiful the huntsman had pity on her and said, "Run away, then, you poor child." "The wild beasts will soon have devoured you," thought he, and yet it seemed as if a stone had been rolled from his heart since it was no longer needful for him to kill her. And as a young boar just then came running by he stabbed it, and cut out its heart and took it to the Queen as proof that the child was dead. The cook had to salt this, and the wicked Queen ate it, and thought she had eaten the heart of Snow-white.

But now the poor child was all alone in the great forest, and so terrified that she looked at every leaf of every tree, and did not know what to do. Then she began to run, and ran over sharp stones and through thorns, and the wild beasts ran past her, but did her no harm.

She ran as long as her feet would go until it was almost evening; then she saw a little cottage and went into it to rest herself. Everything in the cottage was small, but neater and cleaner than can be told. There was a table on which was a white cover, and seven little plates, and on each plate a little spoon; moreover, there were seven little knives and forks, and seven little mugs. Against the wall stood seven little beds side by side, and covered with snow-white counterpanes.

Little Snow-white was so hungry and thirsty that she ate some vegetables and bread from each plate and drank a drop of wine out of each mug, for she did not wish to take all from one only. Then, as she was so tired, she laid herself down on one of the little beds, but none of them suited her; one was too long, another too short, but at last she found that the seventh one was right, and so she remained in it, said a prayer and went to sleep.

When it was quite dark the owners of the cottage came back; they were seven dwarfs who dug and delved in the mountains for ore. They lit their seven candles, and as it was now light within the cottage they saw that someone had been there, for everything was not in the same order in which they had left it.

The first said, "Who has been sitting on my chair?"

The second, "Who has been eating off my plate?"

The third, "Who has been taking some of my bread?"

The fourth, "Who has been eating my vegetables?"

The fifth, "Who has been using my fork?"

The sixth, "Who has been cutting with my knife?"

The seventh, "Who has been drinking out of my mug?"

Then the first looked round and saw that there was a little hole on his bed, and he said, "Who has been getting into my bed?" The others came up and each called out, "Somebody has been lying in my bed too." But the seventh when he looked at his bed saw little Snow-white, who was lying asleep therein. And he called the others, who came running up, and they cried out with astonishment, and brought their seven little candles and let the light fall on little Snow-white. "Oh, heavens! Oh, heavens!" cried they, "what a lovely child!" and they were so glad that they did not wake her up, but let her sleep on in the bed. And the seventh dwarf slept with his companions, one hour with each, and so got through the night.

When it was morning little Snow-white awoke, and was frightened when she saw the seven dwarfs. But they were friendly and asked her what her name was. "My name is Snow-white," she answered. "How have you come to our house?" said the dwarfs. Then she told them that her step-mother had wished to have her killed, but that the huntsman had spared her life, and that she had run for the whole day, until at last she had found their dwelling. The dwarfs said, "If you will take care of our house, cook, make the beds, wash, sew, and knit, and if you will keep everything neat and clean, you can stay with us and you shall want for nothing." "Yes," said Snow-white, "with all my heart," and she stayed with them. She kept the house in order for them; in the mornings they went to the mountains and looked for copper and gold, in the evenings they came back, and then their supper had to be ready. The girl was alone the whole day, so the good dwarfs warned her and said, "Beware of your step-mother, she will soon know that you are here; be sure to let no one come in."

But the Queen, believing that she had eaten Snow-white's heart, could not but think that she was again the first and most beautiful of all; and she went to her looking-glass and said,

"Looking-glass, Looking-glass, on the wall,
Who in this land is the fairest of all?" and the glass answered,
"Oh, Queen, thou art fairest of all I see,
But over the hills, where the seven dwarfs dwell,
Snow-white is still alive and well,
And none is so fair as she."

Then she was astounded, for she knew that the looking-glass never spoke falsely, and she knew that the huntsman had betrayed her, and that little Snow-white was still alive.

And so she thought and thought again how she might kill her, for so long as she was not the fairest in the whole land, envy let her have no rest. And when she had at last thought of something to do, she painted her face, and dressed herself like an old pedlar-woman, and no one could have known her. In this disguise she went over the seven mountains to the seven dwarfs, and knocked at the door and cried, "Pretty things to sell, very cheap, very cheap." Little Snow-white looked out of the window and called out, "Good-day my good woman, what have you to sell?" "Good things, pretty things," she answered; "stay-laces of all colours," and she pulled out one which was woven of bright-coloured silk. "I may let the worthy old woman in," thought Snow-white, and she unbolted the door and bought the pretty laces. "Child," said the old woman, "what a fright you look; come, I will lace you properly for once." Snow-white had no suspicion, but stood before her, and let herself be laced with the new laces. But the old woman laced so quickly and so tightly that Snow-white lost her breath and fell down as if dead. "Now I am the most beautiful," said the Queen to herself, and ran away.

Not long afterwards, in the evening, the seven dwarfs came home, but how shocked they were when they saw their dear little Snow-white lying on the ground, and that she neither stirred nor moved, and seemed to be dead. They lifted her up, and, as they saw that she was laced too tightly, they cut the laces;

then she began to breathe a little, and after a while came to life again. When the dwarfs heard what had happened they said, "The old pedlar-woman was no one else than the wicked Queen; take care and let no one come in when we are not with you."

But the wicked woman when she had reached home went in front of the glass and asked,

"Looking-glass, Looking-glass, on the wall,
Who in this land is the fairest of all?" and it answered as before,
"Oh, Queen, thou art fairest of all I see,
But over the hills, where the seven dwarfs dwell,
Snow-white is still alive and well,
And none is so fair as she."

When she heard that, all her blood rushed to her heart with fear, for she saw plainly that little Snow-white was again alive. "But now," she said, "I will think of something that shall put an end to you," and by the help of witchcraft, which she understood, she made a poisonous comb. Then she disguised herself and took the shape of another old woman. So she went over the seven mountains to the seven dwarfs, knocked at the door, and cried, "Good things to sell, cheap, cheap!" Little Snow-white looked out and said, "Go away; I cannot let anyone come in." "I suppose you can look," said the old woman, and pulled the poisonous comb out and held it up. It pleased the girl so well that she let herself be beguiled, and opened the door. When they had made a bargain the old woman said, "Now I will comb you properly for once." Poor little Snow-white had no suspicion, and let the old woman do as she pleased, but hardly had she put the comb in her hair than the poison in it took effect, and the girl fell down senseless. "You paragon of beauty," said the wicked woman, "you are done for now," and she went away.

But fortunately it was almost evening, when the seven dwarfs came home. When they saw Snow-white lying as if dead upon the ground they at once suspected the step-mother, and they looked and found the poisoned comb. Scarcely had they taken it out when Snow-white came to herself, and told them what had happened. Then they warned her once more to be upon her guard and to open the door to no one.

The Queen, at home, went in front of the glass and said,

"Looking-glass, Looking-glass, on the wall,
Who in this land is the fairest of all?" Then it answered as before,
"Oh, Queen, thou art fairest of all I see,
But over the hills, where the seven dwarfs dwell,
Snow-white is still alive and well,
And none is so fair as she."

When she heard the glass speak thus she trembled and shook with rage.

"Snow-white shall die," she cried, "even if it costs me my life!"

Thereupon she went into a quite secret, lonely room, where no one ever came, and there she made a very poisonous apple. Outside it looked pretty, white with a red cheek, so that everyone who saw it longed for it; but whoever ate a piece of it must surely die.

When the apple was ready she painted her face, and dressed herself up as a country-woman, and so she went over the seven mountains to the seven dwarfs. She knocked at the door. Snow-white put her head out of the window and said, "I cannot let anyone in; the seven dwarfs have forbidden me." "It is all the same to me," answered the woman, "I shall soon get rid of my apples. There, I will give you one."

"No," said Snow-white, "I dare not take anything." "Are you afraid of poison?" said the old woman; "look, I will cut the apple in two pieces; you eat the red cheek, and I will eat the white." The apple was so cunningly made that only the red cheek was poisoned. Snow-white longed for the fine apple, and when she saw that the woman ate part of it she could resist no longer, and stretched out her hand and took the poisonous half. But hardly had she a bit of it in her mouth than she fell down dead. Then the Queen looked at her with a dreadful look, and laughed aloud and said, "White as snow, red as blood, black as ebony-wood! This time the dwarfs cannot wake you up again."

And when she asked of the Looking-glass at home,

"Looking-glass, Looking-glass, on the wall,

Who in this land is the fairest of all?" it answered at last,

"Oh, Queen, in this land thou art fairest of all."

Then her envious heart had rest, so far as an envious heart can have rest.

The dwarfs, when they came home in the evening, found Snow-white lying upon the ground; she breathed no longer and was dead. They lifted her up, looked to see whether they could find anything poisonous, unlaced her, combed her hair, washed her with water and wine, but it was all of no use; the poor child was dead, and remained dead. They laid her upon a bier, and all seven of them sat round it and wept for her, and wept three days long.

Then they were going to bury her, but she still looked as if she were living, and still had her pretty red cheeks. They said, "We could not bury her in the dark ground," and they had a transparent coffin of glass made, so that she could be seen from all sides, and they laid her in it, and wrote her name upon it in golden letters, and that she was a king's daughter. Then they put the coffin out upon the mountain, and one of them always stayed by it and watched it. And birds came too, and wept for Snow-white; first an owl, then a raven, and last a dove.

And now Snow-white lay a long, long time in the coffin, and she did not change, but looked as if she were asleep; for she was as white as snow, as red as blood, and her hair was as black as ebony.

It happened, however, that a king's son came into the forest, and went to the dwarfs' house to spend the night. He saw the coffin on the mountain, and the beautiful Snow-white within it, and read what was written upon it in golden letters. Then he said to the dwarfs, "Let me have the coffin, I will give you whatever you want for it." But the dwarfs answered, "We will not part with it for all the gold in the world." Then he said, "Let me have it as a gift, for I cannot live without seeing Snow-white. I will honour and prize her as my dearest possession." As he spoke in this way the good dwarfs took pity upon him, and gave him the coffin.

And now the King's son had it carried away by his servants on their shoulders. And it happened that they stumbled over a tree-stump, and with the shock the poisonous piece of apple which Snow-white had bitten off came out of her throat. And before long she opened her eyes, lifted up the lid of the coffin, sat up, and was once more alive. "Oh, heavens, where am I?" she cried. The King's son, full of joy, said, "You are with me," and told her what had happened, and said, "I love you more than everything in the world; come with me to my father's palace, you shall be my wife."

And Snow-white was willing, and went with him, and their wedding was held with great show and splendour. But Snow-white's wicked step-mother was also bidden to the feast. When she had arrayed hersef in beautiful clothes she went before the Looking-glass, and said,

"Looking-glass, Looking-glass, on the wall,
Who in this land is the fairest of all?" the glass answered
"Oh, Queen, of all here the fairest art thou,
But the young Queen is fairer by far as I trow."

Then the wicked woman uttered a curse, and was so wretched, so utterly wretched, that she knew not what to do. At first she would not go to the wedding at all, but she had no peace, and must go to see the young Queen. And when she went in she knew Snow-white; and she stood still with rage and fear, and could not stir. But iron slippers had already been put upon the fire, and they were brought in with tongs, and set before her. Then she was forced to put on the red-hot shoes, and dance until she dropped down dead.

Rumpelstiltskin

Once there was a miller who was poor, but who had a beautiful daughter. Now it happened that he had to go and speak to the King, and in order to make himself appear important he said to him, "I have a daughter who can spin straw into gold." The King said to the miller, "That is an art which pleases me well; if your daughter is as clever as you say, bring her to-morrow to my palace, and I will try what she can do."

And when the girl was brought to him he took her into a room which was quite full of straw, gave her a spinning-wheel and a reel, and said, "Now set to work, and if by to-morrow morning early you have not spun this straw into gold during the night, you must die." Thereupon he himself locked up the room, and left her in it alone. So there sat the poor miller's daughter, and for the life of her could not tell what to do; she had no idea how straw could be spun into gold, and she grew more and more miserable, until at last she began to weep.

But all at once the door opened, and in came a little man, and said, "Good evening, Mistress Miller; why are you crying so?" "Alas!" answered the girl, "I have to spin straw into gold, and I do not know how to do it." "What will you give me," said the manikin, "if I do it for you?" "My necklace," said the girl. The little man took the necklace, seated himself in front of the wheel, and "whirr,

whirr, whirr," three turns, and the reel was full; then he put another on, and whirr, whirr, whirr, three times round, and the second was full too. And so it went on until the morning, when all the straw was spun, and all the reels were full of gold. By daybreak the King was already there, and when he saw the gold he was astonished and delighted, but his heart became only more greedy. He had the miller's daughter taken into another room full of straw, which was much larger, and commanded her to spin that also in one night if she valued her life. The girl knew not how to help herself, and was crying, when the door again opened, and the little man appeared, and said, "What will you give me if I spin that straw into gold for you?" "The ring on my finger," answered the girl. The little man took the ring, again began to turn the wheel, and by morning had spun all the straw into glittering gold.

The King rejoiced beyond measure at the sight, but still he had not gold enough; and he had the miller's daughter taken into a still larger room full of straw, and said, "You must spin this, too, in the course of this night; but if you succeed, you shall be my wife." "Even if she be a miller's daughter," thought he, "I could not find a richer wife in the whole world."

When the girl was alone the manikin came again for the third time, and said, "What will you give me if I spin the straw for you this time also?" "I have nothing left that I could give," answered the girl. "Then promise me, if you should become Queen, your first child." "Who knows whether that will ever happen?" thought the miller's daughter; and, not knowing how else to help herself in this strait, she promised the manikin what he wanted, and for that he once more span the straw into gold.

And when the King came in the morning, and found all as he had wished, he took her in marriage, and the pretty miller's daughter became a Queen.

A year after, she had a beautiful child, and she never gave a thought to the manikin. But suddenly he came into her room, and said, "Now give me what you promised." The Queen was horror-struck, and offered the manikin all the riches of the kingdom if he would leave her the child. But the manikin said, "No, something that is living is dearer to me than all the treasures in the world." Then the Queen began to weep and cry, so that the manikin pitied her. "I will give you three days' time," said he, "if by that time you find out my name, then shall you keep your child."

So the Queen thought the whole night of all the names that she had ever heard, and she sent a messenger over the country to inquire, far and wide, for any other names that there might be. When the manikin came the next day, she began with Caspar, Melchior, Balthazar, and said all the names she knew, one after another; but to every one the little man said, "That is not my name." On the second day she had inquiries made in the neighborhood as to the names of the people there, and she repeated to the manikin the most uncommon and curious. "Perhaps your name is Shortribs, or Sheepshanks, or Laceleg?" but he always answered, "That is not my name."

On the third day the messenger came back again, and said, "I have not been able to find a single new name, but as I came to a high mountain at the end of the forest, where the fox and the hare bid each other good night, there I saw a little house, and before the house a fire was burning, and round about the fire quite a ridiculous little man was jumping: he hopped upon one leg, and shouted,

"To-day I bake, to-morrow brew,
The next I'll have the young Queen's child.
Ha! Glad am I that no one knew
That Rumpelstiltskin I am styled."

You may think how glad the Queen was when she heard the name! And when soon afterwards the little man came in, and asked, "Now, Mistress Queen, what is my name?" at first she said, "Is your name Conrad?" "No." "Is your name Harry?" "No."

"Perhaps your name is Rumpelstiltskin?"

"The devil has told you that! The devil has told you that!" cried the little man, and in his anger he plunged his right foot so deep into the earth that his whole leg went in; and then in rage he pulled at his left leg so hard with both hands that he tore himself in two.

The Goose-Girl

THERE was once upon a time an old Queen whose husband had been dead for many years, and she had a beautiful daughter. When the princess grew up she was betrothed to a prince who lived at a great distance. When the time came for her to be married, and she had to journey forth into the distant kingdom, the aged Queen packed up for her many costly vessels of silver and gold, and trinkets also of gold and silver; and cups and jewels, in short, everything which appertained to a royal dowry, for she loved her child with all her heart. She likewise sent her maid in waiting, who was to ride with her, and hand her over to the bridegroom, and each had a horse for the journey, but the horse of the King's daughter was called Falada, and could speak. So when the hour of parting had come, the aged mother went into her bedroom, took a small knife and cut her finger with it until it bled, then she held a white handkerchief to it into which she let three drops of blood fall, gave it to her daughter and said, "Dear child, preserve this carefully, it will be of service to you on your way."

So they took a sorrowful leave of each other; the princess put the piece of cloth in her bosom, mounted her horse, and then went away to her bridegroom. After she had ridden for a while she felt a burning thirst, and said to her waiting-maid, "Dismount, and take my cup which thou hast brought with thee for me, and get me some water from the stream, for I should like to drink." "If you are thirsty," said the waiting-maid, "get off your horse yourself, and lie down and drink out of the water; I don't choose to be your servant." So in her great thirst the princess alighted, bent down over the water in the stream and drank, and was not allowed to drink out of the golden cup. Then she said, "Ah, Heaven!" and the three drops of blood answered, "If thy mother knew, her heart would break." But the King's daughter was humble, said nothing, and mounted her horse again. She rode some miles further, but the day was warm, the sun scorched her, and she was thirsty once more, and when they came to a stream of water, she again cried to her waiting-maid, "Dismount, and give me some water in my golden cup," for she had long ago forgotten the girl's ill words. But the waiting-maid said still more haughtily, "If you wish to drink, drink as you can, I don't choose to be your maid." Then in her great thirst the King's daughter alighted, bent over the flowing stream, wept and said, "Ah, Heaven!" and the drops of blood again replied, "If thy mother knew this, her heart would break." And as she was thus drinking and leaning right over the stream, the handkerchief with the three drops of blood fell out of her bosom, and floated away with the water without her observing it, so great was her trouble. The waiting-maid, however, had seen it, and she rejoiced to think that she had now power over the bride, for since the princess had lost the drops of blood, she had become weak and powerless. So now when she wanted to mount her horse again, the one that was called Falada, the waiting-maid said, "Falada is more suitable for me, and my nag will do for thee" and the princess had to be content with that. Then the waiting-maid, with many hard words, bade the princess exchange her royal apparel for her own shabby clothes; and at length she was compelled to swear by the clear sky above her, that she would not say one word of this to any one at the royal court, and if she had not taken this oath she would have been killed on the spot. But Falada saw all this, and observed it well.

The waiting-maid now mounted Falada, and the true bride the bad horse, and thus they traveled onwards, until at length they entered the royal palace. There were great rejoicings over her arrival, and the prince sprang forward to meet her, lifted the waiting-maid from her horse, and thought she was his consort. She was conducted upstairs, but the real princess was left standing below. Then the old King looked out of the window and saw her standing in the courtyard, and how dainty and delicate and beautiful she was, and instantly went to the royal apartment, and asked the bride about the girl she had with her who was standing down below in the courtyard, and who she was? "I picked her up on my way for a companion; give the girl something to work at, that she may not stand idle." But the old King had no work for her, and knew of none, so he said, "I have a little boy who tends the geese, she may help him." The boy was called Conrad, and the true bride had to help him to tend the geese. Soon afterwards the false bride said to the young King, "Dearest husband, I beg you to do me a favour." He answered, "I will do so most willingly." "Then send for the knacker, and have the head of the horse on which I rode here cut off, for it vexed me on the way." In reality, she was afraid that the horse might tell how she had behaved to the King's daughter. Then she succeeded in making the King promise that it should be done, and the faithful Falada was to die; this came to the ears of the real princess, and she secretly promised to pay the knacker a piece of gold if he would perform a small service for her. There was a great dark-looking gateway in the town, through which morning and evening she had to pass with the geese: would he be so good as to nail up Falada's head on it, so that she might see him again, more than once. The knacker's man promised to do that, and cut off the head, and nailed it fast beneath the dark gateway.

Early in the morning, when she and Conrad drove out their flock beneath this gateway, she said in passing,

"Alas, Falada, hanging there!"
Then the head answered,
"Alas, young Queen, how ill you fare!
If this your tender mother knew,
Her heart would surely break in two."

Then they went still further out of the town, and drove their geese into the country. And when they had come to the meadow, she sat down and unbound her hair which was like pure gold, and Conrad saw it and delighted in its brightness, and wanted to pluck out a few hairs. Then she said,

"Blow, blow, thou gentle wind, I say,
Blow Conrad's little hat away,
And make him chase it here and there,
Until I have braided all my hair,
And bound it up again."

And there came such a violent wind that it blew Conrad's hat far away across country, and he was forced to run after it. When he came back she had finished combing her hair and was putting it up again, and he could not get any of it. Then Conrad was angry, and would not speak to her, and thus they watched the geese until the evening, and then they went home.

Next day when they were driving the geese out through the dark gateway, the maiden said,

"Alas, Falada, hanging there!"
Falada answered,
"Alas, young Queen, how ill you fare!
If this your tender mother knew,
Her heart would surely break in two."

And she sat down again in the field and began to comb out her hair, and Conrad ran and tried to clutch it, so she said in haste,

"Blow, blow, thou gentle wind, I say,
Blow Conrad's little hat away,
And make him chase it here and there,
Until I have braided all my hair,
And bound it up again."

Then the wind blew, and blew his little hat off his head and far away, and Conrad was forced to run after it, and when he came back, her hair had been put up a long time, and he could get none of it, and so they looked after their geese till evening came.

But in the evening after they had got home, Conrad went to the old King, and said, "I won't tend the geese with that girl any longer!" "Why not?" inquired the aged King. "Oh, because she vexes me the whole day long." Then the aged King commanded him to relate what it was that she did to him. And Conrad said, "In the morning when we pass beneath the dark gateway with the flock, there is a sorry horse's head on the wall, and she says to it,

"Alas, Falada, hanging there!"
And the head replies,
"Alas, young Queen how ill you fare!

If this your tender mother knew,
Her heart would surely break in two."

And Conrad went on to relate what happened on the goose pasture, and how when there he had to chase his hat.

The aged King commanded him to drive his flock out again next day, and as soon as morning came, he placed himself behind the dark gateway, and heard how the maiden spoke to the head of Falada, and then he too went into the country, and hid himself in the thicket in the meadow. There he soon saw with his own eyes the goose-girl and the goose-boy bringing their flock, and how after a while she sat down and unplaited her hair, which shone with radiance. And soon she said,

"Blow, blow, thou gentle wind, I say,
Blow Conrad's little hat away,
And make him chase it here and there,
Until I have braided all my hair,
And bound it up again."

Then came a blast of wind and carried off Conrad's hat, so that he had to run far away, while the maiden quietly went on combing and plaiting her hair, all of which the King observed. Then, quite unseen, he went away, and when the goose-girl came home in the evening, he called her aside, and asked why she did all these things. "I may not tell you that, and I dare not lament my sorrows to any human being, for I have sworn not to do so by the heaven which is above me; if I had not done that, I should have lost my life." He urged her and left her no peace, but he could draw nothing from her. Then said he, "If thou wilt not tell me anything, tell thy sorrows to the iron-stove there," and he went away. Then she crept into the iron-stove, and began to weep and lament, and emptied her whole heart, and said, "Here am I deserted by the whole world, and yet I am a King's daughter, and a false waiting-maid has by force brought me to such a pass that I have been compelled to put off my royal apparel, and she has taken my place with my bridegroom, and I have to perform menial service as a goose-girl. If my mother did but know that, her heart would break."

The aged King, however, was standing outside by the pipe of the stove, and was listening to what she said, and heard it. Then he came back again, and bade her come out of the stove. And royal garments were placed on her, and it was marvellous how beautiful she was! The aged King summoned his son, and revealed to him that he had got the false bride who was only a waiting-maid, but that the true one was standing there, as the sometime goose-girl. The young King rejoiced with all his heart when he saw her beauty and youth, and a great feast was made ready to which all the people and all good friends were invited. At the head of the table sat the bridegroom with the King's daughter at one side of him, and the waiting-maid on the other, but the waiting-maid was blinded, and did not recognize the princess in her dazzling array. When they had eaten and drunk, and were merry, the aged King asked the waiting-maid as a riddle, what a person deserved who had behaved in such and such a way to her master, and at the same time related the whole story, and asked what sentence such an one merited? Then the false bride said, "She deserves no better fate than to be stripped entirely naked, and put in a barrel which is studded inside with pointed nails, and two white horses should be harnessed to it, which will drag her along through one street after another, till she is dead." "It is thou," said the aged King, "and thou hast pronounced thine own sentence, and thus shall it be done unto thee." And when the sentence had been carried out, the young King married his true bride, and both of them reigned over their kingdom in peace and happiness.

Iron John

THERE was once on a time a King who had a great forest near his palace, full of all kinds of wild animals. One day he sent out a huntsman to shoot him a roe, but he did not come back. "Perhaps some accident has befallen him," said the King, and the next day he sent out two more huntsmen who were to search for him, but they too stayed away. Then on the third day, he sent for all his huntsmen, and said, "Scour the whole forest through, and do not give up until ye have found all three." But of these also, none came home again, and of the pack of hounds which they had taken with them, none were seen more. From that time forth, no one would any longer venture into the forest, and it lay there in deep stillness and solitude, and nothing was seen of it, but sometimes an eagle or a hawk flying over it. This lasted for many years, when a strange huntsman announced himself to the King as seeking a situation, and offered to go into the dangerous forest. The King, however, would not give his consent, and said, "It is not safe in there; I fear it would fare with thee no better than with the others, and thou wouldst never come out again." The huntsman replied, "Lord, I will venture it at my own risk, of fear I know nothing."

The huntsman therefore betook himself with his dog to the forest. It was not long before the dog fell in with some game on the way, and wanted to pursue it; but hardly had the dog run two steps when it stood before a deep pool, could go no farther, and a naked arm stretched itself out of the water, seized it, and drew it under, When the huntsman saw that, he went back and fetched three men to come with buckets and bale out the water. When they could see to the bottom there lay a wild man whose body was brown like rusty iron, and whose hair hung over his face down to his knees. They bound him with cords, and led him away to the castle. There was great astonishment over the wild man; the King, however, had him put in an iron cage in his court-yard, and forbade the door to be opened on pain of death, and the Queen herself was to take the key into her keeping. And from this time forth every one could again go into the forest with safety.

The King had a son of eight years, who was once playing in the court-yard, and while he was playing, his golden ball fell into the cage. The boy ran thither and said, "Give me my ball out." "Not till thou hast opened the door for me," answered the man. "No," said the boy, "I will not do that; the King has forbidden it," and ran away. The next day he again went and asked for his ball; the wild man said, "Open my door," but the boy would not. On the third day the King had ridden out hunting, and the boy went once more and said, "I cannot open the door even if I wished, for I have not the key." Then the wild man said, "It lies under thy mother's pillow, thou canst get it there." The boy, who wanted to have his ball back, cast all thought to the winds, and brought the key. The door opened with difficulty, and the boy pinched his fingers. When it was open the wild man stepped out, gave him the golden ball, and hurried away. The boy had become afraid; he called and cried after him, "Oh, wild man, do not go away, or I shall be beaten!" The wild man turned back, took him up, set him on his shoulder, and went with hasty steps into the forest. When the King came home, he observed the empty cage, and asked the Queen how that had happened? She knew nothing about it, and sought the key, but it was gone. She called the boy, but no one answered. The King sent out people to seek for him in the fields, but they did not find him. Then he could easily guess what had happened, and much grief reigned in the royal court.

When the wild man had once more reached the dark forest, he took the boy down from his shoulder, and said to him, "Thou wilt never see thy father and mother again, but I will keep thee with me, for thou hast set me free, and I have compassion on thee. If thou dost all I bid thee, thou shalt fare well. Of treasure and gold have I enough, and more than anyone in the world." He made a bed of moss for the boy on which he slept, and the next morning the man took him to a well, and said, "Behold, the gold well is as bright and clear as crystal, thou shalt sit beside it, and take care that nothing falls into it, or it will be polluted. I will come every evening to see if thou hast obeyed my order." The boy placed himself by the margin of the well, and often saw a golden fish or a golden snake show itself therein, and took care that nothing fell in. As he was thus sitting, his finger hurt him so violently that he involuntarily put it in the water. He drew it quickly out again, but saw that it was quite gilded, and whatsoever pains he took to wash the gold off again, all was to no purpose. In the evening Iron John came back, looked at the boy, and said, "What has happened to the well?" "Nothing, nothing," he answered, and held his finger behind his back, that the man might not see it. But he said, "Thou hast dipped thy finger into the water, this time it may pass, but take care thou dost not again let anything go in." By daybreak the boy was already sitting by the well and watching it. His finger hurt him again and he passed it over his head, and then unhappily a hair fell down into the well. He took it quickly out, but it was already quite gilded. Iron John came, and already knew what had happened. "Thou hast let a hair fall into the well," said he. "I will allow thee to watch by it once more, but if this happens for the third time then the well is polluted, and thou canst no longer remain with me."

On the third day, the boy sat by the well, and did not stir his finger, however much it hurt him. But the time was long to him, and he looked at the reflection of his face on the surface of the water. And as he still bent down more and more while he was doing so, and trying to look straight into the eyes, his long hair fell down from his shoulders into the water. He raised himself up quickly, but the whole of the hair of his head was already golden and shone like the sun. You may imagine how terrified the poor boy was! He took his pocket-handkerchief and tied it round his head, in order that the man might not see it. When he came he already knew everything, and said, "Take the handkerchief off." Then the golden hair streamed forth, and let the boy excuse himself as he might, it was of no use. "Thou hast not stood the trial, and canst stay here no longer. Go forth into the world, there thou wilt learn what poverty is. But as thou hast not a bad heart, and as I mean well by thee, there is one thing I will grant thee; if thou fallest into any difficulty, come to the forest and cry, 'Iron John,' and then I will come and help thee. My power is great, greater than thou thinkest, and I have gold and silver in ***abundance***."

Then the King's son left the forest, and walked by beaten and unbeaten paths ever onwards until at length he reached a great city. There he looked for work, but could find none, and he had learnt nothing by which he could help himself. At length he went to the palace, and asked if they would take him in. The people about court did not at all know what use they could make of him, but they liked him, and told him to stay. At length the cook took him into his service, and said he might carry wood and water, and rake the cinders together. Once when it so happened that no one else was at hand, the cook ordered him to carry the food to the royal table, but as he did not like to let his golden hair be seen, he kept his little cap on. Such a thing as that had never yet come under the King's notice, and he said, "When thou comest to the royal table thou must take thy hat off." He answered, "Ah, Lord, I cannot; I have a bad sore place on my head." Then the King had the cook called before him and scolded him, and asked how he could take such a boy as that into his service; and that he was to turn him off at once. The cook, however, had pity on him, and exchanged him for the gardener's boy.

And now the boy had to plant and water the garden, hoe and dig, and bear the wind and bad weather. Once in summer when he was working alone in the garden, the day was so warm he took his little cap off that the air might cool him. As the sun shone on his hair it glittered and flashed so that the rays fell into the bedroom of the King's daughter, and up she sprang to see what that could be. Then she saw the boy, and cried to him, "Boy, bring me a wreath of flowers." He put his cap on with all haste, and gathered wild field-flowers and bound them together. When he was ascending the stairs with them, the gardener met him, and said, "How canst thou take the King's daughter a garland of such common flowers? Go quickly, and get another, and seek out the prettiest and rarest." "Oh, no," replied the boy, "the wild ones have more scent, and will please her better." When he got into the room, the King's daughter said, "Take thy cap off, it is not seemly to keep it on in my presence." He again said, "I may not, I have a sore head." She, however, caught at his cap and pulled it off, and then his golden hair rolled down on his shoulders, and it was splendid to behold. He wanted to run out, but she held him by the arm, and gave him a handful of ducats. With these he departed, but he cared nothing for the gold pieces. He took them to the gardener, and said, "I present them to thy children, they can play with them." The following day the King's daughter again called to him that he was to bring her a wreath of field-flowers, and when he went in with it, she instantly snatched at his cap, and wanted to take it away from him, but he held it fast with both

---

abundance: large quantity

hands. She again gave him a handful of ducats, but he would not keep them, and gave them to the gardener for playthings for his children. On the third day things went just the same; she could not get his cap away from him, and he would not have her money.

Not long afterwards, the country was overrun by war. The King gathered together his people, and did not know whether or not he could offer any opposition to the enemy, who was superior in strength and had a mighty army. Then said the gardener's boy, "I am grown up, and will go to the wars also, only give me a horse." The others laughed, and said, "Seek one for thyself when we are gone, we will leave one behind us in the stable for thee." When they had gone forth, he went into the stable, and got the horse out; it was lame of one foot, and limped hobblety jig, hobblety jig; nevertheless he mounted it, and rode away to the dark forest. When he came to the outskirts, he called "Iron John," three times so loudly that it echoed through the trees. Thereupon the wild man appeared immediately, and said, "What dost thou desire?" "I want a strong steed, for I am going to the wars." "That thou shalt have, and still more than thou askest for." Then the wild man went back into the forest, and it was not long before a stable-boy came out of it, who led a horse that snorted with its nostrils, and could hardly be restrained, and behind them followed a great troop of soldiers entirely equipped in iron, and their swords flashed in the sun. The youth made over his three-legged horse to the stable-boy, mounted the other, and rode at the head of the soldiers. When he got near the battle-field a great part of the King's men had already fallen, and little was wanting to make the rest give way. Then the youth galloped thither with his iron soldiers, broke like a hurricane over the enemy, and beat down all who opposed him. They began to fly, but the youth pursued, and never stopped, until there was not a single man left. Instead, however, of returning to the King, he conducted his troop by bye-ways back to the forest, and called forth Iron John. "What dost thou desire?" asked the wild man. "Take back thy horse and thy troops, and give me my three-legged horse again." All that he asked was done, and soon he was riding on his three-legged horse. When the King returned to his palace, his daughter went to meet him, and wished him joy of his victory. "I am not the one who carried away the victory," said he, "but a stranger knight who came to my assistance with his soldiers." The daughter wanted to hear who the strange knight was, but the King did not know, and said, "He followed the enemy, and I did not see him again." She inquired of the gardener where his boy was, but he smiled, and said, "He has just come home on his three-legged horse, and the others have been mocking him, and crying, "Here comes our hobblety jig back again!" They asked, too, "Under what hedge hast thou been lying sleeping all the time?" He, however, said, "I did the best of all, and it would have gone badly without me." And then he was still more ridiculed."

The King said to his daughter, "I will proclaim a great feast that shall last for three days, and thou shalt throw a golden apple. Perhaps the unknown will come to it." When the feast was announced, the youth went out to the forest, and called Iron John. "What dost thou desire?" asked he. "That I may catch the King's daughter's golden apple." "It is as safe as if thou hadst it already," said

Iron John. "Thou shalt likewise have a suit of red armour for the occasion, and ride on a spirited chestnut-horse." When the day came, the youth galloped to the spot, took his place amongst the knights, and was recognized by no one. The King's daughter came forward, and threw a golden apple to the knights, but none of them caught it but he, only as soon as he had it he galloped away.

On the second day Iron John equipped him as a white knight, and gave him a white horse. Again he was the only one who caught the apple, and he did not linger an instant, but galloped off with it. The King grew angry, and said, "That is not allowed; he must appear before me and tell his name." He gave the order that if the knight who caught the apple, should go away again they should pursue him, and if he would not come back willingly, they were to cut him down and stab him.

On the third day, he received from Iron John a suit of black armour and a black horse, and again he caught the apple. But when he was riding off with it, the King's attendants pursued him, and one of them got so near him that he wounded the youth's leg with the point of his sword. The youth nevertheless escaped from them, but his horse leapt so violently that the helmet fell from the youth's head, and they could see that he had golden hair. They rode back and announced this to the King.

The following day the King's daughter asked the gardener about his boy. "He is at work in the garden; the queer creature has been at the festival too, and only came home yesterday evening; he has likewise shown my children three golden apples which he has won."

The King had him summoned into his presence, and he came and again had his little cap on his head. But the King's daughter went up to him and took it off, and then his golden hair fell down over his shoulders, and he was so handsome that all were amazed. "Art thou the knight who came every day to the festival, always in different colours, and who caught the three golden apples?" asked the King. "Yes," answered he, "and here the apples are," and he took them out of his pocket, and returned them to the King. "If you desire further proof, you may see the wound which your people gave me when they followed me. But I am likewise the knight who helped you to your victory over your enemies." "If thou canst perform such deeds as that, thou art no gardener's boy; tell me, who is thy father?" "My father is a mighty King, and gold have I in plenty as great as I require." "I well see," said the King, "that I owe thanks to thee; can I do anything to please thee?" "Yes," answered he, "that indeed you can. Give me your daughter to wife." The maiden laughed, and said, "He does not stand much on ceremony, but I have already seen by his golden hair that he was no gardener's boy," and then she went and kissed him. His father and mother came to the wedding, and were in great delight, for they had given up all hope of ever seeing their dear son again. And as they were sitting at the marriage-feast, the music suddenly stopped, the doors opened, and a stately King came in with a great retinue. He went up to the youth, embraced him and said, "I am Iron John, and was by enchantment a wild man, but thou hast set me free; all the treasures which I possess, shall be thy property."

MOVIE ADAPTATIONS

Hans Christian Andersen

The Tinder-Box. Das Feuerzeug (original title). Dir. Siegfried Hartmann. Writ. Hans Christian Andersen (fairy tale), Siegfried Hartmann, Anneliese Kocialek and Fred Rodrian. Perf. Rolf Ludwig, Heinz Schubert and Rolf Defrank. Deutsche Film (DEFA), 1959. Film.

The Princess and the Pea. Dir. Mark Swan. Writ. Hans Christian Andersen, Forrest S. Baker III, Ken Cromar. Perf. Dan Finnerty, Jonathan Firth and Lincoln Hoppe. KOAN, 2002. Film.

Thumbelina. Dir. Don Bluth, Gary Goldman. Writ. Hans Christian Andersen (fairy tale), Don Bluth (screenplay). Perf. Jodi Benson, Gary Imhoff and Gino Conforti. Warner Bros, 1994. Film

The Little Mermaid. Dir. Ron Clements, John Musker. Writ. Hans Christian Andersen, John Musker, Ron Clements. Perf. Jodi Benson, Samuel E. Wright and Rene Auberjonois. Walt Disney Pictures, 1989. Film.

The Emperor's New Clothes. Dir. David Irving. Writ. David Irving, Anna Mathias. Perf. Sid Caesar, Clive Revill, Robert Morse. Cannon Films, 1987. Film.

The Tin Soldier. Dir. David Langer. Writ. Hans Christian Andersen (story), David Langer. Perf. Sally Struthers, Frank Augustyn, Stephanie Hutchison. Canadian Broadcasting Corporation, 1992. Television.

H. C. Andersen: The Swineherd. H.C. Andersens eventyrlige verden: Svinedrengen (original title). Dir. Jørgen Bing. Writ. Hans Christian Andersen, Jørgen Bing, Christian Sommer. Perf. Bjarne G. Nielsen. Scanbox Entertainment, 2005. Video.

Angel. Dir. Tatyana Ivanova. Writ. Hans Christian Andersen, Lyudmila Ivanishchenko, Tatyana Ivanova. Lennauchfilm, 1996. Television.

The Tales of Hans Christian Andersen: The Emperor's New Clothes and Nightingale. Dir. Michael Sporn. Writ. Hans Christian Andersen, Maxine Fisher. Perf. Courtney B. Vance, Larry White, Jason McDonald, Peggy Cass, Barnard Hughes. First Run Features, 2007. DVD.

The Ugly Duckling. Gadkiy Utyonok (original title). Dir. Garri Bardin. Writ. Hans Christian Andersen (fairy tale), Garri Bardin (screenwriter). Perf. Khor

Turetskogo, Svetlana Stepchenko, Armen Dzhigarkhanyan. Stayer Studio, 2010. Film.

The Fir Tree. Dir. Martin Hunter. Writ. Hans Christian Andersen (story). Perf. Katie Knox, Nic Labriola, David Hill. Sullivan Entertainment, 1979. Film.

The Snow Queen. Dir. Julian Gibbs. Writ. James Andrew Hall, Hans Christian Andersen (story). Perf. Pax Baldwin, Sydney White, Juliet Stevenson. BBC Worldwide, 2005. Television.

The Red Shoes. Dir. Lindsey Walker. Writ. Hans Christian Andersen, Lindsey Walker (screenplay). Perf. Ian Bell, Katherine Bell, Melissa Clarke. Wright Walker Productions, 2009. DVD.

Andrew Lang

Adventures of Sinbad the Sailor. Dir. Karel Zeman. Prod. Antonin Duchtik, Karel Hutecka. Writ. Karel Zeman. Perf. (voice) Jan Triska. Filmové Studio Gottwaldov, 1971. Film.

"Aladdin and His Wonderful Lamp." *Faerie Tale Theatre.* Dir. Tim Burton. Prod. Shelley Duvall. Writ. Mark Curtis, Rod Ash. Perf. Robert Carradine, Shelley Duvall, James Earl Jones. Showtime, USA. 14 July, 1986. Television.

"The Enchanted Horse." *Mel-O-Toons.* Writ. Art Scott (story) Perf. (voice) Pat McGeehan. New World Productions, USA. 1960. Television.

Ali Baba and the Forty Thieves. Dir. Jacques Becker. Prod. Jean Goiran, René Gaston Vuattoux. Writ. Cesare Zavattini, Jacques Becker. Perf. Fernandel, Samia Gamal. Les Films du Cyclope, 1954. Film.

Brothers Grimm

The Frog Prince. Dir. Jackson Hunsicker. Prod. Patricia Ruben. Perf. Helen Hunt, Amanda Pays, Aileen Quinn, Clive Revill, John Paragon and Eli Gorenstein. Cannon Group, 1986. Film.

Tangled. Dir. Nathan Greno and Byron Howard. Writ. Dan Fogelman (screenplay), Jacob Grimm ("Rapunzel" fairy tale). Perf. Mandy Moore, Zachary Levi and Donna Murphy. Walt Disney Studios, 2010. Film.

Hansel and Gretel. Dir. Len Talan. Perf. David Warner, Hugh Pollard, Nicola Stapleton. Golan-Globus Productions, 1987. Film.

Cinderella. Dir. Clyde Geronimi, Wilfred Jackson. Writ. Bill Peet (story), Erdman Penner (story) Perf: Ilene Woods, James MacDonald, Eleanor Audley. Walt Disney Productions, 1950. Film.

Mother Holly. Frau Holle (original title). Dir. Gottfried Kolditz. Writ. Jacob Grimm (fairy tale), Wilhelm Grimm (fairy tale). Perf. Mathilde Danegger, Karin Ugowski, Katharina Lind. Deutsche Film (DEFA), 1963. Film.

Red Riding Hood. Dir. Adam Brooks. Writ. Carole Lucia Satrina. Perf. Amelia Shankley, Isabella Rossellini, Craig T. Nelson. Golan-Globus Productions, 1989. Film

"The Fisherman and His Wife." *Happily Ever After: Fairy Tales for Every Child.* Dir. Edward Bell. Perf. (Voices). Julia Migenes, Edward James Olmos, Pablo Rodríguez. HBO Family. Hyperion Pictures, USA. 8 June. 1997. Television.

"The Musicians of Bremen Town." *Jackanory.* Dir: Pauline Carter. Prod. Joy Whitby. Writ. Jacob Grimm (story), Wilhelm Grimm (story), Barbara Ireson (adaptation). Perf. (Voice). Dilys Hamlett. BBC1, UK. 31 Jan. 1966. Television.

"Briar Rose." *Grimm Masterpiece Theatre.* Dir. Kerrigan Mahan, Hiroshi Saitô. Prod. Takaji Matsudo. Writ: Robert Benedict, Jacob Grimm, Wilhelm Grimm. Perf. (Voice) Rachael Lillis. TV Asahi. Nippon Animation, Japan. 17 Feb. 1988. Television

Grimm's Snow White. Dir. Rachel Goldenberg. Prod. David Michael Latt. Writ. Naomi L. Selfman (screenplay). Perf. Eliza Bennett, Jane March, Jamie Thomas King. The Asylum, USA. 13 March. 2012. DVD.

Rumpelstiltskin. Dir. David Irving. Prod. Menahem Golan, Yoram Globus. Writ: Jacob Grimm (story), Wilhelm Grimm (story). Perf. Amy Irving, Billy Barty, Clive Revill. The Cannon Group, 1987. Film.

The Goose Girl. Die Gänsemagd (original title). Dir. Fritz Genschow. Prod. Fritz Genschow. Writ. Fritz Genschow, Jacob Grimm (story), Wilhelm Grimm (story). Perf. Rita-Maria Nowotny, Renée Stobrawa, Renate Fischer. Fritz Genschow Films, 1957. Film.

Iron John. Der Eisenhans (original title). Dir. Manuel Siebenmann. Writ. Jacob Grimm (fairy tale), Wilhelm Grimm (fairy tale), Rudolf Herfurtner. Perf. Laurence Rupp, Paula Schramm, Michael Mendl. Zweites Deutsches Fernsehen (ZDF), Germany. 24 Dec, 2011. Television.

www.ingramcontent.com/pod-product-compliance
Lightning Source LLC
Chambersburg PA
CBHW072106170626
46813CB00004B/1472
* 9 7 8 0 9 8 4 4 0 9 8 9 1 *